THE KILLING ROOM

Ryan heard a sound. He turned. He heard it again.

Someone was in the room with him. But he could plainly see he was alone.

But then he heard the sound again. Footsteps. Not from above. Not from outside the room. But from *within* the very room.

Now there was another sound. Metal. It sounded like metal being tapped against the tiles of the floor.

"What is going on?" he whispered again, and for the first time, he felt fear.

He'd break the window. It was the only way. He picked up a heavy marble paperweight and aimed it at the glass. But even as he did so, he heard the sound again. A footstep. The tapping of metal against tile.

He glanced around quickly.

And this time he saw it.

A man. A man with dirty overalls and a straggly beard.

And in his hand the man held an enormous pitchfork, its sharp tines scraping against the floor. . . .

Books by John Manning

ALL THE PRETTY DEAD GIRLS

THE KILLING ROOM

Published by Kensington Publishing Corporation

THE
KILLING
ROOM

JOHN
MANNING

PINNACLE BOOKS
KENSINGTON PUBLISHING CORP.
www.kensingtonbooks.com

PINNACLE BOOKS are published by

Kensington Publishing Corp.
119 West 40th Street
New York, NY 10018

All Kensington titles, imprints, and distributed lines are available at special quantity discounts for bulk purchases for sales promotions, premiums, fund-raising, educational, or institutional use. Special book excerpts or customized printings can also be created to fit specific needs. For details, write or phone the office of the Kensington special sales manager: Kensington Publishing Corp., 119 West 40th Street, New York, NY 10018, attn: Special Sales Department; phone 1-800-221-2647.

This book is a work of fiction. Names, characters, businesses, organizations, places, events, and incidents either are the product of the author's imagination or are used fictitiously. Any resemblance to actual persons, living or dead, events, or locales is entirely coincidental.

PINNACLE BOOKS and the Pinnacle logo are reg. U.S. Pat. & TM Off.

ISBN-13: 978-0-7860-1799-7
ISBN-10: 0-7860-1799-6

First printing: May 2010

10 9 8 7 6 5 4 3 2 1

Printed in the United States of America

THE YOUNG FAMILY

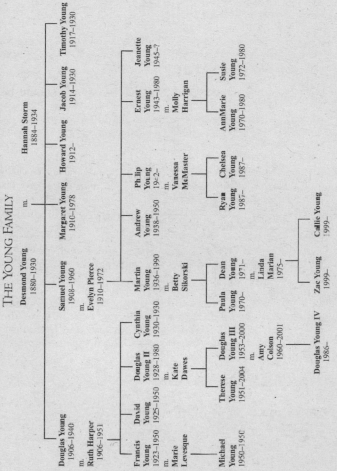

Desmond Young
1880–1930

m.

Hannah Storm
1884–1934

Douglas Young
1906–1940
m.
Ruth Harper
1906–1951

Samuel Young
1908–1960
m.
Evelyn Pierce
1910–1972

Margaret Young
1910–1978

Howard Young
1912–

Jacob Young
1914–1930

Timothy Young
1917–1930

Francis Young
1923–1950
m.
Marie Levesque

David Young
1925–1950

Douglas Young II
1928–1980
m.
Kate Dawes

Cynthia Young
1930–1930

Martin Young
1936–1990
m.
Betty Sikorski

Andrew Young
1938–1950

Philip Young
19-2-
m.
Vanessa McMaster

Ernest Young
1943–1980
m.
Molly Harrigan

Jeanette Young
1945–?

Michael Young
1950–1950

Therese Young
1951–2004

Douglas Young III
1953–2000
m.
Amy Colson
1960–2001

Paula Young
1970–

Dean Young
1971–
m.
Linda Marian
1975–

Ryan Young
1987–

Chelsea Young
1987–

AnnMarie Young
1970–1980

Susie Young
1972–1980

Douglas Young IV
1986–

Zac Young
1999–

Callie Young
1999–

Prologue

Jeanette Young didn't believe what her Uncle Howard had told her. It was all utter nonsense. If her brothers and cousins really believed such things, then they were fools. This wasn't the Middle Ages, after all. This was 1970. And no matter what anyone tried to tell her, Jeanette refused to accept the idea that her father—her wise, beloved, dearly missed father—had ever considered such outlandish tales to be true.

"But perhaps," Uncle Howard had said softly, taking Jeanette's hand, "you can now better understand the manner of your father's death."

That had been an hour ago. Now Jeanette was alone, pondering everything her uncle had said. She threw open the window and breathed in the crisp night air. As always, the sound of waves crashing against the rocks far below the cliff soothed her. They always had, ever since she was a young girl and her father would bring her to this house to visit Uncle Howard. Those were happy days.

The house had been filled with laughter. How could they all have been living with a secret like the one Uncle Howard had just revealed to her?

Uncle Howard and the others—her Aunt Margaret, her brothers, her cousins—were hoping that she would come around and accept their stories as true. That's why they had left her alone, so she could think. But even as she reflected on all she'd been told tonight, Jeanette's ideas didn't change. They simply hardened.

"It's beyond ridiculous," she said out loud, her voice echoing in the empty parlor. "And I'll prove it by spending the night in the room where my father died."

It was the last weekend of September. Only a few tenacious leaves still clung to the branches of the trees. Just as the family had done every ten years for the last half century, the Young clan had gathered at Uncle Howard's great old house on the coast of Maine. As a child and teenager, Jeanette had looked forward to the family reunions. She had enjoyed playing on the grassy lawn that stretched along the cliffs overlooking the Atlantic. With glee she had cracked the lobster claws served up by the cooks, dipping the succulent meat into the bowls of warm butter they brought out from the kitchen. Jeanette had never known about the meeting that took place on Saturday night at midnight in the parlor. Only at this gathering had she learned of that. At twenty-five, Jeanette was finally old enough to be initiated into the family secret, and to take her place in the lottery.

At the stroke of midnight, they had all gathered in the parlor. Jeanette stood beside Uncle Howard, Aunt Margaret, her brothers, and her cousins. The crackling flames in the fireplace filled the room with the fragrance of oak. Aunt Margaret had written their names on slips of paper and placed them into a wooden box. Uncle Howard, being the patriarch, reached in to select one. Everyone had watched in silence. When he pulled out Jeanette's name, the old man's face had gone white. "No," he said, his voice breaking. "She's too young."

Her eldest brother Martin had echoed the objection. "I'll do it in her place," he offered, prompting a little cry from his wife, no doubt thinking of their two small children asleep in rooms upstairs.

"It would only make it worse," Aunt Margaret said. She claimed to know such things, since she and Uncle Howard were the only ones left who remembered how the madness had begun some forty years earlier. "My father tried to shield my brother Jacob when his name was drawn," she told the family. "Jacob had just turned sixteen. Father insisted he was too young, and so he spent the night in the room in Jacob's place. But it was supposed to have been Jacob, since it was his name that had been chosen." She shuddered. "And we all know how that night turned out."

Everyone had nodded except for Jeanette. "No," she said, "I don't know how that night turned out." They had told her about the lottery and revealed the secret in the basement, but they hadn't told her this. She looked from face to face and said, "Tell me what happened that night."

Aunt Margaret's eyes were cold. "If you go down to the cemetery," she said, "you'll see there wasn't just one death in the family that year. There was a slaughter. My father was killed. And Jacob, too, even though he never stepped a foot in that room.

And my youngest brother Timothy as well, and even my newborn niece Cynthia. All as a lesson for us never again to meddle with the lottery."

That's when Jeanette had asked to be alone. In her hands she held a family tree that had been compiled by Aunt Margaret. She saw the death dates of all of those who had died that first night in 1930, and then the series of deaths that occurred in ten-year intervals thereafter. Her uncle Douglas in 1940. Her cousin David in 1950. And then, ten years later, her father. She looked down at his name. Samuel Young. Died 1960.

Jeanette remembered the morning they all started out for Uncle Howard's house. She was fifteen, thrilled to be heading up the coast from their house outside Boston. She loved her uncle and thought his house was fascinating, with all its many rooms and marble staircases and outstanding views of the cliffs and the ocean. She had been excited to see her cousins. But her parents and her two older brothers were glum. At the family picnic that Saturday, the children had turned somersaults on the lawn and splashed in the surf at the bottom of the cliff, but the adults had been somber, talking quietly among themselves. That night, Jeanette was awakened after midnight by her father, slipping into her room to hug her tight. "I love you, Jen," he'd whispered as he kissed her forehead. In the morning she learned he'd died of a heart attack in his sleep.

Now her uncle was telling her a very different story of her father's death.

After Dad's death, Mom had turned to drink. She had chosen not to accompany Jeanette and her brothers to Uncle Howard's this year. Drunk, almost incoherent, she'd clung to Jeanette when she said good-bye. If the stories she'd been told were true, Jeanette could understand why her mother had gone on such a bender.

"But surely it *can't* be what they say. . . ."

Jeanette's voice in the empty room seemed strange to her ears. It was as if someone else were speaking. She shivered. She looked again at the family tree, all those deaths in ten-year intervals. Then, taking a deep breath, she opened the door and called the family back into the room.

Uncle Howard came first, his face a mask of pain under his shock of white hair. Then her brothers, who'd been through all this before, guilt stricken that their names hadn't been drawn. Then her cousin Douglas and his children, who kept their eyes away from hers. Finally there was Aunt Margaret, the bitterest of them all.

"I'll spend the night in the room," Jeanette announced. "And in the morning you'll see all of this was unnecessary worry."

"But, my dear," Uncle Howard said, "it is important that you go in understanding what you face—"

"If what you say has any merit," she said efficiently, "then perhaps it might be *better* if I entered the room with a healthy skepticism. If I remember my history books correctly, Franklin Roosevelt once said the only thing we have to fear is fear itself. Perhaps it has been our own fear that has claimed us in the past."

Yet even as she said the words, she knew her father had not been a man to give in to fear. She might try to cling to an idea that the deaths had all been hysterical reactions to the outrageous tales her family spun, but her theory collapsed when she applied it to her own father, a well-decorated

Navy pilot in World War II who had looked death in the face many times. It hadn't been hysterical fear that had stopped his heart in that basement room ten years ago. Standing there in front of her family, Jeanette began to accept the terrifying fact that what her uncle had told her must be true—no matter how much she still outwardly denied it.

But even if she had wanted to, there was no way to back out now. She steeled her nerves as they all bid her good-bye in the parlor. Her brothers, each in turn, embraced her, saying nothing. Even as she felt the trembling of their bodies, Jeanette did her best to push the stories Uncle Howard had told her far out of her mind. With her chin held high, she followed him across the foyer to the door leading to the basement. She refused to entertain any more thoughts of avenging spirits and haunted rooms. Uncle Howard had relayed to her the origins of what he called the family curse—a long, winding tale of madness and revenge—but she wanted none of it. She refused to keep the details in her mind. She would enter that room a modern, liberated woman, a student of philosophy near to completing her master's thesis at Yale University, a strong, independent soul with a mind of her own. Old folktales had no power over her. It was the only way, Jeanette was now convinced, that she'd get through the night alive.

Uncle Howard pulled open a creaky old door and descended a dark staircase. Jeanette kept close behind, a dim bulb casting a pale orange light, providing barely enough illumination for them to see their way. It was at that moment that she thought of Michael. Michael—with his broad shoulders and piercing blue eyes and strong, reassuring voice. The man she hoped to marry.

"I just wish I could go with you up to Maine," he'd said to her the day before, caressing the long auburn hair that fell to Jeanette's shoulders. "I don't like the idea of us being parted, even for a few days."

"You have an important exhibit in New York," she'd replied briskly, declining to get emotional. "If you're ever going to be recognized as the major artist I know you're going to be, you need to do these things."

"It's just so far away from you."

Her heart was breaking, but she wouldn't admit it. Now she wished she had been more emotional, holding Michael longer. But she had been stoic. It was always her way.

"It's only for a weekend," she'd told Michael. "Besides, I haven't seen my family in so long. It'll be nice to reconnect with all of them."

Michael had taken her in his arms, and they had kissed. Now, in the musty basement air, Jeanette longed for her beloved's arms.

They had reached the bottom of the steps. Uncle Howard turned to see how she was doing. Jeanette nodded that he should continue. He sighed, slowly crossing the floor of the cellar. With a key, he unlocked a door on the opposite wall. He turned and looked again at Jeanette with sad, soulful eyes.

"This is the room?" she asked boldly.

He nodded. Without any hesitation, Jeanette stepped inside. It was a plain room, rather small, no more than twenty feet across. An old sofa squatted beside a table with two chairs. It had been a servant's bedroom back when Uncle Howard had been a boy. That's what he had explained to Jeanette earlier. A servant girl had lived here. . . .

And died here.

Jeanette's eyes came to rest on the wall opposite her.

"There?" she asked her uncle. "Was that the wall?"

He nodded slowly.

That was where the poor girl had been impaled.

Beatrice. Uncle Howard had said her name was Beatrice.

And she was murdered here in this room almost half a century ago.

All of the horrors they had known since came from that fact.

Jeanette approached the wall. She stood in front of it, examining the white plaster. It had obviously been painted many times. How many coats, she wondered? How many coats did it take to cover the bloodstains left behind by that poor woman?

And by the members of the Young family whose grisly deaths had followed?

Her father had been fortunate, Uncle Howard had said. He had merely died of a heart attack. Not so her Uncle Douglas, whose wrists had been found slit, his body drained of blood. Not so her grandfather, the first after Beatrice to die in this place, whose severed head was found on one side of the room and his body on the other.

It had started to rain. She could hear the raindrops hitting against the one window in the room, a dark rectangle of glass embedded in the wall over their heads.

"I would have chosen any other name but yours, my dear," Uncle Howard said. "I would gladly take your place in this room tonight. But in forty years of the lottery, my name has never been drawn. It is my own curse to watch as my kinfolk enter this room, one by one." His voice choked. "Your aunt is right. We learned that first time that substituting someone for the one who was drawn will only bring more destruction."

"I'm the first woman to spend a night here," Jeanette said. "The first who has studied philosophy and science. This first modern Young to face this ancient force." Her eyes fixed on her uncle. "I will survive this night. You will see."

"Your bravery outshines us all," he managed to say. He gripped her by the shoulders and kissed her forehead, much as her father had done a decade before. "May God preserve you."

He hurried out of the room, closing—and locking—the door behind him.

Jeanette looked around the room. A small lamp on the table provided the only light. She sat on the sofa and folded her arms across her chest.

"Well," she whispered. "If something is going to happen, let it happen soon."

There was a small rumble of thunder off in the distance.

The rain was hitting the house harder now. A flicker of lightning crackled by the window. Jeanette thought once more of Michael. She would see him again. She was confident of that. If there was anything to these family legends, she'd beat them. She'd end this so-called family curse. She'd do it for her father.

She'd do it for all of them.

A huge thunderclap made her jump.

"If something's going to happen," she said defiantly to whoever might be listening, "bring it on! I'm not frightened of you!"

There was another loud peal of thunder, and the lamp went out.

"Damn!" Jeanette said. She didn't want to face whatever it was in the dark.

She breathed a sigh of relief as the light flickered on again, just as another thunder boom rattled across the sky.

"I should have anticipated this," she said. There was a small candle on the table as well, and an old book of matches. How many times had this candle been lit by fingers trembling with terror? The candle was little more than a stub. She considered lighting it, but seeing as it was so small, she didn't want to waste the wax when the electricity was still on. Should the power go out again, she'd light it. She kept the book of matches near her hand so she could find it if the darkness returned.

Her name was Beatrice. . . .

Uncle Howard's words echoed in her mind.

And one morning when she failed to come up to set the breakfast table, my brother Timothy and I came down here to look for her.

Jeanette's eyes flickered again to the wall.

I shall never forget what we saw there. Beatrice—impaled to the wall by a long metal pitchfork, driven through her chest. Blood was everywhere. Her eyes were still open, her mouth in anguished fury. It was as if she had died looking at her murderer. Cursing him for all time . . .

The lamp flickered. Jeanette felt her heart flutter.

And in that instant, she looked up at the door—

—and saw a man standing there, in a grass-stained T-shirt, holding a pitchfork.

Jeanette screamed.

It took her several minutes to calm herself, to realize she'd just had a hallucination. There was no man in the doorway. It was her mind, playing tricks.

Was this how it happened? Did those who stayed here in this room work themselves into frenzies of fear? Had her father's heart given out because of it? Had Uncle Douglas slit his wrists rather than face an imaginary ghost?

But her father would not have been spooked.

And there was no way her grandfather could have severed his own head.

Thunder again, the loudest yet, directly over the house. The light struggled to hold—

—shivered—

—and then went out.

Darkness.

Jeanette held her breath.

"Come back on," she whispered.

But the darkness remained.

"Oh, God," she said, a pathetic little cry.

How terribly dark it was. Gripping the box of matches in her left hand, she felt around for the candle with her right. What if the power didn't return? The little stub would never last. . . . She moved her hand over the tabletop. Where was the candle? It had been sitting right there! The darkness was absolute. Deep and thick. The rain kept up its pummeling of the roof. She prayed for a flash of lightning just to show her the candle. But all she got was a low rumble of thunder.

There!

She felt something in the dark. The candle—

She moved her fingers to grip it.

And whatever it was that she touched—moved!

It was a hand! A human hand!

Someone was in the dark with her!

Jeanette screamed.

"Who's there? Who is it?"

Finally, a crash of lightning. The room lit up for an instant. Jeanette saw she was alone in the room.

And there—there was the candle!

She grabbed it as the darkness settled in again. She fumbled for the matches, her hands trembling so much she worried she wouldn't be able to light one. But she managed and lit the wick of the candle. A small, flickering circle of light enveloped her. She sat back on the couch, her heart thudding in her ears.

The memory of that hand—

It was real, she told herself. *It moved.*

No, she argued with herself. *It was just the candle I was feeling. It was just my imagination again.*

She lifted the candle and stood. She was far too anxious to stay seated. Whatever might come, she would face it on her feet. But as she moved into the center of the room, she realized she was stepping in something sticky.

Was rainwater dripping in from the walls?

She lowered the candle.

And she could see plainly that it wasn't water.

It was blood.

Jeanette screamed.

She spun around, just as another bolt of lightning illuminated the room. And there, on the far wall of the living room, just as she'd imagined her, was Beatrice, impaled by that pitchfork, her blood dripping all over the floor.

Jeanette screamed again.

In her terror and panic, she dropped the candle. She was returned to utter darkness.

This can't be happening! This can't be real! I am a student of philosophy at Yale University! I am a liberated woman! I am a child of the twentieth century! This cannot be real!

But her shoes still made sticky, squishy noises in the blood on the floor.

From somewhere in the room came the sound of crying.

A child.

A baby.

Jeanette was paralyzed with fear. Her mind could no longer process what was happening. She simply stood there, trembling, terrified—

Until the door blew open—and she saw the man with the pitchfork again in the doorway.

Jeanette turned and ran. The room was small, but suddenly it seemed cavernous. Such a small space—and yet she ran and ran, for many minutes it seemed, down an endless corridor that stretched farther and farther off into the distance. How could this be happening? How could she keep running for so long? What had happened to this room?

Behind her, the man's footsteps echoed as he pursued her. Thunder clapped overhead. Jeanette just kept on running, down that impossibly long corridor.

Finally she reached what seemed to be the end. There, in front of her, illuminated by a burst of lightning, sat a baby, its round button eyes staring in terror up at Jeanette. The baby began to cry. She tried to speak, but she found herself slipping in the blood on the floor. As she tumbled down face-first, she saw a pair of men's boots hurrying toward her.

She screamed.

Now there was nothing. No sound. No man. No baby.

Her heart thudding in her ears, she began to crawl across the floor. She looked up and saw the window. If she could only get to the window. If she could only pull herself up there somehow and open the window and squeeze herself outside into the rain. She might be safe then.

Or would the man still follow her, across the grounds, over the cliffs?

Something was moving in the dark. In a matter of moments, Jeanette was sure, the man would stand over her with his pitchfork as she lay there helpless on the floor.

The window.

It was her only chance.

No guarantee.

But a chance.

She forced her eyes to look up at the window.

She got to her knees, and then to her feet.

The window. She had to make it to the window.

FORTY
YEARS
LATER

Chapter One

Carolyn Cartwright had met the strange old man with the crooked back only once before, when he'd made his way slowly into her office in New York, one arm swinging at his side, his little tongue darting in and out of his mouth, constantly licking his lips. She had watched him approach her desk with a mixture of fear and fascination. This was the man Sid had told her would change her life.

Now, stepping out of the cab, Carolyn glanced up at the strange old man's house. It was magnificent, just as he had promised. A forty-room stone mansion high on a cliff overlooking the ocean. Carolyn could hear the waves crashing below.

"You sure you don't want me to wait?" the cabbie asked her again.

Carolyn leveled her eyes at him. It was all too much like those creaky old horror movies she used to watch as a kid: the dark old house, the locals warning the newcomer to stay away. The cabbie hadn't exactly warned her to turn back, but he had muttered a few times under his breath about Howard Young being crazy. "Richest man in Maine they say, ayuh," the cabbie told her in his heavy up-state accent. "And all his many far-flung relatives are just waiting for him to kick so they can divvy up the spoils."

Carolyn was not about to engage in idle gossip. She just paid the cabbie and told him that waiting would be unnecessary. "As I mentioned," she said, "I'm here as Mr. Young's guest for a couple of days. I'm doing some work for him."

"Ayuh, so you said, though you never did say what kinda work you had with such a strange old man," the cabbie muttered, taking her money. He handed her a business card in return. "You be sure to use that number on there if you need to make a fast getaway. I'll be back up this hill as fast as I can. A pretty girl like you alone in that big old house with that man . . ." He shuddered.

The cabbie's words frightened Carolyn, though she wouldn't admit it. Mr. Young unnerved her, too. The day they had met in her office, she had sat watching him warily. His rheumy old eyes had moved back and forth; his slithery little tongue had kept darting between his lips. He was ninety-eight years old, he told her, but he insisted that his mind was clear. Jeanette wasn't so sure. The things he said to her that day, sitting in front of her desk, his gnarled hands clasping the wolf's-head handle of his cane, had made little sense to her. But Sid had assured her Howard Young could be trusted.

And for what Mr. Young was paying her, a little unease was worth it.

Carolyn thanked the cabbie one more time,

then gripped her bag and turned to walk toward the house. The sun was low in the sky. Long dark shadows stretched across the grass. Ancient oak trees, their branches bent and twisted by decades of wind off the ocean, surrounded the house like sentinels. Built of granite and brownstone, the house seemed to become less distinct as she approached rather than more, the edges of its stone façade smoothed and muted by time and salt air. The only lights in the entire place were scattered along the lower floor, just to the east of the front door. The glow that emanated from the windows wasn't strong, however. It flickered, almost as if cast by candlelight.

The evening was cool, with a fragrance of impending autumn in the air. Soon those mighty oaks would drop their leaves, blanketing the great lawn with their brown and orange debris. It would turn cold and wet. She was very glad that her business here would be long done by then and she'd be back in her own little apartment in New York.

She reached the front door and lifted the metal knocker in the shape of a wolf. She banged hard against the wooden door three times.

It was as if the old man had been waiting behind the door. Immediately after knocking Carolyn heard a creak, and the door began to swing inward.

"Hello," she said, feeling silly that her heart was fluttering in her chest.

The door opened fully to reveal Howard Young. He stood slightly hunched over, large brown spots marking his face and hands. He was dressed in a silk paisley smoking jacket and gold ascot tie. He was already studying Carolyn with his yellow, watery eyes, just as he had that day in her office. She wasn't sure what he was looking for in her face, but he seemed to be intent on finding something. Finally, he smiled.

"Hello, Miss Cartwright," he said, in the same dry, cracking voice Carolyn remembered, like old leaves being crunched underfoot. He opened the door fully and stepped aside so she could enter.

Carolyn walked into the foyer. A gleaming marble floor led to a curved marble staircase and elegant gold banister ascending to the second floor. A chandelier with thousands of pieces of sparkling cut glass hung from the high ceiling. "One of the richest men in the nation," Sid had told her after Mr. Young had left her office that day. "Probably in the world." Looking at his house, Carolyn believed it.

And where did all of Mr. Young's money come from? "Real estate," Sid told her. "He owns vast tracts of property throughout New England and in other places around the country. The family's property, holdings date back to the early twentieth century, when they bought up entire blocks of cities. He owns a whole section of southern Florida. And when you're as business savvy as Howard Young, you know when to buy, when to sell, when to invest, and where to invest. He's got a magic touch in the stock market. The Young family money has been making money for them for almost a century. I always hope that by hanging around him some of his Midas touch might rub off on me."

Carolyn smiled to herself, remembering Sid's words. Howard Young was gesturing to her to follow him through the foyer toward the parlor. Their footsteps echoed across the marble. Certainly the house had the smell of old money. Carolyn's eyes fell upon upholstery and draperies that she was certain had been in the family for decades, maybe even a century. Portraits of people in nineteenth-century clothing hung along the walls. There was even a suit of armor standing at the foot of the staircase.

"I trust your flight from New York was uneventful," Mr. Young said as they walked.

"Yes, it was."

"And a cab was easy enough to find at the airport?"

"Oh, yes," Carolyn assured him.

"And the driver knew where the house was? We're kind of isolated, as you can see."

Carolyn smiled tightly. "He was aware of the place," she said.

Mr. Young stopped walking and turned, with some difficulty, to look at her. His lips turned up slightly at the corners. "Was he now?"

"Indeed he was," Carolyn told him. "I think he rather enjoyed playing the part of the coachman delivering Jonathan Harker to Castle Dracula."

Mr. Young laughed, an odd little sound down deep in his throat. His tongue darted in and out of his mouth again. "They always do," he said, and resumed walking.

Carolyn smiled to herself, still not quite believing she was there, that she had come all the way up to this windswept, godforsaken place. She wouldn't have agreed to the job if Sid hadn't encouraged her.

"I know he's eccentric," Sid had said, sitting down opposite her desk three weeks ago in her office, "but Howard was very impressed with you. He wants you for the job. And he's offered to pay you very well."

He had indeed. And Carolyn sure could use it.

"It's just the two of us here today," Howard Young informed her as they passed through double doors into the parlor. A fire blazed, obviously the flickering glow Carolyn had seen from outside. "I've given the entire staff the day off. I wanted no eavesdropping. What we have to discuss, as you know, Miss Cartwright, is utterly secret."

Ah yes, Carolyn thought. The old man's "secret." She looked over at him as he shuffled along ahead of her. There was some kind of secret about this house that even Sid knew nothing about.

"But you're his lawyer," Carolyn had said to Sid. "I'd think you'd know *all* his secrets."

"All of his legal and financial secrets, yes," Sid told her. "But this thing about his house . . . it's old family lore, that's all I know. Going back generations. Howard has assured me it's nothing illegal. I'm supposing it's something historical about his family, and Howard is very private about his family."

The old man gestured for her to take a seat on the divan in front of the fireplace. She smiled as she did so, placing her bag at her feet. "Now let me see if I understand your message," she said. "Whatever it is that you're hiring me to do, you want it completed in a month's time. Is that correct?"

"It needs to be taken care of before the last week of September."

"And why is that?" Carolyn asked.

Howard Young was watching her again with

those yellow eyes. "That is when my nieces and nephews are arriving for our regular family reunion."

"I see," Carolyn said, even if she still didn't.

"You travel lightly," Howard Young observed, seeming to notice her small, solitary suitcase for the first time.

"Just a couple changes of clothes and my toothbrush," she said. "Oh, and some pads, pencils, and a tape recorder." She grinned. "That's all I'll need, right?"

The old man returned her smile. "Depends on how much we get done in the next couple of days," he said.

Carolyn shifted uneasily on the divan. Two days. That's what she had told him she could give him. Two days. Whatever the job entailed, she assured him she could finish it in New York.

"Would you like a drink, Miss Cartwright? A glass of sherry, perhaps?"

"Thank you," she said. "And please. Call me Carolyn."

With difficulty, Mr. Young hobbled over to the small bar that sat beneath a pair of rifles mounted in an X on the wall. They looked old, perhaps First World War vintage, but they were in perfect condition, the silver shining, the wood polished. Mr. Young poured two glasses of sherry, and handed Carolyn's over to her. She accepted it, smiling again, hoping her unease didn't show too much.

Howard Young struggled to a chair that was undoubtedly his, a tall, well-worn wingback. On a side table rested several books, an assortment of prescription bottles, and a pair of eyeglasses.

"Enjoy," he said, lifting his sherry to her as he sat down. They both took a sip. The liquid tasted strange, like no sherry Carolyn knew. Sweet, dry, but bitter as well. She set the glass on the coffee table in front of the divan.

"I'm very anxious to hear more about the project you want me to work on," she said.

Mr. Young was studying her again with those ancient eyes. "In good time," he told me. His raspy voice suggested it was rarely used anymore. Carolyn imagined even communication with the servants was infrequent. Surely they knew their jobs and probably had been doing them for decades.

"First," Howard Young said, "I would like to learn a bit more about you. If we are to work together, I must make sure we are a perfect fit."

Carolyn raised her eyebrows. "I thought that was the reason you came down to New York, to scope me out after Sid recommended me. And I thought I passed muster."

He tilted his head slightly. "Oh, you did. But—"

"But?"

"I came back here with a few lingering concerns. Don't worry. If I decide you're not right in the end, I'll more than compensate you for your time and trouble."

"What are your lingering concerns?"

"You're younger than I thought you'd be."

It was like an accusation. Carolyn was momentarily at a loss at how to respond.

"When Sid referred you, I had the image in my mind of a middle-aged lady," he continued. "I expected you to be wearing a plaid business suit with a skirt and sensible black shoes when I met you."

Carolyn felt defensive. She couldn't remember how she'd been dressed the day Mr. Young had come to her office, but today's ensemble seemed appropriate enough. Sharply pleated khakis, a black turtleneck, low-heeled, open-toed black shoes, and a simple strand of pearls around her neck.

"Well, I'm sorry if I disappointed you," she said.

He shook his head. "Not disappointment. Merely mild surprise." He smiled again. "A man my age is never disappointed by a pretty woman."

Carolyn's smile was once again awkward.

He returned to being serious. "As you know, Sid referred me to you because of your work as an FBI investigator."

She nodded.

"And I was delighted to learn how you had been a specialist in some very unusual cases."

Again she nodded. "That specialty continued when I opened my own private investigation service in New York, which is how I met Sid." She laughed. "He hired me for several of his . . . well, stranger cases."

Mr. Young was nodding. "Indeed, Sidney has been an ideal lawyer for me. He has contacts all over the world." He folded his long, twisted fingers in his lap. "And he asks only the most essential questions. He understands the need for secrecy."

"Well," Carolyn said, "Sid has represented many very high-profile clients, like yourself, who don't want their personal business being thrown open to the prurient interests of the public. And I can assure you, Mr. Young, that my experience has also taught me the value of keeping secrets."

He had gone back to studying her face, as if he

saw something there—or wanted to. "You must have been very young when you started at the FBI."

"It was right out of college."

"And you said you were there for . . . four years?"

"Mr. Young," she said, smiling. "If you are trying to discern how old I am, I can simply tell you. I'm twenty-six."

He smiled and took another sip of his sherry. "And you are currently working as a freelance investigator?"

She nodded. "I take on investigative projects if someone like Sid refers me to them."

"Why did you leave the FBI? It would seem to me you had a promising career there."

She smiled tightly. "Personal reasons."

The old man nodded, almost as if he knew what they were. "I told Sid I was looking to hire a smart, thorough, critical thinker to help me with my project and, just as importantly, to write up an account of it all. Those were the criteria. And yours was the name immediately at the tip of his tongue."

He had told her as much that day in her office. "Well, as I said, I'm grateful to Sid for his confidence. . . ."

"What matters," Mr. Young continued, "is that I find someone whom I am able to trust with my deepest secrets. And also one who . . ." His voice trailed off as he seemed to search for the right words. "Who understands the world isn't always governed by forces we can see and hear firsthand."

Carolyn's face betrayed her confusion.

Mr. Young trained his old eyes once more on her. "You have investigated such things, Carolyn," he said. "Such things that live on the other side of our human senses."

"You're referring to—the supernatural?"

He nodded.

So Mr. Young's "secret" had something to do with the supernatural. Carolyn had suspected it might. So many of the cases she had investigated had defied easy solutions. At the FBI, she'd been called several times to investigate "paranormal" activity, so much so that she became one of the "go-to" people in the Bureau for these types of things. For example, there had been a series of strange deaths surrounding an abandoned church on Cape Cod, where a whole town was nearly wiped out by some mysterious killer who was never officially identified, but whom residents believed to be a malevolent spirit. Then there was the eerie haunting of another village not far away, where the ghost of a celebrated killer from a hundred years ago seemed to have returned to kill again. And then, most recently, there had been a series of brutal murders of several students at a girls' school in upstate New York—ritualistic slayings some blamed on the devil himself.

Of course, there was never conclusive "proof" of otherworldly or supernatural forces at work. But sometimes there was simply no other explanation. Investigating such stories had opened Carolyn's mind to the possibility that science and logic could not explain everything. Over the last two years, Sid had gotten her involved in a couple of far-out cases. One wealthy woman, being sued by her husband for divorce, began to practice voodoo on him; although the official investigation could never prove it, Carolyn's meeting with the husband left her convinced he was a zombie, and it was only through a strange woman who called herself a witch doctor that Carolyn was able to "wake him up" from the curse. Maybe he'd been faking; maybe he'd been psychotic; maybe he'd been on drugs. Still, it was all pretty exciting no matter what.

"When Sidney suggested you for my project," said Howard Young, "I had no idea how truly perfect you'd turn out to be."

She smiled. "So have I allayed all your concerns?"

"Most." His face grew solemn. "Because what I need your help with is perhaps beyond any of our understanding."

"Mr. Young, perhaps it's time you finally tell me what exactly it *is*."

"Patience, Carolyn. All in good time. First I must caution you that I have brought others in to help me in the past, and every one of them has failed."

"I see."

"Over the last fifty years I've worked with dozens of experts. And each time—" His face grew sad. "Each time we have met with failure. Now the time comes when we must address this issue again. And, given my age, it is certainly my last attempt to get it right."

Carolyn was starting to feel a little strung along. "Mr. Young, *please*," she said, "I'd like to give you my opinion on whether I can help you, but until I know more details . . ."

"The fact that you came all the way up here after

our brief meeting in New York shows you are at
least intrigued," he said.

"Yes, of course I am."

He smiled. "And I suppose my offer of payment
is also a motivation."

"I can't deny that." Carolyn held her eyes steady
with his. "One million dollars is a great deal of
money."

"For you, perhaps." He gave her a little smile.
"But it is a pittance I'll be glad to pay—if, and only
if, Carolyn, you are successful in what I need you to
do."

"Well, until you tell me what it is, we can't know,
can we?"

Mr. Young looked terribly sad. His eyes glanced
off toward the window. Beyond lay the rocky Atlantic coast. With the room suddenly quiet, Carolyn could hear the crash of the surf far below on
the rocks.

"Mr. Young," she asked, "are you all right?"

His eyes flickered back to her. They were moist.
"I am an old man, Carolyn. How much longer I
have to live is unknown. If I should die—someone
must carry on my work. Someone must find the
answer to the secret I have kept so long."

"Mr. Young, I don't know yet if I'm the right person for you, or even if your project is one that I will
want to take on. But you've certainly left me eager
to find out."

He smiled, clasping his old, veiny hands in his
lap. "That's all I can ask for now. Thank you, Carolyn."

"But I must say . . . if it's something that has
baffled the experts, I'm not sure I can do any dif-

ferently. I'm not necessarily an expert on the supernatural, Mr. Young. I'm an investigator. I go to *other* people for expert opinions."

He nodded. "I wanted you precisely because you are *not* an expert. You are a researcher. You don't pretend to have answers. You go out and *find* them." He chuckled. "Sid said you could be like a dog after a bone. What I like about you is that you will persevere and not rely on what is supposedly known or what is considered the accepted wisdom. You will dig. You will hunt."

He was talking in riddles. What was this secret?

"There is one other reason I chose you, Carolyn."

She raised her eyebrows. "And why is that?"

"Because you're a woman."

She laughed. "How does being a woman qualify me?"

"Because you will understand how a woman feels. How a woman loves."

She considered his words. "So this project—this secret of yours—concerns a woman."

He nodded. "Possibly."

"But how do you know that I will understand how a woman loves? Perhaps I have not experienced what she has. . . ."

"Oh, but you have." His eyes were hard now. "I needed to know something about you before I met you. So I learned a few things." He paused. "Such as your relationship with David Cooke."

A short expulsion of breath escaped her lips.

"I know all about him, Carolyn."

Once again, Carolyn felt on the defensive. Her lips pursed tightly. "Well," she said, "you're a regular FBI investigator yourself."

"A wealthy man can find out anything he wants," Howard Young said. "Believe me, Carolyn. I don't bring up his name to cause you any pain. I will not use the information to hurt you or harass you. It is just to say that I understand you—and I hope you will bring your own understanding and compassion to this project."

David. Even here—even in this strange house, on this faraway rocky coast—his name came back to haunt her. Would she never be free of him? For a second, all the old pain came flooding back—the lies, the tricks, the deceptions, the *fear*. Mr. Young was right about that much. Carolyn knew how a woman loved. She had loved all too well and been burnt for it. A day didn't go by that her heart didn't still ache for David—despite all he had done to her, all the terrible things she'd had to endure.

Not least of which was losing her savings and everything she owned. She was still paying off the debt David had racked up in her name. He had been one very shrewd operator. So the offer of a million bucks, especially with all of the obligations Carolyn had . . . there was no way she could pass that up.

Still, she didn't like that Howard Young had delved into her past. She didn't like being reminded of David. But hadn't *she* researched peoples' lives, uncovered secrets they'd rather not have her know? So she held her tongue. Carolyn let her emotions subside as they sat there in silence for several minutes. Finally, the old man spoke again.

"A wealthy man can find out anything he wants," he repeated, "except, sadly, the one thing that has eluded me now for all these years."

She managed a tight smile. "Which you aren't going to tell me, are you?"

He just looked at her.

"You're expecting me to discover it on my own," she said.

With great difficulty, Mr. Young rose from his chair, steadying himself on the arm. Carolyn stood along with him. He straightened his twisted back the best he could and looked over at her, crooking a finger to follow him.

"I might not tell you," he said, "but I will give you some very important clues."

He shuffled forward, out of the parlor and back into the foyer. Carolyn thought it odd, but she stood and followed him. Once again they crossed the great marble floor, their footsteps echoing in that vast space. At the far end of the foyer there was a door. Mr. Young pulled it open. There was a whiff of mustiness from the darkness within. Then Carolyn discerned the steps going down.

"The basement?" Carolyn asked.

Mr. Young said nothing, just took his first tremulous step down.

He moved down the stone steps with a purpose, even if he seemed at all times ready to topple over. The only light came from small narrow rectangles cut high into the walls of the basement. At the bottom of the steps was a stone floor. The dim pink light allowed Carolyn to make out crates and old furniture, a dressmaker's dummy and a steamer trunk. Everything was covered in a thick layer of dust and draped with cobwebs. Mr. Young didn't pause to look at any of it. He just kept moving as fast as he could, which was not very fast, across the floor. Carolyn followed.

"Where are we going?" she asked.

At the other side of the basement was a rusted iron door. Mr. Young was fumbling with some keys that he had taken out of his pocket.

"This was the servants' quarters when I was a boy, in the years right after the First World War," he told her. "Of course today we are far more egalitarian, and we let the servants go home at night to their own homes and families."

Carolyn tried to smile, but the darkness and mustiness made her uneasy. She had the distinct sense of being watched. It reminded her of her experience with George Grant, the man she believed had been turned into a zombie. Carolyn had been truly unnerved when she'd turned around to see him looking at her. Sid would later try to say he was just a con man trying to spook her. But Carolyn sensed something more. Grant's eyes had been glassy, his skin cold and clammy. For weeks afterward, she had slept with the lights on, thinking George Grant was there somewhere, watching her.

With a shaky hand, Howard Young managed to unlock the door. It swung open with a creak into the darkness within.

"This is where the secret lives," he said.

"Are you trying to frighten me, Mr. Young?" Carolyn asked.

"In your line of work, I imagine you are hard to frighten."

He didn't look back at her, just walked inside. Whether she was spooked or not, Carolyn couldn't tell; it was true that, after episodes like the one with George Grant, she didn't frighten easily. But she could see clearly that Mr. Young was afraid.

The old man was trembling now, so much so that it seemed as if he might fall over. Carolyn watched as he steadied himself against an old sofa covered with spiderwebs. He let out a long breath.

"So what is it about this room?" Carolyn asked. "What do you mean the secret lives here?"

Howard Young seemed lost in thought. "I remember coming down here as a boy. I'd sit up on this bed and listen to the stories she'd tell. We all did. She was the best storyteller."

"Who is *she?*"

Mr. Young was still trembling. Carolyn was now seriously concerned that he'd fall down and break his hip. That frightened her more than some unknown thing in the basement.

"I could not have imagined then what this room would become," the old man intoned. "When I was a boy, this place was filled with laughter. With happiness. With good cheer." His voice broke. "With love."

Carolyn glanced around. A small window high on the far wall had been boarded over. The light was very dim, hardly allowing her to see. But she scanned the walls and the floor. Except for the old sofa and a broken table, there was nothing in the room.

"Mr. Young," she said. "Where is the secret?"

"Here," he said plainly.

"I don't understand."

"You will."

They stood in silence a moment.

And then she saw it.

The words on the wall.

They were not there when they first came in.

She knew that much. The words on the wall had just suddenly appeared.

ABANDON HOPE.

And no matter how dim the light, Carolyn could see they were written in blood. It was still wet and dripping down the wall.

Chapter Two

Douglas Desmond Young IV was determined to arrive at his Uncle Howard's house well before any of his worthless cousins. Leaning forward on his motorcycle, he gave the Harley more gas. The wind rushing at his face and through his hair electrified him. He was looking forward to seeing old Uncle Howie again. It had been a little over a year since he'd last been up to Maine. Uncle Howie liked him because Douglas joked with him and kidded him. He didn't try to kiss his ass the way the others did. Uncle Howie called Douglas his "little hoodlum," and Douglas supposed that's just exactly what he was. And always had been.

Crossing the Maine border from New Hampshire, he accelerated the Harley even more. He knew he was breaking the speed limit. But who the fuck gave a damn? Like one of these hick mountain cops could ever catch him.

Douglas let out a laugh as he sped down the highway. His laughter trailed behind him like his long blond hair. On his right, he passed a young woman driving a white Corvette. He blew her a kiss as he zipped around her car. She waved back at him, but Douglas was in too much of a hurry to even think about stopping, no matter how pretty she had seemed to be.

Douglas had just turned twenty-four. Both his parents were dead, and he had no brothers or sisters. His father had been the grandson of Uncle Howie's older brother, so that actually made the old man Douglas's great granduncle—but to Douglas, he was just Uncle Howie, his closest living relative. Odd, that. So many generations between them and still there was no one more closely related to Douglas than Howard Young. He'd lost his father when he was fourteen. Dad had died of a heart attack at Uncle Howie's house, in fact. A year later, Douglas's mother took her own life by sticking her head in the gas oven. Douglas had gone to live with his father's sister after that, but when he was eighteen, Aunt Therese had followed Mom's example and offed herself with pills. Guess she figured Douglas was finally all grown up and could take care of himself from then on.

And he did. He did just fine. He decided against college, even though Uncle Howie had offered to pay for it. Instead, Douglas worked a series of jobs as a carpenter, a landscaper, and an unlicensed electrician. Then he'd signed on to a merchant ship for a year and sailed from San Francisco to Tokyo to Sydney. After that came a gig as the skipper of a shark-watching cruise off the coast of Maui. That took up another year. But once he hit twenty-four, Douglas figured he ought to start thinking about settling down. He didn't care much about money, but he knew he'd need some if he was ever going to be more than just a gypsy. So he hopped on his bike and headed north to Uncle Howie's. It might be more than a month before the scheduled family reunion in October, but Douglas wanted some time alone with his uncle. He intended to remind the old man that he was the last of his kin, all he had left in the world.

And that was something his prissy cousins could not claim.

Douglas was the last of his branch of the family. If his great-grandfather hadn't died so young, it would have been Douglas living in that big old mansion on the cliff. His great-grandfather had been the eldest son. It was he who should have inherited the estate. But because he died—another one of those mysterious family deaths that seemed to plague the Young family—it had been Howard who became master of the great house, the controller of the family fortune. That's why Douglas's cousins, especially that prissy Philip—and his equally prissy offspring Ryan and Chelsea—brownnosed the old man the way they did. It was always, "Oh, Uncle Howard, can I get you anything?" "Uncle Howard, you look so fit and well!" "Uncle Howard, I'm going to name my first son after you!" It made Douglas want to puke.

Up ahead was the exit for Youngsport. The family was so rich the town was named after them. Douglas angled the bike and slowed down a bit as he headed onto the off-ramp. He thought he could smell the sea from here. He'd always loved the scent of salty air and briny water. It brought back happy memories. It made him think of the days when his dad and mom were still alive.

They'd come up here to Maine from their house in Connecticut and picnic on the great lawn that ran alongside the cliffs. Douglas would watch the seabirds dive into the ocean to catch fish. Sometimes Dad would take him out on a skiff and they'd dive off the sides, swimming in the cold, clear, blue water. Those were good days. Everybody had seemed so happy.

Roaring the Harley down a winding, maple-tree-lined lane, Douglas was glad to be back in Maine. He hadn't called Uncle Howie to tell him he was coming. He didn't want his cousins getting wind of his early arrival. If they did, Ryan would no doubt hop in his Mercedes-Benz and head north to join them, his obnoxious twin sister Chelsea probably in tow. They weren't about to allow their vagabond cousin Douglas any free, uninterrupted time with Uncle Howard. Douglas just laughed. He knew Uncle Howie would be glad to see him. He always was. The one thing Douglas wished was that Brenda had accompanied him. It would have been good for Uncle Howie to see that he was finally serious about a girl, that he might really be ready to settle down.

Except he wasn't. Not really. He didn't love Brenda, and she had figured that out. She was a great girl, but the sparks just weren't there. Douglas had never known sparks. Maybe they were just fairy tales. But Dad had said he'd felt sparks for Mom. "She is my morning, noon, and night," he'd said. Douglas figured Mom had felt the same way, since after Dad's sudden death during a family reunion in Maine, she pulled inward, becoming sullen and depressed. That was why she'd taken her life.

No such passion existed between Douglas and Brenda. "Face it, Douggie," she'd said, when he'd asked her to come with him on this trip. "I'm just an ornament for the back of your bike. You just want to show me off to all those rich relatives of yours. You just want them to think you're gonna get married and be a respectable member of the family. I know you too well, Douggie. I know you don't really want to marry me."

He'd tried insisting that he did, but he couldn't even convince himself. Brenda deserved better. She was a hardworking waitress at a twenty-four-hour diner on the highway outside Syracuse. She had big gorgeous brown eyes and the figure of a model. What guy wouldn't want her? But there just weren't any sparks.

Douglas rounded the bend and started heading up the hill. At the crest of the hill, he knew, was Youngsport, the little village overlooking the sea. And at the very top sat his uncle's house.

Suddenly a person darted in front of him from the side of the road. It all happened so fast that Douglas couldn't see who it was or exactly how far ahead of him the person was. All he could do was instinctively swerve the bike to his right. He careened off the road, bumping over the curb and burning a rut through the tall grass. Only through sheer luck did he avoid hitting a tree. The bike's momentum was slowed by the grass and the swampy muck on the side of the road. He came to a stop with the Harley nearly on top of him, its front tire still spinning.

"What the fuck?" Douglas shouted.

He pulled himself up from under the bike. He glanced out into the road to see if the person was still there. No one. There was silence, except for the hissing of the Harley. Douglas turned back to the bike and righted it, cursing the mud that clung to it as well as to himself, but thankful for it, too. It likely prevented a far worse injury.

He stepped out onto the road, looking around again for the fool who had run in front of him. Once more, he saw no one. Where the hell had they gone? Standing there, looking up and down the road, Douglas was struck by just how quiet it was. Not a sound. No cars in the distance. He wasn't that far from the highway. He thought he should have been able to still hear the rumble of trucks. But it was silent. Utterly, completely silent. There weren't even any birds. The trees were thick with bright green leaves. Shouldn't he hear some chattering from the branches? It was like watching television with the volume turned all the way down. The only thing Douglas could hear was his own heart, still racing from his fall.

Then he saw her.

The person who had run in front of his bike.

It was a young woman. She stood across the street in a white dress, staring at him. Her hair was long and black, blowing in a breeze that made no sound as it danced through the trees. Douglas was caught by her dark eyes. He stood there immobile.

"You okay, buddy?"

Douglas blinked.

A man in a red pickup truck had pulled up alongside him. He hadn't heard him arrive, hadn't seen him until he was there, practically on top of him. The volume had been turned back up. Crows were calling from the treetops. Mosquitoes buzzed around his ears.

Douglas turned his eyes to the man in the truck. He was leaning across the seat, talking to him through the rolled-down passenger window.

"You okay?" the man asked. "Looks like quite a spill you took there."

Still Douglas didn't reply. He moved his eyes past the truck to search out again the dark woman in the white dress.

But she was gone.

"Yeah, thanks," Douglas finally managed to say. "I'm okay."

"How's the bike?"

Douglas turned around to inspect it. "Handlebar's a little banged up. But it could've been worse."

"What made you swerve like that? Fall asleep at the wheel?"

"No. Didn't you see her? Some girl—" Again Douglas's eyes panned the trees across the road. "She ran in front of me. It was all I could do to avoid hitting her."

"Didn't see no girl. Where is she now?"

"I don't know," Douglas said, looking again at his bike.

"You gonna be able to ride it?" the man asked.

Douglas shrugged. "I'm gonna have to try."

"Here." The man turned the ignition off in his truck and stepped outside. He was a big beefy sort, with big arms without any muscular definition and practically no neck. He wore a Red Sox baseball cap and a blue flannel shirt with the sleeves cut off. "We can put it in the back of the truck, and I can drop you off at Stu's Mechanic Shop in town."

"I'll probably be all right," Douglas said.

The man made a face. "Why take a chance, bud?

The sheriff here ain't a very forgiving man. He'll ride your tail if he sees you."

Douglas sighed and steered the bike over to the back of the truck. The man let down the hatch and lowered a ramp. Together they rolled the bike into the truck bed.

"Name's Murphy," the man said. "Reggie Murphy. You're not from around here."

They shook hands. "No, but I have family here," Douglas told him. "Come to visit." He met Reggie Murphy's eyes with his own. "I'm Douglas Young."

"Oh, one of the Youngs," Murphy said. "Back to see the old man, eh?"

Douglas nodded as he slipped into the truck. Murphy returned to his place behind the wheel. He had been smoking a cigar. He placed it back in his mouth now and took a long drag.

"I was up there at the house a few months ago," Murphy said, exhaling smoke as he started the truck. "I work for a contractor, and Mr. Young hired us to do some work on the back terrace. Man, that is one fine house."

"It is indeed," Douglas said, glancing out the window as they drove past the wall of maple trees. Once more he wondered where the woman had gone and why she had just stood there staring at him. That eerie silence perplexed him. He must have been stunned from the impact. That must have been why he hadn't heard anything for several minutes, why the woman's eyes had so entranced him.

Her dark, beautiful eyes.

"You've got your big family reunion coming up this fall, don't you?" Murphy was asking. "That's what your uncle had us doing the work for. You know, fixing up the terrace, laying down some new stonework. A lot of it had started to crumble. That's an old house. When was it built? Like 1900, right?"

"Yes, I think so," Douglas said, still distracted, still looking out the window.

"Mr. Young was quite excited about the family gathering. Happens only once every ten years. So it's quite the event, eh?"

Douglas nodded. "It's the only time all of us are together. I try to make it a point to see my uncle every year or so, and occasionally I'll run into some of the others while I'm there. But the reunion is the one time when every Young is expected to make an appearance."

Murphy laughed. "And if they don't, it could mean being taken out of the will, eh?"

Douglas made no reply to that.

They had turned onto the town road. Maple trees gave way to small houses, then a convenience store, then the white clapboard post office. An American flag whipped in the breeze out front. And next to it was the mechanic shop. The word STU'S was painted in big red letters on its shingled roof.

"Well, here you go, my friend," Murphy said, pulling the truck in for a stop and shutting off the ignition. "Let's roll that bike in and let Stu take a look."

The damage wasn't serious. "I can probably have it fixed for you by tomorrow morning," Stu told him. He was a weather-beaten old man with intense blue eyes, wearing a pair of white overalls stained nearly black with grease and oil. Douglas thanked him. Unhooking his backpack from the side of the bike, he flung it over his shoulder.

"I can give you a ride up to the house," Murphy said.

"No, thanks," Douglas said. "I really appreciate your help. But I can walk from here. Will do me good. Clear my head a little." He smiled. "And it'll be good to check out the town again. It's been a while."

Murphy gave him a salute and headed off in his truck. Douglas took a deep breath. His knees and forearms were starting to ache a little from the fall. But what troubled him more was how fuzzy his mind still felt. He couldn't get over that dreamlike sensation he'd experienced right after the accident. The way that woman had looked at him. The way her eyes had held him. He hadn't ever wanted to look away.

He began to trudge up the hill from the village. He knew there was an old stone staircase cut into the side of the cliff. It led almost all the way up to Uncle Howie's house. He found it without too much trouble. The steps began in the mossy backyard of the town's drugstore. When Douglas was a boy, it was called Andersen's Pharmacy, and he'd sit there with Dad and drink strawberry milkshakes at the counter. Now the old building had been torn down and replaced with a shiny new CVS. But the old staircase was still out in back, even if it was largely grown over with ivy and grass. Douglas started up.

He wasn't a guy who was easily spooked. He'd gone down in that shark cage off the coast of Maui many times and had witnessed plenty of fangs gnawing against the iron bars in front of him. He'd found it thrilling. On the merchant ship, he'd survived many storms; one time, they'd nearly capsized. Even when he'd found his mother's lifeless body in the kitchen of their house, some ten months after his father had died, Douglas hadn't freaked out. He was just fifteen years old, but he calmly called 911 and followed the operator's instructions carefully. He shut off the gas, then checked for a pulse. When he reported that there was none, the operator told him to stay right there, that help was on its way. So he'd sat on the linoleum floor, holding his mother's cold hand, for twenty-five minutes. He didn't cry until the funeral, and then only for a moment.

But his famed self-control had taken a spill back there along with his bike. He couldn't get that woman's eyes out of his mind. Who was she? Why had she run out in front of him? Why had she stood there staring at him? And why hadn't Murphy seen her?

Halfway up the cliff, the staircase was nearly obliterated by intrusive tree roots and years of rockslides. Still, Douglas managed, careful not to lose his footing even if his knees were really starting to ache. He thought maybe he'd scraped his thigh, too. He thought he could sense blood under his dark blue jeans.

He turned as the path led through an old cemetery. And not just any cemetery. Douglas knew it had been the private burial ground for the Young family for several generations. His parents weren't buried here; they were back in Connecticut. But his grandparents were here, and lots of other old relatives dating back to the early nineteenth century. This was where Uncle Howard insisted he would be buried someday as well.

A big black crow alit on top of one old brownstone grave marker. It let out a caw and spread its wings, then folded them against its sides. Douglas squinted to make out the words that were engraved on the stone.

DESMOND D. YOUNG

1880–1930

That was his great-great-grandfather. Uncle Howie's father. He had passed on his middle name Douglas all the way down through five generations. Glancing around the cemetery as the crow let out another cry and took off into the air, Douglas shivered as the bird's shadow passed across his face. Across the way stood a newer stone. This one marked his great grandfather, the first Douglas Desmond Young. Died 1940. And then, off to the right, a shiny marble slab, flush with the earth. This was Douglas's grandfather. Died 1980.

They all died in the first year of a new decade, Douglas thought. He'd never realized that until now. *The first year of a new decade—when the family reunion was held.*

Like this year.

Douglas continued to make his way up the path. Dead leaves crunched underfoot. A blue jay seemed to scold him from somewhere in the trees above.

And then he saw it.

Through the trees, the great stone house on the top of the hill came into view. It was a house that seemed to grow bigger and more impressive every time Douglas saw it. Usually, places you knew as a kid seemed smaller when you saw them again as adults. But Uncle Howie's house seemed to grow another wing every time Douglas visited. Of course it hadn't. There was nothing new about the house, nothing at all, unless one counted that terrace out back that Murphy had said he'd worked on. Uncle Howie's house was like a trip back into time. The stones worn smooth by decades of wind and salt air told the story of its long existence.

Crunching through the leaves up the final bluff, Douglas neared the great lawn of the estate. In the far distance he spied the barn, where Uncle Howie kept his stable of prize horses. To the right were the tennis courts; to the left was the greenhouse, where the old man tended his rare and exotic orchids. Here on top of the hill, the wind whipped hard against Douglas's face. He could hear it howling through the eaves of the house as he got closer. He was happily anticipating the look of surprise when Uncle Howie saw him—a look that would turn to both joy and bemusement, Douglas thought. Joy because his little hoodlum had come for an unexpected visit, and bemusement when he saw the mud all over his clothes.

A small smile had begun to stretch across Douglas's face when suddenly he saw her again.

The young woman who had run in front of his bike.

Douglas froze.

She stood across the lawn. She was just a tiny figure, about a hundred yards away. At this distance Douglas couldn't see her eyes as clearly as he had earlier, but it was her all right. The same dark hair, the same filmy white dress, both blowing in the wind.

"Hey!" Douglas shouted.

She stood there looking at him.

"Hey! Who are you? Why are you following me?"

He began to approach her across the grass. He had made it about halfway when she suddenly turned and bolted. "Hey!" Douglas called again.

The woman ran along the cliffs. Douglas could see now that she was barefoot.

He ran after her.

"I don't want to hurt you!" he cried. "I just want to make sure you're okay! And find out why you're following me!"

She just kept running toward the cliffs.

"Be careful!" Douglas shouted, slowing down himself. "Okay, I won't come after you!"

But still the woman ran. She was just a distant speck on the far side of the cliffs by now, though her dark hair was still discernible in the bright sunlight. She ran as if she were terrified. She ran so fast—

Douglas blinked.

She ran straight off the side of the cliff!

"Jesus!" Douglas cried and began running himself again.

Had he seen right?

That crazy woman ran right off the cliff!

He reached the spot where she had gone over and looked down. There was no sign of a body on the rocks below. The water was just far enough beyond the rocks that there was no way she could have fallen into the surf. If she'd run off this cliff at this spot, she'd be lying right down there, mangled on the rocks below. It was at least a forty-foot drop. No one could have survived that, especially not at the rate she'd been running. There was no way she could have jumped off and then run down the beach. She'd have smashed onto the rocks. But there was no body anywhere.

It was as if she'd vanished into the air.

Douglas ran his hands through his long hair. "Jesus," he whispered to himself.

Has he imagined the whole thing?

He remembered how stunned and dazed he'd felt back on the road, right after the accident. Had he hit his head and not realized it? He must have. This had all been a hallucination. There was no woman. At least not up here. Maybe there had been, down on the road—there *had* to have been, for *someone* had run in front of him—but not up here. Thinking rationally, Douglas concluded he was certain that he'd been alone as he climbed up the cliffside staircase. And if the woman had come by the road, there was no way she would have beat him here. The road from the village up to Uncle Howie's house was long and winding. To walk it would take at least double the amount of time that it took to take the staircase. So there was no way the woman could have gotten here before him.

"Freaky," he murmured to himself, looking down at the rocks. The only sound was the steady crash of the surf and the occasional call of a lonesome gull.

Finally Douglas roused himself. He began heading once again across the great lawn. He wouldn't mention any of this to Uncle Howie. There had been a time, right after his mother died, when Douglas had smoked a bit too much pot. Aunt Therese had reported as much to Uncle Howie. The old man had sat Douglas down and lectured him against the dangers of marijuana. Douglas had nodded, pretending to listen, but it had been the magic of that wonderful weed that had kept him sane not only after Mom's death but after Aunt Therese's as well. A couple of times when Douglas came to visit Uncle Howie after that, his clothes had reeked of pot, and his uncle had noticed. There was a disapproving look for his little hoodlum.

For the last few years, however, Douglas had pretty much cleaned up his act. He'd maybe smoke a joint on a Saturday night with Brenda, but that was all. For this visit to his uncle, he fully intended to present himself as upstanding and serious. If he started telling tales of barefoot women jumping off cliffs, Uncle Howie would assume he'd been smoking that wacky weed again. So Douglas would keep his little hallucination to himself. The muddy clothes were going to be bad enough. Uncle Howie always worried one of these days his nephew would crash his motorcycle.

Douglas decided to blame it on a squirrel.

"I swerved to avoid hitting a squirrel," he said out loud, practicing the line he'd use with his uncle.

He smiled. He thought that would work.

There would be no talk of mysterious women who disappeared into thin air.

Chapter Three

The look in Karen's eyes was enough to shatter Paula's heart, but there was *no way*—no way in heaven or, more appropriately, *hell*—that she was going to give in.

"All my life," Karen was saying, "I've dreamed of having a baby."

"I know, sweetie. I know."

"I don't understand," Karen said. She was angry, but more tearful and sad than anything else. She was a simple girl, a farm girl from Nebraska. All Karen wanted was a home and children. She was old-fashioned like that. But as much as Paula loved her, there was no way she could give that to her.

What made it worse was that she couldn't tell her why.

"You're great with kids," Karen argued, trying for nearly the hundredth time to convince her partner to conceive a child. "You're a teacher! Your students adore you! I've watched you with them. You'd make a great mother."

Paula sighed and looked out her window down onto Commonwealth Avenue. The day was warm, the air pleasant, so she'd opened all the windows of her apartment. Autumn would soon be here, and then winter—and the days of open windows would be over. From the street, taxicabs were bleating. Paula could hear a group of little children laughing. It broke her heart.

There was nothing she could say to Karen. Yes, indeed, she loved kids. In her job teaching English as a second language to immigrants from Puerto Rico, Colombia, Vietnam, and Mexico, she found great satisfaction and joy being with children. She agreed she'd make a wonderful mother, especially with Karen as co-parent. They could raise a wonderful family. If only things were different.

They'd been together five years now. Karen was the love of Paula's life. There had been other girlfriends who had come and gone, but only Karen had truly captured her heart. Right from the start, Paula had wanted to give Karen the world. And she could. Paula had money—her father's will had ensured that at least some of the Young fortune had already made its way to her. But Karen didn't care about Paula's wealth. She cared only about having a baby, a child to love and to raise. She herself was unable to conceive, which was the great sadness of her life. So a child was the one thing she looked to Paula to give her. But it was the one thing Paula could never do.

For a time, Paula had considered telling Karen a lie. She'd agree to go to the doctor and get tested. Then she'd come back and announce that she, too, was sterile. But surely then Karen would want to adopt. Paula had phoned her Uncle Howard and asked him if an adopted child would still face the family curse. He couldn't be sure. Perhaps without the actual bloodline the child would be free. But he could give her no guarantee. That wasn't enough assurance for Paula. She had seen what had happened to her father and to the others. There was no way she could ever bring a child into the family, through birth or adoption, to face that.

So she had told Karen that she simply didn't want children. "A child would change our lives," she said, over and over, a claim she repeated now.

"Yes, it would," Karen said. "It would give us new purpose, a new direction."

Paula turned away from the window to look at her. "Do we need a new purpose? A new direction? Aren't you happy just with me?"

"I love you, Paula. Yes, I'm happy. But I don't feel . . . complete."

Paula couldn't admit that she felt exactly the same way. When she was a teenager, before she'd learned about that room and the terrors it held for her family, she'd dreamed of having kids. Lots of them. How she'd loved watching over her little brother and her little cousins when the adults were inside Uncle Howard's house, talking about those serious things that made them frown and sometimes cry. Paula hadn't understood what all that had been about back then. She'd just been a kid romping in the grass.

Now she was nearly forty. Karen was telling her that her biological clock would soon run out. Paula countered that no kid wanted an old woman for a mother. But it was an argument that didn't hold water. Karen's own mother had been forty-two when she gave birth to Karen. "And Mom was the best mother in the world!" Karen told her emphatically.

A couple of times, Paula had come close to telling her the truth. But each time, she had chickened out at the last possible moment. The secret shamed her. What kind of family had to live with such a thing? She lived the years between those terrible family reunions in a state of denial; she imagined everyone in the family did. To think of it, to actually speak of it, would make it too real. What would Karen *think* if she told her? She might even leave her. At the time of the last family reunion ten years ago, they hadn't met each other. So there had been no reason for Paula to tell Karen about the family's terrible secret. Not until now—because next month she would have to drive up to Maine and face the chance that this time it might be *her* spending a night in that room.

No way would she ever let a son or daughter of hers face that.

"It's just the way I feel," she said to Karen, her eyes growing moist. "I'm sorry if that hurts you, baby. You don't *know* how sorry I am."

Karen said nothing more. Once again the discussion had gone nowhere. She just wiped her eyes and grabbed her purse. "I need to go for a walk," she announced.

"Baby—"

Karen flinched when Paula moved to embrace her. So Paula stood back and let her pass, saying nothing more. The door closed hard on Karen's way out.

Paula looked once more out the window. She

saw Karen emerge from the building onto the sidewalk and hurry down the street. She thought she was crying. Paula's heart broke.

She turned and caught a glimpse of herself in the mirror on the wall. She looked hard. Closed off. She studied her blue eyes, hiding behind lowered lids. Her face was tight, the lines around her eyes more pronounced. Once, Paula had been very pretty. Her hair was still auburn, her eyelashes still dark and thick, but a light seemed to have gone out in her eyes. It was extinguished by the pain and disappointment that she had seen on the face of the woman she loved. Pain and disappointment she had caused.

Paula let out a long sigh. There was no way she could just sit here and wait for Karen to come back. She needed to talk to someone. Someone who would understand.

Paula grabbed her own purse and hurried out of the apartment, locking the door behind her and taking the steps two at a time. In the building's garage, she hopped into her Mercedes CLK 350 and roared out onto the street. In a matter of minutes she was on the Massachusetts Turnpike, headed west. She flew through the suburbs, leaving behind the brownstone of the city for the soft rolling hills of the western part of the state. She dug her phone out of her purse and pressed a number on it, holding the device to her ear.

"I'm sorry I didn't call, but I'm on my way to see you," she said when the person answered. "Is that okay?" She listened, a small, grateful smile creeping across her face. "Thanks. I'll be there in about ten minutes."

Her brother's house was a sprawling white modern structure nestled deep in the woods. Dean had designed it himself. One of the top architects in Boston, Dean Young had been the best baby brother Paula could have asked for. He was the first person she told that she was gay. He had received the news with a warm smile and asked if there was anyone special in her life. At the time, there had not been, but now he and his wife and their kids adored Karen. Little Zac and Callie were always asking when they might have some cousins from Aunt Paula and Aunt Karen. How times were changing. Even in the midst of her distress, Paula smiled, thinking of her brother's family.

But it was precisely because of those two children—Zac and Callie—that Paula needed so desperately to talk to Dean.

"Hey, sis," he called to her from the side yard as her car crunched into the gravel driveway. "We're out back. You're just in time for a barbecue."

She got out of the car and walked through the yard. Eleven-year-old twins Zac and Callie were splashing in the small lake on the side of the house, making their way through the tall cattails that grew there. Even from the yard Paula could see the dragonflies skittering above the lake. Dean's wife Linda was placing a blue-and-white checkered tablecloth on the picnic table. Dean himself had returned to the grill, flipping some burgers and dogs. A typical weekend at the Youngs' house. The perfect picture of a happy family.

As if something dark wasn't lurking in the shadows, waiting to destroy them all.

"Where's Karen?" Linda asked.

"Oh," Paula said uncomfortably. "She had some . . . errands to run today."

Flames crackled from the grill. "You want a hamburger or a hot dog?" Dean asked.

Paula smiled. "Neither, at the moment." She glanced out at the kids in the lake. They were waving up at her, calling "Hi, Auntie!" Paula waved back. Again her heart seemed to splinter into a hundred pieces.

She took a seat at the picnic table as Linda poured her a glass of lemonade from a pitcher. "Something on your mind, Paula?" her sister-in-law asked.

"Well . . ." She hesitated, then smiled. She took a sip of the lemonade. "Yes, there is."

"We figured, given how you sounded on the phone." Linda moved around the table toward the grill. "I think it's time I relieved the cook of his duties. Give you two some time for a good brother-sister chat."

"Thanks, Lin."

She watched as Linda, without saying a word, took the spatula from Dean's hand and nodded for him to join Paula at the table. How comfortable their relationship was. How easy was their communication. There were no secrets between them. There couldn't be. Linda had witnessed the family curse up close and personal. She had been there for the last family reunion ten years ago. She'd been there to watch their cousin Douglas enter that room in the basement. And she'd been there when they'd opened the door the next morning. . . .

Paula shuddered.

Her brother was sitting down beside her. "What I'm *hoping* you've come to tell us," he said, "is that you and Karen have finally set a date to get married."

Paula felt her eyes moisten. "Oh, I *wish* that was what I was here for."

Dean reached over and placed his hand over hers. "Talk to me, sis."

"How do you do it?" she asked him plainly, looking at him directly.

His brown eyes held hers. "How do I do what?"

She gestured over at Zac and Callie splashing in the lake. "How do you go on, knowing that someday they will have to—" She couldn't bring herself to speak the words.

Her brother sighed. "It's a terrible burden. All I can do is pray that soon we will no longer have to deal with that room, that we will find a way to end the curse."

Paula laughed bitterly. "End the curse? Eighty years, Dean! For eighty years—since our great-grandfather's time—our family has tried to find a way to do that. But we have always failed."

Dean's eyes were fixed on his children. A look of profound sadness had settled over his face. "I know, Paula. Sometimes it feels as if there will never be an end."

"How could you even bring them into this world, knowing what they would have to face?"

He turned to look at her sharply. "You know why! We had hope then! After Dad died in that room, we brought in that expert, Dr. Hobart. Remember? Remember how optimistic we were? It seemed as if the curse was over. When Aunt Jeanette—"

Paula raised her hands instinctively, almost as if to cover her ears. "Yes, Dean! I remember all that!

Let's not speak it aloud again!" It was too hard for Paula to remember. Such hope. It hurt now to remember that they all had had such hope.

He nodded. "All right. But it was during that period that Zac and Callie were born."

She studied him. "There was hope then, yes. But there was no guarantee."

He shook his head. "No. There was no guarantee."

"And you and Linda had them anyway."

Once again Dean glanced off at his children. He didn't speak.

"Karen wants a baby," Paula said after a silence of about a minute. "She's been wanting one for some time. And I suspect this time will be decisive for her." She paused. "She's going to leave me if I don't agree."

Her brother moved his eyes back to her. "That's it, Paula. That's the answer to why we need the children."

"What is?"

He smiled wanly. "We can't stop living."

"So you're saying . . . you chose to have children even though there was no absolute guarantee that Dr. Hobart would rid the family of the curse? You chose to still have them because *we can't stop living*?"

Dean nodded slowly.

"And did you ever regret your decision after it turned out that Hobart was wrong—that the curse was still as strong as ever?"

"Look at them in the lake," Dean told her. Callie was splashing Zac and he was laughing, his tinkly little voice echoing through the trees. "How could I regret them?"

"You'll regret it if you ever have to watch one of them go in that room!" Paula charged, her voice getting louder. "The way we watched Daddy! Do you want to open that door one morning and see Zac in there—or Callie—the way we saw Daddy? Or cousin Douglas?"

"Of course not!" Dean stood suddenly, angry now. "Of course I don't want to see that!"

"I don't want to see it either! So if it means losing Karen, then so be it! I will not bring a child into this world if it means that!"

Linda had approached the table. Her face was torn with concern and anguish. "Please," she said. "Don't let the children hear you."

"I have to believe," Dean said, lowering his voice, "that this time, it will end."

"Why this time?" asked Paula. "What makes this time any different from all the other times?"

"Uncle Howard has spent millions in the last ten years. He's met with all sorts of people. And this time he's very encouraged. There's someone up there with him now. . . ."

"How do you know?"

"I phoned him a few days ago, and he told me he was expecting someone." Dean sighed. "He seemed optimistic."

Paula shook her head. "He was optimistic about all the others as well."

"If only we could all just move far away," Linda mused out loud, her eyes on her children. "Sever all ties to the rest of the family. Start over. New names . . ."

Her husband was quick to dismiss the idea. "It was tried. You know that, Linda. Uncle Ernie tried that, and we all know what happened to him."

They were quiet. Yes, indeed, they all knew what had happened to Ernest Young. After attending two successive family reunions, Uncle Ernie decided he no longer wanted to press his luck. He didn't want to end up in that room himself. So he bundled up his wife and two young daughters and disappeared to parts unknown. None of the rest of the family had known where he was or how to contact him. But *something* knew how to find him. When Ernie failed to show for the family reunion, Uncle Howard feared the worst for him. But it wasn't for a couple of weeks that the family learned that his fears were valid. Dental records confirmed that the identities of a family slaughtered by an unknown assailant in their home in the town of Fond du Lac, Wisconsin, were not Jim and Julie Baker and their daughters Kathy and Stephanie, as their neighbors had thought for the past seven years. Rather, they were Ernie, Molly, Ann Marie, and Susie Young. Each had been decapitated, and on the walls of their house, written in their blood, were the words: ABANDON HOPE.

There was no running away. That was the lesson Uncle Ernie had taught them. Instead of just one death that year, there were five. The family did, indeed, abandon hope.

At least until Dr. Kip Hobart, a parapsychologist, had come along. There had been séances. There had been exorcisms. There had been Catholic priests and Wiccan shamans. There had been ghost hunters who vowed the house was "clean." There had been hope. Paula remembered that hope—so painful now that it seemed to burn in her gut. Because the hope had ended the morning they found poor cousin Douglas dead on the floor of that room, his hands tied behind his back and a plastic bag secured over his head.

Poor Douglas. Paula's mind flashed back to the last family reunion ten years earlier. Douglas had had a teenaged son and namesake whom he sent upstairs to bed before they all gathered in the parlor for the lottery. Little Douglas was sound asleep upstairs, unaware of the terror his father faced in the basement. Paula remembered the way the boy's face had crumpled in the morning when he learned the news of his father's death. Little Douglas was now old enough this year to be told the family secret. Uncle Howard surely had plans to sit down with him and break it to him, as gently as possible.

And what happened after Uncle Howard was gone? He was ninety-eight years old. Surely this was his last reunion. Who would take over from him? Paula just wanted to burn the house down—or at least move out. But that had been tried, too. A couple of generations ago, the whole family had tried running away, all except Uncle Howard, who feared such avoidance of the lottery would only bring about more slaughter. He was right. On the designated night, no one entered the basement room—but on the next morning, Francis Young, one of the far-flung nephews, died of a massive heart attack. The morning after, Francis's infant son Michael was found dead in his crib. And on the morning after that, one hundred miles away, twelve-year-old Andrew Young dropped dead face-first into his oatmeal. The remaining members of the clan got the message. Terrified, they all rushed to Uncle Howard's house. The lottery was held as it should have been, and David Young, Francis's younger brother, was chosen to enter the room. The next morning, David was dead of a stab wound to the heart, but the parade of deaths ended after that.

At least for another decade.

What always amazed Paula was how the local Youngsport authorities never seemed to get wise to the odd mortality schedule of the family. Much of it had to do, of course, with Uncle Howard's wealth: if the richest man in the state, indeed one of the richest men in the country, decided that the strange deaths that occurred regularly every ten years in his house were suicides or accidents, then the authorities simply went along. Even this latest sheriff, George Patterson, known to be a hard nut to crack, had been fooled by the death of cousin Douglas. At first he was skeptical that Douglas had accidentally suffocated himself while trying to play a trick, casting suspicious eyes around at all of them. But the family's abject grief had finally absolved them of any blame in the sheriff's mind. They didn't seem like murderers; they seemed like a family decimated by tragedy—which they were.

Dean was calling the kids to come up and eat. Their hamburgers and hot dogs were ready. Paula stood, feeling no better than she had when she left the city to come out here. She had hoped that Dean might be able to say something to her—*anything*—that could have alleviated some of her anguish. But hope was no longer a commodity in her life. She understood that finally. Karen would leave her. She'd be alone. That was her fate. It was, no doubt, better that way.

She watched as Zac and Callie dried themselves

off on the banks of the lake with big white terry-cloth towels. She loved the twins with all her heart. There had to be a way to protect them from that room—a way to free their futures, so they would not spend their lives as trapped as she and the others had always felt.

A flash of movement in the woods just beyond the lake drew Paula's eye.

Was it—a deer?

No.

Paula's blood went cold.

It was a man. In the woods.

He had been watching them.

In that instant a thousand thoughts and emotions flooded her mind. A man. Watching them. A threat.

But no. Why would he be a threat? A neighbor perhaps. A hiker.

Her heart began to race.

She knew that was wrong. The man was no neighbor, no innocent hiker.

He was likely not even a man at all.

Even as the figure faded once more into the shadows of the woods, Paula knew what it was. In the weeks leading up to a reunion, there were often sightings. Apparitions from another time. The forces that had brought upon the curse that ruled over their lives.

Sometimes there were sightings of a woman. Paula had seen the woman with the long dark hair and white dress several days before the last reunion. She had been standing across busy Commonwealth Avenue just watching her. Paula had known right away what it was.

Other times the sightings were of a man. This was the first time Paula had ever seen him, though others had reported seeing him in the past.

A man—holding something in his hands.

Staring into the woods now, discerning the shadow that was surely him, Paula made out the terrible thing that he gripped in his undead hands.

A pitchfork.

Her heart leapt in her chest.

"Zac! Callie!" she called suddenly, bolting down the hill toward them. The children lifted their faces to her, their hair wet and slicked back. "Come along, darlings!" Paula reached them and swept them into her arms.

She didn't think they were in any particular danger from the figure in the woods—at least, not for the moment. But she was letting the man know that she had seen him, and that she would do everything in her power to save those she loved from his grip.

And that included the children she would never have herself.

She ushered Zac and Callie back up the hill, where they settled themselves down at the picnic table and happily devoured the burgers and dogs their father had prepared for them. Paula stood a few feet away, watching them, glancing every so often toward the woods. She could no longer make out the man. But she knew he was there.

Watching them.

And she knew something else.

No matter where they were in the world, something would always be watching them.

Chapter Four

"Helloooo?" Douglas called, stepping into the great foyer of the house. His voice echoed across the marble.

The place was eerily silent. Where were the servants? Usually there was some old housekeeper who scuffed her way out to greet Douglas when he visited. The face was usually different from the last time Douglas visited. Uncle Howie went through staff quickly. There was never anyone who stayed too long. Douglas wondered if his uncle was difficult to work for. Whatever the reason, the staff was usually comprised of new faces every time Douglas visited. But this time, no one—new or old—was around to greet him.

"Helloooo?" he called again. Once more, his only response was his own echo.

He glanced up at the vaulted ceiling. His eyes took in the portraits on the walls, the suit of armor that stood by the great curving marble staircase.

He scratched his head. Odd that the front door would be open if Uncle Howie had gone out.

He took a few steps across the foyer toward the parlor. The double doors were closed. He was about to open them when suddenly they opened inward themselves. He stepped back with a small gasp—

—until he saw that the person who had just opened them was a very attractive young woman, as real as the woman on the cliffs had seemed ethereal.

"Whoa," he said in surprise.

"I'm sorry," the woman said, a little flustered herself. She had reddish hair, green eyes, and a smattering of freckles. The black turtleneck and pleated khakis that she wore showed off her figure quite nicely. A strand of pearls around her neck suggested she was no servant. "I'm a visitor here myself. I heard you come in and assumed Mr. Young would come out to greet you. He's just gone to his room for a moment."

Douglas smiled and introduced myself. "It's okay," he said as he shook hands with the woman. "Uncle Howie wasn't expecting me."

The woman returned his smile. "I'm Carolyn Cartwright. I'm . . ." There was the slightest hesitation, which Douglas noticed. "I'm working with your uncle on a project."

"Well," he said, "I'm glad to see that the house will have a little more life in it than usual. How long are you here for?"

"Just a few days." Carolyn seemed to consider something. "To start, anyway. I'll be back, however. I suspect the project is going to . . . take some time."

He grinned. He was pleased to hear that. As much as he loved Uncle Howie, it sure would be nice to have a pretty woman, and one close to his age at that, around to keep things lively. Douglas had an eye for the ladies. Always had. He liked them, and they liked him. His eyes twinkled at Carolyn. She was looking at him, too—but then Douglas realized that what she was looking at were his muddy clothes.

"Oh," he said, giving a little laugh. "I had a little accident on the way up here. Swerved to avoid . . ." Now it was Douglas's turn to hesitate. "A squirrel. I took a spill on my motorcycle."

"Were you hurt?"

"Just scraped up my leg a bit. Nothing serious. I should probably hop in the shower and change my clothes."

Carolyn was nodding. "Your uncle is just taking a brief rest. He's in his room. We've been discussing the project for the last couple of hours, and it sort of wore him out. So while he rests, I'm in here going through some books and reports. . . ."

"It's okay, I know where his room is," Douglas said, smiling. "I'll pop in on him and surprise him."

Carolyn's face betrayed a hint of concern. "Don't surprise him too much. He's . . . well, a bit overwrought. This project . . . it's . . . stressful."

Douglas made a face. He had never understood Uncle Howie's "projects." Often there were people here, going through books and reports like Carolyn was doing now. Just what Uncle Howie did for his living Douglas had no idea, but even at ninety-eight, the old man still seemed incredibly active in it. Must be a lot of work managing all those investments and properties, Douglas thought.

"Well," he said, flashing a smile, "it was very nice meeting you, Miss Cartwright."

"Please," she said. "Call me Carolyn."

"And you can call me as many times as you'd like," Douglas said, his grin pushing his cheeks up into his face, revealing the dimples that many women had told him were irresistible. He counted on them having the same effect on Carolyn.

Whether they did or not, he wasn't certain. She smiled noncommittally and turned back into the parlor to return to her books and papers. Douglas sighed, heading down the corridor to his uncle's room. Carolyn seemed like one smart, serious lady. No wonder Uncle Howie had hired her to do work for him.

Once again he wondered just what his uncle had done all these years as actual *work*. Oh, he figured managing millions took a lot of time and effort. *Can hardly call it a job, though,* Douglas thought. It sure wasn't like landscaping, or carpentry, or steering a boatload of slaphappy tourists out to see the sharks. That's why Uncle Howie always had "projects," Douglas supposed, and he had "jobs."

Douglas's father had been very different from both his son and the wealthy family patriarch. He'd always worked for his living, even though he expected someday to be a beneficiary of at least some of the family fortune. "You've got to find your own way in this life," he'd told Douglas many times. "You can't rely just on what you hope to get someday. You've got to make it happen for yourself."

Dad was a lawyer, often taking on cases pro bono for clients who couldn't afford to hire representation. Douglas admired his father, wishing he'd inherited his drive and his commitment to do something for the world, to make a difference. But all Douglas had ever really cared about—well, at least after his father had died—was just getting by. His life's goal was just to avoid too much hassle. Living the gypsy life had suited him fine for the last several years. No worries. Just be happy.

But now the idea of Uncle Howie setting him up somewhere, maybe in a little house here in Maine— a little cabin on a brook—sounded very appealing. Maybe he was growing up finally, or maybe some of Dad's sense of stability had finally started to sink in. Maybe, Douglas thought, Uncle Howie could help him set up a carpentry shop where he could build furniture for the locals. Douglas thought he might like that. Maybe he'd even meet a girl up here, someone who might set his heart afire in a way that Mom had once done for Dad, in a way that Brenda, good as she was, had failed to do for him. . . .

He turned the corner into his uncle's room, tapping lightly on the open door.

"Uncle Howie?" Douglas whispered.

The room was dark. The drapes were drawn in the room, blotting out much of the bright sunshine from outside. But as Douglas's eyes adjusted, he could make out his uncle lying on his enormous four-poster bed, fully dressed, even wearing his shoes. He lay on his back, his hands folded over his chest. He looked like he was dead and ready for the casket. A tiny flutter of alarm surged in Douglas's chest.

"Uncle Howie?" he asked again, louder this time, taking a few steps into the room.

The old man didn't move. Douglas stood over him.

"Uncle Howie?" He spoke for a third time, touching his fingers to the old man's hand. It was cold.

But the eyes suddenly slid open.

Douglas made a little gasp and took a step back.

"Douglas!" the old man rasped. He struggled to rise to a sitting position, but couldn't manage. He turned his head instead to look at his nephew. "My little hoodlum. What are you doing here?"

"I . . . I came to visit," Douglas said.

"But the reunion is next month."

Douglas tried to smile. Something about seeing Uncle Howie stretched out like this gave him the creeps. The old man still had not unfolded his hands from his chest. He looked like a talking corpse. "I came early," Douglas said. "To spend some time with you."

Howard Young's tongue snaked out to wet his lips. "Look at you. You are a mess. Why are you so dirty?"

"I had a little accident with my bike."

Finally the old man raised himself with difficulty on one brittle elbow. "I have always feared that motorcycle would bring you to a bad end."

"It was just a little spill. I wasn't hurt."

Uncle Howard was sitting now. "Are you certain?"

Douglas nodded. "I just need a good hot shower."

Uncle Howie grunted. "Well, anyway, I'm glad to see you, Douglas." He smiled. Now that he was sitting up, he seemed warm. Back to life. He was once again the uncle that Douglas knew. "I'm glad you're here."

"You okay, Uncle Howie?" Douglas asked. "The pretty young lady downstairs said you got kind of shook up."

The old man's eyes twinkled. "Oh, so you've met her? Yes, indeed, she's quite pretty." He frowned. "But I wasn't shook up. I just get tired more easily these days."

"Well, don't work too hard. Whatever these projects are, don't let them stress you out."

Uncle Howard sighed. "Would that they would simply go away." He managed a weary smile at his nephew. "I'm glad you're here," he said again.

"So tell me," Douglas said, grinning. "Is this Carolyn married?"

"No."

"Boyfriend?"

"I don't know," Uncle Howie told him. "But I don't think so. Not anymore."

"Good."

"Now, hold on a moment, you hoodlum." Uncle Howie was smiling. "Carolyn is here on a very important matter. I don't want you hassling her."

"Me? Hassle a pretty woman?"

His uncle just gave him a look.

"All right," Douglas said. "I'll go easy on her. But she sure is hot."

Uncle Howard nodded. "Yes, she is lovely. But what she is working on . . . it's going to need her full attention. Which brings me to the reason why I am so pleased you came early to visit me, Douglas . . ."

The old man was struggling to get off the bed and stand. Douglas allowed him to lean on his arm. Once standing, Uncle Howard got quite close to his nephew and looked him directly in the eyes.

"We need to have an important conversation," Uncle Howie said. "In the next day or two. There are many things I need to tell you before the others arrive."

Douglas smiled. *He's going to give me something and doesn't want my cousins knowing about it. I knew I was his favorite.*

"Sure thing, Uncle Howie," Douglas said, walking beside the old man as he shuffled across the floor of his room toward the door. "Anytime you want. We'll sit down and catch up."

"Mm," Howard Young said. "Catch up. I suppose you could call it that."

Douglas escorted his uncle into the foyer, then turned and gave him a jaunty salute. They'd have some dinner once Douglas was cleaned up, Uncle Howard said. Douglas smiled, then hurried up the stairs to the room that he'd always considered his own.

It was the same room where he'd slept the night his father died in this house ten years ago.

He'd come down these very stairs to be met by his cousin Paula. She was crying. "Oh, Douglas," she'd said, turning away.

And he'd known.

Known that his father had died during the night. He'd been trying to play a prank on his cousins, they said. A funny practical joke. And he had suffocated. It was a terrible accident, they told the sheriff.

Except that Dad didn't play pranks. He wasn't that kind of guy.

Douglas pushed the memory out of his mind as

he rounded the top of the staircase. He passed a large plate-glass window on the top landing that looked out over the grounds toward the cliffs. Suddenly he was certain if he looked out he would see the woman in the white dress out there again. He hesitated, then turned to look. He peered outside into the bright sunshine.

She wasn't there.

Of course she wasn't. The woman wasn't real. She was an illusion. A figment of Douglas's imagination.

He headed down the hall to his room.

Chapter Five

Carolyn sat in the parlor with a mountain of books and papers spread out on the table in front of her.

He does not look like David, she thought to herself. Douglas Young did not look *anything* like the man she had loved so much, who had betrayed her so horribly. Douglas was blond; David was dark. Douglas's skin was smooth and unlined; David had had a pink scar running down the side of his face. Douglas was her age or possibly even younger; David had been in his late thirties. But *something* had reminded her of David. . . .

The dimples. It had been the dimples.

And the eyes. The way he flirted with her. The confidence in his appeal. The devil-may-care toss of his head . . .

Damn it, she said to herself, shaking her head. Thinking about David was the last thing she could afford to do at the moment.

Because the case at hand was like nothing she had encountered before.

The blood on the wall had been real. She had seen it, touched it. It had simply appeared—and during the time it took her run up the stairs to fetch her camera to take a picture of it, it had disappeared.

Now, of course, it could have been some kind of ingenious trick. For whatever purpose, maybe Mr. Young was making all of this up. Or someone else was playing a hideous game with him. That's what Carolyn needed to determine first. She'd need to inspect that wall to see if there was some kind of device embedded in it. A screen perhaps. Or maybe the message in blood had been a hologram of some sort.

Except, as she reminded herself, holograms aren't wet and sticky to the touch.

She had walked over to the wall and placed her finger directly into the blood. It was real. And so was the abject terror on Mr. Young's face and the distress he'd felt afterward, which caused him to retreat to his room.

Carolyn sighed as she flipped through the death certificates in front of her. The blood on the wall might conceivably have been a trick, but there was no way that these documents weren't real. To verify them, all Carolyn needed to do was troop over to the clerk's office at the Youngsport town hall—which she certainly planned on doing. Still, every certificate was stamped with the clerk's official seal. Her trained researcher's eye told her these weren't fakes. There were more than a dozen certificates, each from the first year of a decade, with the earliest dating back to 1930. The deaths came in ten-year intervals after that, one to a decade, except in those instances Mr. Young had called "slaughters": when the family had defied the curse and either not sent anyone into the room or sent the wrong person.

The first such slaughter had been at the very beginning. Sixteen-year-old Jacob Young's name had been drawn in the lottery. He had steeled himself to spend the night in the room. But his father—and Howard Young's father as well—Desmond Young had insisted he take his son's place. The result was even greater tragedy. Instead of one death, there had been four. Desmond died, but so did poor Jacob, as well as the two youngest and most innocent members of the family, thirteen-year-old Timothy and the infant Cynthia. Carolyn stared down at their death certificates now. On every one the cause of death was listed as "seizure." Only the wealth and privilege of the Youngs could have staved off the kind of investigation four deaths in the same house on the same night would have prompted otherwise. Even, somehow, the grisly manner of Desmond's death never made it to the official record. That could happen, Carolyn supposed, when a family had its own private graveyard.

The second slaughter came twenty years later, when the family decided to abandon the house and the lottery altogether. On three successive nights, in cities spread across the country, a Young family member died suddenly. Carolyn looked over their certificates now. Howard Young had assembled them all, providing a full record of his family's enduring tragedy. The most recent slaughter had been in 1980. Ernest Young had skipped out on the lottery, breaking with his family and taking his wife and daughters to an undisclosed location. They'd even changed their names. But on the night that one of his cousins died in the basement room, Ernest and his immediate family were also wiped out, murdered savagely in their home. Carolyn felt as if she might cry looking at the death certificates of the little girls. Ann Marie was ten. Susie was seven.

She stood, overcome by all this death. Mr. Young had given her all the particulars. The family reunions every ten years. The lottery. The requirement that one member of the family be chosen to spend a night in the room—a room that had once been a servant's quarters. The inevitable death that occurred during that night. The slaughters that took place if the ritual was not followed exactly, and by everyone.

She walked to the window and stared out at the cliffs and the whitecapped waves of the sea beyond. He had given her all of the particulars but one.

How the whole thing had started. And why.

"Who imposed this horrible thing on you?" Carolyn had asked, but the old man had just shook his head, seeming unable to tell her.

She had looked at him in disbelief.

"You mean to tell me," she asked, "that this is the part you expect me to find out on my own?"

Howard Young had simply nodded, then headed to his room to lie down.

"It can't be that he doesn't know," Carolyn said out loud to herself, still staring out over the cliffs. "He was here when it began. He would have been eighteen years old. He must know how this curse began. Either he isn't telling me for some reason—or he *can't* tell me. Perhaps he is somehow prevented from telling me."

She turned around and looked up at a portrait that hung over the mantel. It was a young man in Edwardian-era clothing, with a high stiff collar and high-buttoned waistcoat. Carolyn suspected it might be Desmond, the father of Howard, who had gone into the room in an effort to save his son Jacob and died in the process.

"Was it you?" Carolyn asked the portrait. "Did you somehow bring this curse upon your family?"

But the portrait was of a young man. Probably not much more than twenty. Desmond Young was fifty years old at the time of his death in that room. Carolyn knew that from his death certificate. The face she was looking at was a face unmarked by future tragedies. Whatever had happened to cause this terrible thing occurred around 1930. The world was mired in the Depression; the movies had just learned to talk; Europe was still holding together in the calm before the storm. So much history between then and now, and yet still, every ten years, the Young family sent one of its own into that room to die.

Why?

Carolyn was not a psychic. She was not even an expert on the paranormal. She was an investigator. She was more Dana Scully than Buffy the Vampire Slayer. She had learned a great deal, of course, investigating the supernatural, but nothing—not even the case with the so-called zombie—had ever definitely proved without a question the existence of things beyond what one could see or hear or logically quantify. It wasn't that Carolyn was a disbeliever. To call her a skeptic would also be wrong. She had seen enough to become convinced that the supernatural could be a real, definable force— but she had also never seen anything that might change that "could be" into a definite belief.

That's what made her a good investigator. She retained an open mind, but a critical one. It was why her first task was to find proof that all this wasn't some terrible hoax, either one set up by Howard Young for some twisted reason or one perpetrated upon him by unknown persons. Yet the deaths—so many of them—couldn't be denied. The deaths were real. What Carolyn had to determine was if they were being caused by normal or paranormal forces. A rather daunting assignment.

She sat back down in front of the papers and books Mr. Young had set out for her. How the hell was she supposed to figure it out? He'd told her to study the results of others' investigations. Several people had tried to end the curse before her, starting in 1930 and continuing up through the years. The latest was Kip Hobart, who'd tried to uncover the mystery of that room a decade earlier. But like all who'd come before him, he'd had no success.

Carolyn knew Kip; they'd worked together on a couple of cases. He was well respected in the paranormal world. If Kip Hobart had been unable to find out and prevent what was going on in this house, how possibly could *she*? Kip was an expert on the supernatural. He had studied with the most esteemed names in the field. She was just a gumshoe.

If not for the million dollars dangling over her head, Carolyn would have walked away from this assignment. It was too big. Too many unknowns. But a million dollars . . .

She'd never had a lot of money. Her father had been a postal clerk who'd died of prostate cancer when Carolyn was eleven. Her mother had soldiered on, trying as best she could to provide her two daughters with a comfortable life. Carolyn's younger sister Andrea had severe Down syndrome, and Mom was insistent she never be sent away and that she attend only the very best special schools. To enable this, Carolyn's mother worked several jobs in their town of Rye, New York, juggling her commissions as a real estate agent with the tips she earned as a waitress at a local diner. When the diner was robbed at gunpoint, forcing Mom to hand over all the cash in the register as well as her diamond engagement ring, Carolyn, just fourteen at the time, had felt a profound sense of violation. At that tender age she decided she wanted to be a police officer, and Mom had scrimped and saved in order to send her to college to major in criminal justice.

But still, on campus, Carolyn had needed a side job to offset expenses. A professor recommended her for a spot as a paid intern to the local district attorney. So impressed was the D.A. with her astute skills at observation and deduction that, upon graduation, he provided a glowing reference to the New York field office of the FBI. Securing a position there, she impressed her superiors almost immediately by solving a homicide case that had perplexed them for years. Carolyn had detected a strong resemblance between a photo of one suspect and the victim's ex-husband. Turned out it was the same man, just made over with thousands of dollars of plastic surgery. "The eyes were the same," she said simply. "They can change the eyelids but not the eyes." The man was arrested, and Carolyn got promoted to Washington.

From there, her rise was swift, with a series of "unusual" cases leading to Carolyn's reputation as the "go-to" person for the paranormal. It was all quite ironic. Carolyn had never even believed in Santa Claus. Neither of her parents were religious. It was simply a coincidence that these cases were assigned to her, but as she proved herself with one, she was given another. Maybe it was because she was so clear, so neutral on the subject. Neither a believer nor a disbeliever, she had exactly the right stuff to be a successful investigator.

Yet her salary never reflected her success or the esteem in which she was held by her superiors. Part of it was the glass ceiling, of course, and she was very aware of that: male agents were always paid better than female agents. Part of it was also the fact that rank-and-file government employees made a lot less money than their critics in the media thought. But perhaps the biggest part of it was the cash she sent back to Rye every month. Mom had developed Amyotrophic Lateral Sclerosis. She'd never had good health insurance, and now her medical bills were exploding through the roof. Carolyn did not want her mother placed in a nursing home, not after all the long years she had labored so that Carolyn could have a better life. So she paid for round-the-clock nursing care to keep Mom at home. Of course, Andrea still needed money for her care as well, living in a beautiful, very expensive assisted-living facility in Dutchess County. So there was very little money left over for Carolyn at the end of each month.

It made sense, then, that Carolyn would leave

the Bureau and move to New York. She told col-
leagues it was time that she opened her own
agency, but in truth it was mostly so she could be
closer to her mother and sister. Rye was just a short
train ride away from Grand Central Station, and
Carolyn went home as often as she could, sitting at
the side of Mom's bed, regaling her with stories of
strange cases, like the so-called haunted houses
and the guy who thought he was a zombie—and
maybe was. Finally, after three difficult years, Mom
passed away. Carolyn had spent a small fortune
taking care of her mother. But she never regretted
one penny.

What she did regret was David Cooke. When
she'd arrived in New York, she was single and
alone. For the last several years she'd been im-
mersed in her work and taking care of her family.
She'd never had time for a real boyfriend. Now
she found herself alone in the Big City, knowing
very few people and susceptible to the charms of a
smooth-talking man. That man was David Cooke.
For all of Carolyn's shrewd powers of observation
on the job, she failed to see through David's shiny,
happy façade. They'd met when she was hired by
the family of nineteen-year-old Lisa Freeman, a
student from NYU who had gone missing. David
Cooke had dated Lisa briefly, and the girl's parents thought he knew more than he was saying.
But after a half hour of questioning, Carolyn concluded that David had nothing to do with Lisa's
disappearance. He was sweet and harmless. David
was able to make her laugh like no man had ever
done before, teasing her about her pug nose and
freckles. She found herself surprisingly attracted
to him. She'd even found the scar on his face

strangely erotic. It was a pink, jagged line that extended from his left temple down to his cheek. A boating accident when he was a boy, David explained.

When she got up to leave after the interview, Carolyn was stunned when David asked her to dinner. She hesitated a moment, then accepted. Eating sushi and strolling through Central Park, they had a delightful time, and as he walked her home, he asked if he could see her again. On the second date, Carolyn slept with him; he was her first lover since college. On the third date, David told her that he loved her. Carolyn was over the moon.

After that, their relationship proceeded quickly. David was being evicted from his apartment; he told Carolyn that the owner was selling the place, so she let him move in with her. Along with David came his instruments: he was a musician who played the guitar and the sax and the drums. Many a night Carolyn was unable to sleep because David was out in the kitchen practicing his music. But she'd stumble groggily to work with a grin on her face the next morning, pausing to kiss the forehead of her sleeping lover before she left. David didn't have a regular job. He'd take the ferry out to Staten Island and play gigs there on the weekend. He never had much money. If only he could finish enough songs to cut his own album, he was certain he could hit it big—and Carolyn was certain, too. She thought she had never heard a more beautiful singer. No one could play the sax like David. But he needed money to buy new mixing equipment, so she put him on her credit cards and authorized him to withdraw money from her account. It only made sense: they were going to get married, after all. This was what committed couples did for each other. This was how they lived.

One night, Carolyn sat transfixed at a music club, her chin in her hands, her eyes trained on the man she loved. David singing for the beer-drinking crowd, pouring his heart into his words. A couple of guys she didn't know sat down next to her. They watched David as intently as she did. Finally Carolyn heard one of them say, "Such stirring words about love and devotion from a guy who killed his girlfriend."

She spun on them. "What the hell are you talking about?"

The man beside her crooked a grin at her. "Come on, everyone knows he killed Lisa Freeman."

"Watch it," Carolyn snarled, "or we'll hit you with a defamation suit."

"Oh," the other man said, smiling himself now. "I take it you're the latest squeeze. Well, honey, I'd keep looking over my shoulder if I were you."

The nightmares began after that. Lisa Freeman would be standing in her closet, staring at Carolyn when she opened the door. Or she'd be drowned in the bathtub. After each horrifying dream, Carolyn would awake with a start—and discover David was awake, looking over at her, his eyes seeming to glow in the dark. "You've been talking in your sleep," he told her one morning. He wouldn't reveal what she had been saying.

She tried to push the idea out of her head. David couldn't be a murderer; it was just idle, cruel gossip. But more and more she began to notice a darker side to the man she lived with. He could be so heartfelt and emotional when he sang his songs, but he was easily roused to anger, once upsetting the entire table when a waitress brought him the wrong order. Another time he'd snapped at a cabdriver who'd taken the wrong route, threatening to break the guy's neck. Carolyn had been horrified, and fearful the cabbie would call the police. That night she couldn't sleep. She just lay there beside David, listening to him breathe, unsure if he was asleep or awake. The scar on his face was no longer erotic. It now seemed like evidence of some terrible encounter. The last scratch of a dying woman. Carolyn no longer believed his stories of a boating accident.

Then one night David didn't come home from a gig. Carolyn called his cell phone; it just went to voice mail. She phoned the club where he was supposed to play, and they said he had left hours ago. Checking his closet, Carolyn noticed several shirts and pairs of pants were gone. His drums were still in the apartment, but he had his guitar and his sax with him. Carolyn pulled open the top drawer in his bureau and realized he had taken his passport. She knew then that he wasn't coming back. She was heartbroken, but after the way she'd been feeling the last few weeks, a part of her was also relieved.

Relief turned to horror the next morning, when she received a notice from her bank that her entire account had been withdrawn and closed out. Her entire savings plus her portfolio of investments. Hundreds of thousands of dollars—gone! Immediately she phoned her credit card companies. Every one of her cards had been maxed out. Her debt nearly equaled the money she had lost. Carolyn stumbled into the bathroom and got sick.

Suddenly she knew without a doubt that David

had killed Lisa Freeman. Her suspicions were confirmed when she got a call two weeks later. David's
old landlord, renovating the apartment he'd lived
in, made a gruesome discovery. A hole had been
cut into one of the walls, then expertly plastered
over and repainted, but not before something had
been placed inside. The landlord had found an
industrial-strength plastic bag in the wall. Unzip-
ping it, he was assaulted by a terrible, toxic odor.
He called police, who discovered inside the de-
composed body of Lisa Freeman. A warrant for
David's arrest for murder was immediately issued.

Of course, David was long gone. He had disappeared without a trace. Carolyn—who knew how
to track people down—had been absolutely stymied.
He must have changed his name, probably even left
the country. With his passport he'd gone over the
border to Canada or Mexico, and who knew where
he headed from there? Carolyn told police he might
be traveling with a guitar or a saxophone, but
he could have stashed them somewhere. Returning
to her apartment, Carolyn had all her locks changed
and double bolts installed. She cried then for the
first time, really let loose with heaving sobs. How
had she not seen? How had she fallen for his sweet
talk? She was too good, too shrewd for that. But
for a year she had slept beside a murderer. Drying
her tears, she began the slow process of digging
herself out of debt and getting her life back.

So Mr. Young's offer of a million dollars was like
a gift from heaven. She didn't need a *million*, of
course, but after living with such financial stress
for the last six months, the idea of never again having to worry about money was a blissful fantasy.

Making everything worse was that Andrea's health had taken a turn for the worse. She'd developed diabetes and a rare skin condition that meant more treatments and more medication. Her disability payments from the government covered some of it, but not everything, and the fees at her home had increased. Carolyn had been seriously thinking of returning to the FBI, even in a lower post since she knew her old job had been filled. Theoretically, working on her own might promise greater rewards, but it also could never afford the kind of security she so desperately craved now. But then one day, out of the blue, Howard Young had walked into her office and offered her a million dollars.

That was, if she could do what he wanted.

Carolyn pushed thoughts of David out of her mind and returned her focus to the matter at hand. She had to figure out how this had all begun. Then perhaps she could understand what was going on down in that basement room. But everyone who might possibly tell her what she needed to know was dead. Except Howard Young, and he was holding back for now, for his own curious reasons. But there was one other person. . . .

Carolyn looked again at the list she had made of those who had spent the night in that room over the years. The names all had several things in common. They were all Youngs, first of all, and had been selected by lottery. But of the eight names, there was one that differed from the rest. Only one was a woman.

And that was not her only distinction.

She was also the only one who hadn't died.

Though from what the old man had told her, Carolyn didn't think "alive" was a suitable way to describe poor Jeanette Young.

She would need to speak with Jeanette. That much was clear. As best she could, Carolyn needed to discover just what had happened to her in that room.

Chapter Six

Philip Young sat by his swimming pool sipping a Beefeater martini with his requisite three olives. It was a warm day. Indian summer. He watched as Carlos, his Salvadoran gardener, trimmed the topiary that surrounded the pool. The sun was hot on Philip's cheeks, so he adjusted the wide-brimmed hat he wore. He'd just had laser resurfacing on his face to blast away the wrinkles and the age spots. He didn't want a sunburn to ruin all that work.

He had a good life, and his life pleased him. Philip watched now as his daughter Chelsea welcomed a couple of girlfriends to sit on the other side of the pool. Such young nubile beauties. One of the girls was dark, the other blond. Philip forgot their names. But he certainly didn't forget how good they looked in their bikinis, which was why he'd encouraged Chelsea to invite them over today. He took another sip of his martini and lowered his sunglasses over his eyes so they wouldn't catch him watching.

"Daddy!" Chelsea was calling from the other side of the pool. "Would it be all right if we took the Bentley into town later?"

"What's wrong with your Beemer?" Philip asked.

"We're going shopping," Chelsea said, "and there's not going to be room for Trisha and Joni and me and all our packages." She giggled.

Trisha and Joni. Those were their names. The two girls waved at Philip as they stretched out on chaises, exposing their long smooth legs.

"Oh, all right, Chels," Philip said. "I don't plan on going anywhere today. I'm staying right here and soaking up this last little bit of summer. Won't be long until fall is here. . . ."

Even as he said the words, Philip knew what the fall season entailed. His mood darkened. The family reunion. He leaned back and closed his eyes. The goddamn family reunion. Every ten fucking years.

He'd lost his father to that room fifty years ago, when Philip was still just a teenager. Then, ten years later, his sister Jeanette had faced something even worse than death in that terrible place. From that moment on, Philip had vowed that he would never again let that room take anything else from him.

He looked over at Chelsea. She was throwing her head back in laughter with her friends, her strawberry blond hair reflecting the sun. How beautiful she was, how full of life. She was just twenty-three. Young enough to have her whole life ahead of her, but finally old enough to be told about the room. Philip didn't relish that duty. But this year, for the first time, both Chelsea and her twin brother Ryan would be required to take part in the lottery. Philip shuddered.

Required they might be—but he would not let anything happen to his children.

"Refill your glass, Mr. Young?"

His eyes flicked up behind his sunglasses to the face of his pretty young assistant. He'd hired Melissa to help him now that he was working mostly from home. The brokerage that bore his name could function quite well without him needing to trek into the city every morning from his home in Cos Cob the way he had most of his career. He was past sixty-five now; he was entitled to leisure.

That didn't mean he didn't work or that he wasn't on top of the market. He could just do it poolside from now on, with a lovely young assistant to help him. "Yes, thank you," he said to Melissa, handing her his empty martini glass.

When he'd hired her, Philip had explained to Melissa that the job would be more than just making telephone calls and filing papers. "I need an all-around personal assistant," he had explained. That meant refreshing his drinks when she noticed he was low. And it meant other things, too— but only when Chelsea or other members of the family were not around.

Philip watched Melissa walk across the lawn to the outside bar. She certainly filled out her tight white jeans well. Chelsea had rolled her eyes when she saw Philip's new assistant—"Trailer trash from Bridgeport, Daddy," she had called her, and Philip supposed she was right—but his son Ryan had given him the thumbs-up. The reaction of his wife Vanessa, however, was considerably more muted.

"Tell me, Philip," she had said, "does the girl know *anything* about the stock market? Or finances in general?"

"All she needs to know is how to make telephone calls and hit print on the computer," Philip had replied.

And she knows how to do those things well, Philip thought. *Other things she does even better.* A small grin crept across his face.

"Darling," he called over to Chelsea. "When are you and the girls going shopping?"

"Maybe in an hour or so," Chelsea called back.

Melissa was handing him his drink. "Ah, thank you, my dear," Philip said. "And how long are you planning to stay today?"

"However long you need me, Mr. Young," Melissa told him, her big brown eyes flashing at him from under her long lashes.

He smiled up at her. "After Chelsea leaves, there's some work I'd like to get done in my office," he said.

"Of course," Melissa said, giving him a broad smile.

Philip settled back into his chair, taking a sip of the martini. Yes, his life pleased him. There was no way he would let anything interfere with his life.

Not even a family curse could stand up against Philip Young.

He was one of the most powerful men on Wall Street. He had spent decades building up his firm. With the money his father left him he had invested wisely and shrewdly and sometimes unscrupulously. He was a very rich man.

But not nearly as rich as he would be one day when Uncle Howard finally died.

Philip planned on bulldozing that house and its accursed room the moment the old man finally kicked off. In the meantime, he kept encouraging Chelsea and Ryan to go up to Maine and visit with their uncle. Butter him up. Get on his good side. Philip worried that the old codger was going to leave the bulk of his billions to that good-for-nothing Douglas. The kid was always winking at Uncle Howard, joshing with him, making him laugh. "Get in there and work your charm on the old coot," Philip had urged his kids. "Don't let that worthless gypsy walk off with everything."

It occurred to Philip as he sat there sipping his gin that this would be the first year Douglas would partake in the lottery as well. He stared across the pool at Chelsea and her friends. Every previous Douglas Young—from the kid's great-grandfather down to his father—had been selected by the lottery to spend the night in that room. And every previous Douglas Young had died in there.

Why shouldn't it be the same for Douglas Desmond Young IV?

A flicker of something passed through Philip's heart. Conscience? No, it couldn't be conscience. He'd long ago surrendered that. One had to if one was going to conquer Wall Street. Maybe it was grief. Philip wasn't so hardened that he didn't regret the deaths of his kinfolk. He'd loved his older brother Martin, of course. They'd been playmates and confidants as children. And growing up, his cousin Douglas Young III had been his hero, the upstanding, courageous public defender who thought of others before thinking of himself.

But Philip came to realize that he'd rather be

alive than upstanding. That being deceitful was better than being dead.

Alone among his generation, he had survived. Every one of his siblings—including Jeanette—had fallen victim to that room. Every one of his first cousins, too, had all been cut down in their youth. One by one, they had been selected to enter the room or they had run off, like his foolish brother Ernie, only to be slaughtered for their mutiny. Philip was the only male Young in nearly a hundred years—except for Uncle Howard, of course—who had made it past the age of sixty.

And he fully intended to ensure that such remained the case. And that Ryan and Chelsea, too, lived to ripe old ages.

Ripe, *wealthy* old ages.

"Mr. Young?"

He lifted an eye. Melissa was standing beside him.

"Mrs. Young is on the telephone. She's decided to stay in the city to have dinner with Gloria Vanderbilt. She wants to know if you have any objection."

Philip crooked a little smile at Melissa. "No objection from me," he said. Melissa returned his smile. She placed the phone to her ear and spoke into it. "Mrs. Young? He says to stay and have a wonderful evening."

Philip laughed. Oh, yes, he enjoyed his life.

So what if he'd had to resort to extraordinary means to do so? He remembered the terror he'd felt as a young man, watching Aunt Margaret prepare all their names and place them in that box. His life—reduced to a slip of paper! He was just eighteen at the time of his first lottery. His whole future might have ended that night. He had felt the sweat bead on his forehead as Uncle Howard took the box from Aunt Margaret. Just hours earlier the old man had told him the secret of that room. At first Philip had scoffed, but he had seen the look in his father's eyes. His father believed it, so it must be true. Sheer panic had gripped Philip then. He wanted to bolt. But his brother Martin, four years older, was brave, even stoic. Philip had never possessed the steel of his brother. Martin could dive from the cliffs into the water below, but Philip had never had the guts. But he couldn't indulge in such terror now. It would forever mark him as a coward. So he trooped into the parlor following Martin and his father, fully expecting it would be his name that would be drawn, his life that would end that night.

When his father's name had been drawn, Philip's first reaction was relief. He didn't like admitting that to himself, but it was true. He loved his father, but better his father than him. When his father was found dead the next morning, Philip wailed like a banshee over his body. But a little voice inside him was also saying, "Thank God it isn't me."

Ten years later it was his sister Jeanette's turn. His baby sister. He saw the fear in her eyes. Martin, of course, volunteered to go in her place. Philip was silent. Only after Uncle Howard had insisted that the lottery forbade anyone from taking the place of the one chosen did Philip speak up, offering great protests that his sister should have to face such a fate, that if only it were possible he would be glad to go in her place.

He took another sip of his drink. There were parts of his past he did not like remembering. But how could he avoid them, with another family re-union looming? With the possibility that Chelsea and Ryan might have to face that room?

Aunt Margaret died two years before the lottery of 1980. She passed away peacefully in her sleep, something for which the entire family envied her. Aunt Margaret had been part of the lottery since the beginning, and each time she had escaped being chosen.

Was it significant that she had prepared the names each time, and burned them afterward in the fireplace?

Philip began to wonder if Aunt Margaret had contrived to keep herself out of that room. Of course, there were always the same number of slips of paper as there were candidates for the lottery. Aunt Margaret wrote all their names out, then folded the papers in half. But what if, Philip had wondered, she had written someone's name *twice* and left out her own? Whether she had or not, no one would ever know.

In 1980, Philip volunteered to take over for Aunt Margaret in writing down the names.

That year there were six of them in the lottery. Philip and Martin. Their cousin Douglas and his two children, Douglas and Therese. And of course, Uncle Howard himself. Philip wrote everyone's name but his own. Then he wrote Douglas Senior's name again. When he handed the box to Uncle Howard, he was giddy—ecstatic—that his plan had worked. Douglas was chosen to enter the room.

Was there guilt? Maybe a flash, when he saw Therese call out, "Daddy! I love you!" But then it was gone. The instinct for survival was a far more potent emotion than guilt. By then, Philip was a hotshot on Wall Street. He was set to marry Vanessa McMaster, heiress to the textile fortune and one of the most chased-after socialites in New York. He had feared they'd never be able to have a family, but now he had found the answer. So long as he kept preparing the names, he could keep himself—and any children he would have—out of that room.

He smiled to himself. And Uncle Howard can only leave his billions to those who are left alive.

The next lottery, there was some regret. Tradition meant something in the Young family, particularly in matters of the lottery, so no one questioned Philip once again preparing the names. He toyed briefly with the idea of leaving out Martin's name this time. But then he'd have to leave out Martin's two children, Paula and Dean, brought into the lottery for the first time that year. And that would cut down the number of available names to the extreme: every name would have to be either that of Uncle Howard or their cousin Douglas, the sole surviving member of that branch of the family. So Philip did what he'd done ten years previously. He left only himself out, and wrote Douglas twice. Hell, the world didn't need another bleeding-heart public defender.

But this time, Martin was chosen. His brother. The fellow who had taught him to ride a bike and to play football. The one who, after their father died, had stepped in and been adviser and supporter as Philip made his way in the world. It had been Martin who'd given him money in the very beginning to make his first investments in the stock market. And now Martin was going to die.

Who's to say his name wouldn't have been chosen even if Philip's name had been in there? That's how Philip rationalized it. How he still rationalized it.

Ten years later, it was easier. This time the lottery got the public defender. They found him in the morning with a plastic bag over his head. This time, Philip had felt no grief at all, not even a flash, not even when Douglas's teenaged son, also named Douglas, had broken down in tears at the news. By now it was clear that he had found the escape hatch from the family curse. His children need never worry. That was all that mattered.

He watched now as Chelsea and her friends stood from their chaises, chattering among themselves, talking on their cell phones, getting ready for their shopping spree. He knew his son Ryan was at the brokerage, working even on a weekend, making millions for himself. If a member of the Young family had to die every decade as a result of some old curse, then it was far, far better that it be someone from a branch that didn't matter as much, that couldn't claim the power and success that Philip's family did.

After Chelsea had blown him a kiss and sped off in his Bentley, Philip stood. He benevolently gave Carlos the rest of the afternoon off. Then he hurried inside the house to find Melissa.

She was in the office, waiting for him in the lacy black teddy he had bought her.

He took her in his arms roughly and began kissing her neck. Melissa ran her hands, with their bright red fingernails, all over his fleshy chest and stomach, playing with the tufts of white hair that grew between his sagging pectorals. Melissa excited him more than any woman had in a long, long time. Yes, indeed, she was trailer trash from Bridgeport. But that only made her more appealing. Philip knew it was his money, his status, that aroused her, and he liked the charge that it gave him. The power. He pulled her tightly into him and bit her neck. She moaned.

Then, another sound.

"What was that?" Melissa asked.

"Nothing," Philip said, but he had heard it too. A baby's cry.

It came again.

"Is there a child in the house?" Melissa asked.

"No," Philip said. "There is no child."

From such hot passion just a moment before, now Philip's blood ran cold.

A baby cried again. It sounded as if it came from the living room.

"There is a child here!" Melissa insisted. "I have to go check!"

"No!" Philip insisted. "Don't go out there!"

She gave him a confused look. "But if someone is here . . . we can't get caught!"

Again the child cried from the other room. It was an insistent cry. Terrified. It grew from a few anxious yelps to one long wail now. Melissa ignored Philip's objections and pulled on her jeans and threw a sweatshirt on over the teddy. She headed out toward the living room.

"Don't touch it!" Philip shouted, following her.

Indeed there was a baby sitting in the middle of the living room. It wore just a cloth diaper. It couldn't have been much more than about six months old. It was crying ferociously, its pudgy little hands in the air.

"The poor child!" Melissa cried.

"Don't touch it!" Philip repeated.

She looked at him as if he were mad. "The child is terrified, maybe in pain. . . ."

"No!"

Suddenly the crying stopped. They both turned to look at the baby. It began to crawl away from them, across the carpet and behind the divan. Melissa hurried to follow it. But as she crossed the room, she discovered the baby was gone.

But in its place were a series of bloody handprints, staining the white carpet in a horrible trail. The handprints ended abruptly in the middle of the room, as if the baby had just disappeared into thin air.

Chapter Seven

Uncle Howie had sure gone all out for this meal. At some point even before Douglas had gotten up, a whole army seemed to have descended on the house. Whereas yesterday there wasn't a servant in sight, today the place was buzzing with them. Housekeepers were doing his laundry and making his bed. An assistant was heading into town with a van to haul Douglas's repaired bike up to the house. And in the kitchen, a dozen cooks and waitstaff were preparing the most elaborate breakfast Douglas had ever seen—let alone tasted.

"The bread is all fresh baked," Uncle Howie was saying from the head of the table. "There are fresh croissants and scones and brioche. The fruit is all local. Strawberries, blueberries, apples, peaches. The eggs will be out in a moment. You'll find an assortment of cheeses and fresh herbs on the table to add to your meals as you choose. Basil, oregano, cilantro, rosemary—all grown here on the estate.

And you have your choice of Canadian bacon or smoked lox—or you can have both, of course."

Douglas was famished. He rubbed his hands together in anticipation. He glanced over at Carolyn Cartwright. She smiled, seemingly overwhelmed by all the food.

"And save room for dessert," Uncle Howie added. "They're making chocolate waffles with maple syrup and fresh cream."

"Awesome," Douglas said, piling his plate high with strawberries and sliced apples with cinnamon.

"All I usually have for breakfast is coffee and a bagel," Carolyn was saying.

"Do you want a bagel?" Uncle Howard asked. "We have bagels."

"No, thank you," Carolyn said, laughing. "These scones are delicious."

"I'm glad you like it," the old man said, watching them both eat.

He himself had little on his plate. When the eggs came, he took a small helping and ate them with a small slice of wheat bread. Douglas, meanwhile, was gorging himself.

The dining room was dominated by a large crystal chandelier hanging over the enormous table, which sat thirty people. On the walls were hung paintings by Renoir and Matisse. An elaborate floral display sat in the middle of the table, a fresh delivery that morning. Fragrant white lilies and purple asters were complemented by a surprising burst of orange birds of paradise.

A server came by to bring Douglas a plate of bacon. He helped himself eagerly.

"You act as if you haven't eaten in days," Carolyn observed.

He grinned. "Well, I haven't, unless you consider Big Macs and Taco Bell eating."

"I do not," she said, smiling.

"Uncle Howie always puts out the best spreads," Douglas said, looking over at his uncle and giving him a thumbs-up.

The old man patted his mouth with his napkin. He had finished his small portion. "Well, you two take your time and enjoy the rest of your meal. I'm going out for my morning walk." He stood. Immediately a valet was behind him, helping him from his chair. Howard Young waved him away, insisting he would be fine on his own. "Douglas, find me afterward. Out on the lawn." He paused. "We need to have a conversation, and I'd like to have it before Carolyn leaves."

"Okay," Douglas said, his mouth full.

Carolyn's eyes moved from uncle to nephew and then back again. *Poor Douglas,* she thought. *He has no idea what Mr. Young will tell him. No idea of how his life will change once he learns about the room . . .*

She watched as the old man walked slowly, and just a little falteringly, out the French doors and onto the terrace. Carolyn presumed he was too proud to use a cane. Outside she could see that the sun was bright. Gulls were swooping in long, languid arcs across the blue sky. The crash of the surf filled the room now that the doors were open.

"What was it like," she asked, "coming here as a child?"

Douglas took a sip of coffee and sat back in his chair. Finally, a break from his ravenous consumption of food. "Well, when I was very young, it was awesome. I mean, what kid wouldn't love coming to a house like this? I'd run through the halls, up and down those marble stairs, hiding in the attic. . . ."

"I suppose attics and . . . basements . . . are irresistible to young boys." She chose her words deliberately.

Douglas shrugged. "We weren't allowed in the basement. I guess that's where Uncle Howie kept all his treasures. But the attic was fun. So many little nooks and crannies where I could hide and jump out from to scare my stuck-up cousins Ryan and Chelsea." He laughed, then returned to shoveling eggs and bacon into his mouth.

"You don't get along with your cousins?"

He shrugged again. "We're just very different. They have an air about them. A certain superiority. I like my other cousins, okay, though. Paula and Dean. But they're older. Ryan and Chelsea are my age." He looked up at her. "I guess they're probably about your age as well." He smiled and winked.

Carolyn felt her cheeks blush. There were those dimples again.

She likes me, Douglas thought. He could always tell when women liked him. He was glad. He hoped Carolyn planned to stay a few days.

"But you said it was awesome when you were little," she commented. "What about when you were older?"

Douglas sat back in his chair again. "Well, it wasn't so great then. You see, my father died here. We had come up for the family reunion. They're held every ten years, and everyone comes. It's something that Uncle Howie insists upon." He made a small laugh. "I guess everybody does it because they don't want to be cut out of the will."

Carolyn was studying him with her beautiful

green eyes. "And your father died while you were all here together?"

Douglas nodded. "Yeah." His voice was tight. "It was an accident. They found him in the morning. When I came down the stairs I remember seeing my cousin Paula's face . . . she was crying. And I just knew. Somehow I just knew that my father was dead."

"I'm so sorry."

"It was ten years ago. Do you know there's another family reunion scheduled for next month?"

Carolyn nodded. "Yes." She paused. "Your uncle mentioned it."

"So tell me about you," Douglas said suddenly. "Enough about me and this house. I want to know about you."

A server had arrived asking if they wanted their waffles now. Carolyn was so full she begged off, but Douglas said he'd have one in a bit. "First," he said, standing, holding out his hand to Carolyn, "I think you might like to see my favorite place in the house. And as we head up there, you can tell me all about who you are and where you come from."

Carolyn smiled and followed him out of the dining room.

As they headed up the grand marble staircase, she explained there wasn't much to tell about her life. She gave him a quick summary of college and the FBI and explained she was now running her own independent investigation agency. She left out everything about Mom and Andrea and, of course, David. But her words had been enough to pique Douglas's curiosity nevertheless.

"Here I was thinking you were some actuary or accountant," he said, "working with Uncle Howie.

on the family investments or whatever. But you're a private eye?"

She laughed. "I guess you can call me that."

"The FBI, huh? You actually worked for the FBI?"

"That I did."

He had stopped walking. They stood on the top landing of the staircase. "So what kind of project does Uncle Howie need a private eye for?"

"I'll let him explain all that," Carolyn said. "It's not my place."

"Very strange," Douglas said, eyeing her. Then he winked and crooked his finger, indicating that she should follow him down the hall.

"This is my favorite spot in the whole house," he said.

At the far end of the corridor was a door. They stood outside the door, and Douglas grinned over at her. His eyes were wide like a little boy's. She couldn't help but smile in return.

He opened the door. Beyond was a small, steep staircase leading up.

"The attic," he said. "But that's not what is so special."

He gripped her hand. Carolyn followed as they bounded up the steps. At the top, to the left, was a small door that led into the attic. But to the right was a bay window. There was a small seat in the window, where one could sit and look out over the cliffs and the ocean.

"Oh, my," Carolyn said.

"Look," Douglas said, his arm now around her shoulder. "You can see the whole estate. The barn. The tennis courts. The road going down to the vil-

lage. And over there, you see, is the village itself.
You can even see the highway through the trees."

"Yes," Carolyn said. "It's a breathtaking view."

"You see there, along the cliffs? You can see the
start of the path that leads down to the village. It's
a shortcut, but rather steep and a little precarious.
It cuts through the family cemetery. If you look
closely you can make out the headstones."

"Oh, yes," Carolyn said, but looking at the cemetery made her uneasy. All those dead Youngs buried
there . . . the ones who had died in this house. She
preferred to glance out over the cliffs to the blue
ocean beyond, the sun reflecting off its whitecaps.

"I would come up here as a boy and sit for
hours, daydreaming that I was a king and this was
my castle," Douglas said.

She smiled over at him. "You had a lively imagination."

He nodded. "I also came up here on the day my
father died. They couldn't get me to budge. I just
stayed here that whole day."

She reached down and squeezed his hand.

"Douglas," she said, her heart breaking. "I think
your uncle would like to talk with you."

He nodded.

Heading back down the stairs, Carolyn thought
about the little boy who had sat in that window,
grieving for his father. She had been up quite late
the night before, reading through the histories of
all who had died in that basement room. Douglas's
father had been a good man. A public defender.
An advocate for the disadvantaged. He had died
by suffocation. His hands had been tied behind his
back and a plastic bag secured over his head. What

kind of vileness lived in that room? What monstrous force could so do such a thing, especially with his young son sleeping in the same house?

Douglas insisted he stop back in the dining room for his waffle before heading out to talk with his uncle. He was still hungry. He asked Carolyn if she'd join him, but she demurred. He told her he'd see her outside then, and reached down and gallantly kissed her hand. Women loved when he did that.

He watched Carolyn head out through the French doors. He liked her. He was surprised by how attracted he was to her. She wasn't like the girls he usually found himself going after. Sure, she was pretty. But she didn't have the va-voom quality that Brenda possessed, the obvious, raw sexuality his girlfriends usually displayed. In the past, the girls on his arm had been one step up from bimbos: shapely bodies, big hair, loud laughs, not a lot of education. Carolyn Cartwright was very different. Smart. Crafty. A private eye, for crying out loud! Sitting back down at the table and licking his lips at the crispy Belgian waffle that was placed in front of him, he figured he'd need to watch himself around Carolyn. There would be no hiding anything from her!

That's why he liked her, he realized as he took his first bite. He was here, after all, to get his life on track. To get serious. A woman like Carolyn, then, held tremendous appeal. Beautiful—but serious, too.

Douglas peered out through the French doors to catch Carolyn looking back at him. He waved. She waved back.

Oh, Carolyn thought. *He saw me looking.*

She was being silly. Acting like a schoolgirl. And acting like a schoolgirl had gotten her in big trouble before. She had vowed never again to trust a man on first impression. Douglas Young might seem charming and sincere, innocent and fun. But so had David. She repeated that mantra as she headed out toward the cliffs. *So had David.*

She found Mr. Young sitting on a stone bench looking out over the ocean. She could hear the surf and even taste the salt on her tongue. The old man turned his yellow eyes up at her.

"I see you are making the acquaintance of my nephew," he said.

Carolyn smiled and sat down beside him. "He's very sweet."

"Mm." Howard Young looked out again over the sea. "He tends to go through women like other men go through undershirts." He was smiling, "Just a friendly word of caution."

"Oh, I'm not—" Carolyn found that her denial of any romantic interest was faltering, and that she actually stammered. "Mr. Young, I'm here on business, not personal pleasure."

"And speaking of that business, you were up quite late last night reading all the material I gave you."

She nodded. "It was absorbing."

"Were you frightened?"

"Of course."

He nodded. "If you had claimed you weren't, I'd have known you were lying."

"I went into the room this morning, with the key you gave me." She looked over at him, but he kept his eyes on the sea. "I could find no trickery, no hint of any kind of contraption in the walls that would have produced the bloody words we saw."

"Well, at least you can retire your skepticism."

Carolyn smiled. "Not entirely. That's not how an investigator operates. You discount nothing. You keep an open mind to all possibilities." She leaned in just a bit closer to the old man. "That's why I need to speak with Jeanette."

"Speak may be a rather high expectation," he replied, still looking out over the waves.

"She survived that night. And yes, I know, survive may be hardly the word to describe what happened to her that night. But she is alive. The only one to make it through a night in that room."

"Of course you can visit Jeanette. The others did as well."

Carolyn was aware that she was following in the footsteps of many others who had tried to do what she was doing and failed. "Kip Hobart is a friend of mine. When I leave here, I plan on going out to see him."

"Dr. Hobart was very bright and gave us all incredible hope." Howard Young slowly turned his face to once again look at Carolyn. "But then poor Douglas's father went into that room and showed how foolish we all were. What did the words say? 'Abandon hope.' "

"But you haven't abandoned hope if you contacted me."

He sighed. "I needed to make one last try. Ten years from now, at the next reunion, I won't be here."

"I wouldn't be too sure," Carolyn said, offering him a small smile.

They sat in silence for a few moments.

"What is your plan?" Mr. Young asked her finally.

"Other than meeting with Jeanette and Kip Hobart, I have none."

He laughed. "Once more, I appreciate your honesty. If you had claimed to know what to do, I would again have known that you were lying."

"It would help if you told me more," she said. "Who are these apparitions that people report seeing in the weeks leading up to the reunion? What were the events of eighty years ago that led to the start of the lottery?"

"You will discover that, if you are meant to."

"Kip made no mention in his notes. Did he not find out?"

"You will have to ask him."

"The woman people report seeing. The one in the white dress and black hair. Is she Beatrice? The servant girl who was killed on the property in 1930? There is a newspaper clipping about her death in the files. There has to be a connection."

"Perhaps there is."

"The newspaper didn't give a cause of death. It just said there had been a 'tragic accident' at the house. It happened right around this time of year, and the first lottery was held a month later."

"You have your chronology correct."

"What was the accident? How did Beatrice die?"

The old man looked pained. A gnarled, spotted hand went to his forehead.

"You won't say, or you *can't*?" Carolyn asked.

"Since my sister died thirty years ago, I have been the only one left alive who remembers those days. It is a lonely burden."

"I imagine it is." Carolyn sat back against the

bench. "If you can't tell me, I'd imagine I can get the information on her death from the records at the Youngsport town hall. Perhaps there was a coroner's report."

"The records won't tell you any more than I have."

She looked over at him. "So there was an attempt to contain scandal, perhaps?"

"To speak of such things to people outside the family is forbidden. That is what has made finding an end to this nightmare so difficult."

Carolyn leaned forward. "*Who* has forbidden it? And by what means?"

"Proceed with your itinerary. Visit Jeanette and Dr. Hobart. It is your only course."

Carolyn sighed. "But if you could just answer—"

"I am stuffed!"

They both turned, Mr. Young more slowly than Carolyn. Douglas was sauntering across the yard, rubbing his belly.

"I ended up having two waffles!" he crowed. "One with syrup and sliced apples and the other with strawberries and cream!"

"It's a wonder you aren't three hundred pounds, given the way you eat, you little hoodlum," his uncle replied. "Ah, the metabolism of youth!"

"Now I wonder what's for lunch," Douglas said, winking down at Carolyn.

She stood. "I'll let the two of you speak."

"No need to hurry off, Carolyn," Douglas said. "I'm happy for you to stick around."

"No, no, my boy," Uncle Howard said, patting the spot on the bench Carolyn had vacated. "She has work to do. And you and I need to have a little talk."

"I'll see you later?" Douglas asked Carolyn.

She nodded. "I suspect you will."

"Good." He smiled at her. He saw her look away.

She seemed upset, Douglas thought. She bid them both good morning and headed back across the lawn. Douglas sat down on the bench. Carolyn and Uncle Howie had been having a rather intense conversation when he'd approached. What kind of business did they have together? Why did his uncle need a private eye?

"So, talk to me, Uncle Howie," Douglas said. "What's the news you have for me?"

The old man did not return his gaze. Instead his eyes remained fixed on the sea.

"I have had this conversation with every member of our family when they have reached a certain age," he said. "It is not an easy one to have." He paused. "All that I ask is that you let me speak, and do not interrupt me until I am done."

"All right," Douglas said. A little flicker of fear had ignited in his gut.

"Very well then. It began on a night some eighty years ago. . . ."

Chapter Eight

It wasn't easy falling asleep by herself.

Karen had, as Paula anticipated, decided to go away "for a little while." She needed time to think, Karen said. It wasn't a breakup. Not yet. She just needed some space from Paula, from this apartment, from the long, unresolved discussion about children. She was staying with their friend Gillian in Jamaica Plain. Paula knew how to reach her. It wasn't as if they had severed all communication.

That didn't make it any easier to fall asleep.

Paula lifted one eye to glance over at the clock, glowing green in the darkness. 1:18. She'd been tossing and turning for almost two hours. Not even an Ambien had helped. She'd felt warm, so she'd kicked off the sheets. Then she'd felt cold, so she pulled them back up again. Now she felt as if she would lie there on her back all night, wide awake, staring at the ceiling.

Maybe it was good that Karen was gone. What business did Paula have trying to salvage the relationship if she knew she could never give Karen what she wanted? Why should she try to change Karen's mind and bring her back? It was better that she stayed far away from the madness of Paula's family.

She was beginning to feel drowsy, but still sleep wouldn't come. Great. The Ambien was making her disoriented but not knocking her out. She turned onto her side and squeezed her eyes shut. She tried to convince her subconscious mind that Karen was right beside her, just as she had been the last five years. All she had to do was reach out her hand and she'd feel her hair. She'd feel her warmth. Paula would know she wasn't alone. That she had someone who loved her. Who wanted to make a life with her.

Tears began forcing their ways out from her tightly closed eyelids.

"Oh, baby," she whispered.

Instinctively she reached out her hand toward the other side of the bed, the place where Karen had slept. . . .

And she felt her.

She felt Karen's hair.

Paula opened her eyes.

Karen was there. She rolled over and looked at Paula and smiled.

"Can't sleep?" she whispered.

"How . . . ?" Paula couldn't form the words. "How did you . . . ? When . . . ?"

"Shh," Karen said, and her eyes seemed to sparkle in the dark. "Do you hear? The baby's crying."

"The . . . baby?"

"Listen."

Paula was silent. There was indeed a baby cry-

ing. From the far distance. So Karen hadn't left at
all. She was right there, right beside Paula. Everything was okay. All their problems were gone.
Karen was there, and they had a baby. They had a
baby. . . .

"The baby's crying," Karen said again, more
forcefully this time.

It was almost like an order. Paula nodded. "Yes,
yes," she said. "The baby is crying. . . ."

She sat up and swung her legs out of the bed.
Her bare feet touched the hardwood floor. The
clock on the side of the bed now read 1:37. Paula
stood.

"Bring me the baby," Karen implored.

Her head was muzzy. *The Ambien,* she thought to
herself. But Paula pushed her way through the
dark, out of the bedroom and into the hallway.
She could hear the baby crying from somewhere
in the apartment. But where? The apartment was
spacious, with two bedrooms, a dining room, a living room, and a study. But the sound seemed to
come from someplace much farther away than any
of those rooms. Maybe from another part of the
building. Where was their baby? Someone had
taken their baby!

Paula began a mad scramble from room to
room. The guest bedroom was empty. Was that
where they had set up the crib? No, no, it was in the
dining room. It was easier to get to the baby. . . .
they'd put the crib there. But the dining room was
empty. Just a roomful of shadows, sliced through
by the moonlight seeping in from between Venetian blinds. Paula was beginning to panic. Where
was the baby? *Where was the baby?*

Through the kitchen she ran into the living

room, but no baby there. She listened. The crying continued. Still far away, but maybe a bit closer. She threw open the door and ran out into the corridor. Upstairs. The crying was coming from upstairs! Someone had kidnapped their baby and taken it to an apartment upstairs! Paula tried to shout, to tell her baby she was coming—but she realized she didn't know her baby's name.

When had they gotten the baby?

Did I give birth? Paula wondered. *Did I . . . bring a baby into this world?*

I shouldn't have.

Oh, God no . . .

She began running up the stairs. They went on and on. She never knew how many stairs there were in this building. She hadn't realized the building was so high. How many floors were there? She just kept running up and up and up. . . .

And always the crying, just a little ahead of her. Her baby . . .

Finally the stairs ended at a single door. She worried the door would be locked, but it wasn't. She flung it open and bounded inside—

And there was Karen, sitting on the couch, bouncing the baby on her knee.

"He's fine, he's fine," she kept saying, even though the baby was still crying.

"What is his name?" Paula asked.

Karen lifted her eyes to her.

"You mean to say," she said coldly, "that you don't know?"

"Please, may I hold him?"

Karen's eyes turned colder. Her lips tightened, and she pulled the baby to her bosom. "No," she spit. "He's not for you."

"He's my baby! I gave birth to him! I gave birth to him for you!"

"So you could give him to that room!"

"No!"

Karen stood up. She was thrusting the baby at her now. "Go ahead then! Take him! Take him!"

Paula took a step backward. "No, not now . . ."

The baby had stopped crying.

She could see that the child in Karen's arms was dead.

Dead and blue. Its head dangled as if its neck had been broken.

Paula screamed.

She sat up in bed, still screaming, her heart pounding in her ears. Even though she knew now it had all been dream, she screamed once more, just to release the last of the terror that had accumulated inside her.

As if one scream could do it.

She looked over at the clock. It read 2:02.

"Dear God," she said, bringing her hands to her forehead. She sat there in her bed, breathing heavily.

And then she realized the nightmare wasn't over.

The baby was crying again.

She looked off into the darkness. Was she still dreaming? Was she going to have to relive that horrible experience again?

She swung her feet out of bed. Bare skin touched hard wood. She padded across the floor, opening the door to the hallway. The crying continued. But closer than it had been before. It was here this time. Here in her apartment.

This was no dream.

She peered into the spare bedroom. Nothing. Out into the dining room. Just as it been in her dream, the moonlight sliced through the darkness in a pattern of stripes from the blinds. Paula steadied herself against a dining table chair. The crying was coming from the living room.

She wouldn't go in there. She knew what she would find. A baby. A bloody baby with its neck broken. Dean had seen such a thing once. Years ago, when Linda was pregnant with the twins. He'd woken up very much like she had tonight and seen a dead baby in his living room.

The creature screamed harder, seeming frustrated and angry that Paula would not come through the door and look upon it. She turned and headed back to her bedroom. She got back into bed and pulled the sheet up to her chin. She would not give it the satisfaction of her fear. Not twice in one night.

It cried harder and harder, breaking her heart. Surely the baby meant her no harm. Surely it was just a terrified creature, trapped between this world and the next.

But it was part of that room. It came from that room. It was part of the curse that had killed her father.

Paula lay awake for a long time, listening to the crying from the living room, refusing to give in. Finally, at 3:15, the crying ceased. Still Paula lay there, not moving, not thinking. Only as the first pink light of morning began to slip into the room did she finally fall asleep.

Chapter Nine

It wasn't until the pilot had lifted the plane off the short runway that Douglas, pressed back into his seat by the force of takeoff, turned to Carolyn beside him and asked, "So what the fuck goes on down in that room?"

Uncle Howie had arranged for his private plane to take them from the small landing strip outside Youngsport to the nearly as small airport in Hyannis, Massachusetts, about forty minutes away by air. There a driver would meet them and take them to see a man named Kip Hobart, who had apparently tried to end the curse ten years before—and failed.

Carolyn turned her eyes to Douglas as the little eight-seater plane rose up into the clouds. "I have no idea," she admitted.

They hadn't discussed what Mr. Young had told him until this very moment. After their breakfast encounter the day before, Carolyn hadn't seen Douglas for the rest of the day. Disturbed by what he'd been told, the young man had hopped onto his motorcycle and zoomed off down the highway. Mr. Young fretted all day, worrying the "little hoodlum" as he called him, would crack up his bike. "He kept saying it wasn't possible," Mr. Young said. "But I could see all of it coming together in his head. The manner of his father's death. The suicides of his mother and his aunt." Douglas hadn't returned until very late in the day. By then Carolyn was hunkered down in the study with all sorts of papers and reports. She had also spoken with Kip Hobart to arrange a meeting. She didn't intrude when she noticed Douglas and his uncle sequestered in the parlor. In fact, she didn't get a chance to speak to him until this very morning, when he'd announced he was going with her to talk with Kip. Mr. Young was agreeable.

But not until they were actually in the air did Douglas bring up the horrors he'd learned about his family.

"I want to say it's all a bunch of superstitious hooey," he said, closing his eyes. "But all those deaths . . . there's no faking that."

"No, there isn't," Carolyn agreed.

"And I saw her, you know." Douglas opened his eyes and turned again to look at Carolyn. "I saw the woman. Beatrice. The servant girl who was killed in that room."

"You did? When?"

"When I got here. She ran across the road, and I fell off my bike. Then she followed me up the cliff. I tried to tell myself she was just an illusion, but now it all makes sense."

"How do you know it was Beatrice? Your uncle wouldn't—or couldn't—admit to me that Beatrice is the apparition that appears to family members."

Douglas seemed puzzled. "He admitted it to me. When he told me about that ghost of a woman, I said I'd seen her—and he nodded and said, 'That's Beatrice.'"

"Odd that he was vague with me." Carolyn glanced out of the window. They were high enough now that she had a grand view of the Maine coastline. "Did he tell you how she died in that room?"

"Yes."

Carolyn was stunned. "He claimed to me that he didn't know. Or at least—that he couldn't say." She looked at Douglas intently. "Tell me how she died."

"She was murdered." He was clearly uncomfortable speaking the words. "Impaled on the wall by an iron pitchfork."

"The man . . ." Carolyn said.

"Yes," Douglas said. "Family members have often reported seeing a vision of a man with a pitchfork."

"It's horrible," Carolyn said, shuddering. "No wonder the room holds such bad energy. But why is your uncle withholding details from me and not from you? What possible reason could he have? It's almost as if he wants to make it as hard as possible for me to find an answer to all this . . . almost as if he doesn't *want* me to. . . ."

Douglas looked at her with surprise. "Uncle Howie wants this horrible curse to end. He wouldn't withhold any details unless there's a reason. I'm sure of it. All the tragedy he's seen . . ." He shook his head. "No, if he's not telling you something, it's because he *can't*."

Carolyn sighed. "Perhaps the curse will permit him only to tell outsiders so much."

"Yes," Douglas said. "It must be something like that."

It might well be, Carolyn thought. But why did she feel that Howard Young had his own reasons to control the flow of information?

She shuddered again. That wall . . . where she'd seen the blood.

A woman had been impaled there.

Douglas was clearly becoming anxious. "I have to ask you, Carolyn. If you have no idea what goes on that room, why did Uncle Howie hire you? No disrespect, but you're a private eye, not a Ghost-buster. You track down missing people, real *live* missing people. You go after insurance frauds—not avenging ghosts."

She smiled. "Well, I have a bit more experience than that." She related the paranormal cases she'd investigated, both for the FBI and on her own. Douglas listened intently, particularly intrigued by the zombie guy. Most people were. "But," Carolyn concluded, "I can't claim to be an expert on the supernatural. That's why we're going to see Kip."

Douglas made a short laugh. "And that's why I wanted to come along. Why should we care what he thinks? He failed last time. How can he help us now?"

Carolyn understood Douglas's bitterness. When Kip had tried to end the curse ten years before, he had given the family hope—and it had been Douglas's father, in a way, who'd been the family's test case. Whatever Kip had done, they had hoped it would allow Douglas Senior to survive the night in that room. But their hopes were futile.

"Kip has trained with the very best psychic investigators," Carolyn said, defending her friend. "He has witnessed some extraordinary things. I'm sure he did his best trying to help your family. Certainly he has some key insights into what goes on in that room. And he may be able to point us to other people who can help as well."

Douglas seemed pessimistic. "The lottery is a month away. We don't have a lot of time."

"No, we don't," Carolyn admitted.

Douglas ran a hand through his blond hair. Ever since he'd learned the secret, he'd felt as if he were carrying around a heavy lead weight tied to his neck. He let out a long sigh.

"Uncle Howie said that for the last decade he's spoken to dozens of people. No one could help. It wasn't until the eleventh hour that he got a recommendation to meet with you. And now, he said, you're our last hope."

Carolyn understood that, and she felt the pressure. Perhaps she had no right accepting this job. What did she know? How could she figure this all out in time to prevent another death from occurring just a month away from now—especially if Howard Young was withholding information from her, willingly or not? She clung to the hope that Kip could help, that he could point her in a direction that might lead to an answer. But all he'd promised her on the phone was to tell her what he knew. "And that," he'd said forlornly, "was clearly not enough ten years ago."

Douglas had closed his eyes again. "In a strange sort of way," he said, almost as much to himself as Carolyn, "learning the secret of that room was a kind of relief. It's like I always knew that something was going on with the family, that there was some deep dark mystery that might explain my parents' deaths."

"It must be a horrible thing to live with," Carolyn said.

She thought of her own family and the hardships they'd faced. Her parents, too, had died painful deaths. But they'd had their children around them. Friends. The goodwill and support of their community. There were no lingering questions after they were gone. Just grief and loss. On that much at least, she could relate to Douglas.

The plane began its descent over the long narrow arm of Cape Cod. Once they were on the ground, the pilot opened the door for them and guided them down the three steps onto the tarmac. Inside the small airport, a man wearing a crisp blue suit waited. He told them he was Mr. Young's driver, and he would take them up to Fall's Church, the tiny village where Kip Hobart lived.

For the entire half-hour ride, neither Douglas nor Carolyn said a word. Douglas gazed out the window, thinking back to the day his father died. He remembered being wakened slightly by his father's kiss on the forehead. That must have been right after he'd been selected in the lottery, and right before he went down to the room. *He was coming to say good-bye,* Douglas thought, his eyes filling with tears at the realization, though he would not let himself cry. And Mom . . . so terrified, so grief stricken, that depression took over and caused her to end her life. *She couldn't bear to live with the thought that I, too, might someday have to spend a night in that room. . . .*

Carolyn sat looking out of the other window, consumed by her own thoughts. *What if I can't find an answer? They'll hold the lottery again. Someone will go into that room. . . .* And what if it was the young man sitting beside her?

At last they pulled up in front of a small cottage along a marshy inlet of the Atlantic Ocean. The sky had gone gray, and Carolyn felt chilled suddenly as she stepped out of the car. The air felt damp. Tall yellow reeds swayed along the soggy banks. A heron touched down into the water ahead of her, flapping its wide wings.

The driver waited in the car as Carolyn and Douglas headed up to the door. Even before they'd had a chance to knock, it was opened by a man wearing a beige cardigan sweater and blue jeans.

"Hello, Kip," Carolyn said.

They embraced. Douglas was surprised by how young Kip Hobart was. He'd expected an expert in the supernatural would be an old man with a white beard. But Kip couldn't have been more than forty, and was quite handsome, with a broad smile and a strong jaw. His sandy hair was fading to white at the temples, and there was a weather-beaten feel to his skin, but his eyes were very young. Watching the affectionate greeting Kip gave Carolyn, Douglas found himself a little jealous. The suddenness of the feeling surprised him.

"Kip," Carolyn was saying, "this is Douglas Young."

The man's eyes filled with compassion as he extended his hand. "Your father was a good man. A brave man. Not a day passes that I don't think of him."

Douglas shook his hand. He couldn't speak. He just nodded.

Inside the cottage, the walls were lined from floor to ceiling with books, many of them old and dusty. Douglas had expected to see skulls and crystal balls in the home of a guy who made his living chasing the supernatural, but the most unusual thing in the place was a framed movie poster of *Freaks*, complete with pinheads. Other than that it was a simple place, with an old sofa covered with a striped afghan, wicker baskets on the walls, and a big conch shell sitting on top of the old television set.

A woman that Kip introduced as Georgeanne served them all hot cups of coffee. "The days are getting cooler out here," Kip said, and they all nodded. Georgeanne was maybe thirty, a beautiful dark-skinned woman with short hair. Her accent sounded Caribbean. From their intimacy, the way they smiled at each other and gently touched each other's arms, Douglas assumed that Kip and Georgeanne were either married or in a relationship. It chased away any lingering thoughts of jealousy.

They sat on the back deck overlooking the marsh. Another heron had joined the first, and a dozen or so ducks paddled along the perimeter. Carolyn held her coffee mug in both hands to warm them. She couldn't shake the chill.

Douglas just sat there, staring at Kip, at this man who knew more about his family's secrets than he did.

"I wish I could have saved your father," Kip said, speaking the words they were all thinking.

"I'm sure you did what you could," Douglas replied. And sitting there now across from the man, looking into his compassionate eyes, he felt certain that Kip *had* done everything in his power. He couldn't blame him for his father's death.

"I've reviewed all your notes and the log you kept," Carolyn said. "But I still have some questions. . . . That's why I felt a meeting would be helpful."

"Of course," Kip said.

Douglas leaned forward. "I haven't read anything, so maybe you can just tell me a couple things first, okay?"

Kip nodded.

"When did my uncle approach you? How long did you investigate the room? What made you think you had ended the curse? And why do you think you weren't successful?"

"Why don't I begin from the beginning, and I'll tell you as much as I can?" He settled back in his chair, and Georgeanne moved down to sit on the arm, seemingly as a gesture of support. "Mr. Young found me through an article I'd written about psychic phenomena. I had investigated a strange case of a woman who was apparently the reincarnation of an earlier self, and was compelled to do things that the earlier self wanted. I wrote about how we can distinguish between true psychic phenomena and mental illness, and I suggested ways in which we can corral the psychic energy, contain it, and if necessary, eliminate it."

"I see why Uncle Howie might have thought you could help."

"Unfortunately, I only had about a year before the lottery was to take place. . . ."

Carolyn made a small, bitter laugh. "Try dividing that time in twelve, and you'll see how much time *I* have."

Kip gave her a sympathetic face. "Your dilemma is far more difficult, Carolyn, as I told you on the phone. Especially because it seems every route has been tried before. If not by me, then by others over the years. There have been a dozen exorcisms conducted in that house, by Roman Catholic priests and Hindu Brahmins and Wiccan practitioners. None of them ended the power of that room."

"So there's no hope," Douglas said, giving in to despair. "No way to end the curse."

Kip sighed. "There is always hope, Douglas." He rubbed his forehead as he struggled for words. "I'm not even sure you can call it a curse, though certainly it feels that way. If it was a curse, we might have been able to end it—because there are ways of removing curses." He looked over at the woman sitting beside him. "Georgeanne is perhaps the best curse remover on the planet."

"He flatters me," she said, a small smile on her lips. "This case was actually how we met. Kip had heard of my work and asked me to accompany him to the house in Maine." She shook her head. "I have never felt such energy in one place before. The hold that woman has over that family is extraordinary."

"Okay, hold up," Douglas said. "What woman? Are you talking about Beatrice? Is she the one who makes the horrible things happen in the room? Because I figured her to be a victim. I figured the bad guy in all this was the creep that people have seen holding the pitchfork. Did he kill Beatrice? Was he the one that did it? Who was he? And why do you say it's Beatrice who has the hold—"

Kip held up his hands as if to calm him. "Perhaps it's best that I continue on with my narrative," he said softly. "Carolyn has read my account. She knows the conclusions that I have drawn. Whether she accepts them or not, time will tell. But for your sake, Douglas, I will continue to share what I experienced and what I believe I discovered."

Carolyn took another sip of the coffee. It felt good going down, warming her. But its effects were temporary. Within moments she was cold again. She began to think it wasn't just the raw air coming in off the marsh that chilled her. It was fear.

"I conducted a series of communications in that room," Kip said. "I did so by rather traditional means, at least in terms of psychic research. I held several séances and brought in two different channelers. I also communicated through untraditional means." He stood and walked back into the cottage for a moment. They watched as he removed a small device that sat on the shelf of the bookcase. The device looked like an old-fashioned walkie-talkie.

"This was invented by a colleague," Kip explained as he came back outside. "It transmits frequencies that are beyond the range of the human ear. It also allows our voices to penetrate that frequency. And as a handy-dandy tool, it also records the communication."

He set the device on a wicker table. Douglas stared at it as Kip pushed a small button. The tape inside the device whirred. Then a piercing sound suddenly filled their ears. It was some kind of a whistle, extremely high-pitched. They all winced.

"What is it?" Douglas asked, covering his ears.

"Listen," Kip told him.

The whistle continued on for nearly a minute, making Douglas want to bolt from his seat. Then it stopped abruptly and was replaced by a voice.

A woman's voice.

"Love," she said.

Even Carolyn looked perplexed.

"Love," the voice said again. "It is love. Love. It is love." The voice sounded sad, terribly sad, as if it might break at any time.

"Are you saying love?"

This was Kip's voice, crackly and higher than the way he spoke normally, but clearly him. The device had recorded him trying to speak to whatever force was in the room.

"Love," the woman's voice repeated. "It is love."

"Love," Kip echoed. "Love. L-O-V-E."

"Love," the voice said once more, and then the whistle returned.

Kip switched off the device.

"That didn't sound like a force intent on the kind of evil that has taken place in that room every ten years," Carolyn said.

Kip shook his head. "Not at all. The voice was sad. Heartbreaking."

"So she's not the one who's killing people then?" Douglas asked. "It's the man with the pitchfork. The one who killed her in real life."

"There's no conclusive evidence that the voice we just heard was Beatrice," Carolyn said. "Kip, I know you made that conclusion, but in the kind of investigations I've been trained to do, we can't make any assumptions. We need direct evidence."

"True," Kip said. "The voice may have been another spirit, or force, or whatever we want to call it. But we held a séance after this communication. I'll let Georgeanne take over from here."

Georgeanne was quiet a moment before continuing the story. "I called upon Beatrice to appear to us. And she did. And she was crying. We asked her if she wished the killings to stop, if she wanted to release the room from her power. And she nodded that she did. So I used the words to invoke the ritual for ending a curse and asked Beatrice to follow along with me. She remained there, visible to both Kip and myself, and seemed to accept the words. Then I asked her to come with me out of the room. She did so. Kip and I walked up the stairs, and Beatrice followed us. I will never forget the experience. She was crying softly. Her long black hair fell over her shoulders. We walked through the foyer and out onto the yard. We walked all the way to the cliffs and turned to Beatrice and told her she was free now, that she was no longer trapped in the place where she had been killed. She smiled and continued walking—directly off the cliff. She vanished then."

"So you can see why we had hope that the curse was ended," Kip said softly.

"She was playing you," Carolyn said. "She played along, let you think that she was really gone. . . ."

Douglas put his hand to his forehead. They all knew he was thinking of his father again.

"Possibly," Kip said. "Possibly she played us for fools."

Georgeanne was shaking her head. "But I felt the energy in the room. When she appeared to us, there was no malevolence in her spirit. I, too, have been trained in my own kind of investigations. And I would recognize malevolence. The energy in that room that day was sadness. Grief. I believed her when she said she wanted the killings to end. But perhaps she is prevented somehow from doing so."

"Yes," Douglas interjected. "She's prevented from doing so by that man with the pitchfork. He's the evil force here! Why do you focus on Beatrice? He killed her. So he's keeping her spirit trapped there and won't let her go."

"It might seem that way, yes," Kip admitted. "But we focused on Beatrice because she was the only one who appeared when we summoned the forces in that room. The energy we felt there was feminine. The overwhelming presence in that room is Beatrice. And although we spoke with family members who reported seeing the man with the pitchfork, we never encountered him ourselves. We never saw him. We never felt his spirit. Only Beatrice responded when we called."

"Though there *is* another force there," Georgeanne said.

Carolyn was nodding. "The baby."

"The baby?" Douglas asked. "What baby?"

Carolyn looked over at them. "In Kip's notes, there was mention of a baby. That some in the family reported seeing the apparition of a baby."

"Uncle Howie didn't tell me anything about a baby," Douglas said.

Kip sighed and stood from his chair, walking over to the edge of the deck. "It appears that Mr. Young picks and chooses the details he shares. For example, we never knew about the man with the pitchfork until other family members reported him to us. Then Mr. Young admitted he knew about him as well. We also did not know the manner of Beatrice's death. Mr. Young only said that it was a tragic accident."

"That was the same for me," Carolyn said.

"So how did you find out?" Douglas asked.

Kip smiled. "Luckily, ten years ago, there were still a few old-timers in Youngsport who remembered the events of seventy years earlier. I'd doubt if you'd find any of them still alive today."

"Why didn't you include any of this in your report?" Carolyn asked. "I had no idea of the manner of Beatrice's death either. There was nothing of it in your notes."

"I discovered it at the very end of my research," Kip told her. "By then, events were proceeding quickly. We had already cast Beatrice out of the room—or thought we had. I never had time to go back and write a conclusive report."

Carolyn thought that was odd. Kip was one of the most thorough psychic investigators she knew. But for the moment, she let it go. "What did these old-timers tell you about what happened?" she asked.

"I could tell you," Kip said, "but I think it would be better in their own words."

Once again he stepped back inside the cottage. This time he returned with a much more conventional tape recorder. Placing it beside the other device, he switched it on.

"I had it ready in anticipation of your visit," Kip said. "Listen."

Kip's voice floated from the machine.

"Will you state your name and age, please?"

"Harry Noons, and I'm eighty-eight," came another voice from the tape recorder. It was a fragile voice, as dry as old leaves.

"And will you tell me everything you remember about the night in question and the events that took place at the Young mansion in September 1930?"

"Ayuh. I'll tell ya what I know and what I can re-membuh." Harry Noons cleared his throat, a loud rattling sound that went on for nearly thirty seconds. "I was working up on the estate as a grounds-man. I was a young man, barely eighteen, and times were tough. We had the Depression back then, you know. And old Mr. Young, the current Mr. Young's father, he hired me and gave me some work trimming hedges and the like, and I was very grateful. And I noticed the girl they had working there. She was very beautiful. I admit I kind of fancied her myself. All the men who saw her did. She was just that kind of girl. To see her was to make your heart stop for a moment."

"And her name was?" Kip asked on the tape recorder.

"Beatrice. I never knew her last name. She lived at the house. She did the housework and all that. She was very young. And here's why she caused such a stir in town in them days. She wasn't married. But she was in the family way."

"She was pregnant?" Kip asked.

"Ayuh, sir, she was. And all the busybodies gossiped in town, wondering why Mr. and Mrs. Young, such pillars in the community, would keep her on. They thought she should have been cast out for disgracing their house in that way. But Beatrice stayed, and I'd see her walking around fluffing clothes and hanging them on the line, and she had her big belly right there, plain as day, for anyone to see it."

"This was how many months before September?"

"Well, I think she had the baby sometime in the

late spring. By September, of course, the baby was born and living there in the house with her."

"Mr. Noons," Kip asked, "there is no record at town hall of a birth of a child born to a woman named Beatrice in that year. Moreover, there's no mention of a child in the newspaper notice of Beatrice's death. Why is that?"

"Dunno. Guess they never filed no birth record. And if Mr. Young didn't want something mentioned in the newspaper, it wasn't."

"Okay. Please proceed with your story."

Harry Noons cleared his throat again, leading to a major coughing fit. The sound of phlegm being hacked up in his throat was plainly audible on the tape. Finally he found his voice again.

"It was getting near to fall, you know, kind of like now. Still hot enough most days to call it summer, but a chill would come in now and then. And I remembuh it was chilly that day. Windy. The skies were gray. And Miss Beatrice, she was crying. All day long, every time I seen her, she was crying. And so I asked Clem—"

"Who's Clem?"

"Well, he was the one who done it."

"Done what, Mr. Noons?"

"Killed her."

"Who was he, and why did he kill Beatrice?"

"Well, that's what I'm telling ya! Clem was kind of a slow-witted man, you know. Big and thick. Body and head, you know. Thick-headed. Clem worked on the grounds, like me, though he did the heavy work and was in charge of the barn. He was always chopping wood or hauling hay for the horses. Those were his jobs. Clem hoped to marry Beatrice, even though that baby was not his. He said he didn't care, that he loved Beatrice and would be a good father to her baby. So one day I asked him what was wrong with Beatrice. He said he didn't know. I believe he was telling me the truth then. But later I saw them arguing."

"Where were they arguing?"

"Outside her room down in the basement," Harry Noons said. "Back in those days the basement was the servants' quarters, and there was an entrance from the back of the house. Nowadays that's been closed off, and you can only get to the basement from the inside of the house. That's because Mr. Young doesn't have any servants who live there anymore. After what happened to Beatrice, all the servants were turned into day staff. No servant ever lived in that house again. The servants' entrance was sealed off."

"But you were inside the servants' quarters to witness this argument?"

"Ayuh, I most certainly was. I had gone inside to wash my hands. I was done for the day and I was going home. And I saw Beatrice and Clem arguing. She was saying she'd never marry him, that she was going to marry a much better man than he was, and it was making Clem angry. He didn't like to be told that anyone was better than him. He was a dumb animal, but like any animal that gets cornered, that gets provoked, he got angry. And I remembuh Beatrice was holding her baby in one arm as she shouted at Clem, and Clem called the baby a bastard. She slapped him then, right across the face."

"What did you do?"

"I was just trying to mind my business, you know, so I didn't say nuthin'. I finished washing my hands and got the hell out of there. I went up the stairs back outside and then walked across the terrace to the kitchen entrance. I stepped inside for just a moment to tell Mrs. Young that I was done for the day. The sun was starting to set, I remembuh. The sky was a bright blood red. Mrs. Young told me that Mr. Young would be down in a moment to give me my pay. He was good like that. Always paid me at the end of each day. But then we heard the screams from downstairs. They were horrible. Really bloodcurdling. Mrs. Young turned all white, and I immediately ran back outside and headed down the stairs into the servants' entrance. There I found Beatrice. . . ."

The old man's voice faltered.

"How did you find her, Mr. Noons?"

"I found her impaled on the wall with a pitch-fork."

He began coughing again, the horror of the memory overtaking him.

"And where was the baby?"

"Don't know that. Nowhere that I could see. But Beatrice . . . she was hanging there on the wall, dripping blood everywhere. . . ."

The old man made a sound of horror and began hacking violently.

Kip switched off the recorder.

"It took him a while to compose himself and be able to speak again," Kip told them, "so I'll just paraphrase the rest of what he told me. The household came running, Mr. Young and all the Young sons, including our current Mr. Young, Howard. Harry Noons told them what he'd seen, and they immediately dispersed across the estate looking for Clem. They searched for hours, but couldn't find him."

"Did they *ever* find him?" Douglas asked.

Kip shook his head. "Apparently not. He never resurfaced, as far as Harry Noons ever knew."

"But the sheriff must have led a manhunt to find him," Douglas said.

"No." Kip sighed. "For the simple reason that your great-great-grandfather never made any accusation against him." Kip sat back down, shaking his head. "The family was terrified of scandal. They only reported that Beatrice had died of an accident. They never let anyone into the house. They never told the sheriff the nature of Beatrice's accident, and reported simply that she'd been buried in the family cemetery nearby."

"And such has always been the power of my family that what they decree is accepted by the authorities." Douglas sighed. "Money has its privileges."

"But the newspaper reports make no mention that she had a baby," Carolyn observed.

"No," Kip said. "That much isn't all that surprising. Back in the day, a bastard child was an unmentionable in the press."

"So what happened to the baby?" Carolyn asked.

"Harry Noons was told that Mr. Young had found a home for the baby."

Douglas seemed aghast. "And the sheriff didn't even inquire further?"

Kip shook his head. "Mr. Young was apparently simply taken at his word. Of course, this was in the days before aggressive child welfare services and things like that."

Douglas stood, unnerved and agitated by all

that he heard about his family. "And so when the high and mighty Desmond Young issued a pronouncement, the local authorities just shook their heads and said, 'Yes, sir.'" He snorted. "I know how it works. And it's not right."

"So there was never any investigation into Beatrice's death," Carolyn said.

"None," Kip said.

"And no inquiry into what happened to her baby."

"None."

Carolyn was adding it all up in her mind. "And Clem disappeared, never to be heard from again."

"Except to haunt members of the family," Douglas said. "Okay. So this tells us some of the history. How did the lottery start? What connection does it have?"

"I'm afraid that I can't tell you precisely," Kip said. "Yet again, Mr. Young was stingy with some details. All he would say is that without the lottery, without the sacrifice of one member of the family every ten years, the entire clan would perish. This is what was told to his father, Desmond Young, who inaugurated the first lottery a week after Beatrice's death."

"*Who* told him?" Douglas wanted to know. "Who told Desmond Young that they had to send someone into that room? The ghost of Beatrice?"

Kip could only shrug.

"It would appear again," Carolyn said, "that certain details are being withheld from us, whether through choice or force."

"Okay," Douglas said, trying to find some iota of logic in all of this madness, "let's suppose it *was* Beatrice who started the curse, or whatever you want to call it. It would seem that it would *have* to be her, right? Because as far as we know, Clem didn't die that day. He escaped. So if it was Beatrice, why would she want to hurt a family who had been so good to her? Who hadn't cast her out when she got pregnant? For a family that feared scandal, that was pretty nice of them. So why would she want to hurt them?"

"Again," Kip said, "your guess will be as good as mine on that."

"Perhaps Beatrice is the force in that room," Carolyn observed, "but perhaps she isn't the originator of the curse. Perhaps it was someone else— someone we have no idea about as yet." She stood, wrapping her arms around herself, still struggling to get warm. "As an investigator, I can only go with the facts as we know them. I cannot add two and two to get four, because there may be another variable to consider in the equation. Maybe it's two plus two plus two again—and we get six." She smiled. "It's not enough for me to say that Clem just disappeared. What happened to him? And for that matter, how do we know Harry Noons is a reliable witness? Why did he wait seventy years to tell his story?"

Kip smiled. "Oh, I'm sorry; I left out a rather salient point." His eyes moved over to Douglas. "Your great-great-grandfather paid him a considerable amount of money to keep quiet. In the midst of the Depression, with five younger siblings in his struggling family, Harry couldn't refuse. Only all those years later, when I found him, did his conscience compel him to tell the real story."

Douglas groaned, putting his hands in his hair and turning to look out over the marsh.

"And you found Noons to be trustworthy?" Carolyn asked.

"I did. As did Georgeanne."

"I held his hand," she said. "He was speaking the truth."

Kip chuckled. "She's rather like a human lie detector. I can't get away with anything with her."

Carolyn managed a small smile. "So we still don't know how the lottery began and what power keeps it in force—or what does the killing in that room."

"If I were still working on this case," Kip said, "I would try to reach the spirit of Clem. Find out what happened. Where did he go? And why did he kill Beatrice?"

"We don't know he killed Beatrice," Carolyn said.

"He was the only one with a motive," Kip said. "Noons said he saw Beatrice turning him down, taunting him."

"But he didn't see him kill her. He left the basement. And when he went down there again, Clem was nowhere to be found."

Kip made a face. "He saw Clem there moments before the screaming began."

"And he rushed down there immediately and found only Beatrice. No Clem."

"He could have been hiding in the basement somewhere."

"Possibly."

Kip looked extremely sad. "I wanted so much to help the family. I wanted so much to end those terrible deaths that they face every decade. I volunteered to continue my research after it was clear that I had failed. I wanted to keep going, to try to find the cause and the solution so that next time . . . but Mr. Young said I was done."

Douglas turned his head at that. "Why wouldn't my uncle want you to continue? After you had already discovered so much?"

"He is a very stubborn man," Kip said simply.

"Did he blame you for not ending the curse?" Carolyn asked.

"Let's just say he wasn't very happy with me." Kip sighed. "I refused to accept any payment from him. But I did promise him that I would speak of it to no one, unless he sent other researchers to me. I heard nothing until I got your call, Carolyn."

"That's why you never wrote a concluding report," Carolyn said. "Howard Young was done with you."

Kip nodded sadly. "I suppose I can understand his distress. I had failed. Another family member of his was dead. The curse went on."

There was nothing much more to say. Carolyn and Kip exchanged a few words as they looked over each others' notes while Georgeanne refilled everyone's coffee cups. Douglas remained where he was, standing looking out over the marsh. The ducks had all taken flight, nearly in unison, and flew in formation over the coastline. The sun was dropping lower in the sky, emerging from the gray clouds to stain the marsh pink.

He didn't like what he'd learned about his family. The secrets were horrible enough. But the way they'd withheld information from the police, picking and choosing details, was reprehensible. That woman's killer was never brought to justice. No wonder she and her baby haunted the family. And the parceling of information that was done eighty years ago was not so different from the way Uncle Howie shared certain details with some people and not with others. What was going on?

They all bid good-bye soon after that. Kip offered to be of service if he could, telling Carolyn to call him. Georgeanne, too, said she would be willing to use her powers of intuition, as she called them, if they were ever needed. Carolyn thanked them both. Douglas shook both of their hands. To Kip he said, "Thank you for trying. I know you did all you could."

Kip seem very moved by his words, and brought him in for an embrace.

On the ride back to the airport both Douglas and Carolyn were silent. As before, it was not until they were airborne that they spoke of what they faced.

"I'm scared," Douglas said.

"I am, too," Carolyn admitted.

"I just wish I knew who—or *what*—I was scared of," Douglas said. "Beatrice? Clem? Or something else?"

Carolyn nodded. That was exactly what she was thinking. She rested her head against the window and looked down at the waters of the Atlantic. She steeled herself, vowing she would do everything in her power to find out what she needed to know. She vowed she would succeed where Kip had failed.

If only she had more time than one slim month.

Chapter Ten

Ryan Young wasn't pleased when he hung up the phone with his Uncle Howard. The old man had told him that his cousin Douglas was visiting. Douglas had been there at the house for nearly a week now. Ryan had tried to seem happy that his uncle had a visitor, but inwardly, he was seething.

Leave it to that gypsy Douglas to sneak in and work on Uncle Howard before any of us could get there, Ryan thought. He was anxious to tell his father about his cousin's sneaky ways. They didn't trust Douglas. He played at being carefree and happy-go-lucky, a hippie on a motorcycle who didn't give a damn about money and inheritance. But he was fooling them all. He wanted that house. He wanted all of Uncle Howard's property. Ryan was certain of it.

Ryan glanced in the mirror at himself and liked what he saw. He'd just come from the pool, and his hair was slicked back against his head, his chiseled body glistening. He had not six abdominals but eight. His eyes brimmed with ambition and desire.

He was as dark as Douglas was fair. Uncle Howard liked to say that Douglas was a lady-killer—in fact, at that very moment, Douglas was charming a young lady who was working for him. That only made Ryan more angry. It was *Ryan* who was the lady-killer, *Ryan* who had every woman in New York chasing after him at nightclubs and restaurants. It was Ryan who often showed up in the gossip columns with some starlet or socialite on his arm. Last he knew Douglas was dating some babe who worked at a *diner,* for Christ's sake! Ryan had dated Paris Hilton—and had his picture printed on Page Six to prove it!

"Chelsea!" he shouted. His sister was staggering out of her room, still sleepy-eyed, her hair a mess. It was two in the afternoon, and she was just getting up after being out on the town very, very late last night. "Guess who's up at Uncle Howard's right at this moment!"

"I don't really care," the girl grumbled. "I have a wicked hangover."

"*Douglas!* Dear cousin Douglas!"

She spun around to look at him, her eyes suddenly coming to life. "No fucking way!"

"*Way.*" Ryan folded his muscled arms across his broad chest. "I just spoke to Uncle Howard. I called just to show what a good nephew I was. Calling in to check up on him, to see how he was feeling and to tell him how very, very much"—here Ryan's eyes rolled comically for his sister to see—"I'm looking forward to the family reunion." He paused, his face puckering as if he'd just bitten into a lemon. "And what does our dear uncle tell me? That *Douglas is there*! Once again, the loser has gotten in ahead of us!"

Chelsea was running fingers through her hair, trying to untangle the knots. "Well, he's not going to be a loser for long if he keeps kissing ass like he is. Uncle Howard will leave him everything. You know Daddy worries about that."

"We have to go up there right away," Ryan said. "I'm not waiting until the actual reunion. There will be too many people around then. Paula and Dean and those obnoxious twins of his." Both Ryan and Chelsea shuddered. "If we leave soon, we can have a couple of weeks with Uncle Howard."

Chelsea made a face. "We have to stay up there a couple of weeks? In that backwoods? There are no clubs, no happening places. . . ."

"Do you want to be in the will or not?"

She nodded. "Okay. You're right." She narrowed her eyes. "But will Douglas still be there?"

Ryan shrugged. "I don't know. Uncle Howard didn't say how long he was staying. But he may well be. But all the more reason for us to get our asses up there! Douglas may be planning to stay up there buttering his toast for as long as he can. He knows he has to work on Uncle Howard. He has to prove that he's more than just a wandering hippie."

"That will be difficult," Chelsea said.

"Yeah, but he's always been able to wrap Uncle Howard around his finger. Remember when we were kids and he'd convince Uncle Howard to let him play in the attic? You and I were never allowed to run free through the house."

"It's true," Chelsea grumbled. "Douglas was allowed to go anywhere he wanted." She thought a moment. "Except the basement."

"Well, no one was ever allowed in the basement," Ryan said.

"What's down there anyway? Why is it always closed off?"

Ryan grinned. "Probably the family jewels. Which can all be ours, dear sister, if we can charm Uncle Howard in the next couple of weeks."

She laughed. "But Daddy has already made us rich. Why would Uncle Howard want to leave us more when Paula or Dean or especially Douglas need it more?"

"Uncle Howard is a businessman," Ryan insisted. "He is a shark. He'd have to be, to accumulate the fortune he has. He respects businessmen. He's told Daddy that many times. He admires the way Daddy has run his business. If he thinks we are just as shrewd and smart and capable as Daddy, he'll make sure we get a good chunk of his change."

"Is he really all that richer than we are?" Chelsea's voice dropped into a whisper. "Does he really have that much more money than Daddy?"

"He makes Daddy look like a pauper," Ryan assured her. "Think about what we could do with Uncle Howard's money. We'd have access to everything and everyone."

Chelsea laughed. "Still burning over the fact that Paris dumped you?"

Ryan's lips tightened. "If we are Uncle Howard's main heirs, we will have so much more money than the Hiltons."

"Well," Chelsea said, heading back toward her room, "I need to sleep off this hangover a little longer. When do you want to get on the road?"

"I have a few things to finish up at the office today, so let's head out first thing tomorrow morning." He was planning on a quick jaunt into Manhattan to issue instructions to his assistants and then to enjoy a late supper with one of his girls. Of course, he'd need to make sure it was the best restaurant and the prettiest girl he could find. If he was heading up to Maine tomorrow, it would be a while before he got back to civilization. "Be ready bright and early tomorrow," Ryan called after his sister. "I mean it! Like eleven o'clock!" She groaned. "Okay, no later than noon!"

She shut her door without answering.

Ryan bolted down the stairs and into his father's study. There were files in here on a couple of business deals he was working on. He'd bring them into the office and dump them in his assistant's lap. He could do things like that. He was the boss. Or more accurately the boss's son. Which was the same thing.

He was standing at his father's desk, riffling though the pages of several spiral-bound files, when he heard the door behind him gently click shut.

He turned. He had left the door open. Now it was closed.

It must have been a breeze. He thought nothing more of it and continued leafing through the files.

Then he heard the unmistakable sound of the lock being turned on the door.

"Dad?" he called out. "Are you there?"

He set the files down on the desk and turned toward the door. Gripping the handle, he saw that it was indeed locked.

"Dad? Hey! I'm in here! Did you lock the door?"

But then he remembered his father was in the Hamptons. "Mom?" he called out instead. But his mother was at their townhouse in the city. She'd been spending more and more time there ever since Dad had hired Melissa. "Melissa?" Ryan called out. But he assumed Melissa was with his father in the Hamptons. As far as Ryan knew, only he and Chelsea were in the house. The servants had all gone home.

"Well, clearly not all of them," he said under his breath. Obviously someone had come back and, finding the door to the study unlocked, thought he or she was doing the right thing by locking it. Ryan began to pound on the door. "Hey! Who's out there? Consuela? Maria? Max? Carlos?"

But there was no answer. The house was eerily silent.

Ryan banged harder, shouting at the top of his lungs. "Hey! Somebody! Open this door!"

But still nothing.

"Jesus Fucking H. Christ," he growled. He turned away from the door, glancing over at the windows. He'd have to crawl out through the window. It wasn't a very high drop; he'd be fine. It was just a frigging nuisance. And very undignified to have to crawl out a window of his own house. Whoever locked that door was going to have his or her ass fired. How irresponsible to lock a room without first checking to see if anyone was inside.

Ryan was barefoot, wearing just a pair of jeans and a sweatshirt. He worried that he might cut his feet on the gravel outside the window. Plus there were rosebushes. Crawling out of the window meant he'd land in a thicket of thorns. There was no way around it. He groaned. He was really going to fire somebody!

"Hello?" he called one more time over his shoulder. "Anyone hear me?"

Chelsea, he was sure, was sound asleep again. He knew how zonked out she could be when she had a hangover. There was no choice but the window.

Except that it wouldn't budge.

"Jesus Fucking H. Christ!" he shouted again. He tried the second window. Same thing.

Had Dad permanently sealed these windows closed? Was it an antitheft thing? He knew Dad kept important papers in the study. But he had a fucking wall safe. Why would he seal off windows?

They were just stuck. That had to be it. Ryan tried again. Once more, the windows wouldn't move.

Ryan Young was not a patient man. In college, one of his girlfriends, a smartass psychology major, had said he suffered from "LFT"—low frustration tolerance. Ever since he was a kid, Ryan had always expected to get what he wanted exactly when he wanted—and ninety-nine times out of a hundred he did. But when things didn't go his way, he got pissed. Instantly. And completely.

"Get me out of this room!" he screamed at the top of his lungs. He picked up a vase and hurled it. It smashed against the door into hundreds of shards of glass.

Maybe that would bring someone running.

But it didn't. The house retained its eerie calm.

Which only infuriated Ryan more.

As a kid, he used to throw temper tantrums Mom always gave in and let him have the candy bar or the extra bottle of Coke after he started screaming and kicking. Sometimes he still threw tantrums. At the office, if his assistants didn't do everything they were supposed to do, or had failed to call a client or move stocks or trade shares, Ryan was known to rip them new assholes right in front of everybody. Often he threw things, like he'd just hurled that vase. Once he threw an assistant's iPhone out the window when it rang while he was speaking. It smashed the glass and dropped twenty-three floors to land on top of a parked cab on Wall Street. Good thing it hadn't hit someone in the head.

But as much as Ryan wanted to pitch a hissy fit, wanted to throw a few more things and break them against the door, he sensed this time a tantrum would do him no good. If he was going to break anything, it would have to be the glass in one of the windows. Then he'd have to crawl out, risking getting cut on the broken glass and rosebushes. This was just too terrible for words.

It was, however, about to get more terrible.

Ryan heard a sound. He turned. He heard it again. He spun around.

It sounded as if someone was in the room with him, though he could plainly see he was alone.

But then he heard it again. Footsteps. Not from above. Not from outside the room. But within the very room.

His father's study was large but very open. The desk was set near the windows, surrounded by wooden cabinets. The other half of the room contained two comfortable chairs positioned in front of a fireplace. There were no closets, no alcoves. If someone were in the room with him, Ryan would have been able to see them. There was nowhere for someone to hide.

The sound this time came from behind him. Spinning around once more, Ryan saw no one there.

But it had sounded as if someone had just walked up behind him!

"What the fuck?" he whispered to himself.

Now there was another sound. Metal. It sounded like metal being tapped against the tiles of the floor. Someone walking around the room, banging something made of metal. Not heavy metal. The sound almost had a musical tone to it. There was reverberation in the air. If Ryan strained his ears, he could still hear it.

"What the fuck is going on?" he whispered again, and for the first time, he felt a little flicker of fear.

He would break the window. It was the only way. He picked up a heavy marble paperweight from his father's desk and aimed it at the glass. But even as he did so, he heard the sound again. A footstep. The tapping of metal against tile.

He glanced around quickly.

And this time he saw it.

A man. A man in dirty overalls and a straggly beard. And in his hand he held an enormous pitchfork, its sharp tines scraping against the floor.

"Who the fuck are you?" Ryan screamed.

The man stood there, gazing at him with eyes so dark that they seemed dead. There was no emotion in the man's face. Only dumb, brute power

"How did you get in here?" Ryan demanded.

It was amazing how many thoughts could rush

in to fill his mind in so short a time. A new land-scaper. That's who it must be. Someone Dad hired. A big old dumbass. Blundered into the house.

Or maybe not so dumb. Maybe he was trying to rob the place. . . .

But why would he be carrying a pitchfork? There were no haystacks on the property. . . .

"Who are you?" Ryan asked again.

The man seemed jolted into movement by his words. He took a step toward Ryan.

Ryan drew his arm back and let the paper-weight in his hands go flying across the room. He watched as the heavy object struck the brute in the forehead. It bounced off easily, leaving no mark, drawing no blood. The man didn't even blink, didn't even seem to notice. He just kept walking toward Ryan.

"Stay back!" Ryan shrilled.

Now the man lifted the pitchfork.

He means to kill me, Ryan thought. *He is going to stick that thing right through me!*

He leapt behind his father's desk just as the pitchfork came crashing down, piercing the wall behind him instead. There was a second's delay as the man extracted the prongs out of the plaster, just enough time for Ryan to yank open his fa-ther's bottom desk drawer and remove the pistol he knew he kept inside. He stood, holding it to-ward the man, his hands shaking terribly.

"Come any closer and you are a dead man," Ryan said.

The words didn't faze the maniac. He just aimed his pitchfork at Ryan and resumed his ap-proach. Ryan fired.

He saw the bullets hit the man. He saw them

tear the fabric of his stained old overalls. He fired three shots. Each one tore through the man's chest. But once again there was no blood. Once again there was no stopping the man.

"Please, don't!" Ryan screamed, crumbling to floor as the man stood over him with the pitchfork. "Please don't kill me! I beg you! I can make you rich! Richer than you ever dreamed of."

The man with the black, dead eyes looked down at him.

"Rich," Ryan cried, tears streaming down his face. "I can make you rich."

"Kill him," came a small voice from somewhere. "Kill him."

The man seemed to hear it. He raised the pitchfork higher, intending to bring it down onto Ryan's chest.

Ryan screamed and closed his eyes, bracing for the impact.

"What's the matter?"

Chelsea's voice. Ryan just continued screaming.

"What the fuck is the matter?"

He opened his eyes. Instead of the man with the pitchfork, his sister stood over him. She looked pissed.

"What is going on?"

"The man!" Ryan shouted, getting back to his feet. "Where is he? We've got to get out of here! He'll kill us!"

"What the fuck are you talking about? Did you do too much coke?"

Ryan glared at Chelsea. "The man! He has a pitchfork! We've got to get out of here!" He grabbed her hand and began pulling her toward the door of the study. It was wide open now.

Chelsea shook off his grip. "Did you drop acid or something? Or are you doing crystal meth again?"

"We've got to get out of here!" Ryan shouted. "The man!"

"There's no man!" Chelsea shouted back at him. "I'm upstairs, trying to sleep off this hangover, and I hear you screaming. And were those gunshots?" She looked down at the floor, stooping to pick up her father's gun. "Who were you shooting at?"

"The man! The man with the pitchfork! He locked me in here and was going to kill me! You had to have seen him! I was right there!" He pointed to the spot behind the desk where he'd been cornered. "He was standing over me with the pitchfork when you came in!"

Chelsea made a face. "You are so fucked up on something, big brother. Don't tell me you didn't snort something up your nose."

"I didn't! I'm totally sober! Totally straight!"

Chelsea laughed. "I came down here, and the door was open, and I saw you cowering behind Daddy's desk. You were alone, Ryan! Alone! No man with any pitchfork!"

"There was a man! I shot at him! The bullets didn't even slow him down!"

Chelsea rolled her eyes, not unlike the way Ryan had done earlier. "Okay, whatever. Just go upstairs and lie down, okay? Just chill. And no more of whatever you were smoking or snorting."

Ryan couldn't form the words. What had just happened to him?

His sister pushed past him. "I'm going back to sleep. Please! No more screaming or shooting guns!"

He grabbed her arm. "He must still be in the house," he told her. "He must have snuck out when you opened the door. We've got to get out of here!"

Once again she shook him off her. "The door wasn't closed, Ryan. It was open. I could see you from the hallway. Listen to me! *There was no man!*"

Her eyes held his. Ryan began to shudder. He wrapped his arms around himself.

Chelsea walked out of the room and headed back up the stairs.

Ryan couldn't stop trembling. He looked around the room, ran out into the hallway, peered out the windows into the yard. There was no man. No sign any man had ever been there. The front door was locked. He checked every room in the house.

There was no man.

He returned to the study and looked around. Was Chelsea right? Had he done some coke? Maybe he had. He often resorted to blow when he was crazed with work and stress. Maybe he'd been feeling stressed out about leaving for Maine tomorrow and had decided to get a little high. Maybe he'd done a line and now he couldn't remember doing it. Maybe it was bad stuff. Crack. Maybe it was crack. And maybe it had done things to his mind. . . .

It was only then that he remembered the wall.

He hurried over to look at it.

He gasped.

They were there.

Five holes.

Five holes where the prongs of the pitchfork had pierced the plaster.

Chapter Eleven

"There is simply no way he wouldn't have seen him," Carolyn mused to herself, reenacting for the third time the order of events as Harry Noons had described them.

She stood on the terrace that led into the kitchen of the great house. Off to her right was the former entrance into the servants' quarters. Once it had consisted of a series of stone steps that led into the basement. Now it was sealed over with concrete. But it was still plainly evident that anyone leaving that way would have had to pass right by this terrace. The place where Harry Noons had been standing when he rushed out of the house after hearing the screams from downstairs.

"And he saw no one come out," Carolyn said to herself. "No one. He ran down there himself and saw no one. No one passed him on the stairs."

Clem may have hid in the basement. That was the only logical explanation. He could have been hiding in the basement when Harry Noons came running back down the stairs. But by then, everyone in the household had come running themselves, and they searched everywhere for Clem. Surely they would have searched the basement. Surely, if Clem had been hiding, someone would have spotted him—if not immediately, then when he tried to make his escape.

No, the only answer was that Clem must have made a run for it up the steps into the main house and escaped through the front door. It would had to have occurred in the few seconds between the time Noons ran out of the kitchen and back down the steps into the servants' quarters. But that was awfully unlikely, too: Carolyn had been up and down the staircase into the main house many times now, and Clem would have had to run out through the front foyer while the house was filled with people. How odd that no one would have seen him. But it was the only logical answer to how he had gotten out of the basement.

That is, the only logical answer if Clem had actually been the one to kill Beatrice.

The morning was cool, with a hint of autumn. The dew was still on the grass when Carolyn had tiptoed out of the house to once again reenact in her mind the day Beatrice was killed. Mr. Young and Douglas were still asleep; the servants had yet to arrive to begin cooking their usual sumptuous breakfast. The sun was still rising over the trees, the sky a wash of rosy pink with flecks of yellow. Carolyn walked back and forth through the wet grass imagining Harry Noons coming out of the sealed-up entrance and crossing the terrace, going inside the house to tell Mrs. Young he was finished for the day, then coming back out here when he heard the screams.

"Good morning."

Douglas's voice startled her. She turned quickly, then smiled. The morning sun cast a soft pink glow on his face. His hair glowed. He looked incredibly handsome in that light.

"Oh, good morning," she said.

"Still perplexed about how the brute escaped?" he asked.

She nodded. "It doesn't make sense."

"He must have run past while Noons was standing in the doorway to the house, talking to my great-great-great-grandmother," Douglas said.

Carolyn shook her head. "Look for yourself. He would have had to run right past here. Right here! This is where Noons would have been standing. He would have seen him!"

"Then when and how *did* Clem make his escape?"

"He could have left the basement immediately after Noons did, in those few moments when Noons was inside the kitchen, talking with Mrs. Young. That was the only moment when Noons might have missed seeing someone leaving the basement."

"But the screams came only *after* Noons was inside the kitchen. If Clem left immediately after Noons did, as you say, he couldn't have been down there killing Beatrice."

"Precisely." Carolyn raised her eyebrows. "In some ways, the timing actually offers a bit of an alibi for Clem."

"Why are you so certain Clem didn't kill Beatrice?" Douglas asked. "Clearly he's involved in all of this. People have seen his ghost. He's the man with the pitchfork."

Carolyn shrugged. "I'm *not* certain he didn't kill her. He may well have. He certainly seems the most likely suspect. Beatrice was murdered with one of the tools of Clem's trade. He was there moments before she died, and they were arguing. She had just turned him down, so he definitely had a motive." She smiled. "I'm just considering all options. It's what investigators do."

Douglas sighed. "And do they also visit sad old ladies confined to mental institutions?"

Carolyn sighed as well. The task ahead of them this day was not going to be pleasant. "When necessary, we do." She glanced over at the rising sun, now seeming to set the trees afire. "You don't have to go with me to see Jeanette. I can go alone."

"No, I want to go." Douglas looked sad. "I remember my father taking me to see her once when I was quite little. He always felt real bad about what happened to her. I remember that he told me that when they were kids, he used to think Jeanette was the most beautiful girl in the world. She was a little bit older than he was, and Dad would just sit there and watch her at family gatherings, transfixed by her. She was like his first crush. And smart, too. He always said Jeanette was so smart. That it was all so tragic because Jeanette had been going to Yale and was going to have this great life. When we went to see her, I remember how sad Dad was afterward. He kept repeating how beautiful Jeanette had been, and how smart."

Carolyn nodded. She'd been reading about Jeanette Young. She had been a master's student at Yale at the time she went into that room. Kip had found several of her student papers, and they were preserved in the files he'd drawn up on every member of the family who had been chosen in the lottery. Jeanette was involved in the women's liberation movement, and had written extremely literate papers on the prevalence of sexism in academia and religious life and the marketplace. This was no timid little woman who could be scared into submission. Indeed, Carolyn found it fascinating that the one person who had made it out of that room alive was a woman. Was it Jeanette's gender or the sheer strength of her willpower that had allowed her to survive? Or possibly was it a combination of both?

Of course, she could hear Howard Young saying to her that it would be hard to say that Jeanette survived, given what she had become.

They heard movement in the kitchen then. The servants had arrived. The smell of cinnamon bread baking was wafting across the yard. Carolyn and Douglas smiled at each other and headed inside.

Howard Young was apparently sleeping late, so they ate breakfast by themselves. Carolyn thought it peculiar that he wasn't up to give her any last-minute advice about her visit to Jeanette. But perhaps the prospect of her visit to his unfortunate niece distressed him so much that he preferred not to talk any more about it until it was all over. Douglas had confirmed that the subject of Jeanette had always made his uncle quite sad. The whole family had always been upset about poor Jeanette.

But she was alive. And that was more than could be said about many members of the family.

Carolyn had been warned that she wouldn't get much out of Jeanette. Kip had been to see her. All he had gotten was a blank stare. He had learned nothing. Even when Georgeanne had touched her hand, she had been unable to pick up anything concrete. "Peaceful," Georgeanne said. "All I can tell you is that she feels peaceful."

At least they could be grateful for that. Jeanette may have been lost to the world, but at least she didn't spend her days in any kind of tortured misery.

After breakfast, they headed outside. Carolyn expected that one of Mr. Young's cars would be brought around for them to use. The home where Jeanette was living was only about an hour away up the coast. But instead of a car, waiting outside in the front driveway was Douglas's motorcycle.

"We're taking that?" she asked, wide-eyed.

Douglas grinned at her, flashing those dimples. "Sure. It's a gorgeous day."

Carolyn gulped. "I've never been on a motor-cycle before," she admitted.

Douglas's smile only broadened. "Then maybe it's time you were." He handed her a helmet. "Strap it on, baby."

Carolyn gave a little nervous laugh, then ex-changed her bag, containing her notebooks and tape recorder, for the helmet. Douglas secured her bag into one of the side compartments of the bike as she awkwardly slipped the helmet onto her head. He smiled.

"Here, let me help you," he said.

Tenderly he adjusted the strap under her chin, tightening it so it was snug but not uncomfortable. It was the closest they had yet been to each other. Their eyes locked.

"Feel okay?" he asked her.

Carolyn nodded.

He patted the black leather pillion on the motorcycle. "You hop up here and just hold onto my waist," he instructed.

Carolyn hesitated. "I won't pull you too much to one side? I mean, my weight won't cause you to lose balance?"

Douglas laughed. "A slim little girl like you? I hardly think so."

Carolyn swallowed, then lifted her leg over the bike. Good thing she was wearing jeans today and low shoes. Douglas followed, settling himself in front of her. She gingerly placed her hands on his waist.

"Hang on!" he called, then started the bike with a roar.

In moments they were zooming down the long driveway and onto the road that led down the side of the hill into the village. Carolyn gripped Douglas tighter around the waist, her face pressed against his back. She was filled with both terror and excitement—terror that she might fall off or cause the bike to topple over, and excitement from the wind in her face and the intimacy of Douglas's body. She realized halfway down the hill that her eyes were squeezed shut. She forced herself to open them and looked around and was rewarded by the sight of the shimmering Atlantic off to her right. Soon they were zipping through the center road of Youngsport, past the little shops and white clapboard village church.

"You okay back there?" Douglas shouted through the wind.

"I'm wonderful," Carolyn replied.

She was grinning widely. She relaxed her grip

around Douglas's waist a bit and settled into her seat to enjoy the ride. Douglas was steering the bike onto the highway now. A tractor trailer rumbled by, and Carolyn flinched a bit. But then the road opened up, and it seemed as if they were the only ones traveling that day. The sun was at ten o'clock overhead. The towering pines on either side of the highway were a deep blue-green. A hawk soared above her through the clear sky. Carolyn smiled again.

She enjoyed being so close to Douglas. For the first time since David, she was feeling drawn to a man. She watched as Douglas's blond hair blew in the breeze. He wasn't wearing a helmet, which worried her a bit. But she had a sense of safety being with him. Nothing bad would happen to them with Douglas at the wheel.

It was almost enough to make her forget what had brought them together. As they sped down the highway, she could pretend that they were just a couple of people enjoying the morning. She was on a date with a guy she liked. That was all. They weren't going to meet a woman whose life had been shattered by a malevolent, murderous force that had lived in the basement of an old house for eighty years.

Carolyn leaned to her right as Douglas gradually slowed the bike down and steered them off an exit ramp. At the end of the ramp, he went left, rattling across a bumpy country lane. They couldn't have been going more than twenty or thirty miles an hour. The fragrance of pine was thick here, and in some places the trees were so tall and so thick that they blocked out the morning sun completely. After about fifteen minutes, Douglas turned right onto an even bumpier road, slowing down to about ten miles an hour. "Hang on," he shouted to Carolyn over his shoulder. She obeyed.

Finally they came to a stop outside a large gate made of stone and wrought iron. On the arch over the gate was the word WINDCLIFFE.

"Hello," Douglas said to the guard seated in the booth. "I'm Douglas Young. We have an appointment to see—"

"Yes, of course, Mr. Young," the guard said, and the gate in front of them magically swung open.

They buzzed through, parking in a space in an area marked VISITORS. Carolyn got off the bike and removed the helmet.

"That was fun," she admitted.

Douglas smiled. "Maybe sometime I can take you for a ride when we're just out for a day of fun."

She returned the smile. "I'd like that."

They said nothing more as they approached the entrance of the place. Windcliffe Sanitarium was an old stone fortress built high on a crag overlooking the ocean. The lobby was sumptuously elegant, with an enormous chandelier and polished marble, not unlike the entrance to Mr. Young's house. No wonder he'd chosen this place for his niece. A bespectacled woman behind the front desk looked up at them without any emotion. When Douglas told her who he was and who he was there to see, she seemed to snap to attention, a wide smile stretching across her face. She rang for someone to meet them. Carolyn had a suspicion that Howard Young was Windcliffe's most important benefactor.

"Mr. Young," came the voice of an old woman hurrying down the corridor. For her apparent years, she moved quite swiftly. She wore a conservative plaid skirt and matching blazer. Her gray hair was swept back into a severe bun. Her hand was extended. "Welcome to Windcliffe."

Douglas shook her hand.

"I'm Dr. Hoffman," she said. "Your uncle telephoned yesterday to let me know you'd be here." Her eyes moved over to Carolyn. "Is this your wife?"

Carolyn blushed. "No," she said, shaking the doctor's hand herself. "I'm Carolyn Cartwright. A . . . friend of the family."

Dr. Hoffman smiled. "Welcome. Come this way." She led them back down the corridor.

"Jeanette is up and waiting for you," she said. "We told her yesterday that she was having visitors."

"Was there any response at all?" Douglas asked.

Dr. Hoffman smiled sadly. "No. There never is."

Douglas exchanged a glance with Carolyn.

"But her friend Michael O'Toole is here. I called him to let him know you were coming. And Michael said he believes she does know that she's having visitors. Michael has a connection with Jeanette that is really quite uncanny."

"Michael O'Toole?" Douglas asked.

The doctor smiled as they turned at the end of the corridor and headed into another wing of the building. Here the rooms were farther apart, and the carpet was thicker and richer. Carolyn deduced it was the section reserved for wealthier patients.

"Michael has been coming to visit Jeanette ever since she first came here," Dr. Hoffman said.

"Three or four times a week. They were to be married, you know, before she had her breakdown."

"No," Douglas said. "I didn't know."

They stopped outside a door at the end of the hall. The plate outside the door read SUITE 1. YOUNG.

The doctor knocked.

The door was almost immediately opened by a stout, balding man with bright red cheeks and thick black glasses. He smiled wide when he saw them.

"Hello, hello," he said, gesturing for all to enter.

The suite was quite large. It looked nothing like a hospital room. There were easy chairs and a sectional sofa, and an enormous painting of what looked like Yale University on the wall. Books lined the shelves, and framed family photographs were everywhere. A flat-screen television was mounted on the wall. But somehow Carolyn felt the books were never read, the TV never watched.

At the far end of the room, facing a large picture window overlooking the ocean, sat a small, white-haired woman in a large wingback chair. She did not stir when they came in. She just sat there very still, her gaze aimed out the window.

"I'm Michael O'Toole," the man with the red cheeks said. Douglas and Carolyn introduced themselves. "I'm very glad you've come. And Jeanette has been looking forward to it all morning."

"I'll leave you alone now," Dr. Hoffman said. They thanked her, and she slipped quietly out the door.

"Jeanette," Michael said to the white-haired woman. "Jeanette, this is your cousin Douglas and his friend Carolyn."

There was no movement, no sense that she even heard him.

"Sit down, please," Michael said, gesturing to Carolyn and Douglas to make themselves comfortable on the soda. He gently turned Jeanette slightly in her chair so that her vacant eyes now looked directly at them. She might as well have been a mannequin.

Carolyn felt her heart sink. She had read this woman's impassioned work. She had followed the career she'd almost had. How vital she seemed in her writings of forty years earlier. Now she was just a shell.

"Mr. Young," Michael said, "I remember your father. I was sorry to hear of his passing."

"Thank you," Douglas said.

Obviously Michael was clueless about the family curse. To him, Jeanette had simply suffered some unexplained breakdown. Carolyn had read the reports from the hospital. Although no brain damage was found, Jeanette had lost all ability to communicate or, apparently, to comprehend. Her body functioned fine. So long as attendants regularly moved her limbs, the muscles remained strong; without such assistance, they would have long ago atrophied. Without outside intervention, Jeanette would simply lie there, not speaking, not eating, not doing anything for herself. Carolyn noticed an IV drip behind Jeanette's chair. She was fed intravenously, but, according to the notes in her file, she would sometimes chew and swallow if nourishment was held to her lips. On a small table in front of her were the remnants of a muffin on a plate and a half-empty glass of orange juice. Michael had apparently been feeding her before they arrived.

He sat now on a hassock at her side, looking solicitously up at Jeanette. "You remember his father, don't you, Jeanette? Douglas. He was a lawyer. Remember when he'd visit? He was such a wonderful man."

Still Jeanette made no sound, revealed no flicker of consciousness. But Carolyn felt somehow that her eyes had moved. They were no longer simply staring blindly. They had fixed on her. She felt Jeanette was looking directly at her.

And more than that.

She felt she was *seeing* her.

"I remember coming here with my father," Douglas said, his voice uneasy. He was directing his words to Jeanette. "I remember meeting you when I was very young. I remember that painting, in fact."

"I painted it," Michael said, pride in his voice. "Jeanette and I met on the Yale campus. She was a divinity student. I was an artist." The sadness shone in his eyes. "We were going to be married, weren't we, Jeanette?"

Her face remained expressionless, her eyes fixed on Carolyn.

"Well, we never got married," Michael said, reaching over to take Jeanette's hand, "but we've still been together for forty-two years, haven't we, my dear?"

Carolyn held Jeanette's gaze. What was she saying with her eyes? There was something . . . something that Carolyn was sure she was trying to communicate.

Georgeanne had been right, though. Whatever thoughts, if any, swirled through Jeanette's head, the woman herself was peaceful. There was nothing about her that seemed in distress.

"Jeanette," Douglas said. "I wonder if I can ask you a few questions."

Michael stiffened. "What kind of questions?"

"We'd like to find out what brought on her current state."

Michael's smile faded. "I was afraid that was the reason for the visit. Why is it that so few ever visit Jeanette just to see her? Your father was one of those few. A good man. Never came prying about what happened that night. Jeanette doesn't know! It was a fluke of the brain. Who can explain the human brain? The human mind?"

"But her doctors have all been stymied," Carolyn interjected. "If we could find out what happened . . ."

"For what good purpose?" He stood. "It would just upset her! Only once in all these years has Jeanette ever gone from the calm, content woman you see before you to a frightened, shaking creature. And I won't allow that to ever happen again."

"Of course, we don't want that," Carolyn said. "We don't want to upset her." She paused. "But Mr. O'Toole, perhaps we can *help* her."

He folded his chubby arms across his chest. "Long ago I gave up any hope that Jeanette will ever change. Long ago I accepted that this is our lot in life."

"But perhaps . . ." Carolyn hesitated, trying to find the words. "Perhaps if we at least know the kinds of things that upset her in the past, we can avoid doing them again now."

His eyes regarded her sternly; then he looked

back over at Jeanette. He seemed to see the way she was looking at Carolyn, and his stance softened.

"I can tell you this much," he said. "Years ago, probably twenty-five years ago now, a man came here. He was sent by Jeanette's uncle. Like you, he wanted to know what had happened to bring Jeanette to such a state. I told him that her doctors had said it was an unexplainable shock. But what brought the shock on? The man wanted to know the answer to that. Possibly nothing, I told him. Doctors say that's rare, but it *is* possible. The brain can experience a shock for no reason. A short-circuiting of nerves, so to speak." He paused for emphasis. "And if there *was* a reason for the shock, I certainly don't want Jeanette remembering it."

"What did this man say when you told him that?" Carolyn asked.

"He kept pushing. And because Mr. Young pays for Jeanette's care here, I couldn't stop him. Even Dr. Hoffman, despite her better judgment, was forced to let him proceed. And he began saying names to Jeanette. Names that upset her. For the first time, she reacted to outside stimuli—"

"Which is actually a good thing," Carolyn observed.

"Not if it makes her upset! I won't have her upset!" He calmed himself, looking anxiously over at Jeanette. "She began to shudder. She began to cry. Her face got red. I told the man if he persisted I would physically throw him out of the room." He smiled. "I was younger then. I could have done it, too. But Dr. Hoffman agreed, and she asked the man to stop."

"But perhaps if we could find the reason for her state, we could reverse it," Carolyn said.

Michael ignored her comment. "Then, about ten years ago, another man came around. He was with a black woman, who claimed she could read minds just by touching someone."

"Kip," Douglas said, and Carolyn nodded.

Michael continued, not hearing. "He wanted to say certain things to Jeanette, too, but I forbade it. And the black woman, she touched Jeanette's hand, and concurred with my judgment. She said Jeanette did not have the information that they sought and they should leave her in peace." He chuckled. "I'm not sure I believe in all that mumbo jumbo, but I was glad to have her as an ally. They left without upsetting Jeanette." His eyes narrowed as he stood over them. "And I will not allow you to upset her either."

Carolyn sighed. "I see in her files that Dr. Hoffman even tried hypnotizing her, but Jeanette remained unable to reveal anything."

"That's because she doesn't *know* anything! Whatever happened that night is gone! All that exists for Jeanette is now! This moment! The moment she lives in. For in the very next moment, it's gone. Every moment is brand new to her. Her only constant is this room . . . and me."

He sat back down on the hassock and took her hand again.

Carolyn looked over at Douglas. "I think he's right. Asking her any questions is pointless."

Douglas sighed, clearly disappointed. "Look, Mr. O'Toole. We came here because we want to help Jeanette. . . ."

"What is it that your family is hiding?" Behind the thick glasses, Michael O'Toole's blue eyes were blazing. "Why is that, in regular intervals, someone comes around trying to find out what caused Jeanette to be this way? Is the story I was always told not true? According to Mr. Young, Jeanette was found one morning during the family reunion simply wandering by the cliffs. She had left the house sometime in the night, and in the morning, no one had been able to find her. Then they spotted her out by the cliffs. When they caught up with her, she didn't know them. She didn't know herself. She didn't speak. This is what was told to me." He glared at Douglas. "Is there more to the story? Is there more that I should know?"

Douglas just looked away.

"That's what they always do when I ask that," Michael said, his anger boiling just under the surface. "They look away."

"Mr. O'Toole," Carolyn said, "what if we spoke with you in private? So that Jeanette couldn't hear, and nothing might upset her?"

He stood. "You can come into the kitchen if you like." He bent and kissed Jeanette's cheek. "I'm just going to show our guests around the place, my dear. We will be right back."

Jeanette remained motionless in her chair. When Carolyn stood, the eyes that had been looking at her did not follow. They simply fell upon the wall behind the sofa. Maybe, Carolyn thought, she had been wrong about Jeanette seeing her.

Once inside the kitchen, Carolyn cut straight to the point. "Mr. O'Toole, I think if we know what the names were that upset Jeanette, it could help us."

"Help you with what?"

"I don't know," Carolyn admitted. "But we would like to help Jeanette."

He frowned. "I can't see where you can help her where so many doctors have failed."

"Please," Douglas added. "Can you just tell us the names?"

"Beatrice." He said the word as if it were bitter on his tongue. "And Malcolm."

Carolyn blinked. She had expected Beatrice. But Malcolm . . . this was a name she had never heard before.

"Malcolm?" she repeated.

"Yes. I don't know if those names were the ones the man and the black woman were prepared to say, because I never allowed them to utter any. But the first man, the one who came here about twenty-five years ago, he used those names. I'll never forget them."

"And what was this man's name?"

"He only identified himself as Dr. Fifer. I'm not sure how it was spelled. With an 'F' or a 'Ph.' But I'll never forget him either, or how he upset Jeanette."

Carolyn figured this Dr. Fifer must have been one of the many investigators Mr. Young had hired over the years to try to find an end to the curse of that room. She would have to go through the papers again to see if there were any files with such a name.

"I think," she said to Douglas with a sense of heavy disappointment, "we've learned as much as we can here today."

"Well, at least come say good-bye to Jeanette," Michael said. "She may not seem it, but I am convinced she is more aware of her surroundings than any of us know. The nurses here tell me there is a certain brightening to her eyes on days she knows I will be here. Her skin is a little more sallow on days when, for whatever reason, I've been unable to make it in. After four decades, you learn to see these things."

Carolyn smiled. "It's really quite touching that you've made such a commitment to her."

He smiled, some of his earlier friendliness returning to his expression. "There was no other way. I love her. She loves me."

Carolyn instinctively reached out and cupped his hand.

Suddenly it seemed as if Michael O'Toole was about to cry. His cheeks flushed even redder, and his lips trembled. "Once, many, many years ago, maybe a year or so after Jeanette was first brought to Windcliffe, I considered maybe . . ." His voice broke. "I considered maybe if I should just move on. You know, my friends and my family, they were saying, 'Michael, you need to pursue your own career, your own life.'" A couple of tears squeezed out of his eyes and ran down his cheeks, collecting into little pools behind his heavy glasses. "I thought I'd never have a real love, you know, if I stayed here with Jeanette. And I was really thinking that way. . . ."

He turned, ashamed of himself.

"But then I had a dream," he continued. "I had a dream of a woman. And the woman told me that if I loved Jeanette, I couldn't leave her. I woke up knowing that I would always stay right by Jeanette's side."

Carolyn was near tears herself. She shook Michael's hand, then Douglas did, too. Back in the living room, they bid good-bye to Jeanette. Douglas leaned in and gave her a kiss on the forehead. "That's from my father," he said.

Jeanette remained still in her chair.

Michael walked them to the door. "I'm sorry if I seemed overprotective. But I guess that's what I am."

Carolyn smiled. "I understand."

She had opened the door to leave when she turned back to him.

"Mr. O'Toole," she asked. "You said you had a dream of a woman. . . ."

He nodded.

"Who was the woman in your dream?"

"I don't know," he said. "I've talked about it with my analyst. He thinks it was a manifestation of Jeanette. It was not the face of any woman I know. Just a female manifestation, my analyst said. A representation of my love for Jeanette."

"Interesting," Carolyn said, her hand still on the doorknob. But she didn't leave. Douglas seemed curious as to why she was delaying. "But could you describe what she looked like, Mr. O'Toole?" Carolyn asked. "The woman in your dream? Do you remember?"

"I'll never forget," he said. "She had long dark hair and dark eyes, and she was wearing a long white dress."

Chapter Twelve

Chelsea pulled her BMW to a stop outside her Uncle Howard's mansion. "We're here," she barked at her brother, who was asleep in the seat beside her.

Ryan just groaned.

Chelsea rolled her eyes. For the last two days Ryan had been a complete and utter mess. "Tragic," she muttered under her breath, getting out of the car and walking around to the passenger's side. She opened the door. "Come on! Get out!"

Slowly Ryan unbent his legs and rose out of the car.

"If Uncle Howard suspects how much blow you've been doing these last couple of days, he'll disinherit you on the spot," Chelsea told him. "You'd better straighten up fast, dear brother."

"I'll be fine," he mumbled.

Chelsea had her doubts about that. Ever since she'd found him quivering in their father's study a couple of days ago, Ryan had been a major train wreck. He went on a bender that night, snorting prodigious amounts of coke and drinking all the vodka they had in the house. So wasted did he become that their trip up to Maine had had to be postponed a day. Chelsea was beyond pissed. Ryan kept babbling about being terrified of "the man with the pitchfork." He insisted such a creature had actually been in their house and had tried to kill him. He even tried to show Chelsea holes in the wall supposedly made by said pitchfork. But of course there were no holes that Chelsea could see.

"You are *tragic*," she told her brother.

Now she hauled her bag out of the backseat, with Ryan barely having the strength to lift his own. His eyes were glassy and his movements awkward. A man had appeared wearing a valet uniform and a broad ingratiating smile. Chelsea tossed him the keys to the Beemer.

"I don't know why Uncle Howard doesn't keep any of the same servants," she said as she headed toward the house. "They're always different every time we visit."

She threw open the front doors. "Helloooo!" she trilled, her voice echoing across the marble. Ryan shuffled along behind her.

"Where the hell is everyone?" Chelsea asked.

Then she spotted a woman she didn't recognize emerging from the study. At first she took her to be another new servant, but the woman had an air of authority. She was an attractive redhead with sharp green eyes. She smiled as she approached Chelsea and Ryan.

"Hello, I'm Carolyn Cartwright," she said. "Your uncle is in the study."

They all shook hands. Chelsea realized her

brother really *was* out of it, because he simply grunted a hello. Usually when he met a pretty woman he was falling all over himself to be charming.

"Mr. Young is very glad you've come early," she said as they headed into the study.

"And you are?" Chelsea asked, a little put off by the familiarity this outsider was showing toward Uncle Howard.

"Mr. Young has hired me to help him with a project," Carolyn explained.

Chelsea nodded. "I guess he can't do everything himself anymore. He's certainly getting up there in years."

"Oh, but he's really quite remarkable," Carolyn observed. "I mean, at ninety-eight, still doing all that he does . . ." She smiled. "He's not slowing down any time soon."

This time it was Chelsea's turn to grunt. How long were they going to have to wait for the old man to kick the bucket and leave them all his billions?

But then she grinned as she caught sight of Uncle Howard sitting in a chair by the window, a book in his lap. Not quite yet did she want him to kick the bucket. She needed a little more time to make sure she was in the will.

"Uncle Howard!" she called, sugary sweet. Rushing ahead, she threw her arms around him as he sat in the chair, planting a big kiss on his mottled old cheek.

"Hello, princess," the old man said, patting her hair. "How lovely that you came early. I'm very pleased you did."

She moved aside so that her brother could

shake Uncle Howard's hand. Ryan stepped forward, his eyelids drooping, a wan smile on his face.

"Good to see you too, Ryan," Howard Young said. "A bit under the weather?"

"Oh, he's just tired from the long ride up here," Chelsea said.

"That's right," Ryan said, trying to summon some of his usual bravado. "A quick shower and change of clothes and I'll be fine."

Uncle Howard just looked at him strangely.

But another voice piped up with an opinion. "If you ask me," Douglas said, sitting up from the sofa where he had been stretched out, hidden from view, "you look better than I've seen you in a long time." He hopped to his feet. "Welcome, dear cousins!"

Chelsea stiffened. Douglas was barefoot, wearing ratty jeans, and it looked as if he hadn't washed his hair this morning. He was disgraceful.

"Hello, Douglas," she said. "Glad you're here. How nice that we'll have a chance to spend a little more time with you than usual."

She knew her voice sounded phony, and she knew that Douglas knew she was being totally insincere. But she hoped Uncle Howard didn't pick up on it.

Ryan hadn't even bothered to say hello. He just excused himself so he could go wash up and change his clothes. Chelsea hoped he would come back downstairs more like his old self so that they could put Douglas in his place.

"So what are you doing now, Douglas?" Chelsea asked cheerily. "You've always had such an interesting, if brief, series of jobs."

"True," he said. "One of the few I haven't tried is Slacker Child Living Off Wealthy Daddy."

"Now, now, Douglas," Uncle Howard said, his voice raspy.

"It's okay, dear uncle," Chelsea said. "Douglas and I just enjoy teasing each other, don't we, Douglas?"

"We adore it," he said, and Chelsea caught the little look he exchanged with that woman, Carolyn. What was their relationship?

"Well," Chelsea announced, "I think I'll go wash up as well, and then we can have a wonderful talk and catch up, dear uncle."

"I look forward to that, Chelsea," the old man said. He hesitated, as if trying to think of exactly how he should phrase something. "I'm glad you're here early, because we need to talk. You and I and your brother."

Chelsea's ears perked up at this. "Really? Well, of course, Uncle Howard."

It had to be about the will. What else would he want to discuss with them?

"But perhaps I should wait until your father is here as well," Uncle Howard said. "He should be here for that."

It has to be the will, Chelsea thought. *Why else would he want Daddy here, too?*

"I'll call him and have him come up early as well," she assured her uncle.

"That would be good," he said.

She bent down and gave him another kiss on his cheek. His dry, flaky skin always grossed her out, but she forced herself. Chelsea smiled over at Douglas as she prepared to exit the room.

Her cousin ignored her. "So, Uncle Howie," he

said, sitting down on the armrest of the old man's chair, "how about if *we* have a conversation, too?"

"All right," Uncle Howard agreed.

Chelsea almost spit. How *dare* Douglas? Trying to worm his way in before Uncle Howard had a chance to talk to her and Ryan?

She was aware that Carolyn had positioned herself close to the old man's chair as well. What business did *she* have listening in?

Unless she was the lawyer drawing up the will. . . .

"Oh, Chelsea," Douglas called sweetly as she left the study and headed into the hall, "will you be so kind as to shut the doors behind you?"

She seethed, but did as he asked. It wouldn't be good to upset Uncle Howard now.

She stood there in the hallway staring at the closed double doors of the study. What did her uncle want to speak to her and Ryan about? *Either to tell us we're in the will . . . or we're out.* She gulped. What were they talking about inside the room at that very moment? Was Douglas brainwashing Uncle Howard against them? That woman . . . there was clearly a connection with Douglas. She was his girlfriend. That must be it! The little sneak had gotten his girlfriend to act as the old man's lawyer!

Chelsea wished she could hear what was taking place inside, but the doors were too thick. But then she remembered something.

Upstairs, the room she always stayed in was directly above the study. One night, sitting on the floor leaning against the bed reading a copy of *Cosmo* she'd stolen from her cousin Paula, she made an exciting discovery. There was a grate on the floor of a heating vent that led down to the study. If you pressed your ear to the grate, you could eavesdrop on the adults below. Chelsea often lay there on the floor listening to the adults in the study below her discussing things she had no clue about. They always seemed to be talking about the lottery. Why, Chelsea didn't know. Her family never played the lottery. They were far too rich for that.

The recollection of that heating vent brought a smile to Chelsea's face. There was no time to waste. She bolted from the spot, taking the stairs two at a time. Flying down the upstairs corridor to her room, she closed down the door behind her and nearly threw herself onto the floor. She pressed her ear up against the grate.

Her smile widened.

She could hear them, plain as day.

"It's just that you haven't been very available since we came back from seeing Jeanette," Douglas was saying.

Jeanette? Why did they go see that crazy old lady? Chelsea frowned. She assumed the old man was obliged to leave poor Jeanette something in the will, some kind of perpetual care. Maybe a trust. She assumed Carolyn, as the lawyer, was setting that up.

"I'm sorry," Uncle Howard replied. "I know I've been keeping to my room of late. But you see, all of this, as I'm sure you understand, is very upsetting for me."

"Mr. Young," Carolyn said. "You hired me to try to find a way to put an end to 'all of this,' as you describe it. And I can't do that without your full cooperation."

All of this? What were they talking about?

"I can only tell you so much," Uncle Howard said. "I expect that whatever else you need to know, you will find out."

"Mr. Young," Carolyn retorted, her voice growing sharp, "we only have a couple of weeks!"

A couple of weeks. Chelsea knew what she was referencing. The family reunion was in two weeks. Less than that, in fact. And apparently Uncle Howard expected to have the will ready by then. *He's probably going to announce who's getting what,* Chelsea thought. But what information was he withholding from Carolyn?

"There are some things we need to ask you about, now that we've seen Jeanette," Douglas said.

"What kind of things?" Uncle Howard asked.

There was the sound of paper rustling. Was Carolyn passing out drafts of the will?

"I've gone through the various reports filed by those who have worked for you previously," Carolyn said. Previous lawyers? Were they looking at old wills? Documents that maybe included Chelsea and her family, which Douglas was now aiming to invalidate? "And I can find none by a certain Dr. Fifer."

"Fifer?" Uncle Howard asked. "Why are you interested in him?"

"Because Jeanette's companion, Michael O'Toole, mentioned he'd visited Jeanette some time ago."

"Indeed, he did," Uncle Howard said. "It was probably 1978 or 1979."

"Why didn't he fill out a final report like the rest of them did?"

"I don't know."

More papers were being shuffled. "It's just curious. I'd like to speak with him. Do you still have a contact number?"

"He's dead."

Carolyn sighed.

"It was a long time ago," Uncle Howard said. "Why are you so interested in Fifer? He came no closer than any of the others to ending this terrible thing."

Terrible thing? Chelsea thought. *What are they talking about?*

"He seems to have come across a name that none of the others did," Carolyn said. "A name I can find nowhere in any of these files. A name that upset Jeanette."

"What name is that?"

"Malcolm."

There was a pause. Chelsea waited, but the seconds ticked by with no response. In her mind's eye, she saw Uncle Howard hesitating. She saw him . . . uncomfortable. She had the sense that the name upset him.

"I don't know that name," Uncle Howard said at last, and even a floor away, even without seeing his face, Chelsea knew he was lying. She suspected the others knew it as well.

"Michael O'Toole said the name upset Jeanette when Dr. Fifer mentioned it to her," Douglas said.

"I suppose poor O'Toole has gone a little stir-crazy all those years watching after Jeanette," Uncle Howard said. "His memory is faulty. That name means nothing to me."

"Mr. Young," Carolyn asked, "are you certain?"

But whatever the old man said in response, it

was drowned out by another sound, this one much closer to Chelsea.

Directly behind her, in fact.

The sound of sobbing.

She lifted her head from the floor with a start. Glancing over her shoulder, she saw a woman sitting on the other side of the bed, her back to Chelsea. A woman with long dark hair, wearing a white dress.

She was holding her face in her hands and crying.

"Excuse me?" Chelsea said, getting to her feet. "Excuse me, what are you doing here? This is my room."

Immediately she deduced the woman to be one of Uncle Howard's servants, one of the nameless revolving cast of nobodies he hired and then let go after a few months. She placed her hands on her hips and scowled. The woman was clearly upset, but that didn't give her the right to walk into a private room. Chelsea looked over at the door. It was still shut. Had the woman come in and closed it behind her again without Chelsea hearing? Not likely. She must have been in the room the whole time.

"Look here," Chelsea said, walking around to confront the woman face-to-face. "You're going to have to leave. I don't know what you're doing here, but—"

The woman simply continued to sob into her hands. Chelsea couldn't see her face. But she noticed she was barefoot. What kind of servant walked around her uncle's house barefoot?

"Hey, listen," she said, raising her voice. "You need to get out of here!"

The woman sobbed harder.

"Stop your crying! I can't take it! I'm going to call my uncle!"

Still nothing but tears.

Chelsea reached down, angry now, grabbing the woman by the shoulders. Immediately the woman's hands fell away from her face and she looked up at Chelsea.

Her eyes were red with blood.

Chelsea screamed, staggering backward.

Now she could see the woman's body. Across her chest were five gaping holes, each gushing blood. The blood was staining the sheets of the bed and dripping into puddles on the floor.

Chelsea screamed at the top of her lungs, then screamed again. She covered her own face with her hands.

She was still screaming when Ryan rushed into the room, shaking her, asking her what was wrong.

"That woman!" Chelsea cried. "On the bed!"

But of course there was no woman on the bed.

And no blood either.

Ryan and Chelsea exchanged looks.

They had been in this position before, only reversed. They said nothing to each other, just continued staring in dumb horror.

In moments, Douglas and Carolyn were at the door, clearly having heard Chelsea's screams. That heating vent worked both ways.

"What's wrong?" Douglas asked.

"What the *fuck* is going on in this house?" Chelsea demanded. She saw Carolyn's face go white.

They heard a shuffling from the hallway, and

within a few seconds, Uncle Howard had made his way into the room.

All he had to do was to take one look at Chelsea's face, and he seemed to surmise what she had seen.

"Perhaps," he said, in a weary voice, "what I have to tell you cannot wait for your father to get here."

Chapter Thirteen

Dean Young wasn't getting any work done today. In front of him, spread all over his desk, were the plans for a major new high-rise development set for Boston's Copley Square. Construction was slated to begin in less than a month, and all sorts of decisions had still to be made. Final dimensions, work orders, schedules. As chief architect, he had to approve all of the minutiae his associates had planned. But he simply couldn't keep his mind on his work. All he could think of was that a month from now, when this project got under way, he might not be alive.

It may be me who's chosen this time, Dean thought, for the thousandth time. *It may be my turn to spend a night in that room.*

Of course it terrified him. What went on in there? What horrible events took place? He remembered his father the morning after his name had been chosen in the lottery. He'd been found sitting on the couch in the room, his eyes bugged out, his hair white. His heart had stopped, and he was cold as ice. Dean would live with that image for the rest of his life.

Would that be how I'd die as well? Terrified beyond all reason? Or would it be even more gruesome, the way cousin Douglas had died, with a plastic bag secured over his head by some unknown creature? Or would there be gore, like so many of the others?

But for all his terror, the manner of his own death was not the worst of it for Dean. It would be leaving Zac and Callie fatherless. He'd made sure to buy all sorts of life insurance policies, with them and Linda as beneficiaries. He was able to get some terrific plans, because, according to everything the insurance companies could see, he was in good health, and was still a relatively young man. Every indicator pointed to Dean living a long life. But Aetna and Travelers didn't know about the room in the basement of Uncle Howard's house.

Sitting at his desk, looking past the blueprints and gazing out his twentieth-story window onto the city below him, Dean thought of his sister. What if it was Paula who was chosen? How could he let her walk in there by herself? He adored his older sister. He had ever since he was a little boy, and asthma had prevented him from playing ball or running too fast. Paula had always been there to protect him when the other boys picked on him. Once, when it looked like they'd miss the bus to school, Paula had swept up the six-year-old Dean in her arms and carried him as she ran, knowing full well he'd never have been able to make the exertion himself. In Dean's mind, that symbolized their relationship. Paula had literally carried him through some of life's roughest moments.

And, he hoped, he'd done the same for her now. He felt terribly bad that the family curse had ended Paula's relationship with Karen. How many lives would it destroy?

He'd spoken with Uncle Howard yesterday. The old man had sounded optimistic that this new investigator might come up with something. Dean wasn't so sure. The investigator, a Carolyn Cartwright, had only been located in the last couple of weeks, at the eleventh and a half hour. "What can she do between now and the lottery?" Dean had asked. "Other people you've hired have had *years,* and they never found an answer."

But Uncle Howard had retained his optimism. It may have been largely an act, Dean surmised. *He has to try to give us some hope,* he thought. But Uncle Howard did keep returning to the fact that Carolyn was a woman. "That will help," he insisted. "I believe that will help."

How Ms. Cartwright's gender could benefit them remained unclear to Dean. But he was encouraged at least that she had good credentials. And that someone—anyone—was trying to find a remedy for them as the date of the lottery drew nearer and nearer.

"Mr. Young?"

His secretary's voice started him as it came through the intercom.

"Yes, Sondra?"

"The image that you asked to be digitized is ready. Should I have them e-mail it directly to you, or should I have it printed out?"

"E-mail it to me, please," he said. "I'll print it."

His mind snapped back into sharp focus. But the image had nothing to do with the plans on his desk. It had everything to do with the thoughts that were consuming his mind this morning.

He heard the little ping on his computer that announced the delivery of a new e-mail. He instantly clicked on it, opening the e-mail and downloading the attached file. As he'd requested, it was a big file. The image had been scanned at a high resolution by the firm's production department. Dean was very curious if such enlargement might allow him to discern something he had long wondered about.

When he and Paula had been young, probably no older than eight and ten, they had broken a very strict rule of Uncle Howard's. While visiting him one weekend, they had snuck down into the basement. That was the one part of the house that was forbidden to them, which of course only made them want to see it more. They were innocent back then, unaware of the dangers and the tragedies of that locked room. But they'd found a set of keys, and while Uncle Howard was in his study, they'd unlocked the door in the foyer that led to the basement and crept down the stairs. They discovered many rooms in the basement, only one of which was locked. All of the rest were open, packed high with crates and boxes. In and out of these rooms Dean and Paula had tiptoed. Nothing exciting to be found. But perhaps in the one room that was locked? The key ring in Dean's hand jingled. They decided to see if they could find the key to the one room they'd been unable to explore. And, after four tries, they'd found the key that fit. . . .

Dean opened the image on his computer.

That day in the basement, they'd recorded their undercover work with a Polaroid camera, a gift Dean had recently gotten from Mom and Dad for his birthday. They'd snapped pictures of the basement staircase and of the various storerooms. They wanted proof that they'd actually made it into forbidden territory. As each photograph slid out of the camera, Dean would hand it to Paula, who would hold it as it dried and the images took shape. But as the door to the locked room creaked open before them, they heard footsteps from above. Uncle Howard was emerging from his study. They would have to forget about exploring the room and hurry back upstairs—but still Dean had time to snap a fast picture of the inside of the room before locking the door again.

That image revealed itself on his computer screen now.

It looked just as it had that day when they'd taken the Polaroid back to Dean's room to look at it. A sofa, a table, and lots of cobwebs. But there had been something else, too. An image in the upper right corner. As kids, they'd enjoyed scaring themselves into believing it was a face. After they learned about the secret of the room, Dean had told investigators about what they had done and what they thought they had photographed—but by then, the relics of their childhood had been lost. Who kept old toys and forty-five records and comic books and Polaroids? The picture was gone, lost. Without it, none of those who tried to end the curse could ever say definitively what the image was. But a couple of weeks ago, going through a box of old school papers, Dean had found the Polaroid. He didn't tell Paula. He didn't tell anyone.

He just brought it to his production department and asked them to scan it for him.

He hit the button on his screen to enlarge the image. And then he enlarged it again.

Dean sat back in his chair, his heart thudding in his chest.

All those years ago, he and Paula had been right.

Their childish imaginings had been absolutely on target.

The image in the corner of the photo was indeed a face.

The face of a crying baby.

Chapter Fourteen

Douglas watched with mounting annoyance as his cousins fluttered around Uncle Howie. Chelsea was adjusting the pillow behind his back as he sat reading in his chair. Ryan kept asking if him if he'd like a brandy, or maybe to share a cigar. They were wide-eyed and attentive to all his stories, asking him to repeat old tales about the family that they'd all heard dozens of times before, acting as if the stories were fresh and new, laughing and telling Uncle Howie how funny and how brilliant he was. It was making Douglas sick.

He knew why they were behaving that way. The old man's will. They had rushed up here when they heard Douglas had arrived. They were afraid that Uncle Howie was going to leave everything to Douglas. They didn't want to get cut out. So they were doing what they always did whenever they visited. They were kissing major ass.

Stretched out on the couch, Douglas just shook his head and went back to reading the notes Carolyn had left for him. He would have thought that finding out about the room—about the lottery, about the ten-year cycle of deaths—would have shaken some sense into Ryan and Chelsea, convinced them that some things were more important than money. Hell, who was to say that either of them would even be *around* to inherit anything Uncle Howie left them? What if one of them was chosen to spend the night in that room? So much for the old man's will then.

But, no. Ryan and Chelsea went on as if unfazed. Oh, sure, that day when Uncle Howie told them the whole story, they had been terrified. Both had seen things that convinced them what their uncle was saying was true. Ryan babbled on about how the man with the pitchfork had tried to kill him. Both of them were shaking like the last leaves on a maple tree on a windy October day. But then they'd run outside to call Daddy on their cell phones. An hour later they'd come back inside with a sense of calm. "We trust you, Carolyn," Ryan grandly announced, kissing the lady's hand. "We trust you will deliver our family from this terrible curse."

Again, Douglas tried to focus on the materials Carolyn had left for him to peruse. So apparently reassured were his cousins that they evinced no interest in reading any of the accounts that had been compiled about the room. They had no desire to help find the solution. They simply went on kissing Uncle Howie's ass. Maybe, Douglas thought, their nonchalance stemmed from the fact that their side of the family had been largely spared any of the tragedies. The luck of the draw had always seemed to favor them. While Douglas's father had died horrifically in that room, their father had survived, decade after decade. Maybe they were counting on that luck to continue.

"Uncle Howard," Ryan was saying, "what do you say about you and I taking a little spin on the yacht? It's still rigged up, isn't it?"

"Yes," the old man said. "It's down at the marina. But I'm afraid I get awfully tired these days. . . ."

"Come on, Uncle Howie," Ryan said, appropriating the nickname Douglas always used. "Just you and I. I've got some girl troubles I thought you might be able to counsel me on." He shot a glance in Douglas's direction. "Rest assured, I'll be popping the question to a very desirable candidate very soon."

Douglas groaned and sat up on the couch.

"Oh, Douglas," Ryan said. "I wasn't aware you were still here."

"I'm heading out," he said, standing. "The air's getting a little soupy in here."

"Will you be back for dinner, Douglas?" Uncle Howard asked.

He nodded. "Sure. I'm just going to take a little walk around the grounds."

There was no way he could concentrate in there. In fact, what he needed to do was take a good long walk and clear his head. It wasn't just his cousins' rapacity that irked him. It was also the growing sense that time was slipping away from them and that they were still no closer to finding any kind of solution. Unless they discovered something, the lottery would have to be held exactly two weeks from now. One of them—possibly Douglas himself—would have to spend a night in that room.

Heading outside onto the great lawn, Douglas looked up at the sun, enjoying its warmth on his cheeks. He tried not to feel despair. They'd discovered quite a bit already; they could still discover more. Carolyn had returned to New York to meet with a couple of psychics with whom she'd worked in the past. There was talk of another séance when she returned, possibly conducted by one of her experts. Also being considered was a more powerful exorcism than the one Kip attempted. But Douglas couldn't shake the feeling that they were just repeating the same steps, going through the same motions that had been tried by so many before. And none of them had ever succeeded.

The strangest sensation of all, however, was how much he missed Carolyn. In the last few days before she headed back to New York, they had spent a great deal of time together. On the night before she left, sitting on the stone bench out near the cliff, she had shared with Douglas the pain of her mother's death. He'd learned of Carolyn's sister, living in a home, and Carolyn's deep sense of responsibility for her. But most significant was hearing about the horrible relationship Carolyn had endured. To think she had been sleeping next to a murderer. Douglas had been unable to restrain himself. He had reached over and placed his arms around Carolyn. She had seemed grateful for his embrace. Slowly, tenderly, he took her chin in his hand and moved his lips to kiss her. . . .

But then a twig had snapped, and they had looked around. Chelsea and Ryan were heading toward them. They had separated quickly, moving apart on the bench. Douglas's cousins were rattling on with questions about whether the curse would end if the house was razed. "I doubt it," Carolyn told them. "Your uncle said he believes that if that were to happen, it would simply cause the kind of slaughter we've seen when periodically the strict rules of the lottery weren't followed to the letter."

"Well," Chelsea said, impatiently, in a tone of voice she never used around Uncle Howard, "eventually, when our dear uncle is gone, someone will have to decide what to do with this house. I wouldn't want it. So many horrific things have happened here."

Douglas thought she spoke as if she had no fears at all about being chosen to enter that room. All she was concerned about was what happened after. As if she knew she'd come out just fine.

The worst part was that he and Carolyn never got to finish what they started. The next morning she was packed and heading out to the airport, being driven by one of Uncle Howie's chauffeurs to the airport. Douglas had offered to take her on his bike, knowing how much she had enjoyed the ride before, but she declined briskly with a smile, saying her bag was too heavy. She seemed cool, a little distant, though she gave him her files to read while she was gone. They barely said good-bye. Uncle Howie was there, so Douglas couldn't say what he wanted to say to her.

That he thought he might be falling in love with her.

It's crazy, he thought as he walked across the grass now. *I've known her for just a couple of weeks.* But her strength, her confidence, her *will* in the face of all this had made a huge impression on him. Never before had he met a woman like Carolyn.

"Terrific," he said out loud. "I finally meet someone I think I could really fall for, and I might have to lose my life to a pitchfork-wielding ghost."

He realized he had walked to the place where the woods began intruding onto the well-manicured lawn. Just ahead lay the path that wound its way down the steep side of the hill into the village.

An enormous black crow high in the tall oak tree in front of him let out a cry, startling Douglas. The bird flapped its wings, then took off soaring down the side of the hill. Douglas kept his eyes on it, listening to the cries it made.

That was the moment he realized he wasn't alone.

He turned his head, and Beatrice stood in the brilliant sunshine not three feet away from him.

"You've got to help us," Douglas said instinctively. "You don't want this killing to go on, do you? It's not you doing it. I know that. So please help us!"

She looked at him with pitiful eyes. She seemed to Douglas the manifestation of sadness, what sadness would look like if it took human form. She cocked her head at him, as if looking for something there. Then she turned and walked away, toward the path.

"Wait!" Douglas called after her.

But she kept walking, the breeze moving her flowing white dress. Douglas realized she was leading him somewhere.

And he thought he knew the destination.

Beatrice disappeared into the trees. Douglas followed, certain that he knew where he'd find her. And he was right. Rushing along the path, skillfully jumping over the protruding roots of trees, he emerged into the old Young family cemetery. And there stood Beatrice, forlornly gazing down upon a patch of tall yellow grass.

Douglas hurried over to her. But even as he approached her, she vanished into the light, a flickering static of incandescence.

He reached the spot where she had been standing. Why here? There was nothing here. The nearest stone was a good three yards away. This was just a stretch of empty ground, covered with grass and the occasional black-eyed Susan.

But then he felt something underfoot.

He bent down, pushing aside the grass.

A sparkle of granite.

There was a stone embedded in the earth. A flat stone overgrown with grass and weeds and moss. He scraped at the moss, peeling it back like a moldy carpet. He saw what was inscribed on the stone.

Just the letter *M.*

And above it, a carving of a small cherub.

Douglas stared at the stone.

"Why did Beatrice want me to see this?" he asked out loud.

He traced the *M* with his finger.

Malcolm.

Perhaps it stood for Malcolm.

Was that Beatrice's last name? Was this the place where they had buried her? Here, in an unmarked grave. Forgotten by the world.

But the cherub . . .

Something about the cherub.

It frightened him. Cherubs were little angels. Symbols of love. Cupid was kind of a cherub. With his little boy's body and his magic arrows of love. There was nothing frightening about Cupid.

But this little winged figure set Douglas's heart racing.

It had been roughly carved. A local stonecutter had most likely been hired to do a rush job. Someone had told him to carve a cherub above the *M*. And so he had etched a rough approximation of a human face and attached two wings in place of ears. The mouth on the face was open, perhaps in song. But it looked as if it were crying.

Or screaming.

Suddenly Douglas felt a terrible chill. He stood up, letting the grass obscure that terrible cherub once again.

M.

What was *M*?

What lay buried under that stone?

Chapter Fifteen

It felt good to be back in New York. Carolyn took considerable comfort in the bleating of taxi-cabs and the rumble of the subway. She felt safe here, far away from the mysteries of Mr. Young's house in Maine. It was good to see Andrea, to spend a little time with her, to hear her laugh. And it was ever so good to get back home, to her own apartment, and pretend for a few stolen hours that the room in Mr. Young's basement was just a fig-ment of her imagination—or at least something so far away that it couldn't touch her.

But touch her it did. Unless she could prevent the lottery, it waited to claim another life.

A life that might be Douglas's.

She closed her eyes now as she waited for the green WALK sign. She was at the corner of Houston Street and Avenue A. This wasn't her neighbor-hood. Carolyn lived in Hell's Kitchen, rapidly transforming itself into one of Manhattan's trendi-est areas. Here in the East Village, bohemia still clung tenaciously to the streets. She opened her eyes and looked across the street. Somewhere in that block lived one of the most unusual people she had ever met in her entire life. And she was depending on her now to provide the solution to the problem that plagued the Young family. It was no longer just an assignment for Carolyn. It was no longer just a means for making money.

It had become personal.

As the light changed, Carolyn began a brisk walk across the street. She couldn't deny the feeling that had surged up inside her the moment Douglas had moved to kiss her. She had shared so much with him. She hadn't felt that comfortable with a man—with anyone—in a very long time. She had told him about Mom, and about Andrea. She had even told him about David. She figured she might as well. who's to say Howard Young would not tell him at some point?

She didn't fully trust Mr. Young. He withheld too much. She still didn't know if he chose to withhold—or if some power prevented him from revealing too much. But she knew that he possessed information that could help her find an answer. By not sharing such information with her, he made her job more difficult—just as he had made Kip's job more difficult, and no doubt Dr. Fifer's job and the jobs of all those who had tried to end the curse before her. It was as if, on some level, Mr. Young didn't want them to succeed.

But that's crazy, Carolyn thought as she reached the other side of the street. *His grief is very real. He has seen so much tragedy. He wants it to end. I have to believe that he wants it to end.*

On the sidewalk ahead of her, a dreadlocked

young man played the xylophone. Carolyn smiled to see a trained gibbon, attached to the man's leg by a leash, dancing to the music its master made. People had stopped to watch and laugh.

If only I could stay here in New York, Carolyn said. *Never go back to Maine.*

Maybe she should have refused the assignment. But she wasn't able to walk away. Not then, not when she realized that someone would die and that she was their only chance. And certainly she couldn't turn her back on the job now, not when it might be Douglas who faced death.

I like him, Carolyn thought. *I like him a great deal.*

That was why she had been distant the day she left. The emotion was too troubling. The last time she had fallen in love, she had been hurt. Badly. Now, she might fall in love only to watch the man she loved walk into that room and never walk back out. And it would be because of her. Because she never found the solution.

"Diana must have the answer," Carolyn said out loud, heading up the brownstone steps and ringing the doorbell. "She *must*."

"Who is it?" crackled the voice over the intercom.

"Diana, it's Carolyn Cartwright."

"Oh, yes, Carolyn. Come upstairs."

The door buzzed, and Carolyn pulled it open.

The tenement was in bad repair. The plaster on the walls was cracking, and the entire building had sunk a bit, leaving the steps at an angle. Diana lived on the very top floor, the fifth. There was a rickety, early twentieth-century cage elevator, but Carolyn preferred the stairs. She had been here several times before. Once she'd gotten stuck in the elevator. She didn't want that experience again.

Only slightly winded, Carolyn finally made it to the fifth floor. Diana's flat was in the rear of the building. She had lived here for more than fifty years, since she was a little girl. It had been her mother's flophouse then, a place where she turned tricks for money. Diana had been born from one such liaison. She never knew who her father was, but she thanked him for one thing: the extraordinary power she had. "It had to have come from my father," Diana told Carolyn. "Because my mother was as ordinary as she could be."

Yet not so ordinary, really. It took extraordinary courage to do what Diana's mother did. Against the furious demands of the state and city welfare departments, she insisted on keeping her baby. She understood that Diana would never be like other girls, but no one else, she said, was going to raise her baby girl.

Carolyn tapped lightly on the door. "Diana?" she called.

As she expected, the lock in the door slid open, and the door opened inward on its specially designed spring. Carolyn's eyes flickered instinctively to the ceiling of Diana's flat, where a cord ran from the door across the length of the room to Diana's custom-made chaise by the window. Diana could lie there and open the door—with her teeth.

Carolyn smiled. Diana held the cord between her teeth, because she had no arms. Nor did she have legs. She was just a head and a small torso, thirty-three inches from top to bottom. She was wearing only an oversized white T-shirt emblazoned with a big Superman *S*.

"Carolyn!" Diana called, spitting the cord from her mouth. "How wonderful to see you again."

Carolyn closed the door behind her, even though she knew, with a different tug of her cord, Diana was perfectly capable of doing it herself.

"Hello, Diana," she said. "How are you doing?"

"Busy writing another book." The walls were lined with Diana's books, volumes describing the various escapades she had assisted with. There were a couple of adventures with Carolyn recounted in those pages. Of course, Diana disguised it all as fiction, changing names to protect both the innocent and the guilty. She didn't want any more freaks coming by her door to bother her. She had enough as it was.

Like Carolyn.

"You're getting rich off these books," Carolyn said, sitting down in a chair opposite Diana's chaise. "Why don't you buy yourself a nicer place?"

"I could never leave the East Village," Diana said. "This is home. I don't need a lot of space, as you know." She winked.

Carolyn smiled. "I've just come back from Maine. So much space up there."

"I've been up there a few times. You know, being in the country makes me nervous. All those crickets and birds." She shuddered. "I can't fall asleep without the sounds of the city outside my window."

Carolyn nodded. "I admit it's been quite a comfort being back."

"It was that bad, huh?" Diana narrowed her round blue eyes. She was a blonde, and rather pretty. Her face looked far younger than her fifty-plus years. "You indicated on the phone that this was one real doozie of a case."

"You know, every other case I've investigated, there has always been that little possibility that a rational explanation could be found, that maybe the supernatural wasn't really involved. Not this time."

Diana grimaced. "Why do you speak as if rational and supernatural are opposites? I would have thought the experience with George Grant would have convinced you that the supernatural is a real, provable, palpable phenomenon."

"Well, Diana, you know, some people say George Grant was just taking drugs, or that maybe his wife had given him drugs, and that's why he appeared that way. . . ."

"He was a *zombie!*" Diana maneuvered herself up with the stubs that served as her shoulders, moving her face forward at Carolyn as she made her point. Her small breasts heaved against the Superman insignia. "Come *on!* You saw him! I was with you that day on the pier. We both saw him!"

It was true. The image of George Grant's face emerging from the shadows had never left Carolyn. At the time, it had been the most terrifying moment of her career. She thought it was possible that Diana saved her life that night. Hidden in a baby carriage, Diana had peered out to see Grant moving toward Carolyn. He walked with the gait of the undead, his eyes blind yet somehow seeing. It was only as he passed Diana's carriage that he slowed down—stopped in his tracks by the words she said and the blood she spit at him. She had held the small balloon in her mouth, waiting for the moment to propel it at him with her tongue. The blood of a chicken. As the balloon popped and the blood stained the front of Grant's shirt,

Diana had uttered whatever mumbo jumbo she had been taught. Carolyn had watched in awe as the man staggered, then fell to his feet. When he awoke, hours later, he was once again himself.

"Good thing you had me with you," Diana reminded her now. "You thought I was just there to observe. But I knew I had to be ready."

"If George Grant really *was* a zombie, then you saved my life," Carolyn said, smiling.

"What do you mean *if?*" Diana sighed.

Carolyn just went on smiling. "Did you ever want to be anything other than a witch doctor?"

"Yeah," Diana cracked. "A ballerina." She hooted a laugh. "Weren't too many options open to me. But when I saw that I had a certain knack—" She hesitated, as if something had just occurred to her. "Okay, what's his name? No, wait, don't tell me."

It was Carolyn's turn to sigh. "There you go, reading my mind again."

"It used to drive Mama crazy, my 'knack,'" Diana said. "I'd know everything she was going to say to me two and half minutes before she actually got it out of her mouth."

"You told me you don't pry," Carolyn chided gently.

Diana frowned. "Sometimes it just pops into my head without me trying. Oh, I know his name. It's Douglas."

Carolyn nodded.

Diana's face turned sympathetic. "And he's one of the ones in danger, isn't he?"

Carolyn nodded again.

"From what you told me on the phone, this is something I don't have a lot of experience with."

Diana rested her head back against the pillow of the chaise. "I mean, when Mama learned of my abilities she brought in lots of teachers for me. Haitian witch doctors and psychics and Wiccan shamans, all sorts of people. I learned all the arcane arts about zombies and voodoo and witchcraft, but I don't know all that much about your run-of-the-mill ghosts."

"Oh, these aren't run-of-the-mill, let me assure you," Carolyn said dryly.

"What I mean is, if this Beatrice person had been a gypsy or something, and had cast a gypsy curse on the family, I might know how to reverse it. There are books on that. Spells you can memorize. Incantations and charms." She closed her eyes, as if thinking. "But Beatrice was just a girl, right?"

"As far as I know."

"Then I'm not sure what I can do. Ghosts are just people, you know. They're people freed from their physical bodies. That means they can act out by levitating things or appearing and disappearing or traveling far distances in a nanosecond." She seemed to consider this, and a wry smile crossed her face. "Gee, can't wait until I'm a ghost."

"Diana, you have to help me," Carolyn said. "Or point me to someone who can."

"Sweetie, I know this is personal for you. Believe me, your thoughts are coming through loud and clear on that." She rested her head back against the chaise and closed her eyes. "The trick is to make contact with the spirit who's causing all this destruction. She's pissed off, and there's no spell to counteract that. You've got to convince her to stop, to end the cycle of death."

"But Kip tried that," Carolyn argued. "He actually was able to walk Beatrice out of the room. It was as if they set her free."

"And then she came back?" Diana smirked. "That's one pissed-off, determined ghost."

"That's just it," Carolyn said. "In every contact with Beatrice, she hasn't manifested as angry. She's sad. She has never been a threatening presence. The word she kept repeating when Kip was able to record her was 'love.' "

"All you need is love, *bum da da da dum*," Diana sang, a snippet of an old Beatles tune. "Then I don't get how she could be killing people."

"Douglas thinks it's the other spirit who's doing the killing."

"The guy with the pitchfork."

Carolyn nodded. "Clem. And there's definitely a case to be made for that. Douglas's cousin Ryan was nearly killed by the ghost of Clem a week or so ago."

Diana made a face of confusion. "But that would go against all precedent, wouldn't it? The killings only happen in the room. If they take place elsewhere, it's because procedures weren't followed in regard to the room. In this case, it's not even time yet to send anyone in there. Why would Clem attempt to kill someone so soon?"

"I don't think Ryan was actually in any danger. I think it was a scare tactic. According to the notes kept by other investigators, it's not uncommon in the weeks before the lottery for family members to have terrifying brushes with the spirits. I think it's just a way to keep the family on its toes, and to make sure they go through with the lottery."

"Well, then it's simple. We contact Clem. Get him to back off."

Carolyn nodded. "I agree we need to try to reach him. And Beatrice, too. At least to gain more information, if possible."

"But you don't think Clem is the one doing the killings?"

"Oh, he may well be. It would seem his energy is far more aggressive and destructive than Beatrice's. He certainly seems capable of doing it. But Ryan said a curious thing." Carolyn paused, wanting to get the words right. "He felt as if Clem was being *led*. In life, Clem was a slow, rather stupid man. I think his brute energy is being manipulated, used for someone else's advantage. Someone else's revenge. Ryan said that as Clem came after him, another voice was heard, urging him on. 'Kill him,' the voice said."

"Whose voice?"

"Ryan didn't know. But it was not a man's voice."

"So Beatrice."

Carolyn sighed. "I suppose."

"It makes sense. You said that Clem was in love with her. Now she wants revenge on the family, so she's using the spirit of a man who, even now, would still do anything for her."

Carolyn shook her head. "But why would Beatrice want revenge on the family? The Youngs were good to her."

"As far as we know," Diana said. "But might there be something lost to history? Something she blames the family for?"

"Possibly the loss of her baby," Carolyn said.

"Apparently Desmond Young gave the baby away after Beatrice's death. Maybe the new parents didn't prove to be good caretakers, because I suspect the baby died soon afterward. Some in the family have reported seeing a ghostly baby over the years. So perhaps Beatrice blames the Youngs for not taking care of her baby, for not finding it a good home."

"I assume this baby, what you keep referring to as 'it,' had a gender?"

Carolyn sighed. "I'm sure it did, but I don't know if it was a boy or a girl. Old Harry Noons, the man on Kip's tape, never said, and there are no records of the baby at all at the Youngsport town hall or in the newspapers at the time. I know this is true. I checked and rechecked before I left."

"Well, it's a theory, anyway," Diana agreed. "A mother's love can be a strong, enduring force. But until you make contact with Beatrice, you can't be sure of why or who or what or when."

"I know." Carolyn smiled "So can you help me?"

"I suppose it could make a good book," Diana said, her eyes twinkling.

Carolyn beamed. "Thank you. I'm heading back up to Maine the day after tomorrow. Mr. Young is sending a chartered plane. I'll tell him we'll have an additional passenger."

"Well, I don't take up a lot of room," Diana said with a wink. "Actually, though, you should make that two additional passengers. Fraulein Schmitz would be very aggrieved if I didn't take her."

Almost as if on cue, the door opened, and a stocky, broad-shouldered, white-haired woman in her seventies huffed inside carrying two brown paper bags of groceries. Huldah Schmitz was Diana's German-born nurse and companion, hired years ago by Diana's mother and at her side fiercely ever since. Huldah was a tough woman of few words, but she made sure that Diana's meals were made and baths were taken and doctors' appointments were kept. Diana could do many things on her own—her disability had never kept her down—but Huldah was there to handle those occasional things that proved too much even for Diana's ingenuity. Carolyn had met her when she'd worked with Diana before. She liked her, even if Huldah's most frequent reply to a question was a grunt.

"We're going to Maine," Diana called over to her as the nurse began putting groceries away in the kitchen. If there was a reply, even a grunt, they didn't hear it.

"Hello, Huldah," Carolyn called, standing. She reached into her bag and withdrew a folder, placing it on the chaise next to Diana. "Here are some photocopies of some of the reports from previous investigators. There are also photographs of the room, of the house, of the cliffs. We can talk more on the flight up to Maine."

"Sounds good," Diana said.

"Rack your brain," Carolyn said. "See if there's anything we can do to protect the family in case we aren't successful with persuading the ghosts to back off."

"If you go in with doubts about your mission, sweetie, then you're doomed to fail."

Carolyn sighed. "I just worry that we're simply repeating steps Kip already took. They thought they had succeeded. Beatrice was free. But still the killing took place."

"She may have been free," Diana said, as Huldah came into the room with a specially designed prop that she set on the disabled woman's chest. "But whatever keeps her wandering between worlds was not addressed. The reason for her grief was not assuaged." Twisting her torso, she grabbed the folder Carolyn had placed beside her with her teeth, maneuvering it onto the prop Huldah had placed on her chest. Again using her teeth, she opened the folder and glanced down at the first page. "I'll start reading right away, sweetie. I promise you I'll think of whatever I can."

"Thank you," Carolyn said, stooping down to kiss her on the forehead.

"We'll do our best to save your young man," Diana said. "It would be nice if you could finally move beyond the past and forget that horrible experience."

Carolyn just smiled. Diana knew all about David Cooke. Some of it Carolyn had shared; some of it Diana had picked up, without even trying too hard to read Carolyn's mind.

She said good-bye to Huldah, who gave her a grunt that seemed a little cheerier than usual. Maybe she was looking forward to taking a trip. Carolyn let herself out of the apartment and headed back down the crooked staircase into the gathering purple evening of the city.

The meeting with Diana had gone well. It should have made her optimistic. But suddenly the sounds and the hustle-bustle of the city no longer felt comforting to Carolyn. Making her way back across town, she couldn't shake the feeling of unease that had settled over her. She felt cold, shaky, even though the night was warm. She felt as if strangers were looking at her, their sharp eyes burning holes into her face. A bus backfired, and Carolyn jumped, letting out a small cry. *This is crazy*, she thought. *Why am I so jittery all of a sudden?*

Heading down into the subway, she had the distinct sense that someone was watching her. Following her. She looked up and down the platform, but saw no one overtly suspect. But she distrusted everyone. The man with the backpack and the shifty eyes. The woman carrying the Macy's shopping bag. The lanky teenager with the sagging jeans and exposed checkered underwear. The heavyset man with the red splotches on his face. The girl with the iPod plugged into her ears.

Getting onto the train, Carolyn clung tightly to the bar. Her heart was racing. *Why am I suddenly so frightened?*

The train lurched and began to move, twisting its way along the underground tracks. Someone was on the train who wanted to kill her. Suddenly she knew that as clearly as anything she'd ever known in her life. She was being stalked. She was the prey, and the killer had her in his sights.

Or her sights.

Or *its* sights.

The entire subway trip was a nightmare of nerves and terror. Every person who pressed against her caused her to recoil. Her hands had broken out into clammy sweat. When she finally reached her destination, she walked quickly out into the night, hoping the sights and sounds of her neighborhood would reassure her. They did not. Walking past the convenience store just a few doors down from her apartment, she decided to pop inside for a moment, hoping some of her usual banter with the clerk, an Indian man with kind eyes, would calm her nerves. But to her dismay, there was a different clerk behind the counter this night, a hard-eyed man who frowned when she looked over at him. Outside she noticed a figure pause outside the store window. The darkness precluded her from getting a look at the figure's face. Was this who was stalking her?

Stop it, Carolyn, she scolded herself. *You are letting your fears run away with all sense and reason.*

This had never happened before. She had been frightened at times. The night seeing George Grant on the pier had been one of those times; the bloody message on the wall in that basement room in Mr. Young's house had occasioned another. But never had she been paranoid. Never had she felt an irrational sense of danger.

That's why she took the emotion seriously.

Someone—something—was out there. She knew that was a fact.

Taking a deep breath, she headed out of the bright lights of the store and back into the purple night. Whoever had paused outside the store was gone. Fighting off a shudder, she hurried around the block and let herself into her apartment, climbing the steps to the second floor. Carolyn unlocked her door and quickly shut it behind her, sliding the bolt firmly in place. She let out a long breath of relief. She was safe here.

But the fear still ate away at her.

He's outside, she thought.

She moved over to her window. Leaving the lights off, she opened the Venetian blinds just a pinch and glanced down at the street.

There was indeed a man standing down there, looking up at her window.

Carolyn gasped.

She knew who it was.

It was no pitchfork-wielding ghost.

It was a far more human, but no less dangerous foe.

It was David Cooke.

Chapter Sixteen

"I'd like to leave the kids with Linda's mother," Dean told her. "I don't want to bring them. . . . I mean if something were to happen . . ."

Paula understood. But sitting across from her brother, glancing out the window at Zac and Callie playing in the yard, she wasn't sure it was a good idea.

"We always went to the reunions as kids," she said. "Mother and Dad always took us. For as long as the lottery has been held, the children have always been in the house. None of us knew about the lottery, of course, until we were older, but we were always there. Not bringing Zac and Callie would be breaking tradition, wouldn't it? Against the rules?"

"I don't know," Dean admitted. "Uncle Howard doesn't know either."

Paula took another sip of her coffee. She'd headed out to her brother's house this morning because she'd spent another sleepless night, dreaming of that baby. The baby who taunted her. Her eyes were puffy and dark with circles. She needed to talk to Dean. He was the only one she could talk to.

"What pisses me off is that we don't even know what the rules are, or who laid them down," Paula said. "It's obscene. Unjust. That some unknown force dictates the rules by which we live and die."

Linda came by to refill both their cups. "I wake up every morning crying," she said. "Thinking that this time, maybe . . ." She couldn't say the words.

"I hope it's me," Paula said. "I hope I'm the one chosen for the lottery."

"Stop it, Paula," Dean said.

"Oh, Paula, no, you can't mean that," Linda said.

She frowned. "Of course I mean it. I have no one now. Since Karen left, there's no one who needs me." She looked out the window again at Zac and Callie.

"I hope it's going to be none of us," Dean said. "Uncle Howard sounded optimistic that this Carolyn Cartwright could—"

"Could what? Oh, Dean," Paula said. "He was optimistic about Kip Hobart, too. And whatever the man's name he had the time before that."

Linda had moved out of the room, her emotions getting the best of her. Brother and sister sat in silence for a while, just staring down at their coffee cups.

Finally Dean reached into a large manila envelope sitting on the table and withdrew the scan he had printed from his computer. He hadn't even shown it to Linda. For some reason, he wanted

Paula to be the first to see it. After all, she had been with him the day he had taken it all those years ago.

She knew instantly what it was. "The Polaroid," she said, almost in awe. "You found it. . . ."

He nodded. "I had it blown up. We were right all those years. It was a face."

Paula held the image in her hands. A short, startled breath escaped her lips.

"A baby," she said. "It's the baby I see in my dreams."

Dean nodded. "I remember before Dad died, he saw a baby. Well, the apparition of a baby. I told him about the Polaroid then, and it seemed to disturb him."

Paula couldn't take it anymore. She stood, a bundle of energy that needed release. She missed Karen terribly. Respecting her wishes, she hadn't tried to contact her. She spent her days and her nights in a constant state of turmoil, grief, fear, and anxiety. She had meant it when she said she hoped she was chosen in the lottery. What did she have to live for now? Dean had Linda and the kids. Her cousins Douglas and Chelsea and Ryan were still in their twenties and had their whole lives ahead of them. It should be her.

But then she thought of her students, the children struggling to adjust to life in this country. She thought of little Quynh-Anh, just six years old and refusing to speak because everything around her was so different from what she knew. Paula had worked with her tenderly and diligently, teaching her words for her favorite things: her doll, a daisy, a glazed donut, a sparkly tiara. Quynh-Anh was making progress, but her mother was still worried about her. Only Paula, the mother insisted, had managed to get through to the little girl.

"Oh, Dean," she said. "What went on in that room so many years ago to cause such enduring tragedy?"

"I don't know if we'll ever really know." Her brother sighed. "All we know for sure is a servant girl was murdered. That's all Uncle Howard has ever admitted."

"But what about the baby? Why is there a spirit of a baby as well?"

"When Kip Hobart was investigating the room, he learned that Beatrice had a baby. But what happened to the baby, none of us know."

Paula shook her head. "Uncle Howard knows. He must. He was there!"

"But he can't say," Dean told her. "Somehow he's prevented from telling all he knows."

"Are you so sure? I love Uncle Howard. He's always been very good to me. And to you and Zac and Callie. Dad adored him. But . . ."

"But what, Paula?" Dean asked. "Do you suspect him of something?"

"I remember the year that Dad died. There was a man investigating the room then, too. Remember? A Dr. Fifer?"

"Yes. I remember him. But he wasn't able to find anything to end the curse. No one has."

Paula pressed her point. "But Fifer accumulated a good amount of information. I remember him saying to Dad once that he thought he understood why the forces in that room were so restless, and that it was up to someone living to put them at rest. That's when he went out to see Jeanette at Windcliffe. Do you remember?"

Dean was nodding. "Yes. He upset her. For the first time, he was able to produce a response from Jeanette."

"Exactly." Paula looked at her brother sternly. "The next day Uncle Howard fired him."

"He said Dr. Fifer wasn't getting anywhere," Dean said.

Paula smiled cagily. "Or maybe he was getting too close to something."

Dean frowned. "Do you think Uncle Howard would abandon the mission to end the curse? That's insanity, Paula. He's spent his whole life trying to end the cycle of death. You can see the pain in his eyes at every family reunion."

"It's true," Paula agreed. "I know Uncle Howard is deeply pained by all of this. But the way he withholds information . . . Dad even commented on it. Dad—who paid the ultimate price in that room."

Dean was silent. He was looking at the scan of the crying baby again.

"Why let Dr. Fifer go just as he was about to tell us something?"

"I admit it's odd," Dean said.

Paula lifted the scan to study it herself. "I think," she said, "I'll have a few questions for Uncle Howard when we see him."

Chapter Seventeen

Philip steered his Bentley up the long driveway outside Uncle Howard's mansion. If he'd had his way, he wouldn't have come to this depressing old place a day earlier than he had to. But Ryan and Chelsea had called a few days ago, all in a state. Uncle Howard had told them about the room and the lottery. Philip cursed the old fool. He should have waited until he was there before revealing the family secret. But apparently something had happened—some sighting of that crazy woman ghost— and Uncle Howard had felt he needed to tell them everything. It had taken Philip a good hour to calm his kids down.

He stepped out of the car and tossed the keys to one of the old man's valets. "Be careful with that car," Philip barked. "Don't think I won't check for dings or scratches, and I've noted the mileage. No joyrides."

He strode imperiously into the house. "Hello!" he called impatiently.

A maid appeared, a big stupid grin on her face. Philip told her to let Uncle Howard know he'd arrived. And where, he demanded, were Ryan and Chelsea? The maid said they were out on the back terrace. Philip made a beeline there.

They have got to be careful, he thought to himself. *They can't give anything away.*

He found his son and daughter stretched out on lounges sunbathing. Chelsea wore a polka-dot string bikini, and Ryan wore flower-print board shorts. Both of them had music plugged into their ears and so they didn't hear him approach. He walked up between them, and with one tug from each hand, he extracted the headphones from their ears.

"You *idiots,*" he spit.

"Daddy!" Chelsea was sitting up, Ryan doing the same.

"You both are complete idiots," Philip said. "Look at you! Lying around acting as if you haven't a care in the world!"

"But, we *don't,* Daddy," Chelsea said. "You told us not to worry about the lottery."

He wanted to strike her. "You stupid girl," Philip said. "The rest of the household will be overwrought with stress and worry, thinking they might be chosen. And here you two are acting as carefree as jaybirds. Do you want to let your uncle—or worse, your cousin Douglas—suspect that we have an ace up our sleeve?"

"I suppose we *should* be acting a bit more concerned," Ryan conceded.

His father glared at him. "I expected more smarts from the appointed heir to the family business. Would you run the company this way? You're far more shrewd on Wall Street, you jackass, than you are here!"

"Oh, Daddy," Chelsea said, in that voice she knew always softened his angry moods, "we'll do better. It was just that it was so nice and sunny, and who knows how many more days we'll have before winter will be here."

Philip looked at her. She truly had no idea of the irony of her words. The rest of the family had no idea how many more days they had to live. But all Chelsea was worried about was how many days she had to sunbathe.

"Listen to me," he told them both. "I want you to go in the house and get dressed. I want you to appear subdued. Quiet. Contemplative." His eyes burned holes as he turned to glare at Chelsea. "Is that something you can even *do*?"

"Oh, sure," she assured him. "It will be kind of like that acting course I took, remember? It'll be fun."

She kissed her father on the forehead, then gathered her things and scampered into the house.

"You're brilliant, Dad, you know that?" Ryan said, preparing to head back inside himself. "When Uncle Howard told us about that room and all that crazy supernatural bullshit, I was like, *we are fucked*. But I should have know you had it all under control. The old bait-and-switch with the names thing. Brilliant. Truly brilliant."

He gave his father a little salute and walked inside the house.

Philip sighed, sitting down on his son's vacated chaise. He felt rotten. Oh, he had no misgivings about the chicanery he intended to work on the lottery. It had served him well, kept him alive. But it had come with some cost. Philip Young could rationalize most things, and most days he lived without any guilt about what he had done. But every once in a while, something would happen—seeing his brother's children, for example—that would cause a flare-up of conscience. He wasn't like his brother, so noble, so upstanding. Nor was he like his father, another good man. There were days that Philip Young almost admitted to himself what he really was: a coward.

His children, he realized, were even worse. They took it for granted that they should not have to face the same risks as everyone else. They had been raised that way. Their entitlement knew no bounds. Unlike their father, they suffered not even a moment's compunction over their trickery. Not once did either Ryan or Chelsea experience even a flicker of guilt or remorse for their cousins. No, to them it was their right, their due, to be excluded from the messy realities of life and death.

Sitting there on his uncle's terrace, Philip was not proud of his children.

Nor was he proud of himself.

But that didn't alter the course he had planned.

"Philip," came a voice.

He looked around. It was Uncle Howard, walking slowly, a little stiffly, onto the terrace.

"Welcome, nephew," the old man was saying. "I wasn't expecting you quite so soon."

They shook hands.

"I came early because I knew Ryan and Chelsea would need me," Philip explained. "They're very upset after learning about the lottery."

"Are they?" Uncle Howard asked. "They seemed to take it surprisingly in stride."

"They are quite good at masking their emotions," Philip lied. "I suppose I've trained them that way."

Uncle Howard sighed, taking a seat in a large wicker chair overlooking the grounds. "Well, I have much faith in this woman that I have hired. She's in New York right now making inquiries about possible solutions. I sense she may be able to finally uncover a way to end the curse."

"Why do you have so much faith in her?"

"Because she's a woman."

Philip laughed. "You've said that on the phone. But I don't understand."

"The spirit that has controlled this family, that has wrought so much destruction, is a woman," Uncle Howard said, his voice hard with resentment. "No man has ever been able to figure out what she wanted or how to control her."

"And so Carolyn Cartwright has a better chance, you think?"

"Possibly. The spirit of Beatrice may allow her to see things that she kept guarded from the men. She has a weakness for her own kind." He moved his yellow, watery eyes to meet Philip's. "Remember, she didn't kill Jeanette."

The mention of his sister's name stabbed Philip's heart, as it always did. "One could argue what she did to Jeanette was even worse."

"Still, she was disinclined to see her die, and that's something." The old man looked back across the grounds. Hummingbirds flitted around the rosebushes. The tall violet cleomes swayed in the soft breeze. "I have great faith in Carolyn. I will finally see an end to this madness before I die."

And when will that be, exactly? Philip's mind raced with the thought. *And who have you decided shall get the bulk of your fortune?*

Just then, as if on cue, a hand was placed on Philip's shoulder.

"Hello, Uncle Philip."

He turned. Douglas had come outside. As usual, the punk looked disheveled and unruly. His hair was straggly, his face unshaven. He wore an Obama HOPE T-shirt. He looked like a filthy hippie.

"Douglas," Philip said, shaking the young man's hand. "And what corner of the world have you blown in from this time?"

"My last address was in Syracuse, but I'm thinking of putting some roots down here in Maine. Come back to my roots, so to speak."

The little sneak, Philip thought. Douglas was implying that he was to be the chief beneficiary of Uncle Howard's will. He probably expected to live in this very house.

"My little hoodlum has visions of opening his own carpentry shop in Youngsport," Uncle Howard said with obvious affection.

Philip stewed. He hated when the old man called Douglas his "little hoodlum." He had no such special nickname for Ryan.

Douglas sat down on the back step at Uncle Howard's feet. The old man placed a gnarled hand on his shoulder.

Any flicker of guilt Philip had been harboring disappeared in that moment. When it came time to draw up the lottery, the names of himself and his children would not be entered. Instead, there would be three additional slips of paper bearing the name "Douglas."

Standing there looking at the old man's hand on Douglas's shoulder, Philip did not feel even the slightest twinge of guilt.

Chapter Eighteen

Carolyn had expected there might be a curious reaction to Diana from the family, but she could hardly have anticipated Chelsea's scream.

"Oh my God!" she cried. "What *is* it?"

"It's only what you would look like, my dear," Diana replied, "if you were thirty years older and had had your arms and legs chopped off."

That shut the girl up.

Diana was strapped into a specially designed motorized wheelchair with a long lever that she could operate with her chin, if need be. But at the moment Huldah was behind her, her hands grasping the handles of the chair tightly, her hard German eyes glaring at Chelsea.

"I apologize for my niece," Mr. Young said, bowing slightly at his waist. Chelsea, meanwhile, was slinking back into the parlor, whether humiliated, revolted, or chagrined, Carolyn couldn't tell. Philip Young stood staring wide-eyed, his look matched by his son Ryan. Douglas stood beside Carolyn. She wondered what thoughts were going through his mind.

"Welcome to my home," Mr. Young was continuing. "And thank you for your assistance with our terrible curse."

"I'm here to do what I can," Diana said. "And one thing that I cannot do is make any promise."

"Understood," Mr. Young said.

"Carolyn has told me of your experience," Douglas managed to say. "Have you ever encountered anything like this?"

"No," Diana told him. "Nothing. But I hope to learn something if I can be brought down into the room. I have a certain . . . knack."

Carolyn turned as she heard Philip Young chuckle. "And what kind of knack would that be?" he asked.

Diana stared at him. "A knack that tells me who I can trust and who I can't."

Carolyn noticed the smile quickly fade from Philip's face.

She didn't like Philip Young any more than she liked his children. She'd known him for just a few minutes, but she'd already marked him as smarmy and untrustworthy. Even without Diana's ability to read minds, Carolyn had known right away that she'd have to keep an eye on him. She'd have to ask Diana later if she had seen anything specific in Philip's thoughts that she should be aware of.

It had been an unsettling few days. Ever since seeing David Cooke on the street outside her apartment, Carolyn had been constantly looking over her shoulder. She had called the police, of course. A massive manhunt was immediately enacted. Guards were stationed outside her house

and followed her at a discreet distance for the rest
of her time in New York. They had accompanied
her and Diana and Huldah to the airport and were
with them until just moments before they boarded
Mr. Young's private plane. There was no way David
could follow them here. He had no idea where she
was going. In a strange twist of fate, she suddenly
felt safer coming back to Maine than she had
when she left it.

They all dispersed to their rooms so they could
clean up after their trip. Huldah wheeled Diana
into a room on the first floor. Carolyn headed up
the stairs to her own room.

"Carolyn, wait," Douglas said behind her.

She paused. Her heart was racing. She turned
and looked at him.

They were alone in the foyer. He approached
her.

"I just wanted to say . . ." His voice faltered.
"That I missed you."

"Oh, Douglas," she said in a small voice.

Before she knew it, they were kissing. They
came together without consideration for who
might see them and embraced each other tightly.
His lips tasted sweet. It took some effort to break
away.

"Not here," Carolyn said.

Douglas took her hand and led her to the study.
He closed the doors behind them. Once again
they fell into each other's arms with a hunger that
surprised Carolyn.

"I wanted to do this so much before you left,"
Douglas said, moving his lips off hers just long
enough to speak.

She smiled. "Oh, Douglas, I'm so glad to be

back here. Even with all of the terrors here . . . to be with you . . ."

He stroked her hair. "What is it, Carolyn? What's happened?"

She told him about seeing David Cooke outside her window.

"Christ," Douglas said, gripping her by the shoulders. "I wish I had gone with you to New York! Do you think he could have followed you here?"

"No, there's no way he could have known where I was going." She smiled wryly. "Even David can't follow an airplane."

She let herself take comfort in Douglas's embrace, resting her head against his chest. Once again, the irony of feeling safe in a place that held only danger for Douglas struck her.

"I think Diana can help us," she said, looking up at Douglas.

His reply was to kiss her again.

"All I want," he said, moving his lips to her ear, "is to spend my life with you. Even if that life just lasts another week . . ."

"Don't say that," Carolyn said.

"But it may be the case," Douglas said.

Their eyes held each other.

Without saying another word, they turned and left the study. They walked silently up the stairs to Carolyn's room. Once inside, the door locked behind them, Carolyn unbuttoned Douglas's shirt. She ran her hands over his chiseled chest. The light blond hairs there seemed to electrify at her touch. He kissed her neck, her ears, her throat. He unbuttoned her blouse, letting it drop to the floor. He kissed her shoulders. He reached around and unsnapped her bra, letting it, too, fall away. Cup-

ping her breasts in each hand, he kissed them tenderly. Then they lay gently down upon the bed.

When they had finished making love, Carolyn
sat up, cradling Douglas's head in her lap. It had
felt good. Very good. Douglas was a kind, considerate lover. He had made sure she was satisfied before thinking about any kind of satisfaction for
himself. Now, in that dreamy state after sex, Carolyn realized she'd never had such an experience.
She had thought David had been a good lover. He
had been exciting. But she realized now she could
never have called him considerate.

She reached down and kissed the top of Douglas's head. He made a sound of contentment.

Once again, Carolyn's thoughts turned to that
room in the basement. She hoped fervently that
Diana could help her find a way to put an end to
the cycle of death.

And failing that . . .

She knew it wasn't right.

But if the lottery went on as scheduled, she
hoped it wouldn't be Douglas who was chosen. Let
it be any of the others.

Just not Douglas.

Chapter Nineteen

Douglas couldn't take his eyes off Carolyn. If he had been looking for sparks, he had found them. Now he understood what Dad had meant when he described falling in love with Mom. Finally Douglas knew what it felt like to be in love. He found himself in the bizarre situation of feeling giddy and joyful—even as he might be facing the most terrible death in just a week's time.

"You'll be all right carrying her?" Carolyn asked.

He beamed. He would do anything she wanted him to. He nodded.

"I don't weigh very much," Diana said, her blue eyes looking up at Douglas.

He smiled down at her. "I'm sure I can manage," he assured her.

With ease, he lifted the small woman in his arms. She couldn't be more than fifty pounds. He held her carefully, like a baby.

"Huldah used to carry me around," Diana said. "But she's got a bad back these days."

The German woman just grunted.

Then they all fell silent, one by one filing out of the parlor and across the foyer to the door to the basement.

Uncle Howie went first, moving slowly down the stairs. Ryan followed, insisting he would be there in case the old man stumbled. Then came Uncle Philip, with a skittish Chelsea close behind. Carolyn went next, followed by Douglas and Diana. Huldah took up the rear, keeping her eyes on the precious cargo Douglas carried in his arms.

The basement was dark and damp. But there was nothing at first glance that gave evidence of the dangers that lurked down there. Douglas looked around at the boxes and cobwebs, the open doors to the various storerooms that had once been servants' bedrooms. But then his eyes fell on the one door that was closed. Uncle Howie was nearing that door now. The keys jingled in his trembling hand.

Off to his right Douglas saw an old sink, and beyond that, an archway that had been sealed over with cement. At one time, Douglas realized, that had been the servants' entrance. And the sink was where Harry Noons had stood, where he had watched as Beatrice and Clem had argued, right in front of that room. Then Noons had left, and Clem had taken Beatrice inside the room and impaled her to the wall with his pitchfork.

Instinctively, Douglas shuddered.

Diana felt it.

"You have reason to be afraid," the woman in his arms told him. "The closer we come to that door, the stronger I feel the force."

"Is it Beatrice?" he asked.

"I cannot tell."

Uncle Howard had managed to unlock the door. With a creak, it swung inward.

The one small window high on the wall gave the room its only light. A shaft of sunshine pierced the dark shadows.

"Place me on the couch there," Diana instructed.

"What is it that you intend to do here?" Philip asked, the impatience obvious in his voice. Douglas knew that his uncle was not used to taking direction—especially not from some strange armless and legless woman who lived in a crumbling tenement on the Lower East Side. But for now Diana was calling the shots. Douglas placed her carefully on the dusty, moldy couch, where, with her remarkable shoulders, she propped herself up against a pillow. Huldah was quickly on hand to make the necessary adjustments.

"I am here to get a reading on the energy in this room," Diana said, her eyes moving all around the place.

"Then why were we all required to come along?" Philip asked.

Douglas looked at the older man. He was clearly uncomfortable being in the room where so many of his family had died.

"You needn't fear, Philip," Uncle Howie said. "No harm has ever come to any of us in this place except on the night of the lottery."

"Then why did you never let us into the basement as children?" Chelsea asked, near tears, hugging herself.

Her uncle looked over at her. "Because I did not want you to see anything that may frighten you." He moved his eyes to the far wall. "Like that."

Douglas gasped. On the wall two words were written in fresh, shiny blood.

ABANDON HOPE.

Chelsea screamed.

"Dear God," Philip uttered.

The blood dripped down the wall.

"It's what I saw the first time I came in here," Carolyn said.

Douglas moved closer to her.

"Who is doing it?" Ryan asked. "Beatrice?"

"No," Diana said, her eyes closed. "It's not Beatrice. She's not here. Kip Hobart was successful in walking her out of this room. She's no longer here."

"Then it's Clem," Douglas said.

Diana just shook her head. "I don't get the energy of a man."

"Then was there another woman involved?" Douglas asked. "Someone besides Beatrice?"

Diana opened her eyes. "Perhaps."

Philip made a sound of exasperation. "This is going nowhere!"

Diana looked at him sternly. "This is why I asked you all to accompany me here. We must together summon the forces of this room. Carolyn, will you close the door?"

"Close the door?" Ryan asked. "What if we can't get back out?"

"We will be able to get back out," Diana assured him.

"Please do as the lady says, Carolyn," Uncle Howie said.

Carolyn closed the door. Douglas admitted that being closed off in this room unnerved him, but he said nothing.

"Ideally, we need all of those who will participate in the lottery to take part in this ritual," Diana said.

"But my niece Paula and nephew Dean have not yet arrived," Uncle Howie said.

Diana sighed. "Then we must make do with what we have."

"What is the first thing we must do?" Carolyn asked.

"You place one hand on my shoulder, Carolyn, and Mr. Young, you place your hand on my other shoulder. Then the rest of you join hands in a circle."

Huldah made a sound in her throat.

"Yes, you too, Huldah," Diana instructed. "We need all the psychic energy we can get." She paused. "Even yours."

Douglas watched as Carolyn stood beside Diana and placed her hand on her shoulder. Then her beautiful eyes found Douglas, and he gripped her other hand tightly.

Chelsea took his other hand, and on the other side linked hands with her brother, who held hands with his father, who reluctantly took the hand of Huldah. The German woman made the circle complete by holding Uncle Howie's hand.

"Now we must free our minds of extraneous thought," Diana said. "Concentrate on feelings of compassion." Douglas thought her eyes moved over to Philip and his children. "Do the best you can to feel nothing but compassion."

"Should we be directing our compassion toward someone?" Carolyn asked. "Beatrice?"

"Just feel compassion," Diana said. "Open your

hearts and practice the feeling of love for all the world."

"Dear God," Philip groaned. "Shall we start singing 'Kumbaya' as well?"

"Philip," Uncle Howie reprimanded. "Let us please give this a try. Nothing else has worked."

Philip merely huffed.

"Compassion," Diana said again. "Compassion for the spirits that reside here. For those who have died here. For those who go on living."

They were quiet. Douglas looked around. Most everyone had their eyes closed. He turned to Carolyn. She was looking at him. So much she was managing to say just with her eyes. She was worried for him. Douglas could see that. She feared he would be the one chosen to spend the night in the room. She wanted desperately for whatever Diana was doing here to work. He gave her a small smile and squeezed her hand.

Then he concentrated on compassion. It wasn't always an easy emotion to summon. It was a cinch when thinking about Carolyn, of course, feeling the pain she had experienced surrounding her family, the fear and grief and wounded pride she had felt regarding David Cooke. It was easy when he looked over at Diana, thinking about the struggles she must have faced growing up. It was easy to feel for Uncle Howie, too, for watching a family member die every ten years as he went on living. But it wasn't so easy when his thoughts moved to Uncle Philip and Ryan and Chelsea. Growing up, they had always been so much more privileged than Douglas's family. And then how he'd envied his cousins for their two living, breathing parents. As adults, money and success had come easy to them, and they seemed to enjoy lording that fact over Douglas. He knew, for example, that they had only come early for the reunion because he was there, and they had their claws out, trying to do everything in their power to push him aside in Uncle Howie's affections.

But still Douglas managed to feel compassion for them. Surely they were as frightened as he was, even if they did their best to hide it. It might be one of them in this room a week from now. And Douglas wouldn't wish that on anyone. Not after seeing his father dead from spending a night here.

He thought of his father then. Where exactly in this room had he died? Where had he struggled? And with whom? Who had tied that bag to his head? Or was he compelled to do it to himself? Douglas would never know. He felt a rush of sadness and love and indeed compassion for his father then. A good man. One of the best. He hadn't been afraid to die, and so Douglas would not be either.

He felt compassion for all of those who had died in this room. Three generations of Douglas Youngs had died here on this dusty concrete floor. His father, grandfather, and great-grandfather. His Uncle Martin had died here, and poor Jeanette had almost died here. He felt a surge of compassion for the woman sitting motionless and voiceless at the asylum.

And lastly he felt compassion for the spirits that controlled this room. Whether Beatrice was still here or not, she had died here, horribly, her heart punctured by the sharp tine of a pitchfork. And Clem . . . he forced his mind to summon compassion for him, too. A simple man. Brokenhearted. Desperate. He had committed a horrible act in the heat of passion. Surely he had been a good man before that. . . .

There was a sound. Almost like the growl of a dog.

Chelsea, panicked, attempted to break the circle by letting go, but Douglas wouldn't let her. He clamped down, causing her to emit a little cry.

"What is it?" she asked pitifully as the growling only got louder.

"Hear us as we hear you," Diana called. "We mean you no harm, even after all this time and all that has transpired here in this room. We forgive the pain you have caused because we know the pain that you feel. The enduring pain and grief that keeps you trapped between this world and the next. You want to be free. You want to move on and leave the pain behind you. We can help you do that! We can help you be free!"

But in reply the growling only increased. It was as if a lion were somewhere in the room, hiding in the shadows, waiting to leap out at them.

"Do not break the circle!" Carolyn called out. "We are safe so long as you don't break the circle!"

"Listen to me," Diana continued, trying to reason with the angry spirit. "We implore you to stop the endless cycle of death! Let us help you move on!"

The growling grew so loud that it now seemed like one long scream. A guttural sound, a frustrated, furious, and yet terrified sound, like an animal with its leg caught in a trap.

"We can help you get free," Diana said, as if she sensed the same image. "We can unchain you from what keeps you here and free you to go—"

But her words were cut short by the door to the

room suddenly swinging open, followed by a burst of cold wind. But what came afterward was far more terrible.

Clem was in the doorway with his pitchfork. His eyes were red and wild.

"He's come back for me!" Ryan shrieked, breaking the circle and running to the far side of the room.

"Fool!" Diana called. "Get him! Bring him back into the circle!"

Douglas bolted, reluctantly releasing Carolyn's hand and grabbing his cousin by the shoulders. Ryan was trying to hide behind the couch. Chelsea was screaming. Even Huldah was making sounds of terror.

"Douglas, watch out!" Carolyn shouted.

Clem had moved forward into the room, his face a mask of rage. He raised the pitchfork over his head and intended to bring it down on both Douglas and Ryan.

"He can't hurt you!" Diana called over to them. "It is nothing but impotent rage!"

Douglas held Clem's glare. The seconds seemed an eternity as the apparition stared back at him. The eyes were red, blazing. Douglas refused to look away while Ryan sobbed into his hands. Then, as if he had never been there, Clem was gone.

Diana let out a long breath. "You can break the circle. Its power was lost the moment the boy left it."

Ryan remained slumped on the floor, shaking all over.

"Oh, for God's sake, get up," his father said derisively, standing over him.

Uncle Howie was as shaken as Ryan. Carolyn helped him to a seat on the couch.

"To see him again," the old man kept babbling. "To actually see him . . . and the rage in his eyes . . ."

"What happened to him in life?" Carolyn asked. "Please, Mr. Young, you must tell us. What happened to Clem?"

"We searched everywhere for him," Uncle Howie said, but his words came out too quickly, as if by rote, an oft-repeated explanation. "My father and brothers and I searched the grounds, but he was nowhere to be found."

"If that were the case," Carolyn said, "why would he still be haunting this place?"

"Guilt," Douglas suggested. "For killing Beatrice."

"Yes!" Uncle Howie said. "That is it! It is his guilt!" He shook a frail fist in the air, looking up as if to seek the vanished spirit. "No matter how much you terrify me, I will always make sure your guilt is known!"

"Are you certain that Clem killed Beatrice?" Carolyn asked.

"Who else *was* there?" he asked, his old rheumy eyes wide.

"There was someone else," Diana said quietly from the couch.

All eyes turned to look at her.

"There was someone else involved that night," she said, "and there was someone else in this room today. Clem's spirit, while it is terrifying and dangerous, is not the one we must fear. The force that controls this room, the one that has killed so many over so many years, controls Clem. And it is far, far worse than any dumb brute with a pitchfork."

Nothing more was said for now. Douglas sensed that every one of them just wanted to get out of the room as quickly as possible. The bloody words on the wall had disappeared, but who knew what might happen next.

Gently Douglas bent down and lifted Diana into his arms. Then they returned one by one upstairs.

Chapter Twenty

As a girl, Paula had felt delight and excitement entering this house, not so different from the enthusiasm Zac and Callie were displaying now, as they ran through the marble foyer, calling out to each other in order to hear their echoes. But now, walking through that front door she felt as if she were entering a mausoleum. The place was cold and dead. The somber portraits on the walls represented a gallery of the dead: her great-grandfather Desmond, her grandfather Samuel, Aunt Margaret, Uncle Ernest, Uncle David. Grim faces all, and most of them murdered in that room downstairs.

Dean and Linda were embracing young Douglas. When it came her turn, Paula couldn't help but get emotional. "You look so much like your father," she said thickly, wrapping her arms around him. He hugged her tightly in return.

She remembered his face ten years ago, when he was just a boy, upon learning of his father's death. Now she pulled back and took his cheeks in her hands, staring into his blue eyes. "You know now?" she asked tenderly. "Uncle Howard has told you about the lottery?"

Douglas nodded.

Paula frowned. Innocence lasted such a short time in this family.

She looked over at Zac and Callie. Douglas seemed to be reading her mind.

"Maybe this year we can end it," he said. "Maybe they'll never have to know."

Paula couldn't reply.

"Maybe," Douglas said, "you and Karen will be able to have a child and never have to worry about the room downstairs."

"Karen left me," Paula said softly.

Douglas gripped her arm in support, just as Uncle Philip strode into the foyer.

"Well, we've been waiting for you all to arrive," he said with some impatience. "You said you'd be here by five, so we scheduled dinner for six. And here it is six-thirty. The food is on the table."

"Traffic was quite bad getting through Boston," Dean explained, reaching out his hand to shake his uncle's. "How are you, Uncle Philip?"

Philip didn't like looking at Dean. He reminded him too much of Martin. He took the hand of his brother's son but avoided direct eye contact. "I'm fine," he said hurriedly, "but hungry. So come along into the dining room. Hello, Linda; hello, Paula. Where is your . . . friend?"

"She's not here," Paula said.

Philip gave her an eye. Tradition called for spouses to be present, even if they weren't included in the lottery. Not that Philip considered Paula's friend, or whatever she wanted to call her, an actual spouse, but they had been careful not to mess with tradition ever since the last slaughter. Paula seemed to intuit what Philip was thinking.

"Don't worry," she said. "We've split up."

He nodded, heading toward the dining room. Of course, his own spouse was still AWOL. He'd called Vanessa three times in the last several hours, always getting her voice mail. He hadn't seen his wife in weeks. She'd been staying at their townhouse in the city, apparently still peeved about Melissa's presence. Philip figured she'd get over it. But Vanessa knew how important it was that she be at the reunion. Spouses always attended. She had promised to have her chauffeur drive her up this afternoon. Why wasn't she answering her goddamn phone?

"Heard from Mummy?" Ryan asked as Philip came into the dining room. Philip just shook his head and took his seat at the table.

"How wonderful to see you both!" Uncle Howard said, greeting Paula and Dean. Embraces were exchanged; then the old man turned to hug Linda. "And where are the youngest members of our family?"

Zac and Callie bounded into the dining room then, each letting out a loud whoop, startling Chelsea so much that she spilled her glass of red wine all over the white tablecloth. As a maid came to wipe up the mess, Ryan looked over at his sister, raised one eyebrow and deadpanned quietly, "Too bad children can't take part in the lottery." Chelsea giggled.

Carolyn, sitting across the table, heard the exchange. Something was up. Before Diana had left with Huldah, she'd taken Carolyn aside and told her to watch out for Philip and his two children. "They're schemers," Diana said. "They're planning something. I couldn't quite make it out. Philip is a major control freak, and he's strong enough to block out the particulars, even preventing me from getting a full read on his kids. But they've got something up their sleeves, and it concerns the lottery. So watch them."

Carolyn was. For three people possibly facing imminent death, they were surprisingly carefree. They had none of the frozen terror imprinted on their faces that was so obvious on these latest arrivals. Carolyn stood to greet Paula and Dean Young.

"I take it you're our savior," Dean said as he shook her hand.

"I am doing all I can," she said. "But time is running out."

"Oh, you have five whole days," Dean joked. "God created the world in less."

Carolyn smiled tightly as she turned to shake Paula's hand.

"Has he told you about Dr. Fifer?" Paula asked quietly.

Carolyn's ears perked up. "Dr. Fifer? What do you know about Dr. Fifer?"

"Let's talk after dinner, shall we?" Paula said. Carolyn agreed readily.

Paula took a seat next to Ryan. He was already eating his salad.

"Oh, I'm sorry," he said. "I'm being piggish, aren't I? Good manners insist one waits until everyone is seated."

Paula smiled. "No, go ahead, Ryan. We were late."

He forked another bunch of endive into his mouth. "So how are you, cousin Paula?" he asked as he chewed.

"The same as you, I imagine."

He made a face of genuine confusion. "The same as me?"

"Terrified," she said. "Uncle Howard said he told you about the lottery."

"Oh, yes. Of course." He took another bite of his salad. "Terrified. It's quite unnerving, isn't it?"

Across the table, Douglas took a seat beside Carolyn. Under the table, he took her hand in his. "Has Diana called you?" he whispered.

Carolyn nodded. "She thinks she's found something. She's having it sent special delivery. It should be here in the morning."

The outcome of their little séance in the basement had led Diana to conclude that there would be no reasoning with whatever forces controlled the room. It was blind rage that ruled down there. So given how close they were to the lottery, the best offense was going to have to be an effective defense. They had to focus their energies on survival, not defeat. As it stood, it was likely the lottery would still be held. But whoever went into that room would go in with something no one else had ever possessed.

Protection.

Diana might not know how to remove curses placed by "run-of-the-mill" ghosts, but she knew how to render those ghosts powerless. "There are certain amulets that can protect the wearer from any kind of supernatural force," Diana explained.

"They were created by witches centuries ago to ward off everything from demons to dead people. I have used them myself in the past and believe I know where to find one."

And she had. An acquaintance of hers ran a voodoo store in New Orleans, and she possessed an amulet of rare power. Only for Diana would she part with it, with the promise that it be returned. Diana had just received it, inspected it, pronounced it genuine, and was shipping it up to Youngsport for delivery tomorrow.

But in the meantime, Carolyn thought, *I still want to piece together what really happened that night.* Only by knowing the full truth, she believed, would they finally be able to end the control of the family by those terrible spirits. Her eyes flicked over to Paula. Perhaps her news about Dr. Fifer might help. Carolyn believed that alone among all those who had tried to end the curse, Fifer had obtained critical information—information now lost, since his report had vanished from the records.

"Let us begin our meal," Uncle Howard said, taking his place at the head of the table. "We are still waiting on Vanessa, but—"

Just then the deep sound of the doorbell reverberated through the house. A servant rushed to answer the door.

"She always did like to be fashionably late," Philip quipped, to scattered laughter at the table.

But when the servant returned he simply bore an envelope that he handed to Philip. "What is this?" Philip asked, irritated. Tearing open the envelope, he read the letter inside. Then he laughed, bitterly.

"Well, Vanessa won't be joining us," he announced. "I've just been served with divorce papers."

"Oh, Mummy," Ryan said disapprovingly.

"Does she get the town house in New York then?" Chelsea asked, obviously trying to figure out if this would affect her comings and goings in any way.

"I'm very sorry, Uncle Philip," Dean offered.

"Sorry?" Philip tossed the letter to the table. "Don't be. I'm not. But I'll tell you, if that woman thinks she's taking me for—"

He stopped, a smile crossing his face.

"Please, everyone. Eat." He stabbed his fork into his endive. "Heckuva way to get out of the family reunion, isn't it?"

"Will it affect things in any way?" Paula asked. Zac and Callie had been allowed to take their meal out on the terrace. The adults could talk about the lottery freely.

Uncle Howard sighed. "Who knows? If a relationship has ended, then I suppose we can't expect the person to join us." He smiled kindly, reaching over and placing his hand on top of Paula's. She smiled sadly in reply.

"As I was saying," the old man continued, "let us enjoy our meal. For tonight, let us simply be glad to be in each other's company. We have reason to be very optimistic this year. Carolyn has made wonderful progress and may have found a solution. A temporary one, but effective nonetheless."

They all looked at her to explain. She told them about the amulet.

"But we don't know for sure that it will work," Philip said.

Carolyn conceded the point. "But Diana has

worn similar amulets, and they have protected her from various supernatural phenomena."

"But it's never been tried on this particular supernatural phenomenon," he countered.

"No," Carolyn admitted. "It has not."

Philip sat back in his chair, as if his point had been made.

"If it's all we've got, I'll take it," Dean said. "No one else who has gone into that room has ever gone in with any kind of protection."

"It's something," Paula agreed. "At least it's something."

"Exactly," Uncle Howard said. "It is something."

"I hope to be able to find out more in the next few days," Carolyn said. "I'm rereading all the notes, and I'm researching the lives of Clem and Beatrice in the town hall archives. If I can find out more about them, about what really happened that night, I believe that we could possibly end this nightmare forever."

"Impossible," Uncle Howard barked. "There is nothing to be found about either of them at the town hall. Others have looked. There is nothing. Our best bet is to simply let history lie, and to use this amulet from now on for our protection. Carolyn, if it works, you tell Diana that I am willing to pay any amount of money—a *fortune*!—to purchase that amulet and keep it in our family forever."

"But how much better if we could actually *end* the curse," Paula said to him. "To actually remove the evil forces that control that room."

Uncle Howard said nothing.

"There is one force there in particular," Carolyn said. "One force that Diana identified as the strongest. It is that force that controls everything. Clem does its bidding."

"And Beatrice?" asked Dean.

Carolyn shrugged. "I still don't fully understand her role in all of this, even though it was clearly her death that set it all into motion."

"But it all must have something to do with the baby," Dean said.

Uncle Howard groaned. "I fail to see how all this talk can help us. We have the amulet. It is the protection we have sought for so long."

Dean had removed a piece of paper from his inside jacket pocket. He unfolded it and handed it over to Carolyn. "You see?" he asked, ignoring his uncle's complaint. "It's a photograph I took years ago of that room."

As Carolyn took the paper, Howard Young's face burned a deep red. "How did you get in there to take such a picture?"

"Uncle Howard," Paula said, "relax. It was a childish prank. We found the keys. We were kids. We had no idea how dangerous it was."

The old man covered his face with his gnarled hands and trembled.

Carolyn was looking at the image. "It's the face of a baby," she said.

"What does the baby have to do with all this?" Dean asked.

Carolyn shuddered, then passed the photo to Douglas. "It was Beatrice's baby. We don't know what happened to it."

"Well, its spirit is in that room," Dean said.

"Yes," Carolyn agreed. "Whatever happened that night, the baby lost a mother. And whatever force exists in that room apparently prevents the baby's spirit from resting as well."

"Who *is* the controlling force?" Douglas asked, passing the photo around the table. "Who could be powerful enough and evil enough to keep these deaths going on for eighty years?"

"Was the baby killed?" Chelsea asked, showing interest in the subject for the first time.

"Who was its father? That's what I'd like to know," Paula said.

"Enough," Uncle Howard said in a raspy voice, refusing to look at the image when it was passed to him. "Tonight we will have no more such talk at this table." He snapped his fingers, and the servants emerged from the kitchen to clear away their salad plates. The main course was served. A huge roast duck. Discussion faded away, and the family ate in relative silence. Every once in a while, Douglas grabbed Carolyn's hand under the table.

When they were finished, they all retired to the parlor for coffee. The others made small talk among themselves, but Paula took a seat beside Uncle Howard. Above them hung a pair of old rifles, still as shiny as the day they were made.

"They were my father's," Uncle Howard said. "He carried them in the First World War. They saved his life many times. That's why I keep them in such good condition." His eyes twinkled. "And loaded."

"Would that we had such weapons to save our own lives," Paula said.

The old man nodded.

"Uncle Howard, I need to ask you about Dr. Fifer."

"I said no more for tonight," the old man said wearily.

"Please, Uncle Howard. I won't be able to sleep tonight if we don't talk."

He made a face. "Why do you bring up Fifer's name?"

"He was the one who was here investigating when you first told me about the room and the lottery. I remember he was a very nice man. Rather eccentric, but nice."

"One of those professor types," Uncle Howard said, raising his coffee cup to his lips, holding the saucer below with shaky hands.

"He asked many questions of all of us," Paula said.

Uncle Howard's eyes were far away. "Yes, indeed, he did."

"And then, right at the end, he said he'd found out something," Paula said. "I remember that so clearly. He said he'd found out something, and that gave me hope. Hope that maybe we wouldn't have to go through with the lottery after all."

Uncle Howard seemed uncomfortable with the conversation. "Well, obviously, whatever he found out didn't amount to anything. Because the lottery still took place. It was the year your father died in that room."

Paula nodded. "That's why I always wondered what Dr. Fifer had found out. He never told us."

"Who knows?" Uncle Howard said. "It was clearly nothing important."

"Why did you fire him before the lottery had even taken place?"

The old man's hands were shaking almost uncontrollably now. He had to set his cup and saucer down on the table beside him.

"Because he upset Jeanette. I couldn't have that."

"But he got a response from her," Paula said. "For the first time in twenty years. That means he was on to something."

"He was not!" Uncle Howard was angry now. "Please, dear, let me be. This all takes so much out of me."

"Of course, Uncle Howard," Paula said. "I'm sorry."

She stood. She noticed that just a couple of feet away, Carolyn and Douglas were watching her. She walked over to join them.

"Did you hear?" she asked.

Carolyn nodded. "Fifer actually said he'd found something important?"

"Yes," Paula said. "Then suddenly he was gone. If only we could find him now . . ."

"He's dead," Carolyn said. "I found an obituary for him online. I wanted to speak to him, too, but it was too late. So I've been looking for his survivors. He left a son and two daughters. But so far, I've been unsuccessful."

"Do you think he may have left notes?" Douglas asked. "Notes that might reveal what he thought was so important?"

"That's what I'm hoping," Carolyn said. "Because any notes he took are not among the papers that Mr. Young has kept. There are notes from every other investigator who has worked on the case, but not Fifer. He's the only one."

Paula glanced back at the old man sitting in the

chair. "He's hiding something, isn't he?" she asked. "He destroyed Fifer's notes."

"Why would he do that?" Douglas asked, still not wanting to believe anything negative of Uncle Howie.

"I think if we knew the answer to that," Carolyn said, "we'd know how to end the curse of that room."

The three of them looked over at the old man in his chair, the flickering light of the fire making strange patterns across his face.

Chapter Twenty-one

Carolyn knew she wasn't alone the moment she turned off the light.

The terror had returned. Since leaving New York, she'd managed to push David Cooke out of her mind, concentrating instead on horrors of a different sort. But now, lying awake in her bed, she had the uncanny sense that he was outside, looking up at her window, much the way he had been in New York.

That's absurd, she told herself. *There is no way David knows where I am.* She had told no one. Not Sid, not Andrea, not anyone she'd worked with. Only the police, and then only one detective she trusted completely. No one knew where she was going when she took off on the plane.

What if he found the pilot and forced him to tell?

What if he broke into Diana's apartment and forced her or Huldah to tell?

Carolyn sat up and switched on the light. Now she was really acting crazy. The pilot of Mr. Young's private plane lived here in Youngsport. There was no way David could find him. And she had spoken with Diana on the phone just a few hours ago, and Diana was fine. There simply wasn't enough time for David to learn Carolyn's whereabouts from her and then make it all the way up here to Maine.

Still, she had to give in to her curiosity. Switching off the light again, she stepped over to the window and pulled back the curtains. She saw no one standing below in the moonlight. She breathed a sigh of relief.

But that sigh became a gasp as she turned around and looked back across her room.

Beatrice stood there. The moonlight reflected against her long white dress.

"Why have you come to me?" Carolyn whispered.

Never before had Beatrice appeared to someone outside the Young family. If she was appearing to Carolyn now, it was because she wanted to tell her something.

"I want to help you," Carolyn whispered, "and I think you want to help me. You want to help all of us, don't you?"

Beatrice lifted her right arm from her side and pointed a finger at Carolyn.

"What is it?" Carolyn asked. "What are you trying to say?"

The apparition took a step forward, her finger pointing directly at Carolyn's face.

"What? I don't understand."

She gently wagged her finger.

"Me. You're indicating me. What about me? What are you saying about me?"

A book suddenly fell from a shelf. It slammed

hard upon the floor, startling Carolyn. She stooped down to retrieve it, and in that fleeting second, Beatrice disappeared.

"Wait!" Carolyn called. "I don't understand your meaning."

But it was no use. Beatrice was gone.

Carolyn lifted the book from the floor. It was a family photo album, and it had opened to one page. Carolyn looked down. It was a photograph of Jeanette Young, probably shortly before she was chosen in the lottery to enter the room. She looked so young and so full of life, a far cry from the pale, shrunken woman Carolyn had met.

"Why did you show me Jeanette?" Carolyn asked out loud. "And why did you point at me?"

She sat there for nearly an hour on the edge of her bed, looking at Jeanette's photo, hoping Beatrice would return, trying to make sense of her message. But all that happened was that Carolyn grew tired. Very, very tired.

Finally she replaced the photo album on the shelf and crawled back into bed. Sleep was forcing itself upon her, even though her mind still struggled with the riddle of Beatrice's appearance. What was she trying to tell her? And did it have anything to do with the feelings of terror Carolyn had experienced, the absurd conviction that David Cooke stood outside, looking up at her window?

Before she knew it, she was dreaming. She was in the room downstairs, the door was locked, and there was someone else in there with her. She didn't need to see him to know it was David Cooke. She could hear his breathing. He was coming at her. She banged on the door, screaming for help.

"You don't have to fear," came a voice.

A woman's voice.

Carolyn knew it was Beatrice.

She turned around. David stood behind her, his eyes blazing.

"Love," Carolyn said.

"Love," came Beatrice's voice.

Carolyn woke up then. It was morning. She had no idea what the dream had meant, and still had no clue what the visitation the night before indicated. She showered and dressed, and headed downstairs for breakfast. Pouring herself a cup of coffee, she took a seat at the table. Already there were Paula and Chelsea. Seeing them gave Carolyn the answer. She understood then what Beatrice had been trying to tell her.

"She won't let him kill a woman," Carolyn said out loud.

Paula and Chelsea turned to look at her.

"Beatrice appeared to me last night," Carolyn told them. "I believe she was trying to tell us that she will do what she can to protect us. She's probably been trying all along, but she was only successful once before. With Jeanette."

"Well, that's crazy," Chelsea said. "Because the way Jeanette came out of that room, I wouldn't say she was protected very well."

"But still," Carolyn said. "Jeanette didn't die."

Paula set down her coffee and looked over at her gravely. "Then further discussion is pointless. Let's just forget the lottery. I volunteer to spend the night myself."

"I'm not sure we can do that," Carolyn said.

"If a woman has a better chance of survival than a man, then I volunteer."

Carolyn looked from Paula over to Chelsea, who blanched.

"No," Carolyn said. "I think we'd risk another slaughter if we don't follow the way the lottery has always been done."

"Who set these rules?" Paula wanted to know. "All these years, we've been like sheep. Herded along, never asking why."

"You're right, Paula," Carolyn agreed. "And it's time we started asking why."

Paula smiled wryly. "And do you think Beatrice is going to tell you?"

"I think she's trying to. I think last night she was trying to give me a clue. About why this all happened. How it all began."

"And what did the clue tell you?" Chelsea asked.

"I think it all goes back to the love of a woman," Carolyn said. "All of this is about a woman's love." She paused. "Beatrice's love."

"Her love for whom?" Paula asked.

"I'm not sure." Carolyn looked at each of them. "But that's precisely what I have to find out."

Chapter Twenty-two

Douglas watched as Carolyn flipped open her laptop and hit the power button. A deep bong inside the machine resonated. They were sitting in the study as rain cascaded against the walls of the house, great sweeping sheets of it. The sun hadn't appeared all day, hidden by a scrim of dark gray haze.

"It struck me last night that none of the previous investigators would have had access to these particular records," Carolyn said as she inserted an Internet-connecting device into the back of her laptop. For all its elegance, Uncle Howie's house had no wireless connection.

"What records do you mean?" Douglas asked, taking a seat beside Carolyn at the long oaken table, peering around to look at her computer screen.

"The United States census of 1930," she told him. "The government releases census records every seventy-two years. The last time the lottery was held, these records weren't yet available."

She was tapping furiously on her keypad. Douglas watched with a keen interest as she accessed a site, then typed in her password. A search screen appeared.

"So," she said, "we simply check for Desmond Young in Youngsport, Maine."

She keyed in the particulars.

"And voilà!" she cried. "There they are!"

On the screen was a digitized image of a census page, consisting of a list of handwritten names in the left column, each followed by various particulars: age, place of birth, occupation, whether married or single, whether they owned a radio. . . .

Carolyn zoomed in so they could easily read the entry for the Youngs.

"Okay, here we can see exactly who was living in this house in 1930," she said as Douglas read along.

Outside the rain and wind continued to pound the house as Carolyn catalogued the Young family of eighty years earlier.

"Head of household, Desmond Young," she read. "He was fifty years old, and his occupation was listed as 'financier.' And after this is his wife Hannah, age forty-six."

"Look at all those children they had," Douglas observed.

They fell quiet. Douglas was quite sure Carolyn was thinking the same thing he was. That most of those children would be dead that same year, taken in the first of the family slaughters.

"Douglas Young," Carolyn read, pointing to a name on the screen.

Douglas swallowed hard. "That's my great-grandfather," he said. "The first of the Douglas Youngs to die in that room."

He saw that he was listed with his wife and four children: Francis, David, Douglas, and Cynthia. The younger Douglas was this generation Douglas's grandfather. He was two years old at the time of this census. Fifty years later, he, too, would die in that room.

Carolyn was reading the names of the rest of Desmond Young's children. "Samuel, Margaret, Howard . . ." She paused. "There's your Uncle Howie right there. A strapping lad of eighteen years old, before tragedy struck."

Douglas nodded.

"And finally there were the children, Jacob and Timothy." Carolyn sighed. "A few months after this was taken, this family would be practically wiped out."

"But what are the rest of the names?" Douglas asked.

Carolyn smiled. "That's the real reason I wanted to see this record. Who else was living in this house in 1930?"

They both peered in at the screen to make out the names.

"Look!" Douglas shouted. "Clement Rittenhouse! That must be Clem!"

"Yes," Carolyn said excitedly. " 'Age: twenty-nine. Occupation: gardener.' And look. It says here he couldn't read or write."

"So he *was* just a dumb old brute," Douglas said. "Probably easily manipulated."

"And look!" Carolyn exclaimed. "Beatrice! It's Beatrice! Her last name was Swan!"

"Beatrice Swan," Douglas said.

" 'Age: nineteen,' " Carolyn said, her voice becoming sad. "She was so young. 'Occupation: servant.' She was single, born in Maine. And unlike Clem, she was literate."

"There's no baby listed with her," Douglas observed.

Carolyn shook her head. "No. The child wouldn't have been born yet. The census was taken in April. Harry Noons said that Beatrice didn't have her baby until the late spring. But she would certainly have been pregnant at the time this was taken."

With her cursor she hit a link to take them to the next page of the census. After it had loaded, she said, "Damn."

"What?" Douglas asked.

"That's it. That's the entire list of the household. There was no one else living here."

"Who were you hoping to find?" he asked.

Carolyn sighed. "Whoever else may have been involved in the events of that night. Remember that Diana picked up on another presence—and she said that presence was the force that really controlled the room. It's not Clem, and it's not Beatrice. I was hoping to find a name of someone else living in the house at that time."

"So who could this other force be?"

Carolyn stood, pacing a little bit. "It could be anyone. A day servant perhaps. Remember Harry Noons worked on the estate, but unlike Beatrice and Clem, he didn't live here. Surely there were others like him, any one of whom might have been involved in what happened that night, and be the force that still holds this family in its power."

"What makes you think it's a servant?"

"I don't think that necessarily," Carolyn explained. "It's just one possibility. It could be anyone. Someone who lived in the village." A thought occurred to her. "It could be the father of Beatrice's baby, whoever he was."

"Yeah," Douglas said. "If only we knew who he was."

Carolyn's eyes were sparkling. "Get your bike. We're going into town."

Douglas stood. "Sure, but why? Where are we going?"

"Back to the town clerk's office."

Douglas made a face. "We've been there before. There's no record of Beatrice's death."

"I'm not looking for a death record this time," said Carolyn. "Last time, we didn't know Beatrice's last name. We could only look up records by date. Now that we know her name was Swan, we can look up some birth records."

Douglas was nodding. "Beatrice's birth record . . ."

Carolyn smiled. "And more importantly, her baby's . . ."

In moments they were flying down the hill on Douglas's bike, both of them wrapped in rubber raincoats. Despite the whipping rain and the chill wind, their spirits were high. And Douglas couldn't deny how much he liked the feeling of Carolyn's arms wrapped around him, her face resting against his shoulder. Suddenly he was filled with the urge just to keep driving, bypass the village, just get on the highway and head to Canada. Surely the forces that had ruled his family for eight decades wouldn't follow them over the border. He laughed to himself at the absurdity of it all and turned the bike into the parking lot of the town hall.

Inside, peeling off their wet raincoats, Douglas realized they didn't have a lot of time. It was nearly four o'clock, and the clerk's office closed at four-thirty. "Clock's ticking," he said.

Carolyn looked at him. "I'm all too aware of that," she said.

He knew what she meant. It wasn't just today's clock that worried her. The lottery would be held in two days. Time was running out.

The clerk brought them a large ledger with the word BIRTHS imprinted in gold on the spine. On the top she had placed a computer printout. Consisting of several stapled pages, it was a list of names. The top sheet had names all beginning with A.

"This helps a great deal," the clerk told them, tapping the printout. "The original records weren't indexed. But this was done not so long ago to help you more quickly get to the record you need."

"Thank you," Carolyn said, eagerly flipping through the list to the page containing the S names. "Here she is," she said within seconds. "Beatrice Swan, born 1911, page 383."

Douglas opened the heavy volume and turned to the correct page. There, in faded handwriting, was the entry marking Beatrice's entrance into this world. Her father was Horace Swan, a farmer. Her mother was the former Jeanne Trudeau, born in Quebec. It seemed terribly odd staring down at the sheet of paper that bore witness to Beatrice's life, when they knew her only as an anguished spirit, roaming the estate, trapped in eternal grief.

But here she was a flesh-and-blood baby, some-body's daughter. Douglas remembered seeing her that day on the cliffs, and his heart broke.

Carolyn told him to write down the information as she flipped through the printout. "Now, we need to find a Swan birth in the year 1930," she said. She flipped ahead a few pages. "Yes! Oh, thank God, yes! It's here! Baby Swan, born May twentieth, 1930, page 785." She looked over at Douglas. "It's marked 'illegitimate.' "

"Will it tell us the father's name?" he asked as he began turning the pages in the old dusty volume.

"Let's pray," Carolyn said.

But there was no page 785.

"That can't be," Douglas said. "Wait a minute." He turned back a page. "Page 783, with 784 on the back." He gulped. "Then it's page 787, with 788 on the back."

"Look," Carolyn said, her voice betraying her disappointment. "You can see there once was a page here, but it's been torn out."

Indeed, in the gutter of the book, there was a faint remnant of a torn page.

"Who tore it out?" Douglas asked. "And why?"

Carolyn made a face. "We might not be able to answer those questions just yet, but we can maybe find out *when*."

She rang the little bell on the counter, and the clerk came back out from her office.

"I'm sorry to disturb you," Carolyn said, "but I have a question. When was this computerized index compiled?"

"I think it was 1990," she said. "I can look for the exact date if that would help."

"It would," Carolyn said. "Tremendously."

The clerk flipped open a ledger she kept behind the counter. "Yes, it was done in the summer of 1990. It was the first year birth records were opened for general research. Now, I don't like to pry, but why does that fact matter?"

"Oh, I just wanted to see whether previous researchers had access to this material," Carolyn explained.

The clerk smiled. She had white hair and blue cat's-eye glasses. "I'm a genealogist myself," she said. "I've traced my family all the way back to the Mayflower, and then for at least eleven generations in England."

"Terrific," Carolyn said.

"What family name are you researching?" the clerk asked.

"My family," Douglas said. "The Youngs."

"Oh!" The clerk's face lit up. "Such an illustrious history! I remember Howard Young himself coming in here at one point to research the family."

Carolyn and Douglas exchanged looks. "Did he now?" Carolyn asked.

"Yes, indeed. In fact, it was about the time that index was prepared. I remember him using it. He was very grateful for it, said it facilitated his research so much."

"I'm sure it did," Carolyn said.

They thanked the clerk and headed back out into the corridor of the town hall.

"What does it mean?" Douglas asked.

"I think I know now what Dr. Fifer found," Carolyn said.

Douglas didn't understand. "Dr. Fifer? What's he got to do with this?"

"Until 1990, no other researcher would have been able to find Beatrice's baby because the records weren't open. But in the summer of that year they were opened and an index was made—just at the point Dr. Fifer was doing his research. So he found the birth record! I think that was what he was so excited about."

"So what happened to the birth record after that?"

Carolyn smiled. "Don't you see? Your uncle fired Dr. Fifer, destroyed his notes, then went to the town hall and tore out the birth record himself."

Douglas didn't want to believe it. "Why would Uncle Howie do such a thing?"

"I don't know why." Carolyn admitted.

"I mean, he wants this curse to end. He would do *anything* to end it. He's spent millions of dollars trying to end it." His voice cracked. "He wouldn't do anything that might keep that room's power alive."

"For now, let's give him the benefit of the doubt," Carolyn said. "Maybe he tore out the record for a good reason."

Douglas shook his head. "What do we do know?"

Carolyn sighed. "I wish I knew. We're at a dead end. I had hoped to find some information, some clue, that might give us an upper hand in dealing with the force in that room. But we found nothing."

She reached into her pocket and withdrew the small amethyst on the gold chain that Diana had sent her.

"For now, this is our only hope," she said.

She started to cry. Douglas wrapped his arms around her.

"I love you, Carolyn," he whispered in her ear.

And he meant it. Never before had he meant anything as much.

Chapter Twenty-three

They gathered in the parlor, as always. A fire was blazing, as always. And according to those who'd been part of the lottery before, the thunderstorm that was raging outside was a part of the tradition as well. "Always," said Philip Young as he carefully wrote the names of the family on slips of paper and dropped them into a wooden box. "There's always been thunder and lightning whenever the lottery has been held."

Carolyn's heart was in her throat. She had failed. Failed utterly. The family had assembled; the lottery was taking place. Despite all her efforts, someone would spend the night in that room. Mr. Young wasn't blaming her. In fact, when they spoke about an hour earlier, he had seemed optimistic, grateful even, that Carolyn had discovered the amulet that Diana had promised would protect them. Carolyn wanted to believe in its power, but the memory of Kip's failure ten years ago remained in her mind.

He, too, had thought it was safe. But he had been proven terribly wrong. So Carolyn clutched the amulet tightly in her hands, hoping for the best, wanting to believe. She was prepared to slip it around the neck of whomever's name was drawn. And though she knew it wasn't right, she was praying that the name drawn from the box would be anyone but Douglas.

Carolyn's eyes glanced around the room as the family members filed in. *I can't think this way,* she said, feeling terribly guilty as Dean Young entered with his wife. *He has two little children asleep upstairs. How can I hope it will be him, or anyone else, instead of Douglas?*

But she did.

She couldn't deny that part of her would exult, would shout a private, inward cheer, if the name drawn was not that of the man she loved.

She'd been unable to reply to Douglas's declaration that he loved her that day at the town hall. She'd simply been unable to form the words. The pain and trauma left over from David was still too real and too fresh. But it was more than that, Carolyn thought. *How can I tell him I love him if I might lose him?*

But that was all the more reason to express how she felt.

The next into the room was Chelsea, her face calm, her body language poised and graceful. *How can she not be terrified?* Carolyn wondered. Her brother, Ryan, too, sauntering in now, winking at his sister. *Are they really so stoic?* The two of them took a seat near the fire, not far from their father, who held the box of names.

Then in hobbled old Mr. Young, helped along by Paula. His face was a mask of pain, his old features twisted like the bark of a knotty tree.

Finally came Douglas. His eyes met Carolyn's as soon as he walked into the room. She felt as if she might cry again. She averted her eyes in time.

"All right," Mr. Young said, his voice frail and week. "Once more we gather for our terrible duty."

He stood, visibly trembling, addressing them all. A flash of lightning suddenly lit up the room, followed by a deep reverberation of thunder.

"Eighty years ago I stood here among a different group of people. Your grandfathers and great-grandfathers. My father stood in the place I now occupy, a position not of honor but of terrible obligation. Every ten years since we have gathered. We have submitted to this horrible family legacy, one we do not understand."

Carolyn could see Philip, standing behind Mr. Young holding the box of names. He sighed, as if impatient. Impatient from annoyance, Carolyn thought, not impatient from fear. As if all of this was one big nuisance, not a matter of life or death.

Watch him, Diana had said.

"This year we have hope," Mr. Young was saying. "Carolyn holds in her hands an object which may mean our salvation. We are grateful to her for locating it."

She tried to smile, but was unable to do so.

"But as she is quick to say, we have no proof that what she holds will protect us. We have had hope before, only to find we hoped in vain. For now, however, let us believe that whoever goes in that room tonight will emerge in the morning alive and well."

Carolyn looked over at Ryan. He had closed his eyes. Out of fear . . . or boredom?

"And so, let us commence the lottery," Mr. Young proclaimed. With difficulty he turned and gestured to Philip to approach with the box. Carolyn noticed Linda take Dean's hand. She understood exactly how Linda felt.

"Nine times this lottery has been held," Mr. Young said, reaching his hand into the box. "Nine times I have been spared. Let it be my name I select this time. My name. I am done with my life. Please let it be my name."

He withdrew his hand.

Carolyn braced.

Her eyes moved over to Douglas. He smiled at her, and mouthed the words again that he had said that day: *I love you.*

"Oh, no," Mr. Young was saying as he looked down at the piece of paper in his hand.

"Who is it?" Linda called out, her eyes wide with terror as she gripped her husband's hand.

The old man looked up, and his gaze told Carolyn what she feared most had come true.

He was looking at Douglas.

"I am so sorry, my little hoodlum." And he began to cry.

"It's okay, Uncle Howie," Douglas said, walking over to him and embracing him. "It's okay."

Paula was sobbing. Linda brought Dean's hand to her lips and kissed it.

Carolyn couldn't move.

No.

A voice inside her was saying it was wrong.

No, it's not Douglas.

She saw Ryan and Chelsea exchange a small smile.

He rigged the lottery.

It was Diana's voice.

Philip rigged the lottery!

Carolyn's eyes darted over to Philip, who was moving toward the fireplace with the box.

Don't let him dispose of the names.

Carolyn bolted. "Stop!"

Everyone in the room looked at her.

"Don't turn that box over into the fire!" she commanded Philip.

"What are you talking about?" he barked.

"I want to see the names!"

Philip's face tightened. "Absolutely not. That is not part of the tradition. Ever since Aunt Margaret began writing the names, the slips of paper were always burned immediately after the lottery took place. We cannot depart from what has always been done."

"Give me that box," Carolyn ordered.

"You are not a family member," Philip said, and he began to tip the box over the flames.

"No, she isn't," said Paula. "But I am."

She had darted over to the fireplace just in time to snatch the box from Philip's hands.

"How dare you?" he shouted. "Give me that box!"

"Philip!"

The voice was Howard Young's. The old man's eyes were black with fury. His face was red, every vein in his neck and forehead pulsing.

"Stand aside, Philip," Mr. Young said. "Paula, bring me the box."

She obeyed.

Carolyn saw Ryan and Chelsea take a few steps toward the back of the room. Philip's face was bright red as he watched the proceedings in mute horror.

Paula handed the box to Mr. Young. With his trembling hands he lifted the lid, slipping his long, gnarled fingers inside. He removed each slip of paper and read the name that was on it.

"Dean," the old man's voice intoned. He removed another slip. "Paula." And another slip. "Douglas."

There was a gasp. Douglas's name had already been drawn. There shouldn't have been another slip in the box with his name.

"Howard," the old man read. His lips curled as he read the two final names. "Douglas." He paused. "And Douglas."

He spun around to confront Philip. Carolyn was stunned that he could move so fast.

"Four times Douglas's name was entered in that box! *Four times*!"

"Uncle Howard," Philip said, his hands imploring.

"And not one slip with the name of Philip!" His eyes were blazing. He spun now to point a crooked finger at the two young people cowering in a far corner of the room. "And neither was there any slip bearing the name of Chelsea or Ryan!"

Thunder boomed from above the house, as if the point needed any emphasis.

"How dare you!" Mr. Young growled.

"Uncle Howard, please . . ." Philip said.

"How many years has this been going on?" Paula pushed forward, only a few inches from Philip's face. "How many years?" Her face contorted in grief and anger. "My father died in that room! Your *brother*, Uncle Philip!"

"I haven't," he stammered. "This is the first time—"

"Liar!" Howard Young snarled. "You are a *liar*, Philip!"

Chelsea was sobbing in the back of the room.

"If I had my way," Mr. Young said, "I'd send you into that room right now, Philip." He turned away from his nephew, as if he couldn't bear to look at him. Paula left Philip's side and helped the old man sit in his chair. "But I don't have my way," Howard Young said. "I only have the way that has been passed down to us for eighty terrible years."

He let out a long sigh. "The lottery needs to take place again."

He closed his eyes as if he wanted to die right there. Then, with apparent effort, he forced his eyes open again. "Dean," he asked, "will you draw up a new list of names?"

"No!" Chelsea cried, crumpling to her knees. Ryan stood beside her, his face white with shock and horror.

"Write the name of every Young in this room," the old man instructed. "And write it only once."

Philip sat down in front of the fire, his face in his hands.

Carolyn hurried to Douglas's side.

"I knew it wasn't you," she said, no longer worried if the family discovered their relationship. "I knew it wasn't supposed to be you."

He smiled wanly. "Oh, but I think it *is* supposed to be me. Every Douglas Young before me has been called into that room."

She took his hand in hers.

Dean was writing the names. "Hurry along, Dean," Howard Young commanded. "It is nearly midnight."

The old man was once again presented the box. He took a deep breath and inserted his hand.

Carolyn squeezed Douglas's hand.

Howard Young looked at the name on the piece of paper he had drawn. "It makes no difference," he said, almost offhandedly. "Philip's perfidy was still an act of cowardice and betrayal, one that none of us will ever forget or forgive."

He handed the paper to Dean, who looked down at it with shock.

"I'm sorry," he said, looking over at Douglas.

"You see?" Douglas tried to smile. "I told you it was meant to be me."

In the back of the room, Chelsea's sobs suddenly ceased. Dean returned to his wife, who embraced him. Paula walked over to the window, softly crying. Philip remained on the hearth, his face still in his hands. And Howard Young simply sat in his chair, his face like stone, staring at Douglas.

"Carolyn," the old man said.

She felt like stone herself. She couldn't move.

"Place the amulet around Douglas's neck," Howard Young instructed. "Then it is time for us to take him downstairs."

Chapter Twenty-four

The amethyst sparkled as it hung around Douglas's neck. He looked down at it, fingering it carefully. Then he looked back into Carolyn's eyes.

"We've just got to believe," he told her.

He had asked his uncle for a moment alone with Carolyn. No questions were asked. Everyone seemed to grasp the truth of their relationship. Everyone had filed out of the parlor, led by the humiliated Philip. Uncle Howie had closed the double doors behind him, but not before cautioning, "We don't have much time."

Thunder crashed overhead as Douglas took Carolyn in his arms and kissed her.

"The amulet will protect me," he whispered in her ear. "Diana said it had great power."

She nodded against his chest. It was as if she couldn't raise her eyes to look at him.

"But whatever happens," Douglas added, "you have got to always believe you did everything you could."

She finally lifted her beautiful green eyes to his.

"I wish it had been anyone but you," she admitted. "I wish it had been Philip."

Douglas shook his head. "It was supposed to be me. Ever since Uncle Howie told me about the room and the lottery, I felt it was going to be me. My father went into that room. My grandfather. My great-grandfather."

Carolyn clutched at his shirt, pressing her face against his chest once more. The amulet brushed against her. She kissed it for luck.

Douglas's mind raced back in time, to the day ten years ago when his father stood in this room, no doubt holding his mother much as Douglas held Carolyn now. Douglas had been sound asleep upstairs, unaware of the drama that was taking place beneath him. Mom surely clutched at Dad's shirt the way Carolyn was doing. She would never be the same after Dad's death. She had loved him that much.

"I need to know," Douglas said, kissing the top of Carolyn's head. "Do you love me? Do you love me the way I love you?"

Carolyn once again lifted her face to look him in the eyes.

"Yes," she said. "Yes, Douglas, I love you."

They kissed, just as Uncle Howie rapped on the door.

"It's time," the old man said, peering inside.

"Yes, okay," Douglas replied.

"I love you," Carolyn said again. She wouldn't move. She just stood there clinging to Douglas.

"I need to go," he whispered gently.

"I love you," she said again, as if only now realizing it fully. "I love you! And you love me!"

He gently caressed her cheek with his hand.

Carolyn's eyes lit up. "That's it! That's what she was trying to tell me!"

"Beatrice? Trying to tell you what?"

Uncle Howie stood in the doorway. "We must hurry," he said.

Carolyn was in a state of agitation. "Love! That's what it was all about for Beatrice! Remember when Kip recorded her. . . . She was saying 'love' over and over again. That's why she didn't let Jeanette die! Because she understands a woman's love! And Jeanette loved Michael!"

Howard Young stood in the doorway, his face hard. "You make no sense, Carolyn. All I know is that it's time. If we delay, we risk far worse."

"Listen to me!" Carolyn cried, tugging even more aggressively at Douglas's shirt. "What will save you more than that amulet is the fact that we are in love! I believe now that Beatrice was a woman in love. Remember what Harry Noons said. She told Clem she wouldn't marry him because there was someone else. She's carried that love with her beyond the grave."

"This is nonsense!" Uncle Howie shouted. "Come along, Douglas! We must go downstairs now!"

"Yes," Carolyn said, releasing her grip on Douglas's shirt. "It's time that Douglas went into the room." She paused, looking from the old man back to Douglas. "And I am going in with him."

Chapter Twenty-five

"That is impossible!" Howard Young declared.

Carolyn eyed him fiercely. "There was never any instruction that forbade a non-family member from entering the room, was there?"

The old man struggled for words. "Nothing was ever written. My father had a dream in which he was told to inaugurate a lottery. It was the only way, he was told, to prevent a full-scale slaughter of the family. We would have to sacrifice one a decade so that the rest of us might live."

"You've never revealed that detail before," Douglas observed.

"What did it matter? All I've cared about is finding a way to end this curse."

"Who gave him the instruction?" Carolyn asked. "Who appeared to him in the dream?"

"He never told us."

"But whoever it was, there was no prohibition of a non-family member accompanying a family member into the room?" Carolyn asked.

Douglas suddenly gripped her forearm. "No, Carolyn," he said. "I can't allow you to go into the room with me."

"I'm not in any danger," she assured him. "Never has a non–family member been killed in the whole eighty years of the lottery. And I believe Beatrice's appearance to me the other night was her assurance that she would protect me."

"The way she protected Jeanette?" Douglas shook his head. "That's not very reassuring."

"It will be different this time." She looked him straight in the eye. "Because we'll be together. Together we will be able to fight off the force in the room." She gave him a smile. "It's all about love. Beatrice has told us that. She's made it very plain."

"No," Douglas said.

"Do you think I would risk doing this if I truly believed we wouldn't survive? You know I would never leave my sister Andrea willingly. She'd be lost without me. You know that, Douglas. I wouldn't leave her alone in this world. So I must honestly believe that I will survive that room—and that the only way you can survive as well is if I accompany you."

"We can't afford to argue any longer," Howard Young said. "It's after midnight, the time when the room has always been entered. Who knows if we've already breached the rules too much? Douglas, whether it's you alone or with Carolyn, you must go downstairs now!"

"Trust me," Carolyn said, her eyes imploring Douglas.

Douglas hesitated for a moment, then grabbed her hand. Mr. Young stepped aside as they hurried out of the parlor and across the foyer, heading for the door to the basement.

"May God protect you both," the old man said as they passed.

There was no time for any further good-byes. Down the stairs they rushed. Carolyn only had time to pick up a flashlight from one of the shelves. The door was open, waiting for them. Mr. Young would be downstairs momentarily after them to lock it.

They entered the room.

It looked just as it had the other day, except that every once in a while lightning flashed from the small window, illuminating the room.

"What do we do?" Douglas asked.

She gave him a small smile. "I suppose we just sit on the couch and wait."

Douglas brought his hands together in a prayerful gesture, his fingertips touching his lips. "So many people have died here," he said. "So many people have stood where we stand now, with the same kind of terror."

They heard a small click. Uncle Howie was turning the key in the lock, sealing them in there for the night.

"Why would he never tell us about his father and the dream he had?" Douglas asked. "Why withhold so much about how the lottery started?"

Carolyn took a seat on the couch. "I'm not sure," she said. "It's as if he's felt the fewer details known by the family, the better."

Douglas sat beside her. "And so decade after decade we've trooped in here to die, without ever knowing why."

"Your cousin Paula said it was like mindless sheep being herded to slaughter."

Douglas looked at her with determination.

"Well, we're not sheep," he said, taking her hand. "We will walk out of this room in the morning."

Carolyn nodded. She believed that. She honestly did.

Then why was she still so terrified?

They sat in silence. She was aware of their breathing. How long before something happened? They had no idea of the sequence of events in this room. Everyone who had ever been selected by the lottery was dead—except for Jeanette, and her voice had been silenced, apparently forever. They might have to wait all night. Perhaps nothing happened until it was close to morning. Perhaps there was no rhyme or reason at all.

"When we get out of here," Douglas said at last, "I want to marry you."

Carolyn just gripped his hand.

Outside the thunderstorm raged. The small lamp that sat beside the couch sputtered and died. They'd lost power. Carolyn switched on the flashlight that she held in her lap. A column of white light shot straight up toward the ceiling.

Only then did they hear the scratching.

"What is it?" Douglas whispered.

"It might only be a mouse," Carolyn whispered back.

But it grew louder. Where it was coming from, they couldn't be sure. Scratch, scratch, scratch. They drew closer to each other on the couch.

"Why don't you just show your face?" Douglas finally said out loud. "Reveal who you are."

But only scratching was heard in return. Louder and louder.

Then a flash of lighting lit up the room. In that brief instant, Carolyn saw a face.

"Dear God," she gasped.

It was the face of a baby. Looking exactly like the face in Dean's photograph.

The baby was crying.

Now its shrieks replaced the scratching. Low at first, then high-pitched. It seemed as if the baby were everywhere in the room. Its cries came at them from every corner.

"The poor child," Carolyn said. "Whatever force controls this room controls that baby's spirit. Refuses to let it find peace."

"Whoever murdered Beatrice must have murdered the baby, too," Douglas said. "What if that was the way it happened? What if the baby was murdered too, and my family never found it a home?"

How he knew this was a fact, he wasn't sure. But he did know it. The baby was killed, too.

Carolyn seemed to grasp this as well. "Set the child free!" she said, standing up, swinging the light from wall to wall. "You can't sate your beastly hunger this time! Beatrice won't have it! There is love in this house again! A love that doesn't hurt people! That doesn't murder children!"

With that, the baby's cries reached a crescendo, as if Carolyn's words had infuriated it. No longer did it sound as if the baby were simply tired or hungry or frightened. Now the cries were angry. Full of rage. As if the child were throwing a furious temper tantrum.

Carolyn took a step back toward the couch, then realized the floor was wet. She turned the flashlight down to get a look.

Blood. The floor was covered with blood.

She swung the flashlight toward the wall. The words had returned.

ABANDON HOPE.

"No," she called out. "We will not abandon hope!"

And in that same moment, the door swung open. Against the forces that controlled this room, mere locks were powerless.

Douglas stood quickly, taking Carolyn by the shoulders.

Even before they saw him, they heard Clem's approach.

The scrape of metal against the basement floor.

The heavy thud of his footsteps.

And his breathing. His loud, labored breathing.

In the doorway appeared Clem's face, red and smiling crazily. His pitchfork was gripped tightly by his dead hands.

Carolyn shone the flashlight in his face. He didn't blink. He just made a sound in his throat and took a step toward them.

"You can't harm us," Carolyn said. "You have no power over us!"

But Clem continued his approach undeterred.

"Show him the amulet," Carolyn whispered to Douglas.

He obeyed. He parted his shirt to reveal the amethyst around his neck.

Clem slowed in his approach, noticing the jewel, and seemingly intrigued.

"You have no quarrel with us," Carolyn said. "It is time that you rested in peace, Clement Ritten-house. Leave us. Rest!"

Clem stared at the amulet. Then he growled, a low sound deep in his throat.

And from somewhere in the dark room came a voice.

"Show them," the voice said.

Light returned to the room. Carolyn gasped. It was no longer a dusty empty cell covered in cobwebs. It was a tidy little bedroom, and on the far wall was a baby's wooden crib. Clem turned, dropping his pitchfork. He walked to the crib and reached down inside. Carolyn and Douglas watched transfixed. He lifted a baby out of the crib. It was wrapped in a baby blanket. It had been sleeping. Carolyn could see its small face clearly. Its little eyes flickered awake. And Clem held it in his hands, staring down at it.

"No," Carolyn murmured, suddenly certain of what they were about to witness.

With ease, Clem reached up and took the baby's tiny head in his enormous right hand. And then he twisted its neck. Carolyn heard the crack, like the snapping of a small twig. The baby's little fingers clutched at the air for a second, then fell still. Carolyn screamed.

And blacked out.

She awoke covered in blood. She was on the floor. The bloody floor. The room was dark again. Douglas was not beside her. She tried to stand and slipped in the blood.

"Douglas!" she cried out.

She found the flashlight, still shining, casting its lonely column of light across the floor. She grabbed it, almost dropping it because it was slick with blood. She swung the light around the room, but did not see Douglas. Once again she called his name.

The room was different. It was longer, wider. It stretched on for a great length, and at the far end she saw the window.

Jeanette had managed to climb out that window. Had Douglas done the same?

But he wouldn't leave me here, Carolyn thought.

She began to run. The bloody floor was slick, but she managed. She ran and ran but seemed to come no closer to the window. As she ran she heard the baby crying again. *It was killed in this room*, she thought. *By Clem. He must have killed Beatrice, too, then.* Perhaps Clem *was* the force that controlled this room.

But, no. She had a heard a voice. A voice commanding him to show them what had happened.

Finally, after what seemed like many long minutes, Carolyn reached the end of the room. There, slumped against the far wall, was Douglas. His shirt was in tatters. The amulet was gone from his neck.

And there was a plastic bag secured around his head!

"No!" Carolyn screamed, lunging at him, ripping the bag with her fingers. Douglas's face was gray. He didn't appear to be breathing.

Getting him onto the floor she began mouth-to-mouth resuscitation. "Breathe, damn it!" she screamed, pressing her lips to his for a second time. "Douglas, I love you!" she screamed, trying it a third time.

Finally he hiccupped a breath, and she could feel the life start moving through his body again.

She looked around. The room was back to normal. There was no more blood on the floor. The far wall was no longer so far. It was just a few feet from where they had been sitting on the couch.

But it wasn't over yet.

The baby continued to cry.

And in the shadows Carolyn detected movement.

She aimed the flashlight.

The spotlight revealed Clem. He stood there, tears running down his face.

Carolyn stood.

"You don't want to do this, do you?" she asked.

The dead man made no reply. He was motionless. The only thing about him that moved were the tears running down his cheeks.

"Someone made you kill that baby," Carolyn said. "Isn't that right, Clem?"

Still no response. Behind her, Douglas staggered to his feet. Carolyn turned to him and asked if he were okay.

He nodded. "Something grabbed the amulet from around my neck," he said, his voice hoarse. "Then there was a plastic bag on the floor in front of me. I couldn't help myself. I put it over my head and tied it. That's the way my father must have died, too."

"But you didn't die," Carolyn told him. "Beatrice was right. Our love is going to save us. Isn't it, Clem?"

They looked over at the figure, still motionless in the corner opposite them.

"For eighty years you have been a prisoner here," Carolyn said. "Why?"

She dared to take a step toward him.

"You loved Beatrice, didn't you?" she asked. "And in a moment of passion, you killed her."

Finally a response from the dead man. His dull eyes flashed for moment as they looked up at her.

"No," Clem said. "I did not kill her."

"Then who did?" Carolyn asked.

But now Clem was silent again.

"Whoever killed her has made you do these terrible things, isn't that right?"

But Clem just went on crying. Carolyn shone the flashlight in his face and continued her approach toward him.

"You can be free," she told him. "Walk out that door, Clem. The love you searched for in your life . . . Douglas and I have it. You don't want to deprive us of that. You're tired. You have done too much that you regret. End it now. Leave this room, just as Beatrice did. You can be free, too."

He looked up at her. There was no longer any malice in his face.

"You know you can't harm us," Carolyn said. "Our love protects us. But not only are you powerless to harm us, you no longer want to. Isn't that right, Clem?"

Slowly, almost imperceptibly, he nodded.

"Go," Carolyn said softly. "Turn your back on the evil force of this room. We have shown that we can be stronger than it is. We came here to free you, Clem. Go. Go now!"

Douglas had come up beside Carolyn. He had placed a hand on her back. He feared at any moment that Clem's rage might surge up again, like bile in his throat. He could pounce again, his pitchfork aimed at them. But he didn't. To Douglas's great surprise the dead man walked. He walked past them, opened the supposedly locked door, and disappeared into the darkness of the basement beyond.

It was only then that they noticed the first pink glimmers of morning filtering through the window.

"We've done it," Carolyn said quietly. "We've survived a night in the room."

"Is he gone?" Douglas asked, approaching the open door and looking out into the basement.

Carolyn came up beside him. "I believe he is."

Douglas turned to her. "Then is it over?"

She looked up at him. "It's over," she said. "We showed that we were stronger than the evil force of this room."

The shaft of sunlight suddenly flooded the room.

They heard a creak. They braced themselves.

But the figure that now appeared in the doorway was only Howard Young.

"Praise God!" he shouted. "Praise God! The curse is over! It is over! Praise God!"

Chapter Twenty-six

"What I surmise," Carolyn said, bringing her coffee to her lips with trembling hands, "is that Clem was being controlled by a force that made him do these things, and that once he was confronted with a greater force, he was finally free to rebel against it and find peace for himself."

"And that greater force was the love between you and Douglas," Paula said, near tears. "That's so beautiful."

"Remember that Beatrice was freed from that room ten years ago by Kip," Carolyn added. "I believe that she exerted her own power to help free Clem, and therefore, save us. Before that, trapped in that room as he was, she was powerless to do anything. But now she could act."

"Then perhaps I owe Dr. Hobart more gratitude than I showed a decade ago," Mr. Young said.

He was seated again at the head of the table. Douglas and Carolyn were on one side, Paula and Dean and Linda on the other. They had been up all night, waiting and hoping. The children were asleep, and Philip and Ryan and Chelsea had retired in shame to their rooms. But Mr. Young had given them strict orders not to leave the house until this morning. He planned to speak to them about their treason and to make a decision about their place in their will.

"But what of the power that controlled that room?" Dean asked. "We still don't know what it was."

"Nor might we ever," Douglas said.

"But how can we be sure it's gone?" Paula asked. "Defeated?"

"They survived, didn't they?" Howard Young barked impatiently. "They have broken the long chain of deaths. We did what the lottery demanded. We drew a name and sent one of our own in there. And he lived."

"And the baby?" Dean asked.

"What about the baby?" Carolyn asked.

"Is it free, too?"

She paused.

"I don't know," she admitted.

And suddenly the terror returned. The relief that had flooded through her body with the coming if the sun was replaced by a cold fear—the same that had gripped her in New York.

She turned all at once then and looked out the French doors onto the terrace.

Standing there, staring in at her, was David Cooke. His eyes were wild. The scar on his face seemed to be pulsing.

Carolyn screamed.

"What is it?" Douglas shouted, standing.

"Outside, on the terrace," Carolyn gasped.

He bolted out the French doors, looked around, then came back inside.

"There's nobody there," he reported. "What did you think you saw?"

"I . . . I don't know," she said.

Howard Young stood. "You're just jittery from the night in that room. It's understandable. You just need to rest."

He hobbled out of the room.

Paula reached over and covered Carolyn's hand with her own. "What was it, Carolyn?"

"Perhaps . . . just my imagination," she said. "It has to be my imagination."

Paula looked from her to Douglas. "Is it really over? Or is there still more?"

"It's got to be over," Douglas said.

"Yes," Carolyn echoed. "It's got to be over."

But she knew now it was not.

Chapter Twenty-Seven

Philip had had enough. He was getting out of the house. Will or no will, family fortune or not, he had taken all he could from Uncle Howard.

Throwing his clothes into a suitcase, he was planning to walk downstairs and tell the old man that he was heading home. "Go ahead and disinherit me," Philip grumbled, slamming the suitcase shut. "But I will no longer be treated like an errant schoolboy."

The embarrassment of last night still rankled. To be treated like a common criminal by his low-class relations. He couldn't get over the contempt he'd seen in Paula's eyes. "The goddamn dyke," he spit. "How *dare* she look at me that way?"

From the shouts of joy he'd heard from downstairs a short while ago, Philip surmised that Douglas had survived the night in that room. Perhaps the curse was finally over. Perhaps Uncle Howard would be in a forgiving mood. But no matter how he might find his uncle, Philip was tired of waiting in his room like a child being punished. He would not tolerate being treated this way.

He hadn't slept a wink, of course. He had consoled Chelsea and Ryan, who shared their father's humiliation. He told them they'd find some way to stay in the will. He wasn't sure he believed it himself, but it was the only way to shut them up and get them to go to bed. He thought about tapping on their doors to tell them he was leaving, but decided against it. He couldn't take any more histrionics. They could fend for themselves.

He glanced around the room one more time to make sure he hadn't left anything behind. Satisfied, he clutched his suitcase with one hand and opened the door of his room with the other.

And he let out a small sound of surprise when he saw a man was standing in the doorframe, blocking his way.

A servant, he thought at first, before remembering that Uncle Howard had given the servants the day off, not knowing what would be found in that room this morning.

"Excuse me," Philip said loudly, officiously.

The man did not move.

He was a tall man, with dark hair and dark eyes, dressed in a black jacket, black T-shirt, and dirty dungarees. A scar ran down the left side of his face.

"I *said*, excuse me!" Philip boomed.

The man's eyes seemed wild. He simply raised one large hand and placed it on Philip's chest, shoving him back into the room.

"How dare you?" Philip bellowed.

The man stepped into the room and closed the door behind him.

Icy terror suddenly began pulsing through Philip's veins.

"Who are you?" Philip asked. "You're something from that room. . . . You're not human!"

The man just glared at him, his eyes glassy.

"Kill him," came a small voice from somewhere above.

The man reached inside his jacket and withdrew a long, wide, sharp knife.

"No!" Philip screamed, backing away. "Help me! Somebody help me!"

The man just grinned. He held the knife out in front of him.

Philip ran to the other side of the room. He heard the rush of air made by the swinging blade. He felt the slice of the knife without seeing it. A sharp stab of pain in his upper left arm. He spun around, mesmerized by the sight of the bright red blood staining his crisp white shirt.

The man moved in closer.

Philip lifted his eyes as he saw the knife glinting in the light.

"No!" he cried.

He felt the sting of the blade cut into his neck. His lips were still moving as his head separated from his body, sliced off by one skillful swing of the knife. For several terrible seconds—an eternity really—Philip was still conscious, aware that he was flying through the air, then watching from the floor as his body staggered forward and fell down hard on its chest. He saw the muddy boots of the man who had beheaded him walk past, and he heard the door open and close. Then his brain shut down from lack of oxygen, and everything faded to black.

Chapter Twenty-eight

Paula couldn't believe her eyes. When the doorbell rang and she opened the door, she had never in a million years expected to see who was standing there. Now she stood, blinking, unable to speak.

"Aren't you going to invite me in?" Karen asked, her smile practically blinding in its brilliance.

Paula just stepped aside, too stunned to say anything.

"I've missed you terribly," Karen said, coming inside the house. "I knew how important this family reunion was to you, and so I wanted to be here. I want to finally meet your extended family." She took Paula's hands and looked her decisively in the eye. "Because nothing is worth losing you, Paula. Nothing."

A week ago—even a day ago—Paula might have struggled with such words. Of course she had missed Karen terribly, too. But it had been better—safer—to have her far away from the family curse and the forces that oppressed them. Now, however, with the danger having been averted, Paula could simply rejoice. Finally she was able to break through her shock and throw her arms around Karen. She kissed her over and over.

"I've missed you, too," she said. "Oh, baby, everything has changed. Everything!"

Karen smiled. "What do you mean? How has everything changed?"

Paula beamed. "We can have a baby!"

Karen's jaw dropped. "What—how—what is different? What has made you change your mind?"

"So many things," Paula said, stroking her beloved's hair.

"Karen!"

They turned. It was Linda, followed by Dean and the children. Happy laughter ensued, with Zac and Callie running into their Aunt Karen's arms.

"We're so happy to see you," Dean said.

"Especially now," Linda added, "when we can finally live free and clear!"

Karen was smiling, but her pretty brown eyes danced with confusion. "What's happened?" she asked. "You seem to be in the midst of a celebration."

"We are," Paula said. "Come meet Uncle Howard. And after that, sweetheart, I have quite the story to tell you."

She looked up and noticed Carolyn and Douglas coming down the marble steps.

"Carolyn! Douglas!" Paula called. "I'd like you to meet my partner Karen."

Carolyn smiled, approaching with her hand extended. Paula watched her, and observed Douglas a few feet behind her on the stairs. But then, almost as if in slow motion, she noticed something else: a dark figure suddenly rounding the stairs. In a blur, the figure leapt upon Douglas, taking him down. It all happened so fast, Paula didn't even have time to scream.

But Karen did. Linda did, too, grabbing her children and running with them into the parlor. Dean, meanwhile, instinctively sprinted to his cousin's aid.

The creature on Douglas's back was a man. He was dressed in dark clothes. Paula finally found her voice to scream when he raised a knife, an enormous shiny silver blade, and held it aloft over Douglas's back.

Carolyn, too, had leapt forward, landing on the man at nearly the same time as Dean. The three of them struggled. Karen kept screaming, clinging to Paula. Their happy mood had changed to terror in a matter of seconds.

Carolyn had grabbed the man's hand, preventing him from plunging the knife down between Douglas's shoulder blades. Meanwhile, Dean had straddled the man's back and was attempting to pull him off of Douglas. But the intruder seemed to have superhuman strength. Carolyn he shook off like a pesky fly. And with a grunt and a backward thrust, he was able to send Dean crashing into the banister.

But it gave Douglas time enough to slip out from under his attacker. He scrambled to his feet as the man growled like a wolf and retrained his eyes upon his prey.

Karen had backed up behind Paula and was frantically pressing numbers on her cell phone.

But as the man flashed that enormous knife, Paula realized he wasn't just after Douglas. He wanted to kill all of them.

It was the room.

The curse was not over.

They had to get out of there. Since the maniac blocked their way to the front door, there was only one other option available to them. Taking hold of Karen's arm, Paula yanked her toward the parlor. Carolyn and Douglas were rushing that way as well.

But that left Dean on the stairs.

The man let out an inhuman roar. He seemed like an ape at the zoo, banging its chest in a raw display of power and aggression. The doors of the parlor opened a crack, and Linda urged them inside. Paula frantically looked around for her brother, but she was pushed along by the force of Carolyn and Douglas and Karen. They literally fell into the parlor as Linda locked the heavy oak doors behind them.

But then she realized her husband was not with them.

"Dean!" she screamed.

"Daddy!" Zac and Callie began shrieking.

"I've got to go back out there and get him," Paula said. She had always protected her baby brother. She couldn't abandon him now.

"No!" Karen said, clutching at her sweater. Her eyes were wide with shock and terror. "You can't go back out there! He'll kill you!"

"What's wrong with the phones?" Douglas shouted, desperately trying to call for help on his cell phone.

"Useless," Carolyn said, looking down at her own.

"Mine has no power either," Karen cried. "What's going on here?"

They heard a scream.

"Dean!" Linda shouted.

"I'm going out there," Paula said. With sudden force she grabbed one of Desmond Young's rifles from the wall. Uncle Howard had told her that he kept them loaded. "The rest of you take the children out through the window," she instructed. "Run as fast as you can down the cliff path and get the sheriff."

"Paula, don't go out there," Carolyn said. "You have no idea how dangerous that man is. I know him. He's a killer."

"Then he's human," Paula said. "Not some apparition from that room."

Carolyn shuddered. "He's human. At least, he *was.*"

Paula gave her a tight smile. "Then he's not so dangerous that a bullet through his heart won't stop him."

"No!" Karen was crying hysterically. "Please, Paula, please don't go out there!"

"Oh, baby." Paula lightly touched Karen's face. "There's no way I can just leave my brother," she said, before opening the door and heading back out into the foyer.

When she was a girl, Uncle Howard had taught her how to shoot, and she'd always had very good aim. She'd have to trust that she hadn't lost the talent. Holding the rifle out in front of her, her eyes scanned the foyer for the maniac. He was nowhere to be seen. Uncle Howard was somewhere in the house. Perhaps he was in danger.

Then she spotted Dean.

Her brother lay on the floor in a pool of blood. Paula hurried over to him. The blood was gushing from his shoulder, and he was struggling to stand. Thank God he was still alive.

"I'll get you into the parlor," Paula said, helping him up, "and they can bind your wound."

"Should've known you'd come for me," Dean said, his voice weak. "But you shouldn't have risked it."

"Where is he?" Paula asked.

"He went outside."

From the parlor now there came screams. Paula rushed forward, flinging open the door, rifle at the ready.

"We were getting ready to go out the window," Linda said, "but he was out there, trying to get in."

"Where is he now?" Paula barked.

"He's gone around the house," Douglas shouted.

The terrace, Paula thought. *He's going to come back in through the French doors on the terrace.* Uncle Howard was out there. He'd kill Uncle Howard.

She hurried down the corridor to the dining room, looking furiously around. She saw no sign of anyone. But the French doors were open. *He's back inside the house. . . .*

Cautiously she moved from room to room, the rifle ready in her hands. Her breathing was labored. Everything was on high alert. Her vision, her hearing. The fine hairs on her arms stood at attention.

And yet she didn't see him until too late.

He was behind the kitchen door, waiting. As she passed him, he lashed out. She felt the sting of the blade pierce her side, and the warmth of the blood flow down her leg. She spun, pointing the gun and firing. But he was too fast. Superhuman fast. She shot an enormous hole in the plaster of the kitchen wall. Then he was behind her again. A part of her brain knew she was about to die. The knife was positioned at the small of her back.

But then, chaos.

Paula heard a shout and then a thud. She whipped around to see her brother, bloodied but unbowed, tackling the man, sending him sprawling across the kitchen. Copper pots and pans, hanging over a counter, clattered to the tiled floor in all the commotion. Paula steadied her hands despite the pain in her side and tried to get the maniac in focus. But now he was tussling with Dean. She didn't want to shoot her brother by mistake.

"Dean, get away from him!" she shouted.

For a second she saw the man's face—his crazy dark eyes, the terrible scar down his left cheek. For that one fleeting second she had a chance to blow his head off. But then Dean grabbed the knife, trying to wrest it from his hands. Instead, the maniac growled like a beast and plunged the blade deep into Dean's abdomen.

"No!" Paula screamed and fired.

The bullet blew a hole in the madman's chest, and he fell back.

Paula rushed forward. Behind her, she realized, were Douglas and Carolyn. Dean was bleeding profusely now.

"We've got to get him to a hospital," Carolyn said.

"Paula, too," Douglas added.

"No, I'm fine," Paula insisted.

She looked down at the man she had shot sprawled on the floor. There was no blood coming from the hole in his chest.

"Paula."

The voice was Dean's.

She bent down.

"You've always been there for me," he managed to say.

She smiled. "You saved me this time, little brother."

"Take care of Zac and Callie for me," he rasped.

The tears began dropping down Paula's cheeks. "We're going to get you to a hospital," she told him. "You'll be fine."

But even as she said the words she saw the life disappear from his eyes.

"Dean!" she cried.

Douglas lifted his body and carried it down the hall to the study. Carolyn followed, helping Paula walk. She could feel the blood still flowing steadily from the wound in her side. But all she was really aware of was the fact that her brother was dead.

Something made her turn back to see the madman who had killed him one more time.

And to her horror, he was no longer on the floor.

Chapter Twenty-nine

"Daddy?"

Chelsea peered into her father's room.

The noise from downstairs had terrified her. She'd run to Ryan's room, only to discover he was not there. There were screams and thuds from the foyer. What was going on? Had the terrors of that room escaped into the house?

Then she'd heard the gunshot. With mounting fear, Chelsea hurried down the corridor to her father's room, barefoot and still in her pink nightie.

"Daddy?" she called again, taking a step into the room.

He didn't seem to be here either. Where had they gone? Chelsea began to panic. Was she the only person left in the house?

She noticed her father's suitcase on the floor. He had packed to leave. But he clearly hadn't left quite yet.

That was when she noticed the splatter of red dots on the wall.

Blood.

She took a couple of steps around to the other side of the bed. The moisture on her feet told her she was walking in blood.

She saw her father lying on the floor. His arms were twisted up in an odd angle.

"Daddy!" she screamed.

Her foot hit something. At first she thought it might have been a boot or a shoe.

But then the object rolled over like a bowling ball.

Dead eyes looked up at her.

It was her father's head.

Chelsea screamed.

Chapter Thirty

"What is going *on* in this house?" Karen asked as she wrapped Paula's wound with a tablecloth.

In one corner of the room, Linda was trying to console her crying, terrified children. At the window, Carolyn kept watch, while Douglas, now holding the rifle, stood guarding the parlor doors.

"Where's everybody else?" Douglas asked. "Uncle Howie, Uncle Philip, Ryan, Chelsea?"

"Last I knew, Philip, Ryan, and Chelsea were still in their rooms," Carolyn said. "Your uncle was in the dining room. But he must have fled when he heard the commotion in the foyer. Let's hope he's hiding."

"Or that maniac got him already," Douglas said.

"Who is he?" Paula wanted to know. "You said you knew him, Carolyn."

Carolyn sighed. It was surreal. The jubilation of just an hour ago had been turned topsy-turvy into a nightmare of disbelief. They had thought they had won. The curse seemed to be ended. They had survived the night in the room; they had sent Clem's spirit to rest in peace. It should have been over. The power that room held over their lives should have been ended.

But instead Carolyn now faced the greatest fear of her life.

David Cooke.

"I was in a relationship with him some time ago," she revealed. "He killed a girl. I found out about it only after he was gone. Then I gave evidence to the police."

"Well, that creature I shot," Paula said, "is definitely not human. I blew a hole right through its chest, but still it got up and walked."

"He's a zombie," Carolyn said. She knew this to be the case; she had experience with such things, after all. "He's not a ghost like Clem, but he's clearly still in the power of whatever force controls that room."

"But you *broke* the curse," Linda said tearfully. "You survived the night. Dean always believed that if someone could survive a night in that room, its power would be broken and we would be free."

"Apparently," Douglas said, "all we did was piss it off."

Carolyn ran her hands through her hair. She realized there was blood on her fingers. "It needs a vessel to act against us," she said, understanding dawning on her. "For eighty years it used Clem. Now that we took Clem away from it, it needed someone else. So it settled on David."

"I don't understand what connection your ex-boyfriend has with that room," Douglas said.

Carolyn shook her head. "I doubt there's a connection. But the room knows more than we gave it credit for. Whether it found David and brought him here—or whether he came here on his own, looking for revenge on me—the room clearly understood he could be used against us, and so it took over his mind and his body." She shuddered. "What that means is that *anyone* could be used against us. The forces that control that room can see into our minds and our hearts."

The children began to cry again. Linda clasped them to her breast.

"I'm sorry," Carolyn said. "I don't mean to frighten them. But they need to understand how serious this is."

"Will someone please explain to me what the *hell* is going on?" Karen cried.

Paula took a deep breath and recapped, as best she could, the long, terrible ordeal of the family curse and the reason why she had been so opposed to having children. Meanwhile, Carolyn once again checked her cell phone and then the house phone. Both remained dead.

"That gun isn't going to be much help to us," she said softly to Douglas.

He shrugged. "Well, it might slow him down a little, and give the kids at least a chance to get away."

Suddenly they both tensed. The doorknobs of the parlor doors had begun to turn.

Douglas aimed the gun at the doors and shouted over his shoulder, "Linda, take the kids and go out the window!"

But just then the doors opened.

"Hold your fire!" Carolyn yelled.

It was Chelsea.

The girl ran into the parlor straight into Carolyn's arms. She was sobbing. Her mascara ran down her face in black streaks.

"My father!" she cried. "My father!"

"What about your father?" Carolyn asked.

"He's dead!" She looked up into Carolyn's eyes. "Someone cut off his head!"

"Dear God," Paula groaned. Linda clapped her hands over the children's ears.

"It's a slaughter," Douglas said, closing the parlor doors securely again. "Just like when the lottery was breached in the past. Until the room had claimed someone, other members of the family were killed off. That's what's happening here."

"But the lottery wasn't breached," Carolyn argued. "It was held as always. Someone was chosen, and someone went into the room."

"But I survived," Douglas said. "That wasn't supposed to happen."

"We've got to find a way of pacifying the room," Paula said, wincing as she headed over to the wall and took down the other rifle that was hanging there. "Give it what it wants, or we all will die."

"No," Carolyn objected. "There has to be another way."

"The amulet," Chelsea said, sitting down on the sofa and hugging herself. "I want that amulet that protects us."

"Didn't do the trick," Douglas told her. "I was simply compelled to rip it off my neck."

"We can't rely on trinkets anymore," Carolyn said.

"What do you suggest then?" Paula asked.

"We were able to send Clem away to rest in peace. We need to do the same to whatever force controls that room."

"We don't even know what it is!" Douglas said.

"No," Carolyn admitted. "But Beatrice does."

She glanced out the window.

"She's out there somewhere. She's the only reason we're still alive. Her power isn't as strong as the power in the room, but she can still manage to have an influence. I'm convinced that if not for Beatrice, David would have been able to burst through those doors and kill us all. But she can only hold him off for so long." Carolyn took a deep breath. "We need to find out what force controls that room."

"What are you suggesting then?" Paula asked, not a little impatient. "We all clasp hands for another séance?"

"Possibly," Carolyn said. "But someone else has the information we need, too. Someone we can simply ask directly and this time demand he tell us."

"Uncle Howie," Douglas said.

Carolyn nodded. Paula, too, seemed to agree.

"If he's still alive," Douglas said.

"I think he is," Carolyn said. "The force has allowed him to live for eighty years. Nine times he's escaped being chosen in the lottery. For some reason, the force wants him alive. And it's time we found out what that reason is."

"But where *is* Uncle Howard?" Paula asked. "How can we get to him? If any one of us leaves this room, surely that madman will kill us."

"That's where you're wrong," Carolyn said. "He would kill any one of you. He will not kill me."

She stepped forward and placed her hand on the doorknob.

"No!" Douglas shouted. "I won't let you go out there alone!"

"I'm the only one not a family member," she said. "As much as I wish it were different, Douglas, right now I'm glad I didn't yet accept your offer of marriage."

He looked at her with wide, terrified eyes.

Carolyn turned the doorknob. "The force in that room has no grievance with me. I'm the only one who can safely step outside this room."

"The force may have no grievance with you," Douglas said, "but David Cooke does."

She steeled herself. "It's time I finally confronted David Cooke."

Chapter Thirty-one

Inside the linen closet Ryan slowly lowered his hands from his ears. The house had fallen eerily quiet. The screaming and crashing and the gunshots had stopped. When the commotion had begun, Ryan had looked over the banister into the foyer below and seen a scar-faced man on Douglas's back raising a knife. Without even a moment's hesitation Ryan had turned on his heel and run down the hall, scurrying into the nearest hiding space he could find. For the next hour—or had it been less than that?—he had kept as still in the closet as possible, his hands clamped over his ears to drown out the sounds of his family being murdered, one by one.

Is it possible they're all dead? he wondered.

And if so, why was I spared?

Surely the killer was some demon from that room. Douglas had apparently survived the night, but something got him this morning instead. And from the screams and thuds that ensued, he wasn't the only one to die.

How long before it comes to get me?

Ryan knew that for something that powerful, a simple linen closet was not going to provide protection for long. It would sense him. It would track him down. He shuddered, tears squeezing out from between his closed eyelids. He remembered the terror he'd felt when the man with the pitchfork had threatened him. He dreaded what might come.

"Please spare me," he whispered—to whom, he had no idea.

He didn't want to die. He had so much to live for. He was going to be the most successful member of his family ever. He'd even thought of running for elected office. Nothing lower than U.S. senator, of course. It wasn't fair that he might die! The evil force of that room could have his cousin Douglas. Douglas was never going to amount to anything. But Ryan was going to be *big*. He was going to be Somebody!

He wondered if his father and Chelsea were dead.

Curiosity was beginning to gnaw away at his fear. What had happened out there? Were bodies strewn everywhere? How long should he wait in here?

A thought occurred to him. *Maybe it's over. Maybe I've really survived the slaughter.*

After all, he reasoned, when the slaughters had happened before, not everyone in the family was killed. There were always survivors. The forces that controlled the room wouldn't want everyone to die. They needed someone who would keep the line going, providing the next generation of victims. Ryan began to think that he really *had* lucked out. Maybe everyone was dead, but *he* had survived.

Slowly, stealthily, he leaned forward, pressing his forehead against the closet door and inching it open just enough to get a glimpse of the hallway.

Nothing. He saw nothing out of the ordinary.

I could make a dash for it, he thought. *Out of the closet, down the hall, down the stairs, across the foyer, out the front door.*

Of course, family members had been killed many miles away from Youngsport. Distance was no guarantee of safety. But if the slaughter was really over, Ryan could rest assured no one would be coming after him. He could forget all about the room.

At least for another ten years.

And if Douglas was dead, maybe the others were dead, too. Maybe even Uncle Howard. That would leave Ryan the sole heir to the family fortune. At that very moment, he might already be one of the richest men in the world.

That alone was enough to get him to stand up and ease his way out of the closet.

He listened. Not a sound. It had to be over.

He took a step down the corridor. The landing overlooking the foyer wasn't far ahead. Stealthily, he approached the banister and looked over. Blood was smeared across the marble. The suit of armor had fallen on its face. But the place was empty and quiet.

He took a deep breath and practically threw himself down the stairs. He ran as fast as he could, taking two steps at a time. When he reached the bottom, however, he lost his footing, slipping in the pool of glossy blood on the floor. He went down on his butt, the blood splashing and staining his white shirt. Panicked, he stood and tried to regain traction, but had the sense he was running in place, like a cartoon character. Only with great effort did he push himself across the foyer to the front door.

But it was locked.

"No," he whispered, spinning around, glancing around the room to make sure he was still alone.

He was. He breathed a sigh of relief.

He'd have to exit by the one of the other doors. He ruled out the terrace door. The trail of blood led that that way. Who knew what he'd find in the dining room or kitchen? He'd have to go out through the side door, accessed through the library.

Carefully he made his way across the foyer. The doors to the parlor were closed. He noticed blood on the doorknobs. Shivering, he headed down the hall. But as he passed the study, he heard a sound.

It was a man.

And he was crying.

Ryan peered in through the half-open doors. He spied Uncle Howard, standing over a sofa, crying softly as he looked down. Ryan couldn't see what he was looking at.

"Uncle Howard?" Ryan whispered.

The old man's eyes flickered up to him, but he did not reply.

Carefully Ryan stepped into the room. He walked around to the front of the couch. Sprawled there was Dean, in a blood-soaked shirt. He was dead.

"Oh, man," Ryan said.

"He was a good man," Uncle Howard said in a thick voice. "Perhaps the best of the lot. Hard-working. Decent. A good father and husband."

Ryan just swallowed, staring down at his dead cousin.

"How many more?" Uncle Howard asked, looking off into the distance. "How many more will you claim?"

"Is it over?" Ryan asked. "Have they killed everybody else?"

"I don't know," Uncle Howard replied. With difficulty he moved away toward the desk that sat at the far end of the room. Bracing himself against it, he let out a long sigh. "I took refuge in the library when I heard the screaming begin. When the house grew silent, I came in here and found Dean. Someone had left his body here. I don't know what we will find in the rest of the house."

"We've got to get out," Ryan said.

The old man just shook his head. "If we're meant to die, there's nowhere we could run. You're too young to remember your Uncle Ernest. But surely you've heard the stories. He ran all the way to Wisconsin, but they found him. No, I'm staying right here. If they come for me, there's nothing I can do." He leveled his old eyes at Ryan. "And the same holds for you."

Once again Ryan felt the old man's imputation of cowardice and betrayal. He looked away.

Uncle Howard took a deep breath. "The house has been quiet for a while now. But I doubt the killing is complete."

"Who's doing it?" Ryan asked. "It's not the guy with the pitchfork. I saw another guy in the foyer. He was attacking Douglas." He rather enjoyed telling his uncle that his favorite nephew had been assaulted.

"Douglas?" the old man asked. "Oh, dear God."

"It was a guy I'd never heard about before," Ryan told him. "A man with a scar on his face."

"Scar?" Howard Young seemed puzzled. "I can't imagine who that might be. There was no man with a scar on his face. . . ." He seemed to think of something. "But that man Carolyn was involved with . . . what was his name? David Cooke. The reports I obtained on him revealed that he had a scar on his face. Could it be the same?"

Ryan looked at him strangely. "But why would some guy Carolyn was involved with be attacking this family?"

"The powers of that room are great," Uncle Howard said. "They can get in your mind. . . . They can cause you to do things." He shuddered. "If it is the same, then it means we are in greater danger than ever before."

They heard a sound. A steady, rhythmic beat. A thud, repeated over and over.

"It sounds as if someone's knocking on the walls," Ryan said.

"No, listen closely." Uncle Howard was straining to hear. "It is the sound of a knife . . . repeatedly stabbing the wall. Close the doors, Ryan."

Ryan obeyed.

"As he walks," Uncle Howard whispered, "he is stabbing the wall. The knife goes in, the knife comes out, and he takes another step toward us."

"No," Ryan said. He began to cry.

"He is coming for us," the old man said.

Thud. Thud. Thud.

The sound grew ever closer.

In his mind, Ryan could see the knife cutting into the plaster of the wall. He could see the brute's hand gripping the handle.

Thud. Thud. Thud.

He was getting closer.

"No!" Ryan cried, running behind the desk and cowering, covering his face.

Thud. Thud.

The sound stopped.

Ryan peered around the desk from between his fingers. Uncle Howard stood in front of the desk, facing the doors.

Suddenly the doors flew open.

And standing there was the man with the scarred face, knife held over his head.

Ryan screamed.

The man walked into the room, directly toward Uncle Howard.

"Go ahead," Howard Young said. "Kill me. Be done with it."

But the man just stood there in front of him, studying his face.

Still peering through his fingers, Ryan saw the maniac's eyes move. They left Uncle Howard's face and found his own. With a snarl, the beast took a step around the desk.

"No, please!" Ryan begged. "Please don't kill me!"

The man simply sneered, raising the knife up over his head, ready to bring it down onto Ryan.

But then—

A gunshot.

Ryan watched in stunned horror and disbelief as the man staggered. Then came another shot. And another. The man swayed on his feet, though none of the shots produced any blood. They simply tore holes in his body. The man seemed bewildered by the bullets rather than pained. His eyes rolled into the back of his head. Then he collapsed, crumpling to the floor.

Ryan leapt up from behind the desk. He saw Carolyn standing in the doorframe, the rifle in her hands still smoking.

"David Cooke had that coming from me for a long time," she said.

Her words made no sense to Ryan. But no matter. He was on his feet and running. He wasted no time asking any more questions or thanking Carolyn for saving his life. He just wanted out of the house. There might be no place that was safe, but at the moment, all Ryan could do was run.

He bolted out of the study and down the hall, his footsteps echoing across the marble.

Chapter Thirty-two

"Come with me," Carolyn said to Howard Young. "He'll soon be back on his feet. The bullets can knock him down, but they can't kill him."

"He's not a ghost?" the old man asked.

Carolyn had stooped down beside the body of the man she had once loved. She had slept beside this creature. She had let him make love to her. She had trusted him.

"No," she said. "He's a zombie."

She pried the knife from his cold hands.

"Might as well disarm him while we have the chance," she said.

Standing, she motioned to Mr. Young to leave the room.

"There's nowhere we can hide," he told her.

"I'm aware of that. That's why we need to have a little talk, you and me. Take advantage of David being out cold for a while." Her eyes hardened. "It's time you told me everything you know, Mr. Young."

He looked away. "Who is still alive?"

"The only ones killed have been Dean and Philip. Everyone else is safe for the moment in the parlor." She glanced out the door. "With the possible exception of Ryan."

"Take me there then," Howard Young said. "I would see my family."

Carolyn shook her head. "Nope. You and I are heading over to the library. Where we can talk privately."

He glared at her.

"Now move," she said, nudging him with the rifle. "We don't have a lot of time."

She led him out of the room and down the corridor. Once inside the library, she locked the door behind them, even though she felt certain David Cooke could break it down if he wanted to. In life he'd been a very strong man. In death, he was even stronger.

"Sit," she ordered Howard Young.

The old man took a seat in a high-backed chair. He looked so small and frail. Carolyn stood over him.

"What happened the night Beatrice was killed? Who else was involved? Who is the power in that room? Who is using David Cooke to try to kill us?"

"I don't know," Howard Young said.

"You're lying. Dr. Fifer found out something, and for that, you fired him. What did he find out?"

The old man just covered his face in his gnarled, veiny hands.

"You claim to want to end all these deaths!" Carolyn said, her voice rising. "But you withhold information! I need to know everything! We may have only a few minutes! But if I could discover who was behind this, maybe we could make some kind of appeal—"

"It doesn't understand logic," Howard Young murmured into his hands. "It cannot be reasoned with."

"Listen to me!" Carolyn shouted. She stooped down beside the chair so that her eyes were level with Howard Young's. "You must tell me everything! Or else we all will die here in this house. One by one. Including you."

"I welcome death," the old man said. "But it will save for me for last. It will make me watch everyone I love die before me. That's the way it has been for eighty years."

"We can end it!" Carolyn insisted. "But first you must tell me everything you know!"

Their eyes held.

Then came the banging on the door.

Chapter Thirty-three

Paula stood at the door of the parlor, listening. The house had once again fallen silent. When the screams had come from the direction of the study, Douglas had rushed out, assuming Carolyn was in danger. His passion to help the woman he loved was understandable—but his departure had left them without a rifle. Paula knew that bullets wouldn't do much to defend them from an undead man. She'd seen that firsthand in the kitchen. But still she wished she were holding that shiny metal in her hands. It provided some comfort, at least.

Karen came up beside her.

"Baby, maybe you ought to come away from the doors," she said, placing her hand on Paula's shoulder.

Paula turned to her. In just the last couple of hours, their world had turned upside down, not once, but several times. She had woken up this morning not knowing what had happened in the room. Then she had learned that Douglas and Carolyn had survived, and for a few blessed moments she had thought them free of the terrors that had ruled their lives for so long. Then, wonder of wonders, Karen had shown up—and everything had indeed seemed right and good and hopeful in Paula's world.

Then all hell had broken loose. Dean was dead. His children were traumatized. And a maniac was trying to kill them all.

"Karen," Paula said. "You might have a chance to survive. End it with me again. Renounce what you said earlier. Take it all back. Then walk out of this house. It won't touch you if you aren't connected to the family."

She smiled wryly. "I'm still adjusting to finding out about this madness. But from what I sense, it— whatever *it* is—would know I didn't mean it. It would know I still loved you. Sorry, Paula. We're in this together." She took her hand. "As we should have been from the beginning."

Paula took her in her arms. It was painful to move; the wound in her side was terribly sore, though she thought they'd stanched the bleeding. Her eyes moved across the room and caught Linda's. Her sister-in-law gave her a small smile. Paula's heart broke. She still had Karen, but Linda had lost her love and her soul mate.

The children remained clinging to their mother. Their tears had stopped for the moment, and they were silent. Paula thought if they were all to die, they should at least try to save Zac and Callie.

But another part of her felt hopeless. What would they save them for? They would inherit the curse.

Unless they could somehow end it this day.

Was it possible? Carolyn seemed to still think it was. She seemed to believe that Uncle Howard possessed some information that could be key. Paula wanted to believe she was right. But right now, hope was a fragile option.

Her eyes moved over to Chelsea. The girl was sitting on the sofa with her knees drawn up to her chest, her arms wrapped around herself. She was still wearing her flimsy pink nightgown, and she was barefoot. Paula's heart broke for her, too, even if she'd been party to a monstrous hoax the night before. She'd found her father's mutilated body. The whereabouts of her brother were unknown. Chelsea was terrified. Alone among the people in the room, she had no one to console her.

From the foyer came a footstep.

"Douglas?" Paula whispered.

It had to be Douglas.

She and Karen took a step backward from the door. It was locked. If it was Douglas, he'd call to them to open it.

But the doorknob just turned. Whoever turned it grew angry when discovering it was locked. The doorknob began to rattle.

It wasn't Douglas.

Suddenly fists were beating against the door.

"Oh God!" Chelsea cried out. The children, too, were crying again.

"Paula," Karen said. "Look! The window!"

Paula turned. A window at the far side of the parlor was open. The frame had opened out. It would be easy to step through it and out onto the backyard.

"It might be a trick," Paula said.

The banging continued against the parlor door.

"No," Linda cried, suddenly. "It's no trick! Look!"

Just beyond the window, standing in the bright sunshine on the grassy lawn, was Beatrice. Her long dark hair and filmy white dress blew in the wind. She was beckoning to them.

"Can we trust her?" Karen asked.

Paula wasn't sure. Carolyn had seemed to think her spirit was benevolent. But she couldn't know for sure.

Just then the banging on the door grew in greater intensity, and at last a fist came smashing through the heavy wood. Chelsea let out a scream.

There was no more time for delay. "Take the children out the window," Paula shouted to Linda. "Go with Beatrice!"

Immediately Linda was pushing the children across the room. Chelsea ran in that direction, too.

"Let the children go first, Chelsea!" Paula commanded.

The girl relented, shaking her hands in frustration. Paula watched as first Callie and then Zac stepped over the windowsill and out onto the lawn. Linda followed, just as the great oak door buckled inward, broken off its hinges, crashing onto the floor.

And standing there was David Cooke, his chest and neck riddled with gaping dry holes made from gunshots. In his hands he held a length of rope.

"Go!" Paula shouted, backing up herself toward the window.

Chelsea was scrambling to get out, but in her terror, she slipped, falling backward on her butt.

In that second, David Cooke lunged, grabbing hold of Karen by her right arm. He tackled her onto the ground, quickly and easily wrapping the rope around her neck. He began to strangle her. Karen's eyes bulged, her mouth open as she tried to breathe. Her small hands clutched at the rope around her neck but to no avail.

Paula jumped onto the maniac's back and began pummeling him with her fists.

"Help me!" she called over to Chelsea, who was once again attempting to step out of the window.

"Help me get him off of her!" Paula screamed. "Please!"

Chelsea looked back. For a second she hesitated. One foot was outside the window.

Paula was struggling now to push David Cooke off Karen. Her girlfriend's face was turning blue.

"Help me!" she called again to Chelsea.

The girl lifted her leg back over the sill and ran to her cousin. Both of them shoved. Paula willed every muscle in her body to come to her aid. She let loose with a primal scream and pushed as hard as she could. With Chelsea pushing beside her, they were able to move the brute. It was just the slightest movement, but it was enough for his grip to loosen on the rope, enabling Karen to gulp down some air.

"Once more!" Paula shouted, and they pushed the creature again. This time he moved a fraction of an inch more, and Karen, small and agile, was able to wiggle out from under him.

"Get out of here!" Paula yelled. Karen, though woozy, managed to get to her feet and stumble over to the window.

Paula and Chelsea were fast on her heels. Paula

practically threw Karen out on to the lawn, then turned to do the same to Chelsea. But by now David Cooke was on his feet—and on them. Paula felt his cold fingers brush her neck. With his other hand he was reaching for Chelsea. But Paula was just a little quicker than her cousin. She was able to pull away from the brute.

No such luck for Chelsea.

Paula watched in horror as David Cooke, enraged now, grabbed Chelsea in his dead hands and lifted her up over his head. With speed and strength that Paula didn't believe possible, he tore Chelsea's right arm off her shoulder, then her left. The girl screamed as blood spurted everywhere. Then the madman let out a loud roar and tore Chelsea in half, splitting her just above the waist. He tossed the bottom half of her body to the floor and raised the armless top half at Paula.

He was tossing the bloody stump at her when she leapt from the window. Out on the lawn Paula heard the sickening thud of her cousin's remains hitting the glass.

Chapter Thirty-four

Douglas peered out of the door of the library into the corridor.

"I'm sure I heard something," he said.

Carolyn looked from him back to Uncle Howie, who sat in his chair with his hands folded in his lap.

"David has probably revived," she said to the old man. "He may be terrifying them in the parlor even as we speak. You must tell us what you know."

"Yes, Uncle Howie," Douglas said, closing the door and turning to face his uncle. "For God's sake, no more stonewalling."

He had finally admitted to himself that his uncle knew more than he was saying, that maybe in fact Uncle Howie had been suppressing information all along. Information that might have saved so many of the people who had died from this long curse. People like his father.

At the moment, his biggest worry was for the

people he had left behind in the parlor, especially Zac and Callie. Douglas had taken the rifle with him. He knew bullets couldn't stop David Cooke, but they could slow him down. The people in the parlor were therefore defenseless. He had seen the madman's body sprawled on the floor of the study before he'd found Carolyn and Uncle Howie here in the library, and he saw that Carolyn had taken the knife. But Douglas knew it wouldn't be long before the zombie was on its feet again, and finding another weapon wouldn't be difficult for it. Even its bare hands were surely weapon enough. Douglas feared that the sounds he'd heard a moment ago had come from the direction of the parlor. Who else, he wondered, was going to die?

"You've got to speak," Douglas shouted at his uncle. "How many more deaths? How many more deaths before you tell us what you know?"

"Are you somehow prevented from telling us?" Carolyn asked. "Is the force of that room so great?"

"It doesn't matter what I know," Uncle Howie said. "Even if I told you everything, we couldn't prevent the killings. My hope was always to find a force greater than it was, something that could overpower it. That was the only way we could end the power of that room. Because there is no appealing to it. It is irrational. It is fueled by instinct and the simplest of emotions, like anger and fear and rage and hunger."

"So are you saying that you *can* tell us," Douglas asked, getting close to the old man's face, "but that you choose *not* to, because you think it's pointless?"

"I'm sorry, my little hoodlum," Uncle Howie said. "Sorry that I have let you down."

They were startled by a sound from the hallway. They all tensed. Douglas moved closer to the door, brandishing the rifle.

He listened. Footsteps. Two people. It was not the heavy clomping of David Cooke.

Still, both he and Carolyn pointed their rifles at the door as it opened.

But who was there on the other side caused both of them to gasp out loud.

Uncle Howie shouted, "Jeanette!"

It was Jeanette Young, with Michael O'Toole close behind her.

"Hello, Uncle Howard," she said calmly. She moved her eyes over to Douglas and then to Carolyn. "Cousin Douglas. Miss Cartwright. It's good to see you both again, though I wish the circumstances were more pleasant."

"Dear God," Uncle Howie exclaimed.

"How is this possible?" Douglas asked.

Jeanette smiled. She still looked frail, and she walked with some stiffness and difficulty. But she seemed in full control of all of her senses. Michael rested a hand on her shoulder for support.

"I awoke this morning and was able to speak," she said. "The veil that had so long separated me from the rest of the world was lifted. I could speak, I could move, I could communicate."

"It was a miracle," Michael said.

Jeanette sighed. "I knew right away that the curse had been lifted, that someone had survived a night in that room." Her face saddened. "We came over here at once, thinking we'd find the house in celebration. I did my best to explain to Michael all of the terrible details on the drive over here. But what we found was no celebration."

"The force is angry that we survived," Douglas explained.

Jeanette nodded. "I deduced that. In the study we saw a dead man."

"Dean," Uncle Howard said with evident grief.

"And in the parlor were the bloody remains of a young woman," Jeanette added.

"Oh, no," Carolyn cried.

"Who?" Douglas asked.

"It was hard to see for all the blood," Jeanette said. Her long years of silence seemed to have left her unnaturally calm. She did not blanch as she described the scene. "The woman had been terribly mutilated. She seemed young, so I wouldn't remember her. No doubt she was born after my own night in that room." She paused. "But she was blond. I could see that much."

"Chelsea," Uncle Howie said, his voice breaking.

"Was there anyone else in the parlor?" Douglas asked.

"No one else," Jeanette informed him. Douglas didn't know if that was a hopeful or an ominous sign.

"Jeanette," Carolyn said, "you need to know you're in danger here. And so is Michael. There is a killer in the house, and unless we can find out a way to stop him, he is bent on taking us all before the day is over."

"We should call the police!" Michael said, whipping out his phone only to see it had lost all service.

"I told you as we walked through the house viewing the carnage that the police were useless," Jeanette said. "In my long years sitting there at

Windcliffe, I saw many things. I saw that what happens here is beyond the control of ordinary humans. I saw things that no one else could see in this house, sitting here all alone, isolated on top of this hill." She paused. "And from everything that I have seen, I think I know who's doing the killing here."

"His name is David Cooke," Carolyn told her. "And I need to tell you again that he is extremely dangerous."

Jeanette shrugged. "I'm not frightened. I survived a night in that room, remember? You did, too, didn't you? I saw you in there, Carolyn. You and Douglas. You saw what I saw. You saw the terrible thing that happened that night."

"The murder of Beatrice?" Douglas asked.

"You didn't see that, because neither did I," Jeanette corrected him. "You saw her dead body. But it was someone else you saw murdered."

"Beatrice's baby," Carolyn said.

Jeanette nodded.

Uncle Howie groaned. They all turned to look at him.

"We saw Clem kill the baby," Jeanette said, approaching her uncle. "It was a terrible thing to see."

The old man was silently crying.

"It's Malcolm doing this, isn't it, Uncle Howard?" Jeanette asked. "It's Malcolm who's the controlling force of that room."

The old man just continued to sob.

"Who is Malcolm?" Douglas asked.

Jeanette looked up at him. "Malcolm," she told him, "was Beatrice's baby."

Chapter Thirty-five

Ryan was getting desperate. He could not find a way out of the house. Doors and windows refused to open; glass refused to break, even with heavy pewter candlesticks tossed at it. What kind of spell had been cast over this place? Were the forces of the room so powerful that they could trap him inside forever?

Ryan shook the knob on the kitchen door again. It didn't budge.

It wasn't fair! Others had gotten out. He'd watched from the window as Linda and Paula and some other woman ran across the yard with those two bratty kids toward the barn. How did *they* get out? How come whatever forces were controlling this house took pity on *them* and not on him?

Because of what we did.

He tried to block the thought from his mind, but was unsuccessful.

When you tamper with the lottery, when you don't follow the rules, you are punished.

Ernest Young had learned that lesson when he'd run away, only to be massacred with his family in their beds.

And now Ryan's family was being massacred.

Running from room to room in the house, he had found the mutilated bodies of his father and sister. It was easy to think they were being punished for their deception. But Dean was dead, too. Ryan understood that, in the end, they were all fair game. They were all just sport for the bloodlust of the thing that was tormenting them.

He tried the French doors that led out onto the terrace. But again they were sealed shut. In frustration, he slammed his fist against one of the panes of glass, but the glass might as well have been iron. He just bruised his knuckles.

A short time before, he'd had a glimmer of hope. A woman and a man had come through the front door. The door had opened easily from the outside, allowing them to enter. Ryan had been watching from an alcove; he had become so paranoid that he trusted no one, so he stayed very quiet, not revealing himself. After the man and woman had passed down the hallway, Ryan ran to the door, hopeful that it was now open. But it had reverted to immobility. He burst into tears.

Now he prowled from room to room, feeling like a caged animal. His mind no longer thought logically or critically. He just wanted to get out.

And then the laughter began.

High pitched and shrill. Like a child's. The laughter came from everywhere, as if an unseen audience were watching his crazy antics and finding them all too amusing.

"Stop!" Ryan cried, wandering into the foyer. "Stop laughing at me!"

But the laughter just went on. The sound assaulted him, almost like spears being tossed at him from all sides of the room. Each gale of laughter pierced him, hurt him. Ryan cried out in pain.

"Stop!" he shouted. "Please stop!"

He fell to his knees, clapping his hands over his ears, but the laughter only increased in volume and intensity.

"Kill me! Take me!" Ryan cried. "Just stop laughing at me!"

That brought about even more hysterical laughter.

Ryan collapsed into a ball, sobbing. Terrified, broken, he pissed his pants.

All around him the room filled up with laughter. It seemed to Ryan that he'd never hear anything else again except the laughter. He fell over onto his side, reduced to a blubbering fool on a floor covered with blood and urine.

Chapter Thirty-six

From the foyer came the sound of laughter.

Carolyn faced Howard Young with new urgency. "You must tell us!" she demanded. "You must tell us everything you know!"

The old man just sat there, yellow tears rolling down the flaking parchment of his cheeks.

Douglas had peered out the door. "Ryan's out there," he reported back to the group. "I can hear his voice."

"Mr. Young," Carolyn said. "Is Jeanette correct? Is all this being done by Beatrice's baby?"

Slowly, the old man nodded his head.

"How is that possible?" Carolyn asked. "For a mere baby . . ."

"Malcolm has learned a great deal in his eighty years in that room," Jeanette explained. "He has learned to mimic our speech, our words. . . . He has even learned how to make letters on a wall."

Carolyn stared at her, dumbstruck.

"He's learned other things as well," Jeanette

continued. "He's learned about the ways in which people seek revenge."

"Dear God," Carolyn said.

"But at his heart, Malcolm is still just a baby, with a baby's emotions. He is angry and frustrated and frightened."

"All of this," Carolyn said, the full realization hitting her, "is merely a baby's tantrum."

"That's right," Jeanette said. "That is an excellent way of putting it."

"How do we stop him then?" Douglas asked.

Jeanette had turned once again to the old man in the chair. "Uncle Howard," she said, "you must tell us everything that happened eighty years ago in this house. There could still be time to do what is needed to end this!"

"Please, Mr. Young," Carolyn begged. "You want this terrible curse to end. I know you do."

Douglas had moved over to confront his uncle again. "No more deaths, Uncle Howie. How many more can you tolerate? My father, and indirectly my mother . . . and just today, Dean and Philip and Chelsea. And now Ryan is out there begging for his life! Please, Uncle Howie! Tell us what you know."

The old man's watery eyes looked at each of them in turn.

"All right," he said brokenly. "I will tell you everything."

EIGHTY
YEARS
EARLIER

Chapter Thirty-seven

Howard Young was not yet eighteen, but already he was a big, strapping fellow, a solid six feet, the tallest and handsomest of the five Young brothers. Of course, Jacob and Timothy were still just sixteen and thirteen, respectively. They might eventually pass Howard in height. But everyone agreed that none of the boys quite matched Howard in looks. His fair hair, wavy and thick, crowned a perfectly symmetrical face, defined by crystal blue eyes, high cheekbones, and a square jaw with a cleft chin.

Howard understood his appeal. He had seen the look in Beatrice's eyes the first day she came to work for them. She had paused, looking up at him from under her long dark lashes. It was a look Howard had returned. Beatrice Swan was exquisite. A year older than Howard, she had mysterious dark eyes and luxurious black hair. Her breasts were full and round, and her smile hinted at pleasures to come. It wasn't long before Howard discovered just what those pleasures were.

Slipping upstairs after the household was asleep, Howard knew she'd be waiting for him. The little alcove in the attic with the bay window had become their secret meeting place. It was here that Beatrice had given herself to him—the first time Howard had known the full joy of making love to a woman. His heart quickened as he climbed the steep steps to the attic.

She turned to him as he entered, her smile bright, her eyes glowing, her arms outstretched. He fell into them, reveling in her sweet fragrance. He kissed her neck, her hair, her lips. His hands moved up her body, cupping her soft breasts.

"Oh, Howard, I do love you so," Beatrice whispered, her lips on his ear.

Did he love her in return? Howard thought perhaps he did, though he had never been in love before, so he had no idea what it might feel like. Certainly he loved the way she felt, and the secret things she did to his body.

"You will be the greatest of all your father's sons," she said. "I know this. I can see things in my mind. It is a gift. My mother had it, too. You will surpass all of them."

Beatrice knew of the rivalry among Howard and his brothers. He had confided in her, telling her how they had always competed, ever since they were children. Whether it be in polo or foxhunting or swimming or lacrosse, the five Young brothers were always trying to one-up each other. It was his eldest brother Douglas whom Howard envied the most. Douglas would inherit this house someday; he would be master here. Douglas stood to take the biggest share of their father's fortune. He had already married, to a woman who was an heiress herself, and produced four grandchildren for their father, the latest being a baby girl, Cynthia. All four could now lay claim to the family wealth, dividing up what might otherwise have been left over for Howard. Many were the times that he rued being born the third son.

"Yes," Beatrice was murmuring, "I see you as the greatest Young of them all. This house will be yours, Howard. I see it."

"There are too many others ahead of me in line," he told her, kissing her neck.

"It will be yours," she promised.

She was unbuttoning his shirt now, slipping her hands inside to caress his chest. Howard leaned his head back and moaned in pleasure. Beatrice was very good at taking the lead in their lovemaking. She pressed his hand to her lips and sucked each finger into her mouth.

"Someday will you marry me?" Beatrice asked, her black eyes locked on his. "Make me mistress of this house?"

"Of course, of course," Howard promised, feeling the hardness swelling in his pants, the urge to have her, possess her.

She kissed him then. Deep and full. He pressed himself down on top of her, unbuckling his belt and lifting her long skirt in nearly the same motion.

"Make love to me, Howard," Beatrice purred.

But suddenly there was a scraping of wood. The door behind them was opening.

"So *this* is what has been going on," a deep voice echoed through the alcove.

Howard spun around. His father stood there glaring over them in his nightshirt.

"Papa," Howard uttered, standing awkwardly, his loose belt dangling in front of him. Beatrice let out a little shriek.

"Go to your room," Desmond Young commanded the servant girl. She quickly pulled her dress back down and scampered out of the alcove. Her frantic footsteps rushing down the stairs echoed through the house.

Meanwhile, his father's eyes never left Howard's face. Even with his own eyes averted, the young man could feel them burning holes in his skin.

"This is not how I raise my sons,' Desmond Young finally intoned. "No son of mine takes up with a scullery maid."

"I'm sorry, Papa."

"Meet me in the study," the older man said, turning and heading back down the stairs.

Howard sighed. He fastened his belt, buttoned his shirt. He had thought he'd been so smooth, so quiet, sneaking up here to meet Beatrice several nights a week. But clearly his father had noticed something. Desmond Young was a very shrewd man. Very little got past him. Howard had been a fool to try.

Trudging into the study, he faced the somber patriarch sitting at his desk.

"She is pretty," Papa said. "I will grant you that. But those French girls . . . they are all witches. They will cling onto you, and expect much in return for their kisses."

"I won't see her again, Papa."

"That is for certain. I know her kind, Howard. She will trick you. She will use you. She will try to get her grubby hands on our money. That is what she is after, son. Your bank account. Not your heart."

Howard knew that wasn't true. Beatrice loved him. He was certain of that. But to dispute his father was futile.

"And if I find you with her again, Howard," the older man added, "I will cut your allowance by half, and the trust that is waiting for you will be reduced. I will take a third and give it to your brother Douglas. Do you understand?"

"Yes, sir."

"So I have your word?"

"Yes, sir," Howard said.

"Go to your room then."

He didn't sleep. In the morning, he came down to breakfast with dark circles under his eyes. Beatrice, carrying the plates out from the kitchen, noticed, and cast him a look from under her dark lashes. After the meal, she passed him in the hallway.

"I need to speak with you," she whispered.

"It's not possible," he said quickly. "My father will be watching with an eagle eye. We cannot see each other anymore."

"But you must talk to me!" Beatrice insisted, her voice rising. "You must! What I have to say can't wait!"

"All right," Howard said, anxious to keep her quiet. "Twenty minutes. In the barn."

She nodded, scurrying away.

Howard stewed as he wrapped a scarf around his neck and slipped into his coat. Winter was coming on fast this year. Already they'd had their first frost. Heading outside, he could see his breath fog up in front of his face. What was so urgent that Beatrice needed to tell him? He began to wonder if his father had been right, if she would do everything she could to cling to him.

In the barn, Clem was feeding the horses, pitching clumps of hay into their stalls with his pitchfork. Howard told him to run along, that he wished to be alone. But when Beatrice came in after him, Clem cast a suspicious eye over his shoulder.

"He'll tell my father that he saw us here," Howard fretted.

"I can take care of Clem," Beatrice said. "He's a simple man, not right in the head. But he's in love with me. He'll do whatever I tell him."

"Then tell him to keep quiet."

"I shall." She tried to smile, to connect with Howard's eyes. "Oh, my love. Your father will *have* to accept us now."

Howard sighed and looked away. "It's impossible. He's not a man who changes his mind."

"But he will—he must!—when he hears that I am carrying his grandchild."

Howard spun around to look at her.

Beatrice smiled. "It's true, my love. I am pregnant."

"No," he uttered.

"Yes! Oh, please, you must be happy!" She patted her belly. "I know it will be a son. A son—born of our love!"

Howard turned away from her.

If I find you with her again, Howard, I will cut your allowance by half, and the trust that is waiting for you will be reduced. I will take a third and give it to your brother Douglas.

"I . . . I can't marry you," Howard stammered.

Beatrice's eyes grew wide. "But you must! Otherwise I'll be ruined!"

"I . . . I'll find some way to get you money. You can go away. Far away."

"No! I love you, Howard! I love you!"

He rushed out of the barn, unable to think. The air slapping against his face was cold as he ran along the cliffs. Below him the waves crashed in a frothy spray against the rocks. He could smell the salt. He had an urge to just jump over the cliffs, crashing into the sea beyond, letting the tide take him wherever it might.

Over the next few days, he avoided Beatrice as much as possible. He knew her parents were dead, that she had noplace to go. For a fleeting second he wondered if maybe he should marry her, if maybe his father would indeed melt when he learned she was pregnant. But sitting in the parlor with his brother Douglas and sister-in-law Ruth, hearing them describe the assets that Ruth had brought with her to the marriage, Howard knew that Beatrice Swan would never make an acceptable Young bride. Taking out his bankbook, Howard calculated that he could pull together a hundred dollars and send Beatrice to Bangor or maybe even Boston. He'd follow that with regular monthly payments. She'd have to accept that.

"I'm not going to destroy my future for some scullery maid," he said out loud, looking at himself in the mirror.

But Beatrice wouldn't leave. She wouldn't take his money. She insisted that she loved him and that she would never leave. When she began to show signs of her pregnancy, the household began to whisper. One night his father summoned Howard into his study.

"What do you know about Beatrice's condition?" Desmond Young asked.

"Nothing, sir. The child is not mine."

He could see that his father didn't believe him. But the patriarch seemed pleased with what would be the official family line. "We will keep her on," he pronounced. "As Christian people, we cannot cast her out for her unfortunate sin. We will keep her with us, where she cannot be the subject of gossip and innuendo."

There were nights when Beatrice's sobs echoed up from the basement and through the house. Howard's brothers smirked in his direction. Nothing had ever been admitted, but it seemed everyone knew, even Howard's mother, who nonetheless presented a placid demeanor. An elaborate pretense was maintained. No one ever commented on Beatrice's pregnancy. She got bigger and bigger, but no one ever said a word.

And through it all, whenever they passed in the hall, Beatrice would pass Howard little notes. *I know you love me,* she wrote. *I know you will marry me when I bear you a son.*

When the time came late the following spring, a midwife from the village was summoned by Clem. The family sat in the parlor, listening to Beatrice's screams from below. But they said not a word, uttered not a single comment—not even when they heard the cries of the newborn. Finally the midwife came upstairs to give the master of the house the news that his servant girl had given birth to a boy. His name was Malcolm. Desmond Young paid the woman, and she left without another word between them.

But in the months that followed, the careful façade they'd all been maintaining crumbled.

The child simply looked too much like Howard. He had the same blond hair, the same cleft to his baby chin. Howard's mother even removed the baby photograph of her son from the mantelpiece, so uncanny was the resemblance to the child downstairs in the servants' quarters. As the summer progressed, the resemblance only became more apparent. It was the eyes that clinched it. As Beatrice performed her chores, the infant strapped to her back like an Indian papoose, family members had to look away. It was as if Howard himself were staring at them from the child's eyes.

Finally someone had to say something.

"I suspect," Desmond Young intoned one day toward the end of the summer, calling Howard once again into his study, "if I asked Beatrice to show me the child's foot he'd have a similar crescent birthmark to the one you have yourself."

Howard could no longer deny such an obvious reality. The child was his. Everyone knew it. He remained silent, his chin on his chest, standing in front of his father's desk.

"You will have to marry her, you know," Mr. Young said.

Douglas's eyes darted up to his father. "You mean . . . you'd accept her as my wife?"

"What choice do I have?" The older man let out an impatient sigh. "The child will grow up, announcing his paternity simply by walking into a room. The girl will have all the ammunition she needs if she decides to blackmail you—or me—simply by showing people her son."

"But if I marry her—"

Desmond Young frowned. "It is not a case of 'if.' You *will* marry her, Howard. But you will have forfeited your place in this family."

"What do you mean?" Howard asked. Desperation was surging up his throat.

"I will find you a house in Bangor," his father told him. "But that is where my largesse will end. You will need to get a job to support the family you have made for yourself. I know jobs are difficult to come by these days. There's a Depression out there for people less fortunate than us. You'll have to find your way best you can."

"You mean . . . you're disinheriting me?"

"That is precisely what I mean."

"Please, no, Papa. I have such plans. I have great ambition. . . ."

His father scowled. "You should have thought of that before you started sniffing around the scullery."

"Please, Papa! Don't do this!"

But pleading was useless. His father ordered him out of the study. Howard walked down the corridor, stunned. He tried to force his brain to work, to find a way out of this terrible predicament.

I've got to make Beatrice go away, he thought to himself.

He pulled open the doorway to the basement and headed down the stairs into the servants' quarters.

He spotted Beatrice heading into her room with the child. He watched through the open door as she laid him in his crib. He'd never so much as held the child. He had kept his distance. Beatrice had fallen quiet around him. The notes had ended. She had either accepted the situation or was simply biding her time, waiting until the moment was right to make her demands of him.

But he had come to make a demand of her.

"Beatrice," he said, standing in her doorway.

"Howard!" she said, her eyes lighting up at the sight of him. She still loved him. He could see that.

He entered the room, closing the door behind him. What they had to discuss was private. Very private.

"I have missed you so much," she told him. "But I have tried to be discreet."

"It is no longer a tenable situation," he said brusquely. "My father knows the truth. And he has insisted I marry you."

Beatrice's face beamed her joy. "Oh, my darling!" She threw open her arms and moved toward him as if to embrace him, but Howard pushed her away.

"I cannot marry you," he said. "I would be throwing away my entire future. My father plans to disinherit me."

"Oh, but I don't care about money," she said. "I will make you a wonderful wife. I love you so, Howard. And Malcolm needs you. He needs a father."

Howard fumed. "No! Don't you see? We would be paupers! The entire world is spiraling down in a depression. There are no jobs! I would lose my place in the family inheritance. I wouldn't be able to go to Yale as my brother Douglas did! I'm just eighteen years old, Beatrice! I can't just throw away my life!"

Her eyes filled with tears. "What of *my* life? More importantly, what about the life of your son?"

"I am making you the same offer I made before. Promise me you'll go away and take the child with you. I will send you money. I will make sure you are provided for. But you must write a letter to my father promising you will never, ever, come back into our lives. You will keep the secret of Malcolm's paternity for all of your life, including from him."

"You're asking me to never tell my son his father's name?"

"That is exactly what I am asking. You must understand my situation here. It is the only choice we have."

Beatrice's expression hardened. "No. It is *not* the only choice. You could marry me." She folded her arms across her chest and stood her ground. "I am not leaving this house except as your wife."

In that instant, Howard knew she would never go away. She would never leave him in peace. He felt the rage boiling up inside him. He wanted to strike her—but just then there was a rapping at the door.

"No one can know I'm here," Howard said, hurrying to hide behind the large armoire on the far side of the room.

Beatrice opened the door. It was Clem. Peering around the side of the armoire, Howard could see the handyman clearly, though he was certain the dumb brute couldn't see him. Clem stood there in the doorway in his ragged, grass-stained overalls, his pitchfork in his hands.

"Beatrice," Clem said, "I heard you cryin' again today and I got to thinkin' . . ."

"Oh, Clem," she said, "I don't have time to talk with you now."

"But I was thinkin' we oughta get hitched. . . ."

She laughed. "Clem, you've asked me that before. You're very kind. But I've told you. I can't marry you."

"Well, you're so sad all the time, you know, carryin' that baby around. If you was my wife I could take care of ya. . . ."

Little Malcolm had started to fuss in his crib. Beatrice bent over and lifted him in her arms. Bouncing him gently, she looked over at Clem and once again told him no, she could never marry him.

"Why not?" Clem asked.

"Because I'm going to marry someone else," she said, her voice raised just enough so that Howard knew she was speaking to him. He seethed.

"Who?" Clem demanded. "Who are you goin' to marry?"

Howard noticed movement in the hallway behind Clem. Another groundsman, Harry Noons, had come in, and was washing his hands at the sink near the servants' entrance. Howard flattened himself against the wall just to doubly ensure he wouldn't be seen.

"Who?" Clem asked again, his voice rising. "Who you goin' to marry?"

Beatrice laughed. "I'm going to marry a man who can offer me much more than you can, Clem."

"I know I may be a simple man," Clem said, angry himself now, "but I would do right by ya. I'd treat ya right."

Beatrice laughed. "I am going to marry a man

who is far your superior, Clem. A great man! Far greater than you!"

Howard could see Clem's face twist in rage. "Fine, then!" the handyman shouted. "Then you can just stay the way you are, and you can keep your little bastard!"

Beatrice reached over and slapped Clem across the face. Harry Noons saw it all, and hurried up the stairs.

And suddenly the solution to his dilemma was clear to Howard.

It came to him so easily. He didn't even have to think it through. It was right there, fully plotted, in the forefront of his mind.

"Clem," he said, stepping out from behind the armoire. "How dare you use such language in front of a lady?"

The groundsman jumped when he saw Howard, dropping his pitchfork on the floor. "I'm sorry, Mr. Howard. I'm very sorry. I just—"

"I should fire you on the spot," Howard said.

He knew the threat of termination would cause great distress for the simple man. Jobs were scarce. Clem wasn't eager to stand in breadlines like so many others.

"No, please, Mr. Howard," he begged, "don't fire me!"

Howard frowned. "Go wait for me in my father's workshop at the other end of the basement. Under no circumstances are you to leave there. I'll be in to speak with you presently."

Clem scurried off into the dark shadows of the basement.

Beatrice was placing the baby back down in his crib. "So you've decided to play the gallant knight, have you?" she asked, smiling at Howard when she turned back to look at him. Her smugness was infuriating. "So perhaps my hope is justified that you will make me your wife."

"I would suggest," Howard said, bending down and taking Clem's pitchfork in his hands, "that you abandon hope, Beatrice."

And with that, he charged at her with the pitchfork, his anger and desperation summoning almost superhuman strength. He plunged its long, sharp, metal tines into her soft chest, piercing the breasts he had once so tenderly caressed, puncturing her heart and her lungs, easily impaling her against the plaster wall.

Beatrice had time to scream only one, but it was a long and terrible wail. Her dark eyes were open wide in shock and accusation. Blood poured down from her wounds, instantly staining her white dress and pooling on the floor.

Howard wasted no time. Rushing out of the room and back up the stairs into the foyer, he felt certain that no matter the commotion, the simpleminded, terrified Clem would not leave the workshop. It would be disobeying a direct order. Once into the foyer, Howard quickly turned around, heading back down the stairs, just as his brothers came running from elsewhere in the house.

"What was that scream?" his brother Douglas asked.

"I don't know," Howard said. "It came from the basement."

They hurried down the stairs just as Harry Noons came rushing in from the servants' entrance. They peered into Beatrice's room and let out a collective gasp.

"Clem!" Harry Noons babbled. "I saw him here just seconds ago—they was arguin'—she slapped him across the face!"

"We'll search the grounds," Douglas said, taking charge as always. Howard felt a vicious delight in tricking him.

"Dear God," Desmond Young uttered when he, too, came down the stairs and saw Beatrice's bloody body. His eyes flickered over to Howard.

"Noons says he saw her arguing with Clem just minutes ago," Howard said.

"Ayuh, I did," Noons agreed. "She struck him. That's when I left. He musta killed her right afterward."

Howard's brothers were already hurrying out the back stairs in search of Clem. Desmond Young turned to Howard.

"Why don't you search the basement for him?" he suggested. "He might be hiding down here somewhere, don't you think?"

Their eyes held. Howard had the distinct impression that his father knew, or at least suspected, the truth, and was colluding with him.

"Yes," Howard said. "I'll search the basement."

His father nodded, then, with Noons, headed outside.

Once he was alone in the basement, Howard walked over to his father's workshop. Opening the door, he saw Clem cowering inside.

Howard took a deep breath. "How could you do such a thing, Clem?" he asked quietly, shaking his head.

"Do what, Mr. Howard?"

"Come with me."

The handyman followed him back to Beatrice's

room, where Howard showed him the carnage. Beatrice's body hung limply from the wall. An enormous glistening puddle of blood had collected on the floor.

"Beatrice!" Clem cried.

"You killed her," Howard said calmly.

"No!"

"Yes, you did." He looked Clem fiercely in the eyes. "I found you, remember? I threatened to fire you!"

"Yes, but . . ."

"She slapped you, didn't she?"

"Yes, but I didn't—"

"You got angry! Very angry!"

Clem's face went white.

"Didn't you, Clem? She slapped you, and you got very angry!"

"Yes," he admitted.

"And then you killed her! With your pitchfork! Look! Look at it sticking out of her!"

"No . . ."

Howard moved in, his eyes wild. "I saw you do it, Clem! I saw you!"

"You . . . you did?"

"Indeed. I saw you drive that pitchfork right through her body."

"I . . . didn't mean to kill her. . . . I don't remember. . . ."

"You're a simpleton. Aren't you, Clem? A simpleton!"

Clem had begun to cry. He nodded his head.

"Your puny brain can't remember what you did," Howard told him. "You've blocked the horror of it from your mind."

"I . . . killed Beatrice?"

"Yes," Howard told him. "And now I must call the sheriff!" He began walking toward the stairs.

"Mr. Howard, they'll put me in jail. They'll hang me!"

Howard stopped walking, turning around to glare at Clem. "Yes, Clem, they will."

"But my ma . . . who would support her then? I take care of my ma, you know. I'm all she's got. What will happen to my ma?"

Howard did indeed know that Clem took care of his sick, elderly mother. He cocked his head to one side and raised his eyebrows at Clem. "They'll put her in the poorhouse, I suppose. Pity, really. The poorhouse is a sickly den of thieves and degenerates. Pity how your poor mother will have to suffer for what you did."

"Please, Mr. Howard, you gotta help me!"

Howard seemed to consider his request. "Well, I don't know. . . . I should just go upstairs and call the sheriff."

"No, please don't!"

"Well, if I'm going to help you, Clem, then you will need to help me."

The poor simple man was nodding absurdly. "Yes, yes, sure, anything!"

"I want you to break the baby's neck."

Clem's eyes nearly bugged out of his head.

"You want me to . . . ?"

"You heard me." Howard was surprised at how easy it was to ask such a thing. But in truth, it was that baby that had caused his terrible dilemma. That baby who stood between him and the kind of life he deserved. To ask for its removal was not so difficult. "I want you to kill Beatrice's baby."

"But . . ."

"Don't argue with me, Clem," Howard said. "I'll just turn around and go call the sheriff. You'll be hanged, and your mother will die a terrible death in the poorhouse."

Clem was crying again. "But why?"

"Really, Clem, you ask the most inane questions. Do you want that child to grow up motherless? We'd have to put it in the poorhouse, too. And babies fare even worse in the poorhouse than do old ladies."

"Oh . . ." Clem said, hanging his head.

"You would be doing the child a great service, Clem. Snapping its neck means its death will be quick and painless. It's the least you can do for killing its mother."

"Really?" Clem asked, his simple eyes wide.

"Yes, Clem. It's quite easy. Just go over to the crib and snap its little neck."

The dumb brute took a step toward the crib.

"Then remain here once it's done," Howard instructed him. "Remain standing there with the child in your arms. I'll be right back to take care of everything."

"Yes, Mr. Howard."

Howard hurried out of the room. His heart had hardened considerably in the last hour, and yet still he could not bear to see what Clem was about to do. The child was his own flesh and blood, after all. He contented himself that death would be quick. Whether it was painless or not as he'd assured Clem, he wasn't so sure. But there was logic in what he had told the simpleton. The bastard child was indeed better off dead.

Whether Clem would actually do the deed or not, Howard wasn't so sure. He was simple, easily swayed, but he had a conscience. In the end, it didn't really matter, Howard thought. Yes, it would be better to have the child out of the way. But if it lived, he'd deal with that. They'd find a home for it somewhere far away, where its resemblance to Howard would never be noticed. In the end, all that really mattered was Clem. And for this part of the plot, Howard needed a witness.

Upstairs in the foyer, he found one. His sister Margaret.

"The rest of them haven't come back yet," she reported, wringing her hands. "They haven't found Clem."

"Well, I have," Howard said. "I just saw him sneak into the basement."

"Oh!" Margaret held a lace handkerchief up to her face. "He's returning to the scene of the crime! All the mystery magazines say murderers always do that."

"Did Papa take his gun?" Howard asked.

"He and Douglas took the rifles from the parlor," Margaret replied.

Howard nodded. "So his revolver is still in his desk in the study."

"Oh, yes, it must be, Howard! Get it! Or Clem could come up here and kill us all!"

It was all working perfectly. Fetching his father's revolver, Howard returned to the basement. Margaret tagged along, terrified but also feverishly excited. She followed a few feet behind, uttering little sounds every few feet. Howard was glad she was with him. He wanted her to witness the little scene he was about to act out.

There, in Beatrice's doorway, stood Clem with little Malcolm in his arms. Margaret screamed.

"Put the child down!" Howard shouted. "Do not harm him!"

"But I did as you—"

Howard pulled the trigger of the revolver. The bullet ripped through Clem's chest. Blood spurted from the bullet hole, and the big, lumbering man staggered once, then fell backward like a great oak. Beatrice's blood on the floor splashed as he made contact.

Margaret screamed again.

Howard stood over Clem's dead body. "I was too late," he announced. "He had already broken the baby's neck."

"Oh," Margaret cried. "We must call the sheriff."

"No," came a voice.

They looked up. Their father had come in from the servants' entrance. He looked down at the three dead bodies on the floor.

"I have never allowed scandal to touch this family, and I am not about to begin now." He looked over at Howard with cold, hard eyes. "The sheriff will not be called until this room is cleaned up, and Clem and the baby are buried on the estate."

The other sons came back into the house at that point, each of them gasping in new horror when they saw the latest atrocities.

"Douglas, Samuel," Desmond Young commanded, "you take the bodies out for burial. Make sure there is no evidence of your work. Leave Beatrice's body here. Remove her from the wall." Again his eyes found Howard. "She should be brought to the barn and placed there with the pitchfork. She fell from the loft and impaled her-

self. The sheriff will be told it was a terrible accident."

Howard recoiled from the idea of touching
Beatrice's body, of having to clean up her blood.
"Can't we simply tell the sheriff that she went
away? Does he need to know she died?"

"Too many questions will be asked if we don't
report her death," Desmond explained. "We can
get away with saying that Clem took off, but the
other servants would know Beatrice would never
go with him. We can say Clem was distraught because of her death, and if suspicions arise that he
killed her, so be it. But we cannot make the claim
ourselves, because I do not want the sheriff here
on the estate nosing around in an investigation."

Howard was now certain that his father knew he
had committed the crime. He was protecting him
by keeping the authorities away.

"The sheriff has always done what I have told
him," the elder Mr. Young said. "He appreciates
the donations I make to his office four times a
year. He wouldn't want to jeopardize that."

Margaret was crying. "But what of the baby?"

"We will say that we gave the baby to a good
home," Desmond explained. "Beatrice has no family who will come wanting to claim him. So we say
that we found a good home for the child in
Boston. No one will question what I say."

So they got to work. The brothers carried the
corpses of Clem and Malcolm out the back entrance, burying them in unmarked graves in the
private family cemetery. It was left to Howard, as
his father intended, to take down Beatrice's body
from the wall, and to carry it out to the barn. He
did this stoically, without any feeling or conscious

thought. It was simply a chore to be completed. Never once did he look down at her face.

But when he returned to the room and began the grisly task of mopping up her blood, he suddenly broke down. He turned to his sister Margaret, standing in the doorway, and gestured pitifully. Beatrice's blood was literally on his hands.

"What have I done?" he cried. "Oh, what have I done?"

Her eyes widened as she realized the truth.

"I was frightened," Howard said. "Mad with fear and desperation. How is it possible that I could do something so terrible?"

"I'd advise you to say no more, Howard," his sister said icily. "No more. Never again. After tonight, none of this exists."

The sheriff came an hour later. As Desmond had predicted, he accepted the story that she had fallen. The official report of her death said she had died of an accident. Nothing more was recorded. Desmond even saw to it that no death certificate was ever signed. After all, Beatrice Swan was just a servant girl.

But Margaret's assertion that the night would put an end to the horror was wrong. No one slept that night. At the breakfast table the next morning the family was solemn. The day passed without anything being spoken. But that night, as they fell into exhausted, restless sleep, the horrors that had taken place twenty-four hours earlier came roaring back to vivid, terrible life.

Howard sat bolt upright in his bed, sweat dripping from his face. And without even needing to wonder, he knew why his father was banging on his door in the middle of the night.

"You had the dream, too," Howard said, getting out of bed and letting his father into his room.

"She will have revenge on us," Desmond said.

"Yes," Howard said, trembling. "That is what she said in the dream."

Beatrice was not gone. She had vowed she would not leave. And so she had come back, appearing in a dream shared by both Howard and his father, a dream that told them their own chance to avoid her full wrath was to sacrifice one of their own every ten years. The exact particulars of the dream were vague and inchoate, fading as both men awoke. But the terms remained clear. A lottery was to be held the next night consisting of every blood family member aged sixteen and over. Whoever was chosen would spend a night in the room where Beatrice, Clem, and Malcolm had died. If this was not done, the entire family would be killed.

"That is *absurd*," Douglas proclaimed when his father announced the plan.

Samuel echoed his brother's disbelief. "You're both just unnerved by the horror of it all," he said.

Desmond slammed his fist down on the table. "Then tell me how both of us could have had the same exact dream! The lottery must be held!"

"Well, I want no part of it," Douglas said.

"Neither do I," Samuel agreed.

Margaret stood up. "We had best heed the dream. There is more here than we know."

Her eyes shot accusation at Howard. He simply looked down at the floor.

And so the lottery was held that night. The brothers went along grudgingly, not really believing in the need for it, or in their father's crazy dream. But no one could overrule a direct command from Desmond. When sixteen-year-old Jacob's name was chosen, his father decreed he would enter the room in his place. Howard protested that they shouldn't tamper with the results of the lottery. But Desmond simply could not bear the thought of sending his son into that room.

Witnessing such a display of paternal solicitude, Howard felt a deep, burning shame for what he had done to his own son.

My own son, he thought to himself, the full dismay of the night before hitting him. *I killed my own son.*

Desmond kissed his wife and made his way down to the basement. Once more, sleep eluded the family. Howard fretted. He was downstairs at daybreak. He and Douglas opened the door. There was the family patriarch, his body spread out on the floor, arms and legs extended in an *X*. All except one part of his body: his head, which lay on the other side of the room. The pitchfork that they thought had been replaced in the barn was stuck through his neck and into the floor, standing straight above him like an exclamation point. Clem walked the earth once more, doing Beatrice's bidding. Once again, the floor of the room was covered in blood.

But that wasn't the worst of it.

Douglas's wife was screaming from upstairs. Rushing back, they discovered Douglas's infant daughter Cynthia dead in her crib, her neck broken just like baby Malcolm's. Down the hall, more horror awaited. Throwing open the doors to his brothers' rooms, Howard found thirteen-year-old Timothy and sixteen-year-old Jacob smothered in their beds. Letting out a long wail, he fell to his knees.

He knew then that his curse was never to be selected in the lottery. Instead, he would live out his days watching his family die, one by one. And he knew he deserved such a fate. Rocking back and forth on the floor, keening like a madman, he knew he deserved all of this and much worse.

For the next eighty years, much worse was to come.

THE PRESENT

Chapter Thirty-eight

"It never stopped," the old man said through his tears. "The horror just continued. All of us were ruined. My mother took her own life a few years later. My sister turned into a bitter recluse. One by one, the rest of my brothers died in that room, and then their sons, too. And I watched it all."

Carolyn looked down at Howard Young with a mixture of revulsion and pity. But for Douglas, there was nothing but contempt in his voice.

"You killed her! You killed your own son!" he shouted. "And all for what?"

The old man looked up at him pathetically. "She gave me what I thought I wanted. She removed my brothers for me. Beatrice ensured that it would be me who became master of this house."

Douglas turned away in utter disgust.

It was Jeanette's turn to speak. "Uncle Howard, your actions that night . . . they cost my father and my brothers their lives. And consigned me to forty years of a silent, terrible prison."

The old man just sat there sobbing, his frail frame convulsing.

"You are beneath contempt," Jeanette said, turning away.

"I tried to end it," he protested. "For eighty years I looked for a way. I hired so many to come here and try to cast Beatrice out of that room. . . ."

"You hoped that the curse could be ended without ever implicating you in your part in it all," Carolyn said. "That's why you withheld so many details. That's why you fired Dr. Fifer."

The old man nodded. "The birth records had been opened finally, and he found the entry for Malcolm. Unbeknownst to us, Beatrice had told the midwife the name of her baby's father, and the midwife included it on the certificate. It was Beatrice's way of holding power over me. We never knew, because the birth records were sealed. But when they were opened, and Fifer got a copy and confronted me, I had to let him go. I couldn't risk the family blaming me. Their love and respect was all I had."

"But you could risk my father going into that room ten years later!" Douglas shouted.

"Oh, my little hoodlum. Fifer had discovered the identity of Malcolm, but had uncovered no strategy to end the curse of that room. Even if I had allowed him to stay on, he wouldn't have been able to end the lottery."

"But you can't really know that," Carolyn objected, "since you terminated him before he could finish his investigation."

Howard Young looked at her, his yellow eyes imploring her to understand. "All I had left was the love and respect of my family!" he cried. "Can't you see that, Carolyn? You *must* understand. Beatrice's revenge was not just in taking away my brothers and their children. It ensured that I would be alone all my life. Never again was I to know the love of a woman. Never would I have the chance again to have children. I was destined to live my life alone here in this lonely house."

"And become a fabulously wealthy man," Douglas interjected, "while everyone else around you was killed off."

"Beatrice's punishment was giving me exactly what I said I wanted," Howard Young said. "Believe me, if I could have exchanged that wealth for the life of just one of my family members, I would have."

"How easily you can say that now," Jeanette said. Michael put his arm around her shoulder, casting a glance filled with contempt at the old man.

"But my role in all this doesn't help solve the problem!" Howard insisted. "I tell you now because I am old, and I can no longer keep it inside. But still the killings go on."

Carolyn considered this. "Mr. Young, you believe that it was Beatrice who controlled that room in the beginning, who orchestrated the deaths. You called it her revenge."

"As it was," he said.

"So when Kip Hobart freed her spirit, allowed her to finally rest in peace, it was her son who took up the cause, so to speak," Carolyn said.

The old man nodded. "Malcolm had seventy years to watch his mother at work. Now he is alone in that room."

"And like any baby, frightened without his mother," Jeanette added.

Carolyn was nodding. "We even took Clem away," she said. "He's all alone. And having a tantrum."

"So how can we possibly reason with *that*?" Howard Young asked.

Carolyn looked at him. "We don't need to reason with him. We just need to give him what he wants."

"And what's that?" Douglas asks.

"His mother," Carolyn said plainly.

"Beatrice," Howard said, his eyes flickering up to look at Carolyn with what she thought was perhaps a glimmer of hope. "But would she . . . help us?"

"She already has been helping us," Carolyn said. "Mr. Young, even after all that has happened, she still loves you. That was clear from the recording Kip made. Yes, she sought revenge on you, but like all lovers scorned, the passion she felt was fueled by her love."

"So now that she's found peace," Douglas asked, "she wants to help us? To end the vendetta she carried on so long against us?"

Carolyn nodded. "Yes, but it's more simple than that. She's helping us because she wants us to help her."

"How can we help her?" Jeanette asked.

"By giving her back her baby," Carolyn said. "Beatrice and Malcolm both want the same thing. They're just going about it in different ways."

"But how can we possibly do what she wants?" Howard asked.

"*We* can't," Carolyn said, looking directly at him. "But *you* can."

He had no time to respond. Outside the room, Ryan's screams had grown only louder. Now there came a terrifying crash. The young man was begging someone to stay away from him.

"David's back," Carolyn said. "And he'll kill Ryan and then come for us."

"I'll go out there," Douglas volunteered. "If I can get in some shots at him, it will at least slow him down and give us more time."

Carolyn held his gaze for a moment. She knew it was likely that the killings weren't over yet, that probably more of them would still die before they had a chance to reunite Beatrice and Malcolm. And in her gut she felt a terrible sensation that one of those who would die would be Douglas.

"Be careful!" she cried as Douglas turned and left the room. "Please be careful!"

She was momentarily overcome, convinced that would be the last time she'd ever see him. Jeanette moved closer to her, touching her shoulder in support.

Then Carolyn summoned all her strength and took a deep breath. She turned her eyes once again to Howard Young. "Let us begin," she said. "We have work to do."

Chapter Thirty-nine

Douglas moved stealthily down the hall, holding the rifle in front of him. He'd loaded up with more ammunition in the library, knowing it might take several shots to bring David Cooke down. He could hear the commotion in the foyer. Leaning his back up against the wall, he peered around the corner.

Ryan was crumpled at the other side of the room. David Cooke stood in the middle of the floor. He had clearly just hurled Ryan against the wall. And from somewhere above—or below, or maybe from everywhere—came Malcolm's laughter. The child was delighted with the show.

The zombie was now beginning to lumber toward Ryan once again. Douglas lifted the rifle and looked through the finder. He steadied his grip, focused his aim. David Cooke stopped walking, seeming to sense he was being watched. He began to turn. Douglas pulled the trigger.

Cooke took a direct hit just above his left ear. A

chunk of his head tore away, exposing gray brain matter. But once again, there was no blood.

But still the zombie walked. He turned, facing Douglas now. Douglas fired again. This time the bullet tore into Cooke's neck. He staggered, but kept approaching. Douglas fired a third time. This time, blowing yet another hole into the undead man's chest, Douglas accomplished what he had set out to do. David Cooke fell over backward with a loud thud, his mutilated head cracking against the marble floor. Malcolm's laughter abruptly ended.

Douglas rushed over to Ryan, who was woozy and confused from the thrashing he'd endured.

"Get up!" Douglas ordered. "Get up before he revives!"

Ryan looked at him. "Did you . . . did you just save my life?"

"Yeah," Douglas said sullenly. "I just did."

He helped his cousin to his feet.

"Hurry up," Douglas said. "I'll take you to the library."

"Is it safe there?"

"It's not safe anywhere until we can unplug the power that keeps that zombie walking," Douglas said.

Even as he said the words, he saw Cooke stirring. The creature was trying to stand. Its right arm flexed as it tried to leverage its body off the floor.

"Hurry!" Douglas urged, pushing Ryan along.

They were crossing the floor of the foyer when Cooke sat up. Ryan screamed.

"Move!" Douglas shouted, and they began to run.

Cooke was on his feet in seconds. With his long legs and extraordinary speed, he was able to sprint across the foyer, blocking their access to the corridor that led to the library. The zombie growled like a bear, its dead eyes fixed on them.

"Quick!" Douglas yelled, grabbing Ryan's arm. "In here!"

He shoved him into the dining room, then turned to aim his rifle at Cooke from the double doors. He fired. He missed. His hands were trembling. He fired again. He barely nicked Cooke's shoulder. The zombie was no more than two feet away from them.

"Goddamn you!" Douglas screamed and fired directly into the creature's chest.

The impact was enough to stop Cooke's approach, but he didn't fall. He swayed for a moment, then regained his balance. Reaching out with a sudden move, he grabbed the rifle from Douglas's hands and snapped it in half.

Ryan screamed. Behind Douglas, he slammed the doors of the dining room closed, leaving his cousin outside. Douglas spun around, banging on the doors.

"Let me in, Ryan!" he called. "Let me in."

But it was too late.

The cold hands of the zombie were around his throat.

Chapter Forty

Inside the dining room, Ryan could hear the maniac banging his cousin's head against the doors. He cowered under the table.

That's when he realized he wasn't alone in the room.

From under the table, he saw the bare feet of a woman wearing a long white dress. She moved across the room almost as if she were gliding. She reached the doors and made a motion to open them.

"No!" Ryan cried, leaping out from under the table. "Don't let him in here!"

But Beatrice paid him no mind. She pulled open the doors, and Douglas tumbled inside. David Cooke, upon seeing her, backed off.

Douglas was on the floor, blood gushing from his nose. He wasn't moving.

Ryan stood over at him, once again in the zombie's sights.

And Beatrice was gone.

David Cooke smiled. His teeth were broken; his head was partially blown off. But he seemed absolutely delighted.

"No, please!" Ryan begged. "You killed Douglas! Isn't that enough?"

The zombie lunged.

Ryan had only a second to realize what was happening. David Cooke had grabbed him around the waist and was throwing him down onto the dining table. The laughter had returned. Suddenly, from the kitchen beyond, a shower of knives descended, each of them piercing Ryan's body, pinning him to the table. Ryan screamed from pain and terror. Then David Cooke very gracefully removed a large serving platter from a hutch against the wall. Placing it on the table, he plucked one of the large knives out of Ryan's shoulder. Then, as if he were a master chef—or the family patriarch on Thanksgiving—he began slicing off pieces of Ryan's flesh. Tenderly he placed each piece on the platter. Blood flowed in rivers across the table and gushed onto the carpet below. Malcolm laughed as Ryan screamed, watching David Cooke slice his body into pieces. First his arms were defleshed, then his legs. The pain was excruciating, but somehow Ryan stayed conscious. Only when the knife was turned to his throat and began the process of delicately cutting out his Adam's apple did his screams finally cease.

Chapter Forty-one

In the library, Carolyn and the others heard the screams and were certain that both Ryan and Douglas were dead. Holding back tears, Carolyn summoned the strength to call on Beatrice to help them.

They were standing in a circle. At first Jeanette had seemed resistant to grasp her uncle's hand, but Carolyn had insisted they needed to make contact, to use their combined energy to summon Beatrice. Once the four of them were linked, Carolyn cleared her mind the way Diana had taught her to do. She struggled to keep thoughts of Douglas—which could only invoke despair, grief, and defeat—far from her mind.

"Beatrice Swan," Carolyn said. "I know now why you came to me. I understand what you have been asking me to do. Help me now to accomplish this task."

There was nothing. Carolyn feared for a moment that Beatrice had abandoned them, if perhaps they were too late.

But then it began to thunder. Rain hit against the windows in a sudden downpour. The day grew ominously dark. Occasional lightning lit up the room.

"Beatrice," Carolyn called. "Help us to reunite you with your son."

The door to the library blew open. A gust of damp air filled the room.

No longer was Malcolm laughing. He was crying. His anguished wails filled the house.

Gently Carolyn broke contact with the circle. "Wait here," she whispered. "I will go out there. Beatrice will protect me."

"Are you certain?" Jeanette asked.

Carolyn gave her a small smile. "No. I am not certain. If I don't come back, try the circle again. Ask Beatrice to help you. At this point, it's all we have." She indicated the second rifle, leaning up against the wall. "That will slow David down, but not kill him. Use it as you need to."

"You should take it with you," Michael suggested.

Carolyn shook her head. "I've got to trust Beatrice."

Slowly she stepped out into the hall. The air in the house was increasingly cold and damp. Carolyn shuddered once, hugging herself. Then she made her way to the foyer.

It was empty. Expensive vases and mirrors were smashed, and tables were overturned. But there was no sign of Douglas, Ryan, or David.

"Beatrice?" Carolyn whispered.

She crossed the foyer and noticed a trail of

blood leading toward the dining room. The doors were open. Blood was everywhere. On the table, she saw the remains of a man, much of the flesh sliced off his body. His face was nearly gone, having been hacked down to expose the skull. Carolyn gasped in horror and revulsion.

Douglas? Was it Douglas?

But then, beyond the table, she saw another man lying on the floor.

She recognized Douglas's shoes.

Was he dead too? She began hurrying toward him. But before she could get there, she felt a hand on the back of her neck. She spun around.

It was David.

All of her old terrors returned, coupled now with new ones. This man she had once loved now glared at her with dull gray eyes. The scar on his face was no longer the most hideous thing about him. Part of his head was torn away. His neck was ripped open, exposing dry gray veins. His body was riddled with bloodless bullet holes.

"Hello, Carolyn," the zombie spoke in a throaty, gravelly voice that bore no resemblance to the one Carolyn remembered. David had been a singer, and a good one; it had been hard to believe, listening to him sing of love, that he was a cold-blooded murderer at heart. Maybe, then, this had been David's real voice all along.

"You're a monster," Carolyn told him, still shaken by what she had seen on the dining room table. "Malcolm may be using you, but only an inherently evil nature could do such a thing."

She managed to pull away from him. David's lifeless eyes studied her as if she were a strange creature he had never seen before.

"I've been looking for you," David said, a grin slowly spreading across his broken face.

She backed away, hoping that Beatrice would show herself and intervene, or at least find a way to keep David from hurting her.

"You can't hurt me, David," Carolyn told him. "I spent many years being afraid of you, but no longer. Your power ends now."

David just continued to smile, taking small steps toward Carolyn. She backed up now, nearly tripping over Douglas's body on the floor.

Beatrice. *Where was Beatrice?*

Had Carolyn been wrong? Was Beatrice not going to protect her?

David's smile grew wider. Then he lunged at her, gripping her throat with his cold, clammy hands.

Chapter Forty-two

What brought Douglas back to consciousness were Carolyn's screams.

Blood was in his throat, so thick he could taste it. He was almost choking on it. At the same time, his shoulder pained him. It felt dislocated. His ears were ringing, and his head throbbed.

But still he knew Carolyn was in danger.

He forced himself to his feet, trying to keep his balance, trying to force his eyes to focus on the scene in front of him.

Carolyn was just outside the door. David Cooke was strangling her to death. Her screams had been replaced by an intense gagging.

Douglas leapt.

He had no idea if he had the strength. He had no idea if he'd even make contact with the brute. But all he needed to do was to dislodge him a bit, make him loosen the grip he had around Carolyn's neck.

Douglas bounced off Cooke and fell back against

the wall of the corridor. But it seemed his effort had done the trick. He could hear Carolyn now gulping in air. But still the zombie had her in his grip. Douglas tried to stand again, but this time the pain in his shoulder flared up so fiercely that it knocked him back to his feet.

In that moment came a huge bang. Douglas had no idea what it was until he saw David Cooke drop Carolyn onto the floor. Then came another bang.

Someone was shooting at Cooke.

Douglas managed to look over his shoulder. It was Uncle Howie, with the second rifle.

David Cooke roared in fury. There were now so many holes in his left shoulder that he could not seem to lift that arm. That's when Douglas realized that if they couldn't kill the creature, they could immobilize it.

Cooke was lumbering across the room toward Uncle Howie. The old man shot again, shrewdly aiming once again for the weakened shoulder. The left arm now hung limply at the creature's side.

But with his right arm he still managed to haul off and backhand Uncle Howie across the face, sending the old man flying backward. The rifle clattered across the marble floor. Douglas knew he had a microsecond to act, or else Cooke would reach the gun first and then snap it in two like a matchstick, just as he had done with the other one.

Disregarding every muscle that screamed out in pain, Douglas threw himself across the floor, landing on the rifle. He could hear the pounding of Cooke's footsteps behind him. Even without looking around, he knew the zombie was standing over him, reaching down to grab him, to twist in his body in half.

"I don't think so," Douglas cried, flipping over and in nearly a simultaneous move, pointing the rifle up at Cooke and firing directly at the beast's wounded shoulder. The left arm blew completely off the body.

Cooke let out a long wail. With his right arm he made a grab for Douglas, but he was off balance now, and toppled to the ground. Douglas stood over him and fired twice more into the hole in his neck. The second shot severed the spine. No matter how much his body ached, Douglas managed one swift kick of the zombie's head, snapping it free of the body and sending it rolling across the floor. All the while the creature's mouth still moved in anger.

The body, too, wasn't ready to quit. It tried to get back onto its feet by using its right arm. But Douglas kept shooting into the creature's back, smashing the spinal cord to bits. Finally the zombie could do nothing but writhe on the floor. They had nothing more to fear from David Cooke.

But then Malcolm began to scream.

Chapter Forty-three

"Mr. Young!" Carolyn called, her voice raspy, her throat painful. "Talk to him! Talk to your son!"

The baby's shrieks threatened to make them all deaf. The sound was like nothing they'd ever heard before. Sharp, shrill, piercing. It seemed to come from every brick, every beam of the house. Now deprived even of his toy—a zombie named David Cooke—Malcolm's tantrum had gone over the edge.

"What am I supposed to say?" the old man asked as Carolyn helped him up off the ground.

"Tell him you will bring him to his mother," Carolyn said.

The pitiful man just looked at her with his watery, bloodshot eyes. "How am I going to do that?"

"Ask her for forgiveness, and Beatrice will meet you halfway," Carolyn told him.

How she knew that, she had no idea. All she could do right now was trust her gut. All the good psychic investigators she had worked with—Kip,

Diana, many others—had told her that there were times when all you had left was your gut. And when that happened, your gut instinct would never steer you wrong.

"How can I dare ask for forgiveness for what I did?" Howard Young lamented. "I was a cowardly, ruthless young man motivated by greed. I coldly took three lives that night and in the process ruined dozens more lives over the course of the next eight decades. How could I possibly stand here and ask for forgiveness? I do not deserve forgiveness. I deserve damnation."

Malcolm's cries had dissolved into stuttering hiccups of fear and frustration.

"Your son is crying for you," Carolyn told Howard.

The old man looked around the room.

"My son," he whispered.

"Yes," Carolyn said. "Your son."

Mr. Young walked unsteadily into the center of the room, looking up at the high vaulted ceiling.

"Malcolm," he said.

The crying flared up louder at the mention of the name.

"Malcolm," Howard Young implored. "The time has come to end all the killing. The time has come when you can finally rest. I am here, my son. I am here to take you to your mother."

The crying just went on, echoing throughout the house.

"Listen to me, Malcolm. I know you are alone. You are alone and frightened. I am your father. Don't think that all these years you have been forgotten. I have lived with the horror of my deeds all my life. Over your grave I had a small stone inscribed with the letter *M*. I had a cherub carved to mark your place of rest, because that is how I came to think of you. As a cherub. But I know now that you were never at rest. And it is all my fault. All mine."

His voice broke.

"But now I come for you," Howard went on. "I will bring you to the mother you seek. Please, my son. Let me finally help you!"

The crying suddenly changed. Instead of being dispersed through the house, it was now localized. It came from one corner of the room. Carolyn looked in that direction. And there, on the floor, wrapped in nothing more than soft white blanket, was a little baby.

"Malcolm," Howard Young gasped.

The baby lay on his back, his little pink hands clutching fistfuls of air. His face was red from crying.

"Go to him," Carolyn told the old man.

Slowly Howard Young crossed the room. He gazed down at the baby on the floor. Then he stooped, and with difficulty, picked him up in his arms.

Carolyn braced herself for what might happen.

But all that occurred was that Malcolm stopped crying.

Douglas had come up beside her. "Where is Beatrice?" he whispered. "Will she not come to take her baby?"

"I don't know," Carolyn admitted.

"I know where she is," Howard Young said, his eyes transfixed by the child he held in his arms. It was the first time he'd ever held his son, the first time he'd ever looked him in the face.

"In the room in the basement?" Carolyn asked. "Is that where you should take Malcolm?"

"No," Howard said. "Not to the place where he died. I will take him to the place where he first came into this world."

Slowly, and with great effort, he began climbing the stairs. Carolyn and Douglas followed a few steps behind. The baby cooed and gurgled in his father's arms. Carolyn worried that after all he'd been through, Howard might fall or lose his footing on the stairs. But the old man didn't waver. He kept ascending the marble staircase, and at the landing turned and continued up the next flight.

The attic. They were going to the attic.

Finally, they reached the top, stepping off into the small alcove with the view of the entire estate below. Carolyn felt Douglas take her hand. He had brought her here. It had been his special place. It had been a special place for Howard and Beatrice as well.

Through the large picture window they could see the storm had passed and the sun was setting. The sky was a liquid mix of pink and gold and blue. Howard stood in front of the window holding the baby.

"I have brought him to you, Beatrice," he said. "Our son."

Outside the window, in the gathering dusk, there was a swirl of white. Carolyn strained her eyes to see.

It was Beatrice.

"It is time we were a family," Howard said. "It is long past time."

Outside, in the darkening air, Beatrice beckoned.

And before Carolyn even knew what was happening, Howard Young, his son clutched to his chest, leapt forward, smashing through the large pane of glass.

Chapter Forty-four

Now that the rain had ended, Paula ventured outside the barn. Looking up at the great house, she couldn't believe what she was seeing.

First came the smashing of glass, then Uncle Howard was plummeting out of a window to the earth below.

And Paula could have sworn he was holding a baby in his arms.

The old man's body hit the muddy ground with a sickening thud. Paula ran to him as fast as she could. As she got near, she saw there was no baby in his arms. It was just Uncle Howard, twisted and broken.

It was clear that he was dead. Paula knelt down to inspect his brittle, broken body. It had been a horrible way to die. But the expression on his face was peaceful.

"Is it over?" Paula asked, clutching the old man's hand. "Or does it still go on?"

Movement caught her eye from several yards away.

She looked up quickly. Darkness was settling. The trees cast long purple shadows across the lawn. But as Paula stood, she could discern the figure of a woman moving toward the cliffs.

It was Beatrice.

And she was carrying a baby in her arms.

Douglas and Carolyn came running out of the house at that moment. Reaching Paula, they exchanged looks that said more than any words could convey. Douglas knelt beside the body of Uncle Howard and saw that he was dead. Still without words, Paula gestured for them to look across the lawn.

There was Beatrice, holding Malcolm. She was walking away from them. She kept on walking, without ever turning back, her black hair blowing in the wind. She walked straight over the cliffs, as if she were walking on air. Paula, Carolyn, and Douglas kept their eyes on her until she had faded away into the reflected light of the setting sun.

Chapter Forty-five

Carolyn's FBI credentials served her well when the sheriff arrived. The multiple murders were easily explained by the presence of the body of David Cooke, a known killer wanted by New York police. The explanation for his rampage in Youngsport was obvious. Cooke had been after Carolyn, and was working his way through the entire household, killing the others in an effort to terrorize her.

But the problem was: there was no blood in Cooke's body.

That's when Carolyn had her former superior at the FBI give the sheriff's department a call. Carolyn's credibility was vouched for, and it was explained, as carefully as possible, that some of the cases she investigated were, to say the least, unusual. The Youngsport sheriff wasn't about to buck the word of the Federal Bureau of Investigation. So he closed the case, classifying the murders

as the work of David Cooke. He accepted the survivors' contention that Cooke was killed in self-
defense.

But the sheriff would never understand why
there wasn't a single drop of blood in Cooke's
body.

Of course, there had been blood everywhere
else. The bodies were removed and buried. Dean's
funeral was especially sad, the sight of Zac and Callie clinging to their mother breaking everyone's
hearts. On the fourth day after the terror had
ended, Sid arrived at the house. He had with him
Howard Young's will. Seated at the old man's desk
in the study, Sid read the will to Douglas, Carolyn,
Paula, Karen, Jeanette, and Michael. The bulk of
the estate had been left to Douglas over a year before, with generous bequests to Jeanette, Paula,
and Dean. Dean's share would now go to Linda
and his children. Sid explained there was nothing
in the will for Philip's family, so they didn't have to
worry about his widow trying to grab anything.

"I don't really care about any of it," Douglas said
afterward, as the six of them sat on the benches
overlooking the cliffs. "I'd still rather just have a
little house by a river as I'd imagined. Run a little
carpentry shop."

"Then that's where we'll live," Carolyn said, taking his hand, kissing his cheek.

Paula smiled. "We could donate the house to
the state. Turn the grounds into a park."

"And bring the kids here to play," Karen said.

They exchanged a smile. Paula had already
arranged for a donor and hoped to be pregnant
within a few months. She'd be forty in a few weeks,

after all; she had no time to lose. She had told them she was praying for twins, since they ran in the family. A boy and a girl. And she'd name them Dean and Chelsea.

Paula took Karen's hand. She would forever be grateful to her brother for risking his life to save her, and to her cousin for giving her life to save Karen's. In the end, Chelsea hadn't been so selfish after all.

"Well, I've finally agreed to marry Michael," Jeanette announced. "I figure a forty-one-year engagement was long enough to make him wait."

They all smiled, looking out over the cliffs.

That sat there in silence for a while. Finally Douglas asked, "We're sure it's over, right?"

"Of course it is," Jeanette said. "They're all at rest now."

"Of course it's over," Paula echoed. "Uncle Howard reunited Beatrice and Malcolm. And he paid for his crime with his death." She shuddered. "It's *got* to be over."

They were all looking at Carolyn for affirmation.

"It's over," she told them.

They seemed to be reassured by her words. Douglas squeezed her hand.

After all they'd been through, it was natural to wonder. It was perfectly understandable that they'd fear this time ten years from now. For the first time in ninety years, no lottery would take place in the house behind them. Carolyn believed it wouldn't matter, that danger no longer threatened them. They'd discover that nothing bad would occur as a result of skipping the lottery. There would be no dead bodies in the morning. They'd know that the curse finally and truly was over.

But still.

Ten years.

It was a long time to wait.

More Books From Your Favorite Thriller Authors

More Nail-Biting Suspense From
Kevin O'Brien